Hans Fallada

Wolf among wolves

First part -The city and its restless -

Roman

First published:

1937

Table of Contents

Chapter 01

- One wakes up in Berlin and elsewhere -

01 01

On a narrow iron bed slept a girl and a man.

The girl's head was resting in the crook of her right arm; her mouth, breathing gently, was half open; her face wore a pouty and worried expression - as of a child who cannot make out what is troubling her heart.

The girl lay turned away from the man, who slept on her back, with limp arms, in a state of extreme exhaustion. On his forehead, all the way into the frizzy blond hair on his head, were small drops of sweat. The beautiful and defiant face looked a little blank.

It was - despite the open window - very hot in the room. Without a blanket and nightgown, the two slept.

It is Berlin, Georgenkirchstraße, third backyard, four staircases, July 1923, the dollar now - at 6 o'clock in the morning - provisionally still stands at 414 thousand marks.

01 02

Into their sleep the dark shaft of the backyard sent the faint smells from a hundred apartments. A hundred sounds, still soft, came through the open window, in front of which a yellowish-gray curtain hung motionless. Suddenly, on the other side of the yard, not eight meters away, a refugee child from the Ruhr cried out in fear.

The sleeping girl's eyelids twitched. The head lifted a little. The limbs tensed. Now the child cried more quietly, a woman's voice shrilled, a man growled - and the head sank back, the limbs relaxed anew, the girl slept on.

There was a stirring in the house. Doors slammed, footsteps slithered across the courtyard. There was a rumbling on the stairs, enamel cans banged against iron railings. In the kitchen next door, the water pipe was running. On the ground floor, in the sheet metal stamping shop, a bell was shrilling, wheels were whirring, belts were grinding ...

The two slept ...

01 03

Over the city - despite the early hour and clear sky - was a cloudy haze. The broth of an impoverished people did not rise to the sky, it clung lazily to the houses, crept through all the streets, seeped through the windows, into every breathing mouth. The trees in the neglected grounds let their leaves hang pale.

An early long-distance train approached the Silesian station, coming from the east of the Reich, with rattling windows, broken panes, cut upholstery - the ruin of a train. The cars drove over the switches and crossings of Stralau-Rummelsburg, banging, clanking.

A gentleman, Rittmeister (ret.) and Rittergutspächter, Joachim von Prackwitz-Neulohe, white-haired and slim, but with dark glowing eyes, leaned out to see where one would be. He backed up - a glowing particle of soot had flown into his eye. With his handkerchief he wiped, he scolded angrily: Miserable dirty city!

01 04

Fire was lit in the stove with ragged yellow paper and matches that stank or the top of which flew off. Damp, spongy wood or low-quality coal smoldered. The adulterated gas burned puffily without heating. Slowly watery blue milk became warm, the bread was soggy or too dry. Margarine softened in the heat of the apartment smelled rancid.

Hastily the people ate the loveless food, hastily as they had hastily driven into the too often stained, washed, worn out clothes. Hastily, her eyes skimmed the newspapers. There had been deprivation riots, unrest and looting in Gliwice and Breslau, in Frankfurt am Main and Neuruppin, in Eisleben and Dramburg, 6 dead and 1000 arrested. As a result, the government has banned open-air gatherings. The State Court sentences a princess to 6 months in prison for abetting treason and perjury - but the dollar stands at 414 thousand marks against 350 thousand on the 23rd. At the Ultimo, in a week, there will be salary - how will the dollar stand then? Will we be able to buy food? For two weeks? For ten days? For three days? Will we be able to buy shoe soles, pay the gas, the fare -? Quick, woman, here's another 10,000 marks, buy something for it. What, is indifferent, a pound of carrots, cufflinks, the record 'Bananas she demands of me' - or a rope to hang us ... Just quickly, run, quickly -!

01 05

The early sun also shone over Rittergut Neulohe. In the fields the rye was in stalks, the wheat was ripe, the oats too. A few machines rattled forlornly in the field's width, above which the larks tirelessly beat their whirls and trills.

Forester Kniebusch, red-brown, wrinkled old-age face, with bald head, but white-yellowish, round full beard, steps out of the heat of the open field into the forest. He walks slowly, adjusting the shotgun strap on his shoulder with one hand and wiping the sweat from his brow with the other. He does not walk cheerfully, not hurriedly, not vigorously; he walks in his own, that is, at least in the forest under his care, gingerly, with soft knees, carefully. His eye sees every branch on the path, he avoids stepping on it, he wants to go quietly.

And yet, in spite of all caution, at a bend in the road, occurring behind a bush, he meets a small procession of handcarts. Men and women. On the wagons lies freshly cut wood, just sheer logs - the branches are too bad for them. Forester Kniebusch's cheeks flush with anger, his lips move, a deeper glow, a bit of fire, comes into his eyes, which are pale with age, from his youth.

The man at the front of the wagon - the Bäumer, of course - bristled. Now he is already going further. Close by, at a distance of barely a meter, the little wagons with the stolen wood rattle past the forester. People stare into the air or to the side, as if he were not there, standing there breathing heavily ... Then they disappear around the bushes corner.

'You're getting old, Kniebusch,' the forester hears Rittmeister von Prackwitz's voice.

'Yes,' he thinks blearily. 'I have grown so old that I would like to die in my bed.'

Think it and move on.

He will not die in his bed.

01 06

In Meienburg Prison, the alarm bells are ringing, the guards are running from cell to cell, the warden is on the phone to the Reichswehr for reinforcements, the administrators are strapping belts with pistols around their bellies and grabbing rubber truncheons. Ten minutes ago, Prisoner 367 threw his bread at the constable's feet: I demand bread, prescribed weight, and no damn plaster mush! he shouted.

In the same second the tumult, the riot had broken out. From twelve hundred cells it had screamed, shouted, wailed, sung, howled: Cabbage steam! Hunger! Cabbage steam! Hunger!

The small town of Meienburg lay crouched under the gleaming white walls of the high penitentiary - in every house, in every window the roar penetrated: Coal steam! Hunger! Now there was a crash, a thousand prisoners had run against the iron doors with their stools.

Through the corridors ran the constables and calactors, whispering imploringly at the doors of the rebellious. The cells of the well-meaning were unlocked: Be reasonable, no one in Germany gets other food ... the dollar ... the Ruhr district ... Harvest squads are immediately assembled and sent to the large estates. Every week a package of tobacco, daily meat ... for those with good leadership ...

Gradually, the noise subsides. Harvest commandos ... Meat ... Tobacco ... good leadership ... It seeps through the walls, it soothes the growling stomachs, a prospect, a hope of satiety, open skies, perhaps escape ... The last noise-makers, those enraged by their own rage, are dragged by the constables to the holding cells: There, try how to live without the plaster porridge!

The iron doors fly shut with a crash.

01 07

Despite the early morning hour, the maid Sophie is already awake in the apartment of Countess Mutzbauer in the Bavarian Quarter of Berlin. Her chamber, which she shares with the cook, who is still fast asleep, is so narrow that, apart from the two iron beds, there is only room for two chairs - so she writes her letter on the board of the open window.

Sophie Kowalewski has beautifully manicured hands, but they wield the pencil clumsily. Base stroke, hairline, check mark, comma, hairline, base stroke ... Oh, she would like to say so many things ...: how she misses him, how time doesn't want to pass, almost three more years and barely half a year around .... But nothing comes of it; Sophie Kowalewski, daughter of the bailiff Kowalewski in Neulohe, has not learned to translate feelings into writing. Yes, if he were here, if it were a matter of speaking, of touching -! She could express everything, she could make him wild with a kiss, happy with a soft touch.... But so!

She stares ahead of her. Oh, she wants to make him feel it in this letter! From the window pane, she looks dully at a second Sophie. Involuntarily, she smiles quickly at her. A few curls have come loose, hanging darkly in the forehead. The shadows under the eyes are also dark. She would have to take the time once again to sleep thoroughly - but is there a bedtime in this time, when everything so noticeably slips away, hardly since it became clear -? Everything is falling apart, make the most of the minute, today you're still alive, Sophie!

She may be so tired in the morning, her feet are burning, her mouth tastes stale after all the liqueurs, the wine, the kisses - but in the evening she is drawn back to one of the bars. Dance, drink and frolic! Cavaliers enough, limp as their money, hundreds of thousands, fifty times maid's pay, loose in a jacket pocket. She also went with one of the cavaliers last night - what does it matter? Time slips, runs, chases. Perhaps she is also looking for Hans, the Hans lost for three and a quarter years (imposture) in all the ever-repeated embraces, in all the faces leaning over hers, as greedy-restless as hers ... But Hans, radiant, quick, superior to all, there is no second time!

Sophie Kowalewski, having escaped the hard work on the manor, is looking for something in the city - she doesn't know what, anything - that will make her work even harder. This life is unique, fleeting; when we are dead, we are dead for so long; and when we are old, already, when we are over twenty-five, no one looks at us anymore. Hans, oh Hans ... She wears the evening gown of the madam, it is no matter if the cook sees it. What she makes schmuh at the suppliers, she steals silk stockings and silk lingerie. No one has anything to blame the other. It's almost seven, quickly still the conclusion ... And I remain with hot kisses your eternally loving bride Sophie ...

She does not attach any importance to the word bride, she does not even know if she wants to, to marry him, but she has to write it, so that they also hand over the letter to him in the penitentiary.

And the prisoner Hans Liebschner will receive the letter of his bride, he was not one of those who were taken to a holding cell for too wild roaring.

No, although he had been living in the Meienburg penitentiary for barely half a year, he had already advanced to the position of calf factor, completely against all house rules, and had understood how to talk about harvest commandos with particular conviction. He could do that, he knew: Neulohe was not far from Meienburg, and Neulohe was the home of a sweet doll named Sophie ...

'I'll rock the boat,' he thought.

The girl had awakened.

Resting its head in its hand, it lay looking over at the window. The yellowish gray curtain did not move. The girl thought she could feel the smelly heat coming from the yard. There was a slight shudder.

At the same time it looked down at itself. Not that it had shivered from cold - it had shivered because of the ugly heat, because of the foul smell. It looked at his body; the body was white and flawless; one had to wonder that in an air that was as decomposed, as putrid, something could remain so flawless!

The girl had no exact idea what time it was, by the sounds it could be nine or ten or even eleven - the mid-morning sounds stayed pretty much the same after eight. It was possible that the landlady, Mrs. Thumann, came in right away with the morning coffee. According to Wolfgang's wishes, she should have gotten up and dressed herself decently, and also covered him up. Very well, she would do it right away. Wolfgang had such surprising bouts of decency ...

It's all the same, she said to him, for instance. The Thumann is used to it in this way and still quite differently. If she just gets her money, nothing bothers her ...

Disturb -? Wolfgang had laughed tenderly. Disturbing when she sees you like this -?!!!

He had looked at her. Always under such looks from him she became weak and tender. She might have pulled him to her, but then he said more seriously: "It's for our sake, Peter, for our sake! Even if we are sitting in the mud now; we are only really in the mud when we no longer take care of ourselves ...

A dress does not make decent, no dress does not make indecent, she began.

Even if it's just a dress! It doesn't matter! he had said almost vehemently. If it's just anything that reminds us. We are not dirt, I am not and neither are you. And once I've made it, everything will be much easier for us if we didn't feel comfortable here, in this shithole. We just can't go along with them here!

He only mumbled, his words lost in the incomprehensible. He thought again about how he would 'make it', he was away from her. (He was away from her, his Peter, a lot).

When you've made it, I won't be with you anymore, she had once said.

There had been silence for a while, but then what she had said had reached him in his brooding.

You will be with me, Peter! he had answered fiercely. Always and always. Do you think I'll forget how you wait for me night after night?! I forget that, how you sit here - in the hole - without anything?! I forget that you never ask me and never push me, however I come?! O Peter!!! he had cried, and his eyes shone with that brightness which she did not like, for it was a brightness which she did not kindle. Last night it was almost time! It was a moment, like a mountain the money lay before me ... I felt it was almost time, just once, twice more ... No, I'm not fooling you. I wasn't thinking of anything in particular, not a house, not a garden, not a car, not you ... It was like a sudden brightness before me, no, a radiant brightness within me, life was so wide and clear, like the sky when the sun rises, it was all pure....

Then ... he lowered his forehead ... a hooker approached me, and from then on everything went wrong ...

He had been standing at the window with his forehead lowered. She felt, as she took his twitching hand between hers, how young he was, how young his enthusiasm, how young his despair, how young and without all obligation what he told her ...

You will make it! she said softly. But when you will have made it, I will no longer be with you.

He pulled his hand out from between hers.

You will stay with me, he said coldly. I do not forget anything.

She knew he had just thought of his mother, who had once punched her in the face. She did not want to stay with him because his mother had once beaten her.

And now, from today on, she would stay with him after all, forever. He hadn't made it yet, and she had known for a long time that nothing would ever come of it the way she had. But what did that? Further this greasy room, further not knowing how to live tomorrow, to dress, further everything unclear - but bound to him from noon one o'clock today!

She reached on the chair next to her bed, grabbed the stockings and began to slip them on. -

Suddenly she was overcome by a terrible fear that nothing could come of it, that everything had gone wrong yesterday, completely wrong, down to the last thousand mark bill. She did not dare to get up to see for herself, she looked with burning eyes at Wolfgang's clothes hanging over the chair next to the door. She tried to correctly estimate the thickness of the right jacket pocket where he kept his money.

'Fees must be paid,' she thought fearfully. 'If the fees can't be paid, nothing will come of it.'

It was a futile effort. Sometimes he also had his handkerchief in this pocket. What could there be now again for new bills -? Five hundred thousand mark bills -? Million dollar bills? What did she know -? What would a wedding ceremony cost - a million? Two million? Five million - what did she know -?! Even if she had had the courage to reach into her pocket, to count, she still knew nothing! She never knew anything.

The bag was not thick enough.

Slowly, so that the bedsprings did not creak, slowly, cautiously, fearfully, she turned around to face him.

Good morning, Peter, he said in a cheerful voice. His arm pulled her against his chest. She put her mouth on his mouth. She didn't want to hear it, now she didn't want to hear what he was saying:

I am completely blank, Peter. We have no more marks! And the flame rose and rose, silently. Her pure, whitish-blue heat burned clean the stale air of the room. Still merciful arms lifted the lovers from every love camp of haze and turmoil, of struggle, hunger and despair, of sin and shamelessness, up into the pure, cool heaven of fulfillment.

Chapter 02

- Berlin makes itself weak

02 01

Many streets around the Schlesischer Bahnhof are bad; at that time, in 1923, the desolation, the foul smells, the misery of the barren, arid stone desert were joined by a wild, desperate shamelessness, feasting on misery or indifference. Horniness from the greed to feel oneself for once, to be something oneself in a world that carried everyone along in a whizzing, crazy ride, towards unknown darknesses.

The Rittmeister von Prackwitz, dressed far too elegantly in a light gray suit made for him by a London tailor according to measurements sent, looking far too conspicuous with his slender figure, the loop-white hair on his head above his brown burnt face, with the dark, bushy brows and the dark glowing eyes - the Rittmeister von Prackwitz walks along the sidewalk, careful not to brush anyone. He looks straight ahead of him, at an imaginary spot far away down the street at eye level, so as not to have to see anyone or anything. He would also like to be able to listen away with his ears, for example into the heavy rustling of his still barely mown, harvest-ripe Neuloh cornfields, he strives to listen away from what scorn and envy and greed call after him.

Suddenly it is like the unfortunate November days of 1918, when he marched with twenty comrades - the rest of his squadron - along a Berlin street, near the Reichstag - and suddenly from windows, from roofs, from dark gateways, a wild gunfire pelted down on the small platoon, a ruleless, wild, cowardly banging. They had marched on like that then, too, chin thrust forward, mouth firmly closed, eyes fixed on an imaginary point at the end of the road that they would probably never reach. And the cavalry captain feels as if in the five mad years since then he has actually always marched on like this, fixing an imaginary point, waking as well as sleeping - for there was no sleep without a dream in these years. Always down a desolate street full of enemies, hatred, meanness, lack of dignity, and when, against all expectations, the corner came, then only a new, quite the same street opened up, with the same hatred and the same meanness. But again there was the point to march towards, this point that didn't exist at all, a mere imagination - .

Or was the point something that was not outside, outside of him at all, but inside him, in his own chest - do I say it then: in my heart? If he marched, because a man must march without listening to hatred and meanness, even from a thousand windows ten thousand evil eyes look at him, even if he is all alone - because where are the comrades?! Was he marching because only in this way can you get closer to yourself, become what you have to be on this earth, namely not what others expect of you, but yourself -? Man himself!

And suddenly is to the cavalry captain von Prackwitz, here on the Lange Straße at the Schlesischer Bahnhof in Berlin, a cursed city, is to the cavalry captain and knight tenant, in the face of ten screaming coffee signs, which indicate nothing but brothels - is to the cavalry captain and manor tenant and man Joachim von Prackwitz-Neulohe, who came here, came here very much against his will, to raise at least sixty people for the harvest, it is to him as if now really the end of his marching were very near. As if he could now really soon take back his chin, lower his gaze, rest his foot and say like the Lord God: behold, it was all very good!

Yes, there was a good, almost a bomb harvest in the fields, a harvest that those starving people in the city could very well have used, and he had to leave everything, hand it over to a young, somewhat ragged brat of an inspector, and go to the city and beg for people. For it was strange and completely incomprehensible: the greater the misery in the city became, the scarcer the bread there and the more only the countryside offered at least the adequate food, the more people pushed into the city. It was really like the moths lured by the killing flame!

The cavalry captain laughed. Yes truly, it really looked as if the heavenly Lord's rest from the sixth day of creation beckoned him close by! A mirage, an oasis-preview mirror, when the thirst gets really bad!

The woman, whom he thoughtfully laughed in the face, pours out behind him a whole bucket, a cesspool, a whole cesspool of foul-mouthed swearing. But the cavalry captain enters a store, above which, filthy and crooked, hangs a sign 'Berliner Schnitter-Vermittlung'.

02 02

The flame rises and sinks, the fire that was just burning is extinguished - happy the hearth that keeps the embers long! Sparks run over the ashes, the flame sank down, the embers burned out, but there is still heat.

Wolfgang Page sits at the table in his field-grey, already badly worn tunic. He put his hands on the empty oilcloth plate. Now he points with his head to the door. His one eye winks, he whispers: "Pottmadamm has already had a thunderstorm.

What? asks Petra, and: I told you not to call Mrs. Thumann Pottmadamm! She's still putting us out.

Certainly! he says. Today there's already no breakfast. She already smelled it.

Should I ask, Wolf -?

I wo. If you ask a lot, you don't get coffee. Let's wait.

He tilts the chair back, rocks and starts whistling: Rise from the earth, sleepers all ...

He is completely unconcerned, completely without worries. Through the window - the curtain is now drawn back - some sun comes into the gray, barren cave, what they call sun in Berlin, what the haze layer still left to the sunlight ... As he rocks back and forth, once the broad, slightly wavy strands of hair light up, once the face with the bright, now funny sparkling eyes, gray-green.

Petra, who has only put on his scuffed summer coat, one still from the pre-war period - Petra looks at him, she never tires of looking at him, she admires him. She wonders how he manages to wash himself in a little bowl with half a liter of water and yet look as if he has been scrubbing himself in a tub for an hour. She feels old and used up against him, even though she is a year younger than he is.

Suddenly he stops whistling, he listens to the door: the enemy is approaching. Is there coffee? I am still and still hungry for cabbage.

(She would like to say that she is also hungry for cabbage, for days, because the little breakfast with the two rolls has been her only food for many days - no, she doesn't want to say it!) The shuffling step in the hallway faded away, the floor door clanged shut. You see, Peter! Pottmadamm just went to the bathroom with the pot again. Also a move of the times: all business is done in a roundabout way. Pottmadamm runs with her pot.

He tilted the chair back again, he starts whistling again, unconcerned, funny.

He does not deceive them. She doesn't understand everything he says for a long time, she doesn't even listen that closely. It is the sound of his voice, the slightest vibration, hardly even conscious to himself, she hears it nevertheless: he is not as funny as he pretends, not as carefree as he would like to be. If he did speak out - with whom should he speak out, if not with her?! He doesn't need to be ashamed in front of her, he doesn't need to lie to her, she understands everything about him - no, don't! But it approves everything, a priori and blindly! Forgive. Pardon? Nonsense! It's all right, and if it came over him now to rage, to beat her - it would have been necessary already.

Petra Ledig (there are such names that seem to be a destiny) had been an unmarried child, without a father. Later, a small saleswoman, just suffered by her now married mother, as long as she delivered her monthly salary down to the last penny as board money. But the day came when the mother said: Feed yourself with the dirt! and called out: and where you can sleep, you will also know!

Petra Ledig (it can be assumed that the demanding name Petra was the only contribution of her unknown father for her life equipment) - Petra Ledig was no longer a blank sheet with her twenty-two years. Their maturity had not fallen into a peaceful time, war, post-war, inflation. She already knew what it meant when the gentlemen in the shoe store pressed the shoe so meaningfully against the saleswoman's lap. Sometimes she nodded, met this one and that one in the evening, after closing time; and she steered her little ship through a whole year quite courageously, without sinking completely. She even managed to make a certain selection, a selection determined not so much by her taste as by fear of illness. Once the dollar went up very badly, and everything set aside for rent devalued to nothing, she also once strolled through the streets, always in fear of the 'vice'. During such a stroll she had met Wolfgang Pagel.

Wolfgang had had his good evening. He had a little money, he had a little drink. Then he was always cheerful, up to a thousand things. Come along, little dark one, come along! he had shouted all over the street, and there had been something of a race between a mustachioed vice squad and her. But the cab, a horrible car, had taken them to an evening, nice, but actually an evening like all such evenings.

Then the morning had come, that gray, dreary morning in the room of a flophouse hotel that always made one so despondent. Where it really gets into your head at one point to ask: What's the point of all this? What do you live for?

As was proper, she had still pretended to be asleep when the gentleman hurriedly dressed, he too quite quietly so as not to wake her. Because morning conversations afterwards were unpopular, unedifying, because you discovered that you suddenly didn't have the slightest thing to say to each other, indeed, most of the time, that you were obnoxious to each other. She only had to blink through her eyelids to see if he also put the money on her bedside table. Well, he had put the money down. Everything took its orderly course, no word of goodbye had been said, he was already at the door.

She doesn't know how it happened, what came over her, she sat up in bed and asked softly in a faltering voice: Would you - would you - oh, can't I come?

He had not understood at first, quite puzzled he had turned around. Excuse me -?!

Then he had meant that, newly in such a position, she might have been ashamed to walk past the boarding house mother and porter. He had agreed to wait if she made it fast. But while she was hastily getting dressed, it had become apparent that it was not something as simple as getting out on the street unmolested. She is used to that. (She was completely honest with him from the first minute.) No, she wanted to go with him completely, at all. Would it not work? Oh, please, please! Who knows what he was thinking. Suddenly, he was no longer in a hurry. He was standing in the gray room - it was just that awful morning hour shortly before five, which gentlemen always choose to leave, because that's when they get the first electricity in their apartment. They can then freshen up before going to the office, and many also pretend to have lain in their beds, quickly turning over in them once more.

He tapped his fingers thoughtfully on a table. With his bright, greenish eyes, he looked at her thoughtfully from under his lowered brow. Surely you don't expect him to have money?

No. She had not thought about it. Let it also be the same for her.

He was a retired ensign, i.e. without any pay. Without position. Without a fixed income. Yes, actually without income.

Yes, it was right, not why she asked.

He did not inquire why she had asked. He asked nothing more at all. Only later did it occur to her that he could have asked a great many questions, very unpleasant ones. About whether she had already asked more men like that, whether she was expecting a child - a thousand disgusting things. But he just stood there looking at her. Even then she was convinced that he would say yes. Would have to. It was something too mysterious that she had had to ask him. She had never thought of it before. She was also - at that time - not the slightest bit in love with him. It had been an ordinary night.

Do you think Konstanze is behaving properly? he had quoted the title of a play that was much performed at the time. For the first time, she saw the twinkle in one eye when he joked, and the wrinkles in the corner of his eyes.

Yes, she did!

All right, he said stretched, where one does not get full, two can hardly starve. Let's go! Are you ready?

It had been a strange feeling to descend the stairs beside him, in a disgusting apartment building, beside a man to whom one now belonged. Once, when she tripped over a poorly laid runner, he had said Oops! but quite thoughtlessly, probably not quite aware of her proximity.

Suddenly, he then stopped. She remembered clearly. They had reached the bottom, it was in the false marble splendor and plaster stucco of the entrance. By the way, my name is Wolfgang Pagel, he said with a softly implied bow.

Very pleasant, she replied, just as she should. Petra Ledig.

Whether it is pleasant, remains to be seen, he had laughed. Come, little one. I will call you Peter. Petra is on the one hand too biblical for me, on the other hand too stony. But single is good and can stay that way.

02 03

When Wolfgang Pagel had spoken to her like that, Petra had still been far too full of what had happened to pay much attention to his words. Later she learned from him that the name Petra meant rock and that it had first been borne by that disciple Peter on whom Christ wanted to build His Church as on a rock.

She learned a lot from Wolfgang during the one year they lived together. Not that he had anything doctrinal. But it was inevitable that he would talk to her a lot during the long hours they spent together - for he was without real occupation - simply because they could not always sit together in silence in their cave. And once Petra had gained confidence, she often asked him something, just to keep him from brooding, or because she enjoyed hearing him talk. Like this: Wolf, how is cheese actually made? Or: Wolf, is it really true that a man lives in the moon?

He never laughed at them, nor did he reject their questions. He answered her slowly, thoughtfully, seriously - because even with his science from the cadet school it did not look famous. And if he did not know, he would take her and go with her to one of the great libraries and look up and read. She sat there quietly, some booklet in front of her, in which she was not reading, and looked solemnly into the large room, in which the people sat so quietly and gently turned over the leaves, so quietly, as if they were stirring in their sleep. It always seemed like a fairy tale to her that she, a little saleswoman, an illegitimate child who had just been sinking, was now allowed to go into such houses where the educated people sat, who had certainly never known anything of all the dirt she had had to get to know so well. Alone, she would never have dared to come here, although the - mutely tolerated - miserable figures on the walls proved to her that not only wisdom was sought here, but also warmth, light, cleanliness and precisely what also rose to her from the books: solemn peace.

When Wolfgang knew enough, they went out again and he told her what he had explored. She listened to him and forgot it again, or even kept it, but not the right thing - but that was not what mattered. What mattered was that he took her so seriously that she was something else to him than a body he liked and which was good for him.

Sometimes, when she had said something quite thoughtlessly, she could exclaim, overwhelmed by herself: Oh, Wolf, I'm so terribly stupid! I learn and I also learn nothing! I will remain eternally stupid!

But then again, he did not laugh at such exclamation, but dealt with it in a friendly serious manner, saying that basically, of course, it does not matter at all if you know how cheese is made. After all, you'll never know as well as the cheese maker. Stupidity, he believes, is something quite different. If one does not know how to arrange one's life, if one does not learn anything from one's mistakes, if one is always unnecessarily annoyed about every dirt and knows exactly that it will be forgotten in two weeks, if one cannot deal with one's fellow men - yes, all this seems to him to be right stupidity. A true prime example was his mother, who, as much as she had read and learned and as clever as she was, had now happily driven him out of the house with love and knowledge and badgering, and he was really a patient, sociable person. (Said he.) You, Petra, stupid -? Well, they would not even have quarreled, and even if they often had no money, they would not have had bad days because of it, nor would they have had grim rages. Stupid -?! What Peter then my -?

Of course, that's exactly what Wolf meant! Bad days? Grim expressions? They had had the most glorious time in the world together, the most beautiful time of their whole lives - it couldn't get any more beautiful now! After all, she didn't really care whether she was stupid or not (smart was out of the question, despite all his explanations), as long as he just liked her and took her seriously.

Bad days - truly! She had learned well enough in her life, and especially in the last year, that days without money need not be bad days. Exactly at this time, when everything was feverishly awaiting the dollar exchange rate every day, when almost all thoughts revolved around money, money, around numbers, around printed paper, around paper printed with more and more zeros - exactly at this time, this little, foolish girl had made the discovery that money is nothing at all. That it is nonsensical to worry about money - namely the missing - even for a minute - it was quite indifferent!

(Only this morning not, because she had such a nauseating hunger, and because nevertheless at 1 o'clock 30 the fees had to be paid).

How could she have lived, trembling for the next day's livelihood, even a quiet minute of happiness at the side of the retired flag junkie Wolfgang Pagel, who had now already managed for an abundant year to fetch her entire livelihood - with the smallest operating capital in the world - evening after evening from the gambling table? Evening after evening, around eleven o'clock - he gave her a kiss and said: So then, little one! and left, while she only nodded at him with a smile. Because she was not allowed to say a word, because every word could have an unlucky meaning.

In the first time, after she had learned that these eternal nightly walks did not mean 'cheating' but 'work' for both their livelihoods, she had sat up until three, four ... Only to see him arrive: pale, with nervous movements, his temples sunken, his hair still damp, his gaze flickering. She had listened to his feverish reports, his triumph when things had gone well, his despair when he had lost. Silently she had listened to his scolding of such and such a woman for taking away his stake, or his brooding wonderment as to why that very evening the black had come seventeen times in a row and hurled her, already on the threshold of wealth, back into utter poverty.

She didn't understand anything about the game, his game, roulette, as much as he told her about it (he had flatly refused to take her 'there' once). But she understood very well that this was his toll he was paying on her life, that this was why he could be so friendly, so unconcerned, so calm with her, because in the hours at the gambling table he could pour out all his strength, all his despair about this his blown, aimless and yet so unique life.

Oh, she understood far more! She understood that he was deceiving himself, at least he was deceiving himself when he kept passionately asserting that he was not a gambler ...

Say yourself, what better can I do!?! As an accountant, should I scribble numbers in a book to get a salary at the end of the day that will starve us? Should I sell shoes, write articles, become a chauffeur? Peter, the secret is: have few needs and you have time for your life. Three, four, oh, often just half an hour on the roulette, and we can live for a week, a month! Me a player? But it's a dog's work, I'd rather carry bricks, instead of standing there waiting and not letting myself be carried away, luck beckons for once. I am cold and calculating, you know they call me the Pari-Panther. They hate me, they make sour faces just by seeing me. Because I'm not a gambler, because they know there's nothing to get from me, because I pick up my little winnings every day, and when I have them, I call it a day, never letting myself be tempted to keep playing ...

And with a wonderful inconsistency, completely forgetting what he had just said: Just wait - let me do the big blow first! A real sum worthwhile! Then you shall see what we start! Then you shall see that I am not a gambler! Never again will I be taken in by them! Why should it be - it's the nastiest cattle show there is - who will voluntarily go to something like that if he's not a gamer -?!

Meanwhile she saw him coming home, at night, at night, with hollow temples, damp hair, shining eyes.

It was almost time, Peter! he shouted.

Hans Fallada   -26-   Wolf among Wolves

But his pockets were empty. Then he hocked everything they had, kept only what he wore on his body (she was condemned to bed rest in such days), left, with just enough money in his pocket to buy the minimum of tokens. Came back, with a very small profit or even once - very rarely - stuffed his pockets full of money. When everything seemed to end, she had to admit, he always brought money, little or much, but he brought money.

He had some 'system' about the rolling of the roulette ball, a system of systemlessness, a system built on the fact that the ball often didn't do what it in all probability should have done. He had explained this system to her a hundred times, but since she had never seen a roulette, she couldn't really get a picture of all that he was telling. She also doubted that he always adhered to his own system.

But be that as it may, he had still managed to do it. Long ago she managed - trusting it - to go to sleep quietly, not waiting for him to come. Yes, it was even better to pretend to be asleep if she happened to be awake for once. For once he came home from the game, hot from the game, and started talking, there was no sleep for the night.

How do you manage girl, could sometimes the Thumann, the Pottmadamm, be heard, head shaking. Always all nights away and always all that money in your bag! And it should be swarming here from noble whores! Mine I would not let go gambling!

But you also let yours go to construction, Mrs. Thumann! A ladder can also slip or crack through a board. And hookers are everywhere.

God, don't jinx it, while they are doing brickwork on the fifth floor! Where I am already so scared! But it's a Schiedunta, girl! Building must be, but gambling doesn't have to be.

But if he needs it, Mrs. Thumann!

Needs, needs! Ick hear imma needs! Mine also tells me a lot of things he needs. Skat and a cigar and Molle strong and possibly still small girls (but he tells me not!). But I tell him: what you need is a firm command and on Fridays the pay packet in front of the construction office in my hand! Det brauchste! - You're just too good, girl. But jut comes from weak, and when I look at you like this, morjens, when I serve you the coffee, and I see you rolling your eyes at him, only he doesn't notice it at all, then I also know how this turns out. Gambling as work - when I hear that! Gambling is not working and working is not playing. And if you really mean well with him, girl, you'll take his money away and he'll go to work with Willem. He will probably still be able to carry stones.

God, Mrs. Thumann, now you're talking just like his mother! She also thought I was too good and still supported him in his vice, and even gave me a pop for it.

Snap pea is ooch wieda not right! Because are you the Schwiejatochta? Nah, you just make it your vajniejen, so to speak, and if it gets too stupid for you, then you eun. Nee, Knallschote was ooch nich fine, on Knallschote can sojar sue!

But it didn't hurt at all, Mrs. Thumann. Such little fingers as his mother has. My mother was different. And anyway ...

02 04

There is a wooden barrier dividing the space of the Berlin reaper's agency into two halves, two very unequal halves. The front part, where the Rittmeister von Prackwitz now stands, is quite small, and the entrance door also knocks in. Prackwitz can hardly move.

The rear, larger half is held by a short, fat, blackish man - the cavalry captain can't quite tell, does the man seem so blackish because of his dark hair or because of uncleanliness? The blackish fat man in the dark cloth suit talks fiercely, gesticulating wildly, to three men in Manchester suits who have gray hats on their heads and cigars in the corner of their mouths. The men respond just as fiercely, and although they don't speak loudly, it seems like shouting.

The Rittmeister doesn't understand a word, of course they speak Polish. Even if the Neuloh tenant farmer employs half a hundred Poles every year, he has not learned Polish, apart from a few commands.

I admit to you, he could say to Eva, his wife, who radebrechte Polish, I admit to you that I would have to learn it already for practical reasons. Nevertheless, I refuse, for today and always, to learn this language. I reject that. We are sitting too close to the border here. Learn Polish - ah bah!

But people are making the most outrageous remarks to your face right now, Achim!

Well - and? Should I learn Polish so that I can understand their insolence as well -?! I don't even think about it! So what these four were negotiating so fiercely in the corner, the cavalry captain did not understand, nor was he interested. But he was not a very patient waiter; what had to be done should be done quickly. He was going back to Neulohe at noon, with fifty or sixty people, a bomb crop was out in the fields, and the sun was shining so that he thought he could hear the pattering of the wheat in his ears - customers! Economy! shouted the cavalry captain.

They kept on talking, it looked exactly as if they were fighting to the death, soon they would probably go for each other's necks.

Heh! You there! the cavalry captain shouted sharply. Good day I said. (He hadn't said hello.) Just the right company! Eight years ago, oh, five years ago, that had whimpered before him and slavishly tried to kiss his hand -! Damn times, damn city - just wait! Once I get you out!

Listen, you there! he shouted in his sharpest commanding voice and struck the barre with his fist.

Yes - and how they listened! They knew that kind of voice! For this generation, such voice still meant something, the sound evoked memories.

Immediately they had stopped talking. Inwardly, the cavalry captain smiled. Yes, the old Ruck-Zuck, it did and still does its job - most of all with such losers. Probably drove them like a pre-trombone of the Last Judgment into the dissolute bones! Just always had a guilty conscience.

I need reapers! he said to the fat blackish one. Fifty to sixty. Twenty men, twenty women, the rest girls and boys.

Yes, Panje, the fat man bowed, grinning politely.

A capable reaper - must be able to post bail worth twenty hundredweight of rye. The woman has to cook for the people for women's wages.

Yes, Panje, grinned the other.

I pay the outward travel money and your commission; if people stay until after the beet harvest, the travel money is not deducted from them. Otherwise ...

Yes, yes, Panje ...

So - and now a little dalli! At 12:30 the train leaves. Dalli. Printgo! Understand? The cavalry captain, a burden off his heart, nodded even to the three figures in the background. Get the contracts ready now. I'll be back here in half an hour. Just want to have breakfast.

Yes, Panje!

So everything would be all right then? the cavalry captain said in conclusion. Something in the other's attitude made him wonder, the devoted smile suddenly seemed not so devoted, more devious. Everything is fine - or -?

Everything is all right! reassured the fat man, with a quick flash of his gaze to the others. Everything according to the orders from the Panje. Fifty people - well, they are here! Railroad - 12:30 - well, she departs! Neat, punctual, according to orders - but without people! He grinned.

Hans Fallada   -30-   Wolf among Wolves

What?! the cavalry captain almost shouted, his face contorted into a thousand wrinkles. What are you saying?! Talk German, man! Why without people -?!

And the Lord, who can command so well, will he also command where I get the people? Fifty men - gutt, gutt, find them, make them, quick, fix, printgo, what?!

Now the captain took a closer look at the man. His first amazement was over, also already the first anger, because he realized he should be irritated. 'He's quite good at German,' he thought, as the other talked more and more grotesquely, rashly. 'He just won't.'

And the ones in the back? he asked, pointing to the three in Manchester, who still had their cigars hanging from the corner of their mouths as if they had gone out. You are Vorschnitter, aren't you? Why don't you come and see me? New reaper barracks, decent beds, no bug traps.

For a moment it seemed pathetic to him that he was bragging like that. But it was about the harvest, one day, one very near day there could be rain. Yes, it was actually already like thunderstorms in the air here in Berlin today. He could no longer count on the fat blackish one, with whom he had spoiled it, probably by his voice of command. Well, how is it? he asked encouragingly.

The three stood motionless, as if they had not heard a word. They were Vorschnitter, the Rittmeister was sure of his cause. He knew those thrust-forward jaws, those determined, somewhat fierce yet bleary-eyed looks of drivers by trade.

The blackish one stood there grinning, looking at the cavalry captain from the side, not looking at the people at all, so sure was he of his cause. (There's the road and the point I'm looking at. I have to go along!) Loud: Good work - good pay, good piecework - good deputation! How is it -? They heard nothing. And for the reaper thirty, I say thirty good real paper dollars in the hand!

I mediate the people! shouted the blackish one.

But already too late. The forecutters stood at the barrier.

Take mine, Panje! People like oxen, strong, pious ...

No, not the one from Joseph. All lazy crooks, early not out of bed, strong at Marushka, limp at work ...

What are you talking about, Panje, with Jablonski?! Has just come from jail, has stabbed with knife Panje inspector ...

Psia krew, pierunna -!

One on top of the other, Polish word fall - should there be a stabbing here too? The fat one in between, talking incessantly, gesticulating, shouting, pushing back, also glaring at the cavalry captain - while the third one stalks the cavalry captain without noticing.

Good paper dollars, like, what? Thirty? In the hand on departure? Be the Lord at twelve on the Silesian, I also there, with people. Say nothing! Go away quickly! Bad people here!

And already he is back with the others, voices shouting, four figures swaying back and forth, tugging ...

The cavalry captain is glad to find the door close and unobstructed. He steps back onto the street, redeemed.

02 05

Wolfgang Pagel is still sitting at the oilcloth table in his den, bobbing his chair, mindlessly fluting his entire repertoire of soldier songs and waiting for the Thumann enamel coffee pot.

His mother, meanwhile, in the well-appointed apartment on Tannenstrasse, sits in front of a beautiful, dark Renaissance table. On a yellowish bobbin lace ceiling stands a silver coffee set, fresh butter, honey, real English jams - it's all there. Only in front of the second place setting nobody is sitting yet. Mrs. Pagel looks at the square, the clock. Then she reaches for the napkin, pulls it out of the silver ring and says: Minna, I'll start. Minna, the elderly, yellowish, dusty creature at the door, with Mrs. Pagel for over twenty years, nods her head, also looks at her watch, and says: Certainly. Who does not come at the right time ...

He knows when our breakfast time is ...

Certainly - the young gentleman can't forget that!

The old lady, with the energetic face, the clear blue eye, from which age has been able to take nothing of her taut bearing, nothing of her firm principles, says after a pause: I actually thought I would see him for breakfast today.

Since that quarrel, at the end of which the least involved Petra got a slap in the face, Minna has had to set the place for the only son every day, every day she has had to put it away unused and every day the madam has pronounced this expectation. But Minna has also seen that the daily disappointment of the old lady has not taken away any of the certainty with which she always awaits the son anew (without taking a step towards him). Minna has known for a long time that all the talking doesn't help, so Minna keeps quiet.

Mrs. Pagel strikes her egg. Well, he can still come later today, Minna. What do we have for dinner today?

Minna reports, and the madam is pleased: all things he likes.

Anyway, it will come very soon now. Once he has to fail with this damn gimmick. An end with horror ... Well, from me he shall not hear a word of reproach ...

Minna knows better, but she doesn't have to say that, so she keeps quiet. But Mrs. Pagel is also not without brains and not without scent. She turns her head sharply to the old faithful under the door and asks: "You had your afternoon off yesterday, Minna. They were probably again - there -?

Where is an old person to go? Minna says grumpily. He's like my boy too!

The madam angrily bangs the spoon against the cup. He's a very stupid boy, Minna! she says sharply.

Youth has no virtue, Minna replies completely unmoved. When I think, madam, of all the stupid things I did in my youth -!

What kind of foolishness have you done, Minna?" exclaims the madam indignantly. You have made none at all! No, when you talk about foolishness, of course you only mean me - and I forbid myself that, Minna!

Minna is silent in response. But if one is dissatisfied with oneself, the silence of the other can also be oil on the fire - precisely the silence.

Of course I shouldn't have slapped her, Mrs. Pagel continues even more heatedly. She's just a silly little girl, and she loves him. I do not want to say how a dog loves his master, yet she does just that, yes Minna, do not shake your head, just that ... (Mrs. Pagel did not turn to Minna, but Minna really shook her head). ... she loves him as women should not love a man!

Mrs. Pagel stares angrily at her loaf of jam. From an obvious consideration, she sticks the spoon into the jam can and makes the spread finger thick. Sacrifice yourself! she says indignantly. I believe that! That's what everyone wants! Because it's convenient, because then there's no trouble! But to say something unpleasant: Wolfgang, my son, I'm through playing around, you won't get a penny more from me, to say something like that to him, that would be real love ... But, ma'am," Minna says, "the girl doesn't have any money to give him, and he's not her son either....

There!! exclaims Mrs. Pagel angrily. There!! Get out of here, you ungrateful person, you! You have spoiled my whole breakfast with your eternal know-it-all and contradicting! - Minna. Where are you running to? Cover on the spot! Do you think I can still eat when you tease me like that?! You know how sensitive I am with my bile! - Yes, the coffee away too. I'm

Hans Fallada Wolf among Wolves

going to have some more coffee now - I'm excited enough as it is! For you, this girl might as well be like a daughter; I'm old-fashioned, I don't believe that you can be mentally clean if you ... before marriage.

You have just said, Minna thinks quite unmoved by the outburst, for such outbursts are daily fare for her, and the madam is just as quick to be peaceful as she is to get angry.... You just said that when you like someone, you sometimes say something unpleasant to them. I was allowed to tell you that the wolf is not the son of Petra?

And with that Minna departs, the clinking tray in her hands, and as a sign that she now wants to have peace 'in her kitchen' for the time being, she slams the door firmly shut.

Mrs. Pagel also understands this and she respects this old familiar sign of the faithful. She just calls out quickly behind them: Sheepshead! Always immediately offended! Always the same angry! She laughs to herself, her anger gone. 'Such an old owl, now imagines, love consists in saying unpleasant things to the other!' She walks back and forth in the room once, she is full, because the outburst of anger came only after she had already eaten enough, and she is in the best of moods, because the little quarrel has refreshed her. Now she stops in front of a cabinet, carefully chooses a long black brasil, burns it long and carefully, and then goes over to her husband's room.

02 06

On the apartment door above the bronze bell ring (lion's mouth) hangs a chipped porcelain nameplate 'Edmund Pagel - Gesandtschaftsattaché'. Mrs. Pagel is already approaching seventy, so it doesn't look like her husband has made it very far in life. Aged legation attachés are a rare article.

By the way, Edmund Pagel had made it as far as the most capable embassy councilor and authorized envoy can go - namely to the cemetery. When Mrs. Pagel goes into her husband's room, she is not visiting him, but what remained of him in this world - and that has its reputation in the world, far beyond the walls of the little home.

Mrs. Pagel pushes the windows of the room wide open: Light and air enter from the gardens. Here in this small street, so close to the traffic that in the evening you can hear the elevated train coming into Nollendorfplatz station and the buses rumbling by day and night - here is a sprawling interweaving of old gardens with tall trees, lost gardens that have hardly changed since the eighties, nineties. It is good to live here - for aging people. The elevated train may thunder and the dollar climb - the widowed Mrs. Pagel looks calmly into the gardens. The vine leaves have risen up to their windows, down below everything keeps growing, blossoms further, sows itself - the frenzied, hasty, restless over there with their rumbling and operation just don't know it. She can watch and remember, she does not need to rush, the garden may remind her. But that she can still live here, that she doesn't have to rush along - he did that, whose work is here in this room.

Forty-five years ago they saw each other for the first time, made love, later married. There was nothing more radiant, more cheerful, more swift than him. When she thinks back, she always feels as if she walked with him through flower streets in a bright wind. From the walls the branches descended on them. They ran faster. Above the top of the hill covered with houses - between two cypress trees - the sky was blowing like a tent ...

If they only ran, soon the blue silk curtain would open in front of them.

Yes, what was really the sign of his nature was his speed, which had nothing of haste, which came from the strength, the well-being of complete health.

They came to a meadow with autumn crocus. For a moment they held still on the festive green, lila-streaked carpet. Then she bent down to pick - but she had hardly twenty blossoms in her hand, when he came with the bouquet, lightly, quickly, without haste, with the big, cheerful bouquet.

How do you do that? she asked breathlessly.

Hans Fallada   -36-   Wolf among Wolves

I don't know, he said. I always feel as if I am very light, woe is me with the wind.

The curtain rustles. Half a year has passed, they have been married for a while now, the young woman hears a plaintive call in her sleep. She wakes up. Her young husband is sitting in bed, he looks completely changed, she does not know this face yet.

Is it you -? she asks so quietly, as if she fears that her words could turn the dream into truth.

The strangely familiar man next to her tries to smile, an embarrassed smile that begs for forgiveness. Sorry if I interrupted you. It's so strange, I don't understand it. I am really scared. And after a long pause, while he looks at her doubtfully: I can't get up ...

You can't stand up? she asks incredulously. It's so unreal, a joke, nonsense from him, bad nonsense of course. There is no such thing as suddenly not being able to get up.

Yes, he says slowly and doesn't seem to believe it either. I feel as if I have no legs left. Anyway, I don't feel them anymore.

Nonsense! she shouts and jumps up. You caught a cold, or they fell asleep on you. Just wait, I'll help you ...

But even as she says this, even as she walks around the beds to him, an icy feeling enters her ... Even as she speaks, she feels: it's true, it's true, it's true....

Does she feel -? Still the old woman at the window makes an angry shoulder movement. How can she feel the impossible?! The fastest, the happiest, the liveliest - and not being able to walk, not even being able to stand! Impossible to feel.

But the icy cold remains in her, it is as if she breathes the cold deeper and deeper into herself with the air of life. The heart wants to fight back, but it's already getting cold, too, and the ice shield is tightening around it.

Hans Fallada   -37-   Wolf among Wolves

Edmund! she calls imploringly. Wake up! Get up!

I can't, he mumbles.

He really couldn't. Just as he sat in bed that morning, he now sat there day in and day out, year after year - in bed, in a wheelchair, in a recliner.... sat there, completely healthy, without any pain, only: he could not walk. The life that began so flamingly, the hurried, swift, shining life, the laughing happy life, blue silk tents and blossoms - over! Gone! Once and not again. Why not again -? No answer. Oh, my, my, why -? But if it had to be, why so suddenly -? Why without all warning, without transition -? Happily slipped into sleep - and woke up miserable, immeasurably miserable!

Oh, she didn't put up with it, no way she put up with it! All twenty years that this lasted, she did not find herself in it. When he had long since given up all hope, she still dragged him from doctor to doctor. Their hopes were ignited by reports of a miracle healing, by a newspaper notice. One after another, she believed in baths, irradiation, packs, massages, medicines - miraculous saints. She wanted to believe in it, she did.

Leave it, he smiled. Maybe it's just as well.

That's what you want! she cried angrily. Find yourself in there - humble, huh?! That would be convenient! Humility may be good for the overconfident, the fortunate who need a rein. I keep it with the ancients who fought for their happiness with the gods.

But I am happy, he said kindly.

But she did not want this happiness. She despised it, it filled her with anger. She had married a legation attaché, an active man, person in dealing with people, a future ambassador. But on the door hung a sign 'Edmund Pagel - Gesandtschaftsattaché' and that's how it stayed! She did not have a new one made: 'Pagel - painter'? No, she had not married a paint driver and blob.

Yes, there he sat now and painted. He sat in his wheelchair and smiled and whistled and painted. An angry impatience filled her. Didn't he realize that he was wasting his life with these funny descriptions that everyone was just smiling about?

Let him be, Mathilde, said the relatives. For a sick person, this is very good. He does have his occupation and distraction.

No, she wouldn't let him. When she married him, there had been no talk of times. She was not aware that he had ever held a paintbrush. She hated it all, already the smell of the oil paints. She kept bumping into the stretcher bars, the easel was always in her way. She never came to terms with it. In the guest rooms of the baths, on the floors of the rented apartments, she forgot his pictures, the charcoal drawings lay around, decayed.

Sometimes, in the middle of a work, out of worries, out of the very narrow prison of her own self, she could look up and look at such picture on the wall as if she saw it for the first time. Something wanted to touch her then quietly, as if something was stirring in her sleep - towards awakening. Stop! Why don't you stop? It was very bright, a tree about, in the sun, in the air, against a clear summer sky. Why don't you stop? But the tree seemed to lift, wind blew gently, the tree moved - was it flying? But, the whole earth flew, the sun, games of light and air, quietly, hurriedly, tenderly - stop, grim, dark earth!

She stepped closer. The curtain of mystery blew. It was canvas, smelling oil paint, earthen cloth, solid, solid earthen cloth. But eddies sounded, wind blew, the tree moved the branches, life flowed, blew - fly, do not stop, flee and fly, as we poor earthly ones flee and fly. In vain we hang the lead weights of worries, hopes, designs on our soles to arrest us to the hour. We flee there, we run into the sea ...

Painted by a paralytic, created from nothing. Of course, from a man who knew and loved movement, who is now nothing more than a lumbering body that you roll out of bed into the chair - no, do not stop, we flee, we fly.

Hans Fallada   -39-   Wolf among Wolves

Yes, it stirs gently in the contemplating woman. A presentiment wants to overtake her, as if she had her husband more imperishable, more radiant, more rapid than ever before - but she shakes it off, she sinks back into sleep. Canvas and paint, a flat surface made colorful according to certain rules, nothing of movement, nothing of the man!

On to the baths! To even more doctors! What does the world say? There have been two or three small exhibitions - you heard nothing about it, you saw nothing about it - never was a painting sold. Thank God that at least that was not necessary! And whoever knew how to find her now and then on the restless journeys through the sanatoriums of the earth: some young person, silent, clumsy, gloomy or another, suddenly breaking out into a stream of words, with agitated movements, announcing a new time - that did not exactly encourage her to take his descriptions seriously!

Come on, the day is so beautiful, let's go out!

The light is good. Let me paint for another hour.

I don't even know what it's like outside anymore. I'm dying of air hunger!

Well, sit at the window, open it - I wanted to paint you once for a long time ...

He was like that, friendly, cheerful, never angry - but not to be shaken. She talked, she asked, became angry, good again, devious, asking for forgiveness - he was like a field over which wind, thunderstorm, sunshine, night frost, rain pass. It absorbs everything, it does not seem to change, in the end there is a harvest.

Yes, a harvest was there. But until she matured, something else happened, something for which she had struggled, wrangled, pleaded for twenty years: one day he was standing there! He walked a few steps, hesitantly at first, with the same somewhat trepidatious, asking-for-pardon face as twenty years ago: I really think it works!

As they came, the disease had dwindled, incomprehensible why. All their zeal, all their worries had not been able to add anything to this progress; all this was removed from human influence, from their influence - it was despairing!

In the meantime, half a life - and the better part of life - had passed. She stood in her early forties, a forty-five-year-old legation attaché beside her - withered, withered, gone! An active life, a zealous life, without rest, full of plans, full of hopes ... Now the hopes are fulfilled and there is nothing left to hope for. All plans, all worries have become formless. A whole life crumbled into dust the moment Edmund got up and left!

Incomprehensible woman's heart:

There's your picture, Edmund. You only have a few strokes left to do - don't you want to -?

Pictures, yes, pictures ... he said thoughtlessly, glanced at it and went out, already quite outside.

No, he didn't have time to paint for half an hour. He had had twenty years to be patient, to be sick without complaint, now he had not one minute more! All of life was waiting for him outside, with a whirl of festivities, one more radiant than the other, with hundreds of people who were delightful to talk to - beautiful women, young girls so beguilingly young that it trickled down your spine just to look at them....

And wasn't he himself young -? He was twenty-five; what had come next didn't count, it had just been waiting. He was young, life was young, grasp, hold, taste the fruit - hold on, do hold on! Next ...

Paint? Yes, yes, it had helped him, it had been a pleasant pastime. Now nothing more needed to drive away the tough, burdensome time - sparkling, shining from a thousand eyes, millions of songs rejoicing, the stream chased along - with him, still with him, finally with him again!

Sometimes, at night he would drive up, dead tired, barely sunk into the first, feverish sleep of over-watching. He propped his glowing temple in his hot hand. He thought he could hear time rushing. She de-noised. He was not allowed to sleep; who was allowed to sleep, since time flowed so quickly -? Sleep was called neglect. And quietly, quietly, not to wake her, he got up, went into the city, went once again into the city where the lights were burning. He sat at a table, looking breathlessly into the faces. This one there -? Or you -? Oh, don't disappoint - do comply!

She let him go. She heard him, but she let him go, day and night. In the beginning she had gone along, she whose hope had now been fulfilled, whose struggle had yet become victorious. She saw him at the garden party of a family friend, at a diner - impeccably dressed, slim, quick, cheerful - with gray hair, two razor-sharp, deep wrinkles from the wings of his nose, over the corners of his mouth to his chin. He danced, impeccably, with a certainty, a playful perfection - 'forty-five' it said in her. He joked, chatted, talked - always with the youngest, saw them. A shudder almost came to her. Wasn't it almost as if a dead man had come to life, as if a departed man were demanding life food, in whose mouth the dust was already crunching? Why don't you stop? That which her jealous, angry heart held most dearly, that which had been her bread of happiness and food of life for twenty years: the memory of her first, festive time - was now melting away. She could no longer hold it.

The night is like a wall around them, a narrow prison with no way out. The clock on the nightstand ticks away useless time that needs to be waited through. The trembling hand lets the light shine - and from the walls his bright, hurried pictures greet them.

She looks at them as if seeing these images for the first time. It is like the world outside, which at this time also begins to stand still before his paintings, to see them. Suddenly the time of these pictures has come - but for their creator the time is over. Contradiction, counterpart, nonsense of time, contradiction - since he created his work, twenty years, unceasingly,

Hans Fallada Wolf among Wolves

patiently, mildly, he was the only one who saw it. Now comes the world, with letters and illustrations, with art dealers and exhibitions, with money, with golden laurels but his time passed, he has exhausted them, the well is empty ...

Yes, pictures ... he says and leaves.

The woman who is expecting his child is lying in bed, and now it is she who is staring at the pictures. Now it is she who sees his true image in them. His quickness, his cheerfulness, his mild seriousness - gone! There! There -? Here they are, enhanced, with a radiance that eternity lends to life.

There is one, painted shortly before his 'recovery', the last completed before he put away the brush. He had her sit down at a window, the window was open, she sat there rigid and still as hardly ever in her active life. It is her picture, it is her, since she was still with him, painted by him, when she was still something to him. Nothing more: a young woman at the window, waiting, perhaps waiting, outside the world rushes. Young woman at the window, she - his most beautiful picture!

Painted by him, since he was still with you. Where is he now? The morning is in the rushing world, radiant, full of sunshine (but the sun becomes pale to you), as they carry the man home, soiled, the clever hands bent, the chin limp, at the temple a blood clot. Oh, they are very careful with her, the policemen and the criminalists, it happened in a street whose name, of course, does not tell her anything. An accident - yes, a case. Silence!

Flee away, time, make haste! Here comes the son. The father rose as a radiant star, then shone mildly for a long time and abruptly went out. He is extinguished, we are waiting for the Son! A small light in the night, a nothing, heatless fire. But we are not so alone.

The woman in the window, the old woman, turns around. There is the picture. Yes, everything is right: young woman at the window, waiting.

The old woman puts the rest of her cigar in the ashtray.

I really feel like that stupid kid could come today. Time to go!

02 07

The Thumannsche, marital sweetheart of the bricklayer Wilhelm Thumann, spongy, flabby, in flowing robes, with a spongy flabby face, in which nevertheless a trait of sour austerity prevails - the Thumannsche shuffles with the inevitable pot across the corridor, to the loo, downstairs, half a staircase below, loo of three parties. The Thumanns, completely unhesitating in the accommodation of girls of ill repute with appendages (at present the racy Ida from the Alex occupies the room opposite Pagels), is full of sanitary misgivings as far as the toilet is concerned: "That's where they discovered these bacilli, Liebecken. They could have left it alone, but now that they have, and we don't have the finest people here, and sometimes when I go to the toilet, I think I'm running out of breath, and who knows what's swirling around in there, and once there was a black beetle, and it looked so dangerous to me ... No, how then, what then, I who know no bugs, no house bees! You can't tell me that, love, where me and the bugs, we grew up together. But since they have discovered them, I say to my Willem: Pott remains Pott, and: Health is half the life! Willem, I say to him, watch where you put yourself. The beasts jump at you like tigers, and eh de dir umsiehst, bring de eene janze Mikrokosmetik int Haus! But what can I say to you, love basin, man is strangely inferior after all, since I've been living with the pot, I've been saying all the time. Not that I'm complaining, just: it's wonderful! I know, our young gentleman, who has the small, pale dark one, but she is not his wife, only, she imagines she will be, and some people like such a formation as us cakes from Hilbrichen, he calls me imma Pottmadamm. Only, she forbids him, which I find again hochreell. But let him sar it quietly, from meinswejen! Because why does he say it? Because he wants his jokus! And why does he want his jokus? Because he is young! Because when you're young, you don't think about anything, not about the priests, which I don't, and not about the bacteria. But how does it happen? Like me with a pot, they go to the counseling center later, but with what, I don't know, because we both know, love basins, and some people just call it a sniff. And there se, as stupid as they are, have suddenly become smart, and wat den Schnuppen anjeht, so se would suddenly like to be able to sneeze and have someone to tell them Jesundheit. But that is perdü and therefore I loofe lieba with 'em pot ...

So this sort of Thumannsche, flabby-flabby, but marked by too much stomach acid in the face, shuffles along the corridor with her pot.

The door to Pagel's room opens, and in it stands young Wolfgang Pagel, tall, with broad shoulders and narrow hips, the bright, cheerful face, in his field-gray litewka with the narrow red stripes - it is a fabric that even now, after five years of use, still looks good, soft-silvery shining like some linden leaves ...

Good morning, Mrs. Thumann, he says cheerfully. How about a little palaver over coffee?

You. You! says the Thumann indignantly and pushes past with her face half averted. As you can see, I'm busy!

But of course, excuse me, Mrs. Thumann. It was just a hurried request because of cabbage. We like to wait. It only goes to elfe.

Don't just wait for the twelve, says Thumann like a warning goddess of fate in the entrance door, and the pot sways in her hand. At twelve the new dollar comes, and as the Olle in the Jemüsekeller jesacht, he will come strongly and Berlin makes itself weak once again. Then you can give me an extra million marks on the table of the house without batting an eyelash. And coffee without Jeld is not at all!

With that, the door slams shut behind her, the verdict is in, and Wolfgang turns back to the room and says thoughtfully, irresolutely: Actually, she's right, Peter. Before I smooched them around for coffee, I'm sure it's twelve, and if the dollar really goes up - what do you think?!

However, he does not wait for her answer, but says half-embarrassed: Lie down comfortably in bed, I'll take the things to uncle in a minute. And in twenty minutes, at the latest in half an hour, I'll be back here and we'll have a leisurely breakfast of ribs and liverwurst - you in bed and me on the edge of the bed, what do you think, Peter?

Oh, Wolfi, she says weakly, and her eyes get very big. Just today ...

Although they had not spoken a word of this matter this morning, he did not pretend for a moment that he did not understand it. A little guiltily, he said, "Yes, I know it's stupid. But it is truly not my fault. Or almost not my fault. Everything went wrong tonight. I had already won quite a bit, but then I suddenly had the insane idea that zero had to win. I no longer understand myself ...

He paused. He saw the game table in front of him, nothing more than a worn green cloth, spread over the dining room table of a well-bourgeois room. In the corner stood chunky, with towers, carved knights and noble ladies, knobs and lions' mouths the buffet. For the gambling clubs, gambling dens of those days led - on the constant run from the gambling department of the Krimpo - an unsteady existence. From one night to another - it smelled sour in the old place - they rented the dining room, the salon from some impoverished employee. Just for the few hours of the night - you don't need it after all. And you lie in bed and sleep; what we do is none of your business!

So it happened that for that senior accountant, for that department head, the pre-war room, which mother-in-law had still chosen, became the meeting place of tuxedos and jacket suits, blouses and evening dresses - from eleven o'clock at night. In the quiet, quietly decent street, touts and peeping toms were doing their thing, they gathered the audience that mattered: provincial concubines, drunken gentlemen, undecided where to go now; stock market jobbers, who had not yet had enough of the daily value hype. The porter had his money and slept soundly, the front door liked to go as often as it wanted. In the sober hall checkroom with its greened brass hooks stood a small table with a large box of tokens, which was managed by a bearded, sad-looking giant of the constable type. On the door of the W. C. hung a cardboard sign 'Here!' It was only whispered, everyone had an interest that no one in the house noticed 'anything'. There was also nothing to drink. Drunks could not be used because of possible noise. There was only the game, intoxication enough.

It was so quiet that the purr of the ball could already be heard from the forecourt. Behind the croupier stood two men in jacket suits, ready at any time to intervene and settle any dispute by the dreaded expulsion to the street, by exclusion from the game. The croupier wears tails. But they all three look alike, he and his two aides standing behind him, these three men, lean or fat, dark or light. All have cold, quick eyes, crooked, wicked noses like hawk beaks, thin lips. They hardly speak to each other, they communicate by glances, at most a gesture with the shoulder. They are evil, greedy, cold - adventurers, robber barons, bagmen, brooders - who knows! It is impossible to imagine that they have a private life, a wife, children who shake their hand and say 'good morning'. You can't imagine what they are like when they are alone with themselves, getting out of bed, looking at themselves in the mirror while shaving. They seem destined to be behind the gaming table, evil, greedy, cold. It didn't exist three years ago, and it won't exist a year from now. Life has flushed them up, since they were needed; it carries them away again, incomprehensible, to where, when their time is over, but life has them, life has everything that is needed.

Around the table sits a row of players, the rich, the people with the fat, swelling wallets to be gutted, the newbies, the green herrings. The three silent, ruffled birds of prey make sure that they always find a seat. Behind them, in two or three rows, are the other players, crowded together. She took her bets off over the shoulders of the front men, under the arms, onto a patch of pitch they could just spy. Or they hand the tokens away high above the heads of the others, to one of the three men, with a muttered instruction.

But despite this confusion, this crowding, there is hardly ever a dispute, because the players are far too absorbed in their own game, in the rolling of the ball, to pay much attention to the others. And besides, there are so many varieties of different colored tokens that even with the heaviest crowds, at most two or three players play the same color. Closely packed together they stand: beautiful women, handsome men are there. They lean against each other, hand touches breast, hand touches silky hip: they feel nothing. As a great blaze makes the glow of the small fire pale and dark, the tightly packed hear only the purr of the ball, the clatter of the legged tokens. Still stands the world, the chest can not breathe, time stands still while the ball runs, steers into a hole, reflects, jumps on, rattles ...

There! Red! Unequal! Twenty-one! And suddenly the chest breathes again, the face relaxes - yes, this girl is beautiful ... The stake, ladies and gentlemen! The stake! The stake! - Nothing more! And the ball runs, purrs, rattles ... the world stands still...

Wolfgang Pagel has moved into the second row of standing players. Further forward he never comes, the three birds of prey already pay attention to that, which exchange dissatisfied looks with each other, they see him only enter. He is the most undesirable gambler, he is the pari-panther, the man who, playing cautiously, does not get carried away; the man with the smallest working capital in his pocket, which is not even worth looking at, let alone taking away; the man who comes night after night with the firm intention of taking from the bank just enough to have life the next day - and who usually succeeds.

It is quite useless for Pagel to change clubs (for there are gambling clubs a dime a dozen these days, as there is heroin and coke everywhere, snow; as there are nude dances, French champagne and American cigarettes everywhere; as there is flu, hunger, despair, fornication, crime everywhere). No, the birds of prey at the head of the table always recognize him the same. They recognize him by the way he enters, the scrutinizing gaze that strangely sweeps all faces to stick to the pitch. They recognize him by his exaggerated

Hans Fallada   -48-   Wolf among Wolves

calm, his feigned indifference, the way he sets, by the long pauses he makes to skip the leaps of chance to catch a series: they recognize the same bird in different plumage!

That evening Wolfgang was nervous. Twice the touts had locked the front door in his face to scare away the unwanted gambler until he managed to sneak in with company. The man with the sad constable's face had pretended not to hear his request for tokens; Wolfgang had had to pull himself together very hard not to raise his voice. After all, he had gotten his tokens.

In the game room, he had immediately seen that a certain half-world lady, called the foreign exchange vamp by those in the know, was present. He had already had several run-ins with this demanding, loud girl in different places, because, in a losing streak and near the end of her means, she used to dispose unquestioningly of the stakes of her fellow players. He would have preferred to be the other way around. A token had fallen to him, which was of ominous significance, for it said that this room wished to keep its money. (There were many portents of this kind - all but one or two of dire foreboding).

Then he had stepped up to the table to play after all. At least he could try - within the scope of his habits - since he was here now. Like all players, Wolfgang Pagel was of the unshakable conviction that what he was doing was not a real game at all, that it 'didn't count'. He firmly believed that at some point, in a flash, in a second, the feeling would come over him: now is your hour! In this hour he would really be a player, the darling of blind luck. The ball in the wheel would purr as he set, the money would come pouring in -: Everything, everything I will win! - When he thought of this hour, sometimes, not very often, as one does not want to make the enjoyment of a great happiness worthless by tasting it too often - when Wolfgang thought of it, he felt his mouth become dry, the skin above his temples parchment.

He thought he saw himself, slightly bent over, with shining eyes - and between his hands, spread a little apart, slipped the paper, as if blown in by a wind, all this diverse paper with the enormous numbers, zeros upon zeros, a stupefying wealth that could never be fully understood - astronomical!

Until that hour came, he was a small-timer of fortune, a starveling who had to make do with the meager odds of winning at par. He was happy to make do, because the prospect of great things beckoned!

That evening he was not badly off by his standards. If he played a little carefully, a sufficient profit had to be carried home. Wolfgang Pagel had his particular system at play, devised on the basis of careful observation. Of the thirty-six numbers in the roulette, eighteen were red, eighteen were black. If we did not take into account the thirty-seventh chance, the zero, where all the bank's bets were forfeited, the chance for red and for black was equal. In an infinitely played roulette, according to the probability calculation, red had to come as often as black. It certainly did. But the way in which red and black replaced each other in the course of the game seemed to be governed by a much more mysterious rule, which one had to half observe, half feel.

When Wolfgang stood at the table - as he always did before he made his first bet - watching, he saw that red came, and red again, and red again. A fourth, fifth, sixth time red, it could go up to the tenth time, up to the fifteenth time, yes, in very rare cases even higher: red, always red. It was against all sense and reason, it contradicted all probability calculation, it was the despair of all 'players with system'.

Then all of a sudden black came, after six, eight times red came black! Came two, three times; now came red again, and now it went back and forth with a tiring, perpetual alternation: red and black, black and red.

Wolfgang, however, was still waiting. Nothing was to be said, no wager to be ventured with some prospect of gain.

But suddenly he felt something tense inside him. He looks at the patch of game table that is free to his gaze. He feels as if he has been away for a while with his thoughts, without knowing where, as if he has not followed the game. Nevertheless, he knows that now black came three times in a row, he knows that now he has to bet, that now a series black has started - he bets.

He bets three, four times. More often he does not dare. Oh, twelve, fifteen times red are an exception, that's where the big odds are: stand the bet and win - doubled! Stand - doubled ... on and on, into fabulous numbers. But his capital is too small, he cannot risk failure, he has to make do with home-baked security. But once - once for sure the night will come, and he will continue, continue, continue ... He will know that seventeen times red is coming, he will put it seventeen times and no more.

And then he will never play again. Then they will start something quiet with the money, an antique store for example. He has a sense for that kind of thing, he likes to deal with those things. Life will then flow gently and calmly, no more extreme tension, nothing of deepest despair, no more bird of prey faces eyeing him ruffled, no more quite undoubted half-world ladies stealing his stake ...

He has sought his place at the other end of the gaming table so as not to be near the Valutenvamp, but it does him no good. He is just about to sit down when he hears her voice: Why don't you make room? Don't stand there so broad! Others also want to play.

He makes a bow, does not look at her and clears the field for her. He finds another place and starts to sit down again. He remembers that he must play especially carefully today, bring home a little more than usual: tomorrow at half past twelve they want to get married.

Very well. Very well. She is an excellent girl, there will never be one who loves him more selflessly as he is, without comparing him to a troublesome ideal. So you are going to get married tomorrow, why actually is not ascertainable at the moment. It doesn't matter, it will be right. But he wished he would play a bit more attentively, just now he should not have bet Black under any circumstances. There! There! So now ...

Suddenly he hears the angry, irritated voice behind him again. She is now arguing with another gentleman, speaking very high and indignant. Of course: her nose is all white, she snorts snow, the bitch, coke. No point in tying up with her, she already soberly doesn't know what she wants or does. And now more than ever -!

He again looks for another place and starts playing again.

This time everything goes well. He sets cautiously, and recovers what he has added so far, yes, he can already withdraw all his working capital and operate with the profit. Next to him stands a youth with flickering eyes and erratic movements, making his maiden game sure as death. Such bring good luck. He manages to stroke the young man's back without him noticing, with his left hand, his left hand - such a thing increases the chances of winning! As a result, he leaves the insert in place once longer than he would otherwise have dared. He wins again. The bird of prey shoots him a quick, evil glance. Good.

He now has enough for tomorrow, for a few days longer (if the dollar doesn't rise too much), he could go home. But it's still very early; he knows he'd just lie awake in bed for hours thinking about the game, he knows he'd be gripped with regret that he didn't take advantage of this lucky streak ...

He stands quietly, his won chips in hand, listening to the ball, the croupier's calls, the soft, scratchy scrape of rakes on this gambling floor, but maybe he's somewhere else entirely. The clattering of the ball is reminiscent of a rattling mill wheel. Yes, it is soporific; life, when you feel it, always reminds you of water, flowing water; panta rhei, everything flows, it was said at the Penne, even before the Cadet School. Also flowed away.

He feels that he is very tired, moreover, his oral cavity is leathery with dryness. A mess that there is nothing to drink here. He would have to go to the tap on the toilet. But then he does not know how the game continues. Red - Black - Black - Red - Red - Black ... Of course, there is nothing else: red life

Hans Fallada   -52-   Wolf among Wolves

and black death. Something else is not handed and invented, they may invent as much as they want, life and death, beyond that there is nothing ...

Zero!

Of course - he had forgotten zero, there was that, too. The pari players always forgot zero, and suddenly their money was gone. But if there was zero, zero was death, and that was quite right. Then red was love, a bit of an exaggerated thing, but well: pleasant when you had it. But black - what was black then? Well, for Schwarz there was still life, again exaggerated, but towards the other side. Not completely black, gray would have sufficed. Often a light, almost silvery gray. Certainly, Peter is a good girl.

I do have a fever, he suddenly thought. But I have a fever, I think, every night. I would really have to drink water. Now I'm leaving right now.

Instead, he shook the tokens in his hand, hurriedly added the one from his pocket, and bet everything just as the croupier called: Nothing more! to zero. To zero.

His heart stopped. 'What am I doing?" he asked himself, confused. The feeling of dryness in his mouth intensified to the unbearable. The eyes burned, above the temples parchment stretched the skin. The bullet purred for an incomprehensibly long time, he felt as if everyone was looking at him.

'Everyone is looking at me. I set to zero. Everything we have I have set to zero - and zero means death. Tomorrow is wedding ceremony ...'

The ball was still purring; it was impossible to hold one's breath waiting any longer. He took a deep breath - the tension eased ...

Twenty-six! shouted the croupier. Black, unequal, passe ... Pagel pushed through his nose the air, almost relieved. It had been right: the gambling hall had kept its money. The valute vamp had not confused him for nothing. Just now the girl said half aloud: These little nebbichs! Play they want - in the sandbox they should play! The predatory croupier shot him a sharp, triumphant look.

For a moment Wolfgang stood waiting. The feeling of release from agonizing tension passed. 'If I had another token,' he thought. 'Well, it doesn't matter. One day the day will come.'

The ball was purring again. Slowly he went out, past the sad constable, down the dark staircase. For a long time he stood in the entrance to the house until a tugboat let him out.

02 08

What could he tell his good little Peter about all these things? Almost nothing. It could be compressed to the sentence: First I won, then I had bad luck. So there was nothing special to report, lately he had had to say this more often. Of course, she could hardly imagine anything about it. She may have thought it was something similar to when someone loses at skat or comes out with a blank in the lottery. Nothing of the ups and downs, the happiness and the despair could be made comprehensible to her. Only the result was to be communicated: an empty bag - and that was meager.

But she knew much more about all these things than he believed. Too often she had seen his face, at night when he came home, still half heated. And the exhausted face in sleep. And the evil, moving face when he dreamed of the game. (Didn't he know that he dreamed of it almost every night, he who wanted to convince himself and her that he was not a gambler -?) And the distant, thin face, when he didn't listen to her talk, thoughtlessly asked 'How?' and yet didn't hear, the face on which his vision found such a strong expression that one thought one could lift it off like something that had taken shape. And the face when combing his hair in front of the mirror, when he suddenly saw what kind of face he had.

No, she knew enough, he didn't have to say anything, didn't have to torture himself with explanations and excuses.

It doesn't matter, Wolf, she said quickly. We have always been indifferent to money.

He just looked at her, grateful that she took this explanation from him. Of course, he then said. I'll make up for it. Maybe tonight already.

Only, she said, and was insistent for the first time, that we have to go to the registry office at half past twelve today.

And I, he said quickly, want to take your clothes to your uncle. - Can't the registrar marry you as a seriously ill woman in bed?

You will have to pay for seriously ill people, too! she laughed. You know, not even death is free.

But maybe with sick people you have to pay afterwards, he said, half laughing, half thinking. And if then nothing is there: trusted is trusted.

For a while they were both silent. The stale air, increasingly overheated as the sun rose, stood almost palpably in the room, making itself felt dry on the skin. In the silence, the noise of the tin-punching shop could be heard louder, then suddenly the whining, tearful voice of Mrs. Thumann, who was chatting with a neighbor outside the door. The crowded human honeycomb of the house hummed, screamed, sang, rattled, shouted, cried with many voices into it.

You know you don't have to marry me, the girl said with a sudden resolve. And after a pause: No one has done as much for me as you have.

He looked to the side a little embarrassed. The window glistening in the sun glowed with a whitish glow. 'What did I actually do for her?' he thought, embarrassed. 'Taught her how to hold a knife and fork - and proper German.'

He turned his head and looked at her. She wanted to say something else, but her lips twitched as if she were fighting a sob. He felt such intensity in the dark gaze that looked at him that he would rather have looked away.

By then she was already talking. She said, "If I knew you merely felt obligated to marry me, I never wanted it.

He shook his head, slowly, negatively.

Or out of defiance against your mother, she continued. Or because you think it gives me pleasure.

He continued in the negative.

('But does she know why we're getting married?' he thought in wonder, lost.)

... But I always think you want it too, because you feel we both belong together, she said suddenly. She pushed it out, now there were tears in her eyes. She could speak more freely, as if the hardest thing had been said. Oh, Wolf, dear, if it is not so, if you marry for any other reason, leave it, I beg you, leave it. You won't hurt me with that. Not as hurt, she said hastily, as when you marry me, and we don't belong together at all.

She looked at him, suddenly she started to smile, there were still tears in her eyes. You know my name is 'Ledig', I have always been called Ledig - you always agreed with the name, only Petra was too stony for you.

Oh, Petra, Peter, Peter Ledig! he cried, somehow overwhelmed in his lonely, selfish cave by her humble loveliness. What are you talking about?! He took her, wrapped her in his arms, rocked her like a child, and laughingly said, "We don't have the money for the registry fees, and you're talking about the deepest things?!

And don't I have to talk about it? she said more quietly, holding her head close to his chest, don't I have to talk about it, since you yourself are silent about it - always and all days, all hours -?! I think so often, even when you hold me in your arms as you do now and kiss me as you do now, that you are very far away from me - from everything -.

Now you're talking about the game, he said, holding her looser.

No, I'm not talking about the game, she hastily objected, leaning tighter against him. Or maybe that's what I'm talking about. You must know that, I don't know where you are and what you think. Play all you want - but if you don't play, couldn't you be here for a bit -? Ah, Wolfi, she said, and now she had slipped away from him, but held both his arms clasped above the elbows and looked at him firmly. You always think you have to apologize or explain something to me because of the money - nothing you have to explain and nothing you have to excuse. If we belong together, everything is right, and if we don't belong together, everything is wrong - with and without money, with and without marriage.

She looked at him expectantly, she hoped for a word, oh, if he had only pulled her into his arms in the right way, she would have felt it already -!

'What does she want from me anyway?" he had thought above her talking. But he probably knew what she wanted. She had given herself entirely into his hands, from time immemorial, from that first morning when she had asked him if she could not come with him. She had nothing left. Now she asked him to open his dark, distant heart to her once, but just once....

But how do I do that?" he asked himself, "How do I do that?" And in a flash, relieved: "The fact that I don't know that shows that she is right: I don't love her. I just want to marry her like that. 'If only I hadn't set it to zero yesterday,' he hurriedly continued to think. Then the money would have been there for the registry office. There would have been no such dispute. Of course, now that I know this, it would be more correct if we did not get married. But how am I going to tell her? I can't go back. She is still looking at me. What should I tell her -?'

The silence had become heavy and oppressive between them, she was still holding his arm, but only loosely, as if she had forgotten that she was holding him. He cleared his throat. Peter ... he began.

Then the hall door opened and the shuffling of the Thumanns became audible.

Quick, Wolf, close the door! Petra said hurriedly. Mrs. Thumann is coming, we can't use her now.

She had let him go. He went toward the hallway, but before he had even grasped the door to the room, the landlady came into view.

Are you still waiting? she asked. I've already said: coffee is not without money.

Listen, Mrs. Thumann, said Wolfgang hurriedly. I don't want coffee at all. I'm going to my uncle's right now with our things. And in the meantime, give Petra some rolls and coffee, she's half-starved.

Not a sound in his back.

And with the money I'll come to you right away and pay for everything, keeping only enough for myself so that I can go to Grunewald. I have a friend from the military, his name is Tick, from Tick, who will surely pump me something ...

He now ventured a look into the room. Noiselessly Petra had sat down on the bed, sitting there with her head bowed, he did not see her face.

So? replied the Thumann, half questioning, half threatening. Breakfast for the girl should not be lacking - today not and tomorrow not yet - but how is it with the wedding -? She stood there, in flowing robes, with melting forms, the pot in her hanging hand - and as she stood there like that, she could now of course drive out everyone's desire for all marriage and civility for a long life.

Oh! Wolfgang said lightly and was on top again in an instant. If it's okay with breakfast for Peter, it's okay with the wedding ceremony.

He quickly looked after the girl, but Peter was still sitting as before. You will have to queue at the pawnshop and Jrunewald is far, said the Thumann. Ick hear imma wedding, but ick trau nich!

Yes, yes! Petra suddenly said and stood up. You may already marry, Mrs. Thumann, because of the money and because of the marriage ceremony, both. - Come on, Wolf, I'll help you pack the things. We take the suitcase again, then he only has to take a look inside and sees that everything is together again. He already knows it now. And she smiles at him.

Mrs. Thumann turned her head observingly from one to the other, slowly, like an old, wise bird. Wolfgang cried out with infinite relief: "Oh, Peter, you're always the very best, and maybe I really will make it until half past twelve. If I hit tick now, he sure pumps me enough that I can take a car ...

Certainly! said Thumann instead of Petra. And then out with the girl from the beds and in with her to the registry office, as she stands and stands, with 'em men's paletot, without everything underneath. We're big time!!! She sparkled venomously. When ick so wat just hear! And the bad thing is, the girls aren't all who give you men such a hard time, and if I know the girl, she sits around in the kitchen with me the whole time afterwards and acts as if she wants to help me. But she doesn't want to help me, not a bit, she just wants to have an omen on the kitchen clock, and half past on time she says: I feel he's coming, Mrs. Thumann! - But he doesn't come, and probably he just sits with his highborn friend and they take care of him in peace and quiet and puff one, and when he really thinks something, he thinks: they trust every day! And what is not today, does not need to come tomorrow ...

And with that, the Thumann shot a withering look at Wolfgang, a contemptuous-pitying one at Petra, made a small movement with the pot as a final point, exclamation and question mark in one, and pulled the door shut. The two of them, however, were quite embarrassed and hardly dared to look at each other, for one might think what one wanted of the landlady's outpouring: it was not pleasant.

Finally, however, Petra said, "Don't worry about it, Wolfgang. They and everyone else can say what they want, it doesn't change anything. And if I was so whiny earlier, forget it. Sometimes you have a mood like you're all alone, and then you're afraid and you'd like to hear some comfort.

And now you are no longer alone, Peter? Wolfgang asked, strangely moved. Now you don't need any more consolation?

Ah, she said, looking at him in lost embarrassment. You are there ...

But, he suddenly urged, perhaps Pottmadamm is quite right that I sit at half past twelve and think: do they mourn every day - what do you think?

That I trust! she exclaimed, raising her head and looking at him boldly. And if I didn't trust you either, does that change anything? I cannot bind you. Marriage or not - if you like me, it's all good, and if you don't like me ... She broke off and smiled at him. Now run along, Wolf. Uncle breaks for lunch at noon, and maybe there really are a lot of people in line. She put the suitcase in his hand, she gave him another kiss. Take care, Wolf!

He would have liked to say something else to her, but he couldn't think of anything. So he took the suitcase and left.

Chapter 03

- Hunter and hunted -

03 01

On the Neulohe manor, the little field inspector Meier, called Negermeier, is so tired again between the eleventh and twelfth hour of the morning that he could fall into bed, as he is, in his jacket and spats, and sleep until the next morning. But he is just sitting on the edge of a rye field, well covered from view by a few pine snugs, in the long and dry forest grass, dozing away.

Up at three, into the warm haze of the barn (so tired, oh, so tired!), put out feed, supervised feeding, supervised milking, checked on grooming. From four o'clock rape brought in, which must be brought in the morning dew, so that it does not fail. At three quarters of seven, drank a cup of coffee standing up, hastily gulped down something (still tired). And from seven the usual day's work.

Then came word from the rye beat that both tying machines were broken. Hunted with the blacksmith, messed around with the things. Now they clatter again, they still clatter - oh, what he is tired, now he is not only still tired from yesterday, now he is already tired from today! Oh, how he would love to fall asleep here now, roasting in the sun -! But he has to go back to the sugar beet field before noon to check whether the bailiff, Kowalewski, is hoeing properly with his column and not tinkering ...

Meier's bike lies in the ditch a few steps around the pine grove. But he's too lazy to go on now, he just can't. Like a thick, woolly, somewhat aching mass, fatigue sits in all his limbs, but especially in his throat. When he lies very still, she sort of falls asleep. But if he moves only one leg, it scratches and rubs the same as with bristles.

He slowly lights a cigarette, takes a few blissful drags, and stares at his dusty, faded shoes. New ones would also do, however the Rittmeister is a big man, five hundred thousand marks is an unheard of salary for a field inspector. But let's just wait and see how the dollar comes to the first, then we may not even be able to sole our shoes! Many things are needed at the Neulohe manor - at least two more officials are needed. But the cavalryman is a big man and has discovered that he can do everything on his own - he can't do a damn thing! Today he went to Berlin to pick up reapers. In any case, he can't chase a poor inspector up from his morning doze like that - 'But I'm curious to see what people he brings in. If he brings any at all. Oh, shit -!'

Meier lies back, the cigarette slips all the way into the corner of his mouth, the Trillerbibi is pushed over his eyes against the sunburn ... The women in the sugar beets can be boiled sour with their Kowalewski for his sake, a cheeky gang is that! But you wouldn't think Kowalewski had a smart daughter. The can come quiet times again on vacation from Berlin, he would rock the child already! Warm is that, hot is that, an oven is that. If only no thunderstorm comes, then all the grain gets wet, and he has the mess -! Of course, we should have driven in today, but the cavalry captain is a great man and weather prophet by the way: it's not raining, we're not driving in, Sela!

Thank God, the binding machines are still rattling, so you can keep lying here. Just don't fall asleep, then you won't wake up again before evening. The cavalry captain would find out right away, and tomorrow they would be sitting outside. It would be even so, at least you could sleep off -!

Yes, the little Kowalewski is not bad, she won't make any bad bitches in Berlin either - but the Amanda, Amanda Backs is not without her! The little negermeier throws himself on his side, he finally represses the piercing thought that the cavalry captain did not actually say that one should not drive in, but rather that the negermeier should do as the weather dictates.

No, Meier doesn't want to think about that now, he'd rather think about Amanda. Some life comes into him, he tightens his knees and emits a grunting sound of pleasure. The cigarette falls out of his mouth, but it doesn't matter - what does he need a cigarette for, he has Amanda! Yes, they call him the little Meier, the Negermeier - and when he looks at himself in the mirror, he has to agree with them. Behind the round, large, domed glasses sit round, large, yellowish owl eyes, he has a depressed nose and beaded lips, a forehead barely two fingers high, his ears stick out - and in addition, the whole man Meier is one meter fifty-four high!

But that's just it: he looks so great and forbidden, so grotesque in his ugliness, and he has such a cheeky cute snout to boot that the girls all fall for him. When she passed him with her friend - he was still fresh on Neulohe - the friend said: Amanda, you need a kick to get started! But Amanda said: It doesn't matter, he has such a sweet notch! - That was their kind of declaration of love, that's how the girls were here: cheeky and of heavenly insouciance. They had an appetite for one or not, but in any case they did not make a fuss about it. Good they were!

How the Amanda joined him in the window last night - actually he didn't feel like it, he was too tired - and the madam drove out of the bushes. (Not the young lady from the cavalry captain, she would have just laughed, she was not without her own. No, the old madam, the mother-in-law, from the castle). Anyone else would have shrieked or hidden or called for his help, not so the Amanda. He could remain completely uninvolved and enjoy himself. Yes, madam, Amanda had said innocently. I just go through the poultry bills with the inspector, he never has time during the day.

And you're going through the window?" shrieked the old lady, who was very pious. You shameless person!

But if the house is already closed, the Amanda replied.

And when the madam was still not fed up and did not want to see that she could no longer stand up to the young things of today, not with piety and

Hans Fallada   -63-   Wolf among Wolves

not with severity, she had said: And now, by the way, it's closing time, madam. And what I do after work is my business. And if you find a better poultry maid than me (for such a disgraceful wage) - but you don't find any - then I can go, but only tomorrow!

And she had wanted him not to close the window. If she wants to stand and listen, let her stand, Hansel! We don't care, and she might enjoy it - she didn't get her daughter from praying!

Little Meier gnawed away most amusedly and pressed his cheek more firmly against his arm, as if he felt the soft yet firm body of his Amanda. Such was just right for a have-not and bachelor like him! No talk of love, fidelity, marriage, but always on top of things, at work and with his mouth. And keß! Keß that sometimes the shudder came on! But in the end, no wonder how she had grown up, with four years of war and five years of post-war and:

If I don't eat something, I don't get anything. And if I don't slap you, you slap me. Always show your teeth, young man, even against 'ne olle woman, does not matter at all. She has had her good - and I am not supposed to have my good, just because they make a stupid war and an inflation -? Don't make me laugh! I am me, and when I am no more, there is no one! And for the tears that she cries into my grave as a good girl (but they are only tears of pressure) and for the tin wreath that she puts on my maggot box, I can't afford anything either, and that's why we'd rather be happy today, eh, Hansel? Pity the old woman and a little gently -? Well, you know, who felt sorry for me? Always over 'n head, and when the Neese bled, it was just beautiful. And when I just wanted to cry a bit, I was immediately told: Shut up, or there will be more from the same bag! Nah, goosebumps, I said nix if there was any point. But it has no sense, and as stupid as my chickens, which lay the eggs for our pleasure, and then in the end still rin in the cooking pot - I do not, nope, thanks! If you like, please, I do not!

That's right, the girl! laughs little Meier once again and is already fast asleep and would really have slept on into the evening dew - business or no business, Rittmeister or no business - if it hadn't suddenly become too hot and, above all, too stuffy for him.

Riding up - but with a jerk that was not at all tired and immediately on both legs - he saw that he was in the middle of the most beautiful, incipient forest fire. He saw a figure jumping and trampling and beating through the whitish, deep, acrid smoke, and already he himself was jumping along, also trampling into the flames and beating them with a spruce branch and shouting to the other: That burns sweetly!

Cigarette! said the only and continued to extinguish.

I almost got burned too, Meier laughed.

Not a pity either! said the other.

Say. Meier shouted, coughing from the smoke.

Hold the edge, man, ordered the other. Smoke inhalation is also not without.

And now they both continued to extinguish the fire at the top of their lungs, while Negermeier listened intently to his two binding machines to see whether they were also continuing to rattle. For it would not have been at all pleasant for him if people had noticed something and told the cavalry captain.

But, contrary to expectations, they calmly kept on cutting their way down, and this should have annoyed the inspector again, because it proved that the guys were dozing on their seats and left not only the work but also the mind to the horses, and that because of them the whole Neulohe manor with all its buildings and eight thousand acres of forest could have burned down - they would have stared at their incinerated stables when they came home from work as if witchcraft was involved. But for this time, Meier was not annoyed, but was happy about the rattling on and also about the decreasing smoke. Finally, he and his rescuer stood facing each other in a room-sized black spot, a little breathless and bruised, looking at each other.

The rescuer, however, looked a bit wild, young still, but with a flutter and gun of reddish hair around his nose and chin, quite strong looking blue eyes, an old gray tunic and pants just like it, but with a nice yellow leather belt around his waist and an equally nice yellow leather pistol pouch. There had to be something in it, too, namely in the pistol pocket, and not just sugar candy, so heavy it hung down.

Would you like a cigarette? the incorrigible greyhound Meier asked the other and held out his case to him, because he thought he had to do something for his savior.

Give it to me, comrade, said the other. My fins are black.

Mine too! laughed Meier. But he reached out with two pointed fingers, and immediately the cigarettes burned, too, and the two of them sat down a little away from the charred spot in the sparse pine shade, nicely tucked into the dry grass. But they had learned so much from the experience that one took an old pine stump, the other a flat stone for an ashtray.

The field gray did a few deep lung breaths, stretched and stretched, yawned unabashedly with a few deep A sounds and spoke profoundly: Yes ... yes ...

Modest, huh? agreed Inspector Meier.

Modest -? Shit! said the other one, examining the heat-scorched landscape once again with narrowed eyes and falling backwards into the grass, seemingly bored beyond limits.

Actually, Meier had neither the time nor the inclination to become a partner in another morning snooze, but he still felt obliged to hold out for a while next to this man. So he remarked, not wanting the conversation to completely peter out: Hot, huh?

He just grunted.

Meier looked at him scrutinizingly from the side and guessed: Baltic, eh?

But this time he didn't even get a grunt in response. Instead, it rustled in the pines. The forester Kniebusch, white-bearded but bald, appeared, leading Meier's wheel, threw the wheel in front of Meier's feet and said sweatily: "Man, Meier, are you going to leave your wheel on the open road again? And it's not even yours, but Dienstrad - and when it travels, the Rittmeister rages and you -.

But about this the forester had seen the black-burnt spot, inflamed himself on the spot angrily red (because with a fellow official he could afford what he was not allowed to dare with wood thieves because of danger to life) and began to scold: Have you damned louse smoked your damned Stinkadores again and burnt my forest?! Well, wait, friend, there can be no more talk of friendship and evening Skatkloppen - service is service and tonight still learns the captain ...

But it was written that for this time the forester Kniebusch should not finish a sentence. For now he spotted the apparently sleeping, highly suspicious, dissolutely field-grey subject in the grass and said: Have you caught a bum and forest arsonist, Meier? Great, that's praise from the cavalry captain; and for a while he has to shut up about slackness and not taking action and being afraid of people. - Wake up, you bastard! the forester shouted and jabbed his foot hard into the guy's ribs. Go! Up and off to Father Philip -!

But the kicked one only pushed the field cap from his face, shot a sharp look at the angry one and spoke in an even sharper voice: Forester Kniebusch -!

It was very surprising for Negermeier and even more amusing to watch the effect this mere name call had on his skat brother, the lecherous and scaredy-cat Kniebusch. He was literally thunderstruck, all his ranting died away and he said, standing at attention for the first time: Lieutenant -!

The other slowly raised himself, brushed the dry stalks and twigs from his skirt and trousers and said: "Tonight at ten o'clock at the schoolmaster's

Hans Fallada   -67-   Wolf among Wolves

meeting. They notify people. You can bring that little guy with you. He stood, moved to his coop and still said: You can also report how much weapons are available on Neulohe, usable weapons and ammunition, understand -?!

At your command, Herr Leutnant! stammered the old Rauschebart, but Meier noticed how it gave him a puff.

The indeterminate individual, however, nodded briefly to Meier, said: Goes all right, comrade! and disappeared into the bushes, pine huddles, pine poles, forest - gone he was like a dream!

Golly! Meier spoke a little breathlessly and stared into the greenery. But that was already motionless again, flickering in the midday glass.

Yes, by golly you say, Meier," the forester scolded. But I have the running around the village this afternoon. And whether it's right for everyone is far from clear. Some pull such funny faces and say it's all nonsense, and they've had enough of Kapp. -ä But ... the forester continued, perhaps even more miserably ... you've seen him as he is, no one dares tell him to his face, and when he whistles, they all come. Only I always hear the backtalk.

Who is he? Meier asked curiously. He doesn't look that big!

Who is he supposed to be? the forester cried angrily. It doesn't matter what he calls himself, he won't tell us his real name. He is just the lieutenant ...

Well, lieutenant is not so much nowadays, Meier said, but he was impressed by the way he had stomped the forester.

Do I know if lieutenant is much or little! grumbled the forester. Anyway, people parry him. And ... he continued mysteriously, surely they are up to something big, and if it succeeds, it's all over with Ebert and the whole red bubble!

There, there! said Meier. Some people have already thought that. Red seems to be a real color, you won't scratch it off easily!

Hans Fallada   -68-   Wolf among Wolves

But this time! whispered the forester. They are supposed to have the Reichswehr behind them, and they call themselves the Black Reichswehr. The whole area is full of them, from the Baltic States and from Upper Silesia, and from the Ruhr as well. They are called work commandos and they are also disarmed. But you've seen and heard for yourself ...

So a coup! said Meier. And you want me to join in? I'll have to give that a lot of thought. Just because someone says: 'It's okay, comrade!' - no, that's not why!

The forester had already moved on. He mused anxiously: the old man has four hunting guns and two triplets. Then the can. The cavalry captain ...

Right! said Meier, suddenly relieved. What is the Rittmeister's opinion? Or does he not know anything about it -?

Yes, if I knew that! said the forester plaintively. But I just do not know! I have already asked around everywhere. To Ostade the Rittmeister goes and sometimes tipples with the Reichswehr officers. We might get ourselves into trouble and, if things go wrong, I might lose my job and end up in jail in my old age....

Well, don't you cry, old walrus! laughed Meier. The matter is quite simple: why shouldn't we just ask the captain if he wants us to join or not?

O God! Oh God! cried the forester, and now he really threw his hands together in despair. You really are the biggest greyhound in the world, Meier! Afterwards, the cavalry captain doesn't know about the whole thing, and we told him. And you should know that from the newspapers: Traitors fall to the Feme! - And I - suddenly came to his mind, and the sky went all black, all the skins swam away rushing, his arm went with ground ice ... And I sheep's head told you everything! Oh, Meier, do me a favor, give me your word of honor right now that you won't tell anyone anything! I will also not tell the cavalry captain that you burned the forest ...

First of all, said Meier, I didn't burn the forest, but your lieutenant did - and if you betray him, you know. And secondly, if I had really set fire to the forest, I'm also going to the Schulzen tonight at ten, so I'm also part of the Black Reichswehr. And if you then betray me, Kniebusch, you know that traitors fall into the trap of fame....

There stood Meier, grinning, in the middle of the forest aisle, looking cheekily and challengingly at the gossip and the scaredy-cat Kniebusch. 'And if this whole coup story is good for nothing at all,' he thought, 'it settles this wretched earwig - who shall not risk another sound about me to the old gentleman or the cavalryman -!'

Opposite him, however, stood the old forester Kniebusch, and redness and pallor rose alternately in his face. 'Now,' he thought, 'one has wriggled through forty years of service with hanging and choking and thinks: it's getting calmer. But no, it's getting worse and worse, and the way I now wake up from sleep at night terrified something has happened, it's never been like this before. Earlier it was only the wood bills and the fear whether I had also added correctly, and sometimes a buck whether he also went on his bill when the old man sat on decency.

But now you lie the night in the dark and the heart beats worse and worse, and it's wood thieves and lieutenants and this insolent carrion is now also becoming insolent, and it is to be couped ... And after all, I am sitting in it, whereas I have nothing at all against the Herr Reichspräsident ...'

But he said aloud: "We are colleagues, Meier, and have played many a good game of skat. I have never said a word against you to the Herr Rittmeister, and the thing about the forest fire, that just came out in my anger. I would never have betrayed you, of course not!

Of course not! Meier said and grinned cheekily. Now it's almost twelve and I won't get to the sugar beets after all. But I have to go to the feeders, so I get on my bike. You can run after it, Kniebusch, you don't mind, do you?!

And Meier was already sitting on the wheel and competing. As he drove off, however, he shouted once again: "It's all right, comrade," and he was gone!

But the forester stared after him, shook his head gloomily, and considered that he would rather take the sneaking path instead of the big road to the forester's house. On the road he might still have met timber thieves, and that would have been embarrassing - for the forester!

03 02

The pawnbroker, the uncle, sat on a high Kontorbock and wrote in his books. A clerk was half-negotiating with two women, one of whom was holding a bundle of beds wrapped in a sheet. The other, however, had embraced a black mannequin of the kind used by dressmakers. Both women had sharp faces and the emphatically carefree look of rare pawnshop visitors.

The loan itself, located on the mezzanine floor of an over-busy house, looked as always greasy, dusty, untidy, although it was scrupulously tidy. The light filtering through the white frosted glass of the windows was gray and dead. As always, the huge strongbox stood wide open, opening the view to small piles of packets wrapped in white paper, at the sight of which one could dream of precious jewels. As always, the keys were in the small walled-in safe that held the loaner's cash.

Wolf saw it all with one look. From dozens of corridors, it was so familiar to him that he saw it without quite seeing it. It was also the usual thing for the uncle to shoot away a quick glance at him over his narrow gold glasses and then continue writing.

Wolfgang Pagel turned to the employee, who apparently could not come to an agreement with the woman who wanted to move her mannequin, lifted the case onto the table and said half aloud - lightly: I'll bring the usual again. Please, if you want to check ...

And he flicked open the locks on the carry-on case.

Everything was really there as usual; everything they owned: a second pair of trousers from him, already thin in the bottom; two white men's shirts; three dresses from her; her linen (scanty enough) and - the pièce de résistance - a real silver purse, probably the gift of an admirer to Petra, he had never asked for it.

Not true, three dollars as usual? he still said, just to say something, as the employee, it seemed to him, looked a little hesitantly at the things.

But then he already said, "Yes, Lieutenant!

And now, when everything seemed to be in order, quite surprisingly the high voice from the Kontorbock called out: No!

Wolfgang, who was only called the lieutenant here, and the clerk looked up in surprise.

No! said the uncle again and shook his head vigorously. I'm sorry, Lieutenant, but we can't oblige you this time. It's not worth it for us. They always get it back the very next day, all that rigmarole - and, you know, those clothes do go out of style! - Maybe another time again when you have something - more fashionable.

The uncle looked at Pagel once more, raised the pen, with the point against him, so it seemed to Wolf, and already continued writing. The clerk slowly, without looking up, closed the lid of the suitcase and let the locks snap into place. The two women looked at Wolfgang sheepishly and yet a little gleefully, the way students look at their classmates from the side when they are reprimanded by the teacher for a mistake.

Listen, Mr. Feld, said Pagel briskly, and walked across the lend towards the quietly continuing writer. I have a rich friend in the West who will definitely help me out. Give me the fare. I'll leave the things here, come by tonight before closing time, give you the money back, five times as much if I have to. Or ten times that.

The uncle looked thoughtfully at Wolfgang through his glasses, frowned and said, "I'm sorry, Herr Leutnant. We don't give loans here, we only lend on pawns.

But it's only the paltry few thousand fare, Wolf insisted. And I'll leave you with these things.

Without a pawn ticket I am not allowed to keep the things, the lender said. And I don't want them in pawn. I'm sorry, Lieutenant.

He looked attentively at Wolfgang once more with a furrowed brow, as if to read the effect of his words off his face, then nodded slightly and returned to his books. Wolfgang had also frowned, nodded slightly to the writer, as if to indicate that he did not take the refusal amiss, and turned toward the door. Suddenly something occurred to him. He quickly turned around, approached Mr. Feld once again and said: You know what, Mr. Feld?! Buy all the putty off me. For three dollars. Then the dear soul has rest. It occurred to him that the rich tick would surely help him out with a larger sum. It would be a blast to surprise Peter with a whole new outfit. What else was she going to do with the old junk? No, get rid of that stuff!

Mr. Feld continued to write for a while. Then he put the feather in the barrel, leaned back a little and said, "One dollar, with the suitcase, Herr Leutnant. As I said, the things are - not modern. His gaze fell on the wall clock. It was ten minutes to twelve. And on yesterday's dollar exchange rate.

For a moment Wolfgang wanted to get angry. It was the most impudent swindling of the world! For a moment it came over Wolfgang quietly, quietly, as if he also had to think of Peter - washing clothes and his ancient summer paletot were their only possessions at the moment, but just as quickly came the thought: 'Tick gives money. And if not him, I still managed money!' - And he said with a quick movement of the hand, which was to show how little it mattered: So, all right! Give me the dough! Four hundred and fourteen thousand!

It was really dirt when he considered that he had gambled away nearly thirty million to zero last night. And one had to laugh at such microbe as the field, which struggled for this dirt, for these ridiculous amounts!

The uncle, the evil, tough uncle, the microbe, slowly climbed down from his Kontorbock, went to the safe, rummaged in it for a while, and then counted out four hundred thousand marks to Wolfgang.

Fourteen are still missing, said Wolfgang.

Four percent cash discount comes off as customary for cash payments, Mr. Feld said. Actually makes three hundred and ninety-eight thousand. Two thousand I give you because you are old customer.

Wolfgang laughed: "You are very capable, Uncle! You come to what, watch out! I'll be a chauffeur with you then, right?

Mr. Feld took it seriously. He protested: Let you drive me, Lieutenant! No, not even for free! When you don't care about anything, not even your stuff. No, no ... And again quite the pawnbroker: So if there is something again, Herr Leutnant. Until then!

Pagel let the bills crackle in his hand with the beautiful Holbeinian picture of the merchant Georg Giße - who also could not defend himself against the abuse of his person - and said laughing: Who knows, maybe this will help me to get my own car!

The pawnbroker's expression remained worried, he wrote. Laughing, Wolfgang stepped out onto the street.

03 03

After the disgusting negotiation at the Schnitter mediation, Rittmeister von Prackwitz thought, he deserved a little relaxation. But where did one go, so early in the morning? This was a time around which the Rittmeister had not often been out and about in Berlin before. Finally, he remembered a hotel café in Friedrichstadt, where one could sit pleasantly and perhaps see a few well-dressed women.

The first person the cavalry captain saw in the hotel lobby was, of course, an acquaintance. (Prackwitz always met acquaintances in 'his' neighborhood - not at the Silesian Station, of course. Or acquaintances of acquaintances. Or relatives. Or acquaintances of relatives. Or comrades from the regiment. Or comrades from the war. Or Baltic. Or 'Schnöffels', as the pussycotes used to be called in the Rrrr'ment. He knew all the world in all the world).

This time it was even a regimental comrade, First Lieutenant von Studmann.

Herr von Studmann stood in the hall, impeccable frock coat, mirrored shoes (at such an early hour!), and seemed somewhat embarrassed for a moment at the reunion. But the cavalry captain, in his joy at having found a companion for the two-hour wait, noticed none of this.

Studmann, dude - great to see you again! I have two hours for you. Have you had coffee yet -? I just want - for the second time, that is. But the first on the Silesian does not reckon, it was gruesome. When was the last time we actually saw each other? In Frankfurt - for the officers' meeting? Well, anyway, I'm glad to see you again. But come on, in there you sit quite comfortably, if I remember correctly ...

Oberleutnant von Studmann said very quietly and clearly, but somewhat laboriously: Gladly, Prackwitz - as soon as my time permits. You see, I'm a - uh - receptionist at this store. I just want the guests from the nine-forty train first ...

Damn it! said the cavalry captain suddenly, just as quietly and quite somberly. Inflation, what -? Those crooks! Well, I can sing a song too!

Von Studmann nodded bleakly, as if singing songs had long since passed him by. Faced with the long, smooth, energetic face, Prackwitz wanted to remember a certain evening when they had celebrated the E. K. First of this same Studmann - it had been early fifteen, in fact the first E. K. First that had fallen to the regiment ... He wanted to remember the laughing, happy, high-spirited, but about eight years younger face of this same Studmann, but then the grade said: Jawohl, Portier, sofort ... He turned to von Prackwitz with a regretful, putting-off motion and then approached a rather substantial lady in a dusty gray silk coat: "Here you are, madam -?

For a moment the cavalry captain watched as his friend stood there, leaning slightly forward, listening with a serious yet friendly face to the lady's vehemently made requests or complaints. At this, a feeling of deep sadness rose in him, shapeless, all-pervading sadness: 'Good for nothing better?' it asked in him. Something like shame came over him, as if he had observed his comrade doing something degrading, dishonoring. He quickly turned away and stepped into the café.

In the hotel café, the early morning silence that always reigns there when only the house guests are there first, the street crowd had not yet made its entrance. Few guests sat in pairs or singly at tables far from each other. A newspaper rustled, a couple spoke half aloud, the nickel silver coffee pots gleamed dully, a spoon clinked on a cup. The less busy waiters stood quietly at their places; one cautiously counted cutlery, avoiding any unnecessary noise.

The cavalry captain had quickly found a suitable place. The coffee that immediately followed the order was so good that he took it upon himself to say a few words of appreciation to Studmann.

But he immediately dismissed the thought: 'That could put him to shame,' he thought. 'Lieutenant von Studmann and a really freshly brewed hotel coffee!'

The cavalry captain tried to find out why he was again overcome by this feeling of shame, as if Studmann were doing something forbidden, even indecent.

'It's work like any other,' he thought in wonder. We are all no longer so limited that we value one job less than another. After all, I am only sitting on Neulohe by the grace of my father-in-law, scraping together his rent - with many worries. So what is the reason -?'

Suddenly it came over him that perhaps it was because Studmann was only doing this work under duress. A man must work, certainly, if he wants to have a right to be before him. But there is free will in the choice of work; hated work, just for the sake of money, disgraces. - 'After all, he would never have chosen this job,' he thought. 'There was no choice for him.'

And a feeling of helpless hatred overtook Rittmeister Joachim von Prackwitz. Somewhere in this city there was a machine - of course a machine, humans would never let themselves be abused for something like that! - and vomited paper day and night over the city, the people. 'Money' they called it, they printed numbers on it, wonderful, smooth numbers with lots of zeros, getting rounder and rounder. And if you have worked, if you have toiled, if you have saved something in your old age - it has all become worthless already, paper, paper - dirt!

And for the sake of this dirt, Comrade Studmann stood in the hotel lobby and made servants. Well, should he stand there, he should do servants - but not because of dirt. Painfully clearly the cavalry captain saw again the friendly-serious face of his friend as he had just seen it.

Suddenly it became dark, then slowly brighter. A small beet oil lantern dangled from the raw, unhewn deck beam. It cast its warm, reddish glow directly into Studmann's face - and that face laughed, laughed! The eyes sparkled with joy, a hundred wrinkles jumped and twitched in their corners.

'The restored life is also in this laughter,' spoke a voice in the cavalier.

It was nothing, just a memory of a night in a shelter - where had it been -? Somewhere in Ukraine. It was a rich land, pumpkins and melons grew by the hundreds in the fields. They had taken from the abundance into the shelter, laid on wall boards. They were sleeping, a rat (there were thousands of rats), a rat knocked a pumpkin off the board. He fell on the head of a sleeper, in the sleeping face. The sleeper cried out horribly, the pumpkin rolling on did blow after blow. They lay, all awake, breathless, pressed flat into their blankets, awaiting the blasts of the impact. Seconds of mortal fear - life rushes, now I'm still alive, I want to think something worthwhile, the wife, the child, the girl Weio, I still have a hundred and fifty marks in my pocket, better I had paid my wine bill, they are now also gone ...

And now the laughter of Studmann: Pumpkin! Pumpkin!

They laugh, laugh. 'Life given again is also in that laughter.' Little Geyer wipes his bleeding nose and laughs, too. That's right, Geyer was his name. He fell a little later, pumpkins were exceptions in the war.

But that's what it had been: real fear and real danger and real courage! Trembling - but then jumping up, discovering it was just a pumpkin, and laughing again! About himself, about fear, about this foolish life - going on, down the street, towards the non-existent point. But to be threatened by something that spewed paper, to be forced by something that added zeros to the world - that was shameful! It hurt the man who did it; it hurt the man who saw the other do it.

Prackwitz looks attentively at his friend. Von Studmann has already entered a while ago and is listening to the waiter who was so attentively counting the cutlery a while ago and who is now excitedly bringing up something. Surely a complaint about some colleague. Prackwitz knows from his own experience this quarrelsome, heated talk. (He did not fare any differently with his officials at Neulohe. Eternal bickering, eternal gossip. He would prefer to continue managing with only one official, so that he would at least be spared this hassle. But he really needs to see that he gets someone else. Thefts are rampant, Meier can't make it, and Kniebusch is old and used up. Well, next time. This time there is no more time, at twelve he must be at the Schlesische Bahnhof).

The waiter is still talking, talking himself into fire and flames. Von Studmann listens to him, friendly, attentive, now and then he says a few words, nods sometimes, shakes his head. 'There's no life left in him,' the cavalry captain decides. 'Burned out. Canceled. - 'But,' he thinks with sudden dismay, 'maybe I'm burned out and extinguished too - don't you notice?'

Then suddenly - quite surprisingly - Studmann says a single sentence. The waiter, completely flustered, abruptly breaks off. Studmann nods to him once more and goes to the friend's table.

So, he says, and sits down - and immediately his face becomes more animated. Now, I think, I have half an hour. If nothing comes up. He smiles encouragingly at Prackwitz. But actually something always comes up.

You have a lot to do? Prackwitz asks, a little embarrassed. God, to do! Studmann laughs briefly. If you ask the others, here the elevator boys or the waiters or the doormen, they will tell you that I have nothing to do, just standing around. And yet in the evening I'm as dog-tired as I was only back then when we had squadron drill and the old man grinded us.

There is probably something like an old man here?

One -? Ten, twelve! General director, three directors, four sub-directors, three managing directors, two authorized signatories -.

Please, stop!

But in the end, it's not so bad. It has a lot of similarity with the military. Command, obey - impeccable organization ...

But still civilians ... von Prackwitz said apprehensively, thinking of Neulohe, where obedience did not always follow orders for a long time.

Of course, Studmann also confirmed. It's a little looser than it was back then, more casual. Therefore more difficult for the individual, I would say. He orders something, and you don't know for sure whether he has a right to order it. Not very clearly delineated powers, you know?

But Prackwitz said that was also the case with us. Some officer on special assignment, you know?

Certainly, certainly. But on the whole, one can say that it is an amazing organization, an exemplary giant operation. You should see something like our linen closets sometime. Or the kitchen. Or the shopping check. Amazing, I tell you!

So you're having a little fun? the captain asked cautiously.

Studmann's liveliness went out. God, fun! Well, maybe. But that's not what matters, is it? We must live - how? - live on, after all that. Just keep on living. Nevertheless, one thought it once differently.

Prackwitz looked scrutinizingly into the shadowed face of the other. 'Yeah, why have to?" he thought fleetingly, a little annoyed. And he found the only possible explanation, asked aloud: You are married? Have kids?

Me? Studmann asked, very surprised. But no! No thought!

No, no, of course not, said the cavalry captain, a little guiltily.

After all, why not? But it didn't turn out that way, von Studmann said thoughtfully. And today? No! Where the mark becomes more worthless every day, where people have to scrape together a little money for themselves ...

Money -? Dirt! said the cavalry captain sharply.

Yes, of course, Studmann answered quietly. Dirt, I get your point. I also understood your question earlier quite correctly, or rather your thoughts. Why I do for such 'dirt' this, reluctantly, you mean ... Prackwitz wanted to protest in dismay. Oh, don't talk, Prackwitz! said von Studmann warmer for the first time. I know you! Money - dirt, this is not just inflationary wisdom from you, you used to think a bit like that. You -? All of us! In any case, money was something that went without saying. One had his change of house and his few pennies from the rrrr'ment, one did not speak of it. And if something could not be paid for immediately, the man had to wait. Isn't that how it was? Money was something that did not reward reflection ... Prackwitz swayed his head doubtfully and wanted to object. But Studmann said more hurriedly: I beg you, Prackwitz, it was something like that. But today I ask myself - not at all, I am quite sure of myself - that we were all completely wrong before, had no idea of the world. Money, I have since discovered, is something very important, something that makes all thought worthwhile ...

Money! said von Prackwitz indignantly. If at least it was still real money! But this paper stuff ...

Prackwitz! said Studmann reproachfully. What does real money mean! There is no such thing, just as there is no such thing as incorrect money. Money, that's simply what you need to live, the basis of being there, the bread we have to eat every day to be there, the suit we have to wear to not freeze to death....

But that is mysticism! exclaimed von Prackwitz angrily. Money is a very simple thing after all! Money is just - in the past, anyway, I mean - if you had a gold fox there, but paper also went, paper was something else back then, because you got gold for it ... So money, I mean no matter what money - you understand ... Now he was getting angry at himself, at this stupid stammering. Shouldn't you be able to say what you felt so rightly and clearly -? So, he concluded, if I have money, I want to know what I can buy with it.

Yes, of course, Studmann said, and had noticed nothing of his friend's confusion, but was blithely continuing his own thread of thought. Of course, we were wrong before. I discovered that ninety-nine percent of people have to agonize a lot over money, that they think about it day and night, talk about it, budget it, save it, start again - in short, that money is what the world revolves around. That it is simply ridiculously out of touch with life not to think about money, not to want to talk about it - the most important thing there is!

But is that right?! Prackwitz exclaimed, distressed at his friend's new state of mind. Is that beautiful -? Just live to get the little bit of hunger full?!

Certainly it is not right. Certainly it's not pretty, Studmann agreed. But it is not asked about it, for the time being it is so. And if it is, you can't squint your eyes, you have to deal with it. And if you don't like it, you have to ask yourself, how do you change it?

Studmann, von Prackwitz asked, quite dismayed and in despair, Studmann, you haven't become a sociologist, have you?

The former lieutenant looked for a moment as dismayed and stunned as if he had been suspected of an assassination. Prackwitz, he said, old comrade-in-arms, the Socialists think about money the same way you do! Only they want to take it away from you so they can have it. No, Prackwitz, I am certainly not a socialist. And will not.

But what are you? asked von Prackwitz. You have to belong to some group or party, after all.

Why? asked von Studmann. Why do I have to?

Yes, I don't know, said von Prackwitz, a little taken aback. After all, every one of us belongs to something, if only because of the elections. Somehow you have to fit in, join the ranks. It is, in a sense - neat!

But if there is still no order for me? asked von Studmann.

Yes ... Prackwitz said thoughtfully. I remember, he recalled, I once had a guy in the squadron, a Schnöffel we used to say, a sectarian, what was his name? Grigoleit, yes, Grigoleit! Quite a proprer, neat man. But he refused to touch a carbine or sidearm. Pleading didn't help, upsetting didn't help, punishing didn't help. 'At your command, Herr Leutnant,' he said - I was a lieutenant, it was still at peace. 'But I'm not allowed to. You have your order and I have my order. And because I have my order, I must not sin against it. One day, after all, my order will be your order ...' And stuff like that, some sectarian, pacifist, but of the decent sort, not these shirkers who shout 'Never again war!' because they're cowards .... Well, you could have made his life hell, of course. But the old man was also reasonable and said:

'He's just a poor idiot!' And so he was written D. U. 15, you know, because of existing mental illness ....

The cavalry captain was thoughtfully silent, perhaps he saw the fat, round-headed Grigoleit with the white-blond hair in front of him, who did not look like a martyr at all.

Studmann, however, laughed out brightly. O Prackwitz! he shouted. You're still the same! And the way you have just innocently certified my idiocy and existing mental illness - without even noticing it - reminds me very vividly of the time when, after the maneuver, you told our old man, who had done insanely badly, about a major who had even fallen off his horse during the maneuver review in front of the assembled generals, and yet had not received the blue letter! And do you remember -?

With that, the two friends lost themselves in shared memories, their voices becoming more animated. But that didn't matter. Now the café began to fill up. Busily the waiters ran, already carried the first beer glasses, voices buzzed. The conversation between the two was just one of many.

After a while, however, when they had remembered enough and laughed enough, the cavalry captain said, "I also want to ask you something, Studmann. I'm sitting there all alone on my flat, and all I ever hear and see are the same people. But you are here in the big city and in such company, and surely you hear and know more than all of us.

Oh, who knows anything today?! Studmann asked and smiled. Believe me, even Prime Minister Cuno has no idea what tomorrow will bring.

But Prackwitz was not deterred. He sat back a little, his long legs crossed, smoked with pleasure and said: "You may think that Prackwitz is fine, he has a manor and is a great man. But I'm not stuck, I have to be very careful. Neulohe is not mine, it belongs to my father-in-law, the old gentleman von Teschow - after all, I married little Eva Teschow long before the war - oh, forgive me, you know my wife! Well, I leased Neulohe from my father-in-law - and the old boy didn't make the rent cheap, I can tell you. Sometimes I have disgusting worries. - Anyway, I have to be very careful. Neulohe is our only existence, and if something happens to me - the old man doesn't love me, he takes the chink away from me at the slightest occasion.

And what can happen to you? Studmann asked.

Yes, look, I'm not a hermit and Eva certainly isn't, and so we have our little bit of traffic in the area, and of course also with the comrades from the Reichswehr. And then you hear all kinds of things. And whispers are also heard, directly and indirectly.

And what do you hear and what do you see?

That something should go off, Studmann, once again. After all, you're not blind. The whole country is full of people, they call themselves work commandos, but you just have to see them. 'Black Reichswehr' is whispered.

This can be because of entente and control commission, snooping commission, said von Studmann.

Of course - and that they bury weapons and dig them up again and take them away, that can also be why. But it's not just about that, Studmann, there's more whispering, there's more to see. No doubt: it is also recruited in the civilian population, perhaps already in my own village. The owner is always the last to know that the farm is on fire. Neulohe is bordered by Altlohe, and there are many industrial workers there, and that of course means enmity to the knife with us from the farm and with the farmers in Neulohe. For where some have food and others are hungry, it is like a powder keg - and if it blows up, I fly with it.

I don't quite see how you can stop anything there yet, von Studmann said.

Obstruct ... But maybe I will have to decide whether to participate or not? You don't want to be uncompanionable. It's the old comrades in the Reichswehr, Studmann, and if they wanted to take a risk and get the car out of the mud, and then you wouldn't have been there - you'd have to be ashamed to death! Yes, and maybe it's all just talk, the machinations of a few adventurers, a hopeless coup - and therefore risking your farm and livelihood and your family ...

The cavalry captain looked questioningly at Studmann. He said: Don't you have anyone in the Reichswehr whom you can take aside and ask on honor and conscience?

God, ask Studmann! Of course I can ask, but who knows what? Only three or four people really know about this kind of thing, and they certainly won't answer you. - Have you ever heard of a Major Rückert?

No, Studmann said. From the Reichswehr?

Yes, you see, Studmann, that's just it! This Rückert is supposed to be the man who ... But I can't even get out whether he belongs to the Reichswehr or not. Some say yes, others say no, and the very smart ones shrug their shoulders and say, 'Maybe he doesn't know that himself!' And that sounds again as if others are behind him - it's really exasperating, Studmann!

Yes, Studmann said. I get it. If necessary, immediately, but for crazy adventures - thank you!

Right! said Prackwitz.

Then they both fell silent. But Prackwitz continued to look expectantly at Studmann, the former first lieutenant and current hotel receptionist. (Wore the nickname 'the nanny' at the Rrrr'ment.) Finally, a man with recently very strange, actually already suspicious views about money and God-ordained poverty. Looked at him as if expecting from his answer release from all doubts.

And finally this Studmann also slowly said: I think you shouldn't worry so much, Prackwitz. You should just wait. We actually know this from the field. Worry and even sometimes fear were only felt when lying quietly or still in the trench. But when it was then: Out and forward! - then you were there and off you went and everything was forgotten. You won't miss the signal, Prackwitz. After all, we learned it in the field, the calm waiting without brooding - why shouldn't we be able to do it now?

You're right! said the captain gratefully, and I want to remember that too! It's funny that you can't wait now! I think it's that stupid dollar doing it. Run, run, quickly buy something, rush, chase ...

Yes, Studmann said. Hunting and being hunted, hunter and game at the same time, that makes so angry and impatient. But you don't need either. Yes ... he smiled, but now I have to go again, I am not completely free of it. I see the doorman waving there. Perhaps a director is already hunting for me, why and why I am nowhere to be seen. And I will hunt the parlor maids a little again, so that the rooms of the departures will be ready at twelve. So weidmannsheil, Prackwitz! And if you should still be in town at seven today and have nothing planned ...

I'll be back in Neulohe by then, Studmann, von Prackwitz said. But I was really nonsensically happy, directly nonsensically happy to see you again, Studmann, and when I come to town again ...

4

The girl was sitting alone, motionless, busy, still on the bed in the parlor. The head was lowered a little, the line leading from the back over the neck to the head was yielding, soft. The small, clear, pure-lined face stood softly in the air, the lips were half open, the gaze directed at the scraped floorboards saw nothing. Under the coat that had slipped apart, the naked flesh shimmered, slightly brownish, very firm. The air was stuffy, full of smells ... The fully awakened house marched through its day screaming, shouting, crying, slamming doors and pounding stairs. Life expressed itself here mainly through sounds, and further still through decomposition, through stench. In the sheet metal stamping shop on the ground floor, cut sheet metal cried out, sounding as if cats or tormented children were screaming. Then it was almost silent again, only the drive belts purring and whirring on the transmissions. The girl heard a clock strike twelve.

Involuntarily, it raised its head and looked for the door. If he looked in at her again after the 'uncle', perhaps to bring her something to eat, he had to come now. He had said something like that about having breakfast together. But he didn't come, she had the definite feeling he wasn't coming. He drove safely straight to his friend. If he got money there, he might still go to her, maybe directly to play, and she wouldn't see him again until morning, cleaned out or with money in his pockets. No matter, she saw him again.

Yes, it suddenly came over her, was it so certain that she would see him again -? She had gotten used to it: he had always gone away, and he had always come back. Whatever he had done, wherever he had been, his path had always ended here with her in Georgenkirchstraße. He had crossed the courtyard, climbed the stairs - and he had reached her, joyfully excited or completely exhausted.

But, she thought for the first time, deeply frightened: but is it sure that he always comes back -?! It was possible that he would not come back one day, perhaps today. No, today he came back, of course, he knew how she was sitting there, very hungry, naked in his shabby summer paletot, without the simplest necessities of life, with debts to the landlady. Today he came back for sure - but tomorrow maybe already -?

'I never asked anything of him,' she thinks. 'Why shouldn't he come back? I was never a burden to him!'

Then she remembers that she has asked something of him, that she always asks for it, not in words, but she asks for it no less: that he come back to her.

'Even that can be a burden for him one day,' she thinks, filled with a boundless sadness. 'Even my love can be a burden to him one day, and then he doesn't return home.'

It gets hotter and hotter. She gets up from the edge of the bed with a jerk, goes to the mirror and stops in front of it. Yes, she is - Petra Ledig - but even that can't hold him. Hair and flesh, a hurried smell, desire, fulfillment - but the world is full of it. Fleetingly she remembers the thousand rooms, into which at this hour the morning desire returns: kisses are exchanged, women slowly undress, bedsteads creak, the fleeting sigh of lust becomes loud and escapes. It is attached and completed, one separates - at every hour, every minute - in a thousand rooms.

Did she think she was safe from it? It could go on like this? Deeply she knows, she has always known, it would not last.

They were running on the streets, they were all in a hurry, running to catch the train, to meet the girl, to spend this bill before its total devaluation. What took -? And love should last -?!

Suddenly she realizes that everything she has her heart set on is nonsense. This civil wedding, which seemed so important to her this morning that she made a scene for it - what did it change? Gone! There! And that she sits here without anything, half-naked, over-starved, with debts - that's why he should come back today?! But if he doesn't come back, it doesn't matter how she stays - with a car and a villa in the Grunewald, for all I care - he won't come back, that's the only important thing! And what she starts then, whether she jumps out of the window or sells shoes again or goes on the street - that is then also the same, he does not come back!

She still stands in front of the mirror and looks at herself as if there were a dangerous stranger standing there who must be watched carefully. The one there in the mirror is very pale, a brownish pale consumed from within, the dark eyes burning, the hair hanging with a few loose strands in the forehead, sighs sleepily once more and falls silent. She is still breathing.

Hans Fallada   -88-   Wolf among Wolves

She closes her eyes, an almost aching shower of happiness washes over her. She feels heat rising in her cheeks, she gets hot. A good heat, a nice heat! O life, desire to live! It has led me from there over there to here. Houses, faces, beatings, bickering, dirt, money, fear. Here I stand - sweet, sweet life! He can never leave me again. I have him inside me.

It purrs, it whizzes. It runs tirelessly up and down stairs. It stirs in every stone cube. It spills out of the windows. It squints and it scolds. It laughs, yes, it laughs too. Life, sweet, glorious, everlasting life! He cannot leave me again. I have him inside me. Never thought, never hoped, never wished. I have him inside me. In the hollow hand we lay, and life ran, ran with us. We never got anywhere. Everything slipped away. All over. All there. But something remained. Not over all footsteps grass grows, not every sigh blows away. I stay. And he stays. We.

She looks at herself. She has opened her eyes again and looks at herself. That's me! she thinks for the first time in her life, yes, she points her finger at herself. She is without any fear. He'll be back. He, too, will one day understand that she is 'I' as she understood. She understood it since she is no longer 'I' but 'we'.

5

As often as Rittmeister von Prackwitz came to Berlin, one of his main pleasures was to stroll down Friedrichstrasse and a stretch of Leipziger and look into the stores. Not that he made or even intended to make big purchases, no, the shop windows delighted him. They were so wonderfully dressed up for a provincial. In some of them, there were adorable little things to see, things that tempted you to just walk into the store, point your fingers at them, say, This! And in others there were such gruesome abominations and horrors that one could possibly stand in front of them even longer, always provoked to laugh anew. And again, one was tempted to bring such piece home, just to see once how Eva and Weio would amuse themselves over this glass man's head, whose mouth served as an ashtray. (You could also connect the head to the light line, and it would glow eerily red and green).

But the experience that these things stood around in the house completely unnoticed after only one day had made the cavalry captain cautious - he was content with his own laughter. If something was to be brought, and you may be a white-knuckled cavalry officer, however farewell, you bring a little something for the women, he preferred to stop in front of a linen store and choose something silky or a trifle with lace. It was a delight to buy something like this. Every time he stepped into such a store, everything had become even lighter and more fragrant, even more delicate in color. You could squeeze such panties in one hand into a light, tiny ball, and then it spread out again, slightly crackling. No matter how gray and bleak life had become, women's beauty always seemed to become lighter, more tender, more unearthly. Such a brassiere made only of lace - the cavalry captain could still remember very well the gray Drillich corsets of the pre-war period, into which the husband had to tie up the wife as if he were bridling an unruly horse!

Or the cavalry captain went into a delicatessen - and no matter how worthless the money had become, here all the shelves were full to bursting: green asparagus from Italy, artichokes from France, fattened geese from Poland, Helgoland lobster, horseradish from Hungary, English yams - the whole world was here. Even the caviar from Russia was back - and the rare, scarce foreign currency, which one got only out of 'friendship' and senselessly expensive, here one could eat it up by the hundredweight - completely puzzling!

The cavalry captain had plenty of time after his discussion with Studmann, so he once again strolled along the old path. But this time the joy was spoiled for him: it was going on on Friedrichstraße as one would imagine an Oriental bazaar. Almost man to man they stood on the walls of the houses and on the edge of the sidewalk: merchants, beggars, prostitutes. Young people flipped open carry-on cases in which polished perfume bottles

Hans Fallada   -90-   Wolf among Wolves

gleamed softly. Suspenders waved another, jeering, shouting. A woman, shaggy and greasy, handled endlessly long, shimmering silk stockings, which she offered to the gentlemen with a cheeky smile: Wat for de Kleene, Herr Jraf. Just put it on her, and you'll see what fun you'll have for that lumpy bit of paper, Mr. Jraf -!

A Schupo came into view, looking glum under his painted Landwehr shako. Pro forma the suitcases were closed and were already open again, barely he was two steps further. Beggars sat, squatted and lay on the walls of the houses, all of them war wounded, if you believed the signs they carried. But there were so young among them that they must still have gone to school during the war, and old people who had certainly been invalids before the war. Blind men bawled bleakly monotonous, shakers shook their heads or arms, wounds were on display, horrible scars shone fiery from a gray, scaly flesh.

But the worst were the girls. Everywhere they roamed, shouted, whispered, hooked up with everyone, ran along, laughed. Some were exposed to such an extent that it was hardly bearable. A market of meat - fat, white, swollen with liquors; and lean, dark, which the sharp liquors seemed to have burned. But the worst were the completely shameless, the almost sexless: the morphinists with the sharp pinhead of the pupil, the snuffers with the white nose, and the cocaine injectors with the screaming voices from unrestrained twitching faces. They bobbed around, they flicked their flesh in the wide-cut or sophisticated openwork blouses. When they swerved or went around a corner, they gathered their skirts, which in themselves did not reach the knee, and showed the strip of pale white flesh between the stocking and the pants, under which ran the green or pink garter. They unabashedly exchanged remarks about the passing men, threw jokes across the street to each other, and their greedy eyes looked for the foreigners in whose pockets they hoped to find foreign currency in the crowd that slowly drifted past them.

And among vice, misery and beggary, among hunger, deceit and poison, the young girls, barely out of school, ran out of the stores with their boxes and stacks of letters. Nothing escaped their quick, sure glances, and their ambition was to be just as bold as those, not to be impressed by anything, not to shy away from anything, to wear just as short skirts, to gather just as much currency.

'Nothing impresses us!' said their looks. You old people don't fool us anymore. Yes,' they said, waving folders or boxes, 'now we are still shopgirls, saleswomen, clerks. But it only takes one to keep an eye on us, that little Jap there, or that fat guy with the sideburns, waving his belly in a pair of plaid flannel pants - and we'll drop our cardboard box, right here on the street, yes, and tonight we're already sitting in a bar, and tomorrow we'll have a car!'

To the cavalry captain it was as if he heard them all shouting, screaming, chasing: nothing counts but money! Money!!! But even the money counted for nothing, in every minute the greatest possible enjoyment had to be squeezed out of him! Preserve for what - for tomorrow? Who knows how the dollar will stand tomorrow, who knows if we will still be alive tomorrow, tomorrow younger, fresher people are already pushing to the starting line - come on, old man, you already have white hair - all the more you have to stick to it! Come on, sweetie!

The cavalry captain spied the entrance to the passage from the Linden to Friedrichstraße. He had always liked to look at the Panopticon once, he escaped into the store aisle. But it was as if he had gone from limbo to hell. A densely packed crowd pushed its way endlessly slowly through the brilliantly lit tunnel. The stores were emblazoned with huge oil hams of naked women, disgustingly naked, with disgustingly sweet, rosy breasts. Naughty postcards hung in long strings of pennants everywhere. There were joke articles that would have made an old lecher blush, and the shamelessness of the nude photos that moistly whispering men pressed into your hand could no longer be surpassed.

But the worst were the boys. In their sailor suits with the smooth bare chest, the cigarette free in the mouth, they glided everywhere, not speaking, but looking at or touching.

A tall, light blonde woman in a low-cut dress, very elegant, pushed her way through the crowd, led by a whole gaggle of such guys. She laughed uproariously, speaking fiercely. The cavalry captain saw her very close, his gaze falling on the shamelessly exposed, thickly powdered breast. The lady looked at him laughing with her unnaturally dilated pupils, her eyes were blue-black underlined - and suddenly a body-shaking disgust overtook him at the realization that this bloated woman was a man, the wife of all those disgusting brats and yet a man -!

The cavalry captain ruthlessly pushed his way through the crowd. A whore shouted: The old man is beeping! Emil, hit him! He jebufft me! But the Rittmeister was already outside, caught a cab, Schlesischer Bahnhof! he said and leaned back into the cushions, completely exhausted. Then he pulled a white handkerchief, still quite unused, from his skirt and slowly wiped his face and hands.

'Yes,' he forced himself to think intensely of something else - and what more intensely than his worries? 'Yep, it's really not easy to farm new land at this time.'

Quite apart from the fact that the father-in-law was a carrion (and only the mother-in-law with her piety!), the rent was really too high. Either nothing grew, like last year, or if something grew, you had no people like this summer!

But after the conversation with poor Studmann, whom it had also already infected and who was really getting plenty of twisted ideas, and after this little walk through Friedrichstraße and Passage, the cavalry captain thought of Neulohe as a pure, untouched island. Certainly, there was always trouble: people trouble, tax trouble, money trouble, craftsmen trouble (and the worst of all was the in-law trouble!), but there were now Eva and Violet, who since her childhood days was called only Weio.

Certainly, Eva was a little very fun-loving, the way she danced and flirted with the officers in Ostade would have been quite unseemly in former times, and Weio had also taken on a richly rude tone (her grandmother probably fainted sometimes!) - but what was that against this misery, this shamelessness, this corruption of morals that was spreading in Berlin in broad daylight?! Rittmeister Joachim von Prackwitz was like that and he stayed like that, he had no intention at all to change in this respect: a woman was made of finer stuff than a man, something delicate, to be pampered. Those girls there on Friedrichstraße - oh, they weren't women anymore. A real man could only think of them with a shudder!

In Neulohe they had a garden, they sat in this garden in the evening. The servant Hubert brought lanterns and a bottle of Mosel, at most the gramophone with 'Bananas, of all things bananas!' sent a metropolitan wave into the rustle of leaves and the scent of flowers. But the women were preserved. Pure, clean.

Truly, one could no longer walk along Friedrichstraße with a lady, especially if the lady was one's own daughter! And to think that a splendid fellow like Studmann wanted to somehow please this rabble there from the street, to somehow put himself on a par with them, if only because he had to earn money like them! No, thank you. At home in Neulohe, people might have found it exaggerated when the Deutsche Tageszeitung called Berlin a sinkhole, an asphalt swamp, a Sodom and Gomorrah. But if you smelled it only once, you found everything was still much too weak. No, thanks! -

And the cavalry captain had calmed down enough to light a cigarette and head for the train station, satisfied that his business had been accomplished and that he would soon be returning home.

Of course, he first drank a few strong cognacs in the waiting room, because he had the fairly certain feeling that the inspection of his newly acquired reapers would not be a pure pleasure. But then it wasn't so bad. Actually the usual, the faces maybe a bit more cheeky, raw, shameless than usual - but what did that mean? If only they worked, brought in the harvest! You should not have it bad with him, decent deputat, every week a mutton, once a month a fat pig!

Only the Vorschnitter was exactly the kind of person that the Rittmeister completely hated - the Radler brand: pedal down, hump up. He waved around the cavalry captain, spurted out a torrent of half-German, half-Polish words praising the strength and prowess of his men, and in the process unawares kicked a girl in the butt who couldn't get through the door fast enough with her pack.

By the way, when the cavalry captain wanted to buy the collective ticket, it turned out that the foresnitter had brought not fifty, but only thirty-seven people. But in response to a question from the Rittmeister, he again poured out buckets of confused phrases that became more and more Polish and incomprehensible ('Of course Eva is quite right, I should have learned Polish, but I don't think about it -!'). The Vorschnitter seemed to affirm something, he tensed his upper arm muscle and sparkled at the Rittmeister laughing, flattering with small, mouse-quick black eyes. Finally, Prackwitz shrugged and loosened the bill. Thirty-seven were better than nothing, and in any case they were skilled farm workers.

Then came the noisy, shouting procession onto the platform; the loading onto the already waiting train; the scolding conductor, who wanted to stuff a door-blocking bundle into the carriage, while it was being pushed out again from inside, together with its carrier; the quarrel of two boys; the wild gesticulations and shouts of the foreman, who in between talked continuously to the cavalry captain, asked for his thirty dollars, demanded, begged ...

At first, the cavalry captain thought that twenty would be enough, since a quarter of the people were missing. They began to calculate heatedly, and finally, tired of arguing, the cavalry captain counted three ten-dollar bills into the hand of the foreshitter after the last man had also found his place. Now the reaper overflowed with gratitude, bowed, stepped back and forth, and finally really managed to catch the hand of the cavalry captain and kiss it fervently: Marjosef. Holy benefactor!

Somewhat disgusted, the cavalry captain looked for a seat at the very front of the train in a smoking compartment Second, he sat comfortably in a corner and lit a new cigarette. All in all, it was a good day's work that he had accomplished. Tomorrow the harvest could begin properly.

Rumbling and blowing, the train finally got going, pulling out of the sad, sooty, dilapidated hall with its shattered windows. The cavalry captain just waited for the conductor to pass, then he wanted to take a nap.

Finally the conductor came, snapped the card and gave it back to the cavalryman. But he did not go yet, as if waiting he remained standing.

Well? asked the captain sleepily. A little hot out, isn't it?

Aren't you the gentleman? asked the conductor, with the Polish reapers?

Yes, sir," said the captain, straightening up.

Then I just wanted to report to you, said the conductor (a hint of gloating), that the people all got off again right away at the Silesian station. Quite stealthily.

What? yelled the cavalry captain and jumped to the compartment door.

6

The train went faster and faster. He dived into the tunnel, the illuminated platform remained behind.

Wolf Pagel sat on the extinguisher box of the crowded smoker's car, burning a Lucky Strike from the pack he had just purchased from the proceeds for all their belongings. He took a deep drag.

Oh, beautiful, beautiful! He had smoked the last cigarette the previous night on his way home from the game, so this one tasted all the better, almost twelve hours later. Lucky Strike meant, if his school English didn't completely fail him, as much as lucky strike, lucky hit - this auspicious cigarette was to be of prophetic significance for the whole day!

The fat man snorts cholerically, rustles with the newspaper, shoots uneasy glances - all this doesn't help you, we already know it: the dollar comes today with 760 thousand, over fifty percent markup. Thank goodness the cigarette uncle didn't know yet, otherwise we wouldn't have been able to afford this cigarette. You were wrong too, fatty, your panting betrays you, you are outraged! But that doesn't help you. This is quite a great, completely modern post-war invention: they steal half the money you have in your pocket - and yet don't touch the pocket or the money - yes, brains! Brains! Now the question was whether friend Tick had been right or wrong. If he had been wrong, he would hear something hard (though not even that was certain); but if the new devaluation suited him, a handful of million-dollar bills would not matter. For a few days there had even been two-million bills - Pagel had seen them at the gambling club. They were once again properly printed on both sides, looked like money, not these one-sided white scraps - people were already saying that this should now remain the highest bill forever. Said - because of such saga snorts the fat man, had believed in sagas.

It was hardly likely that Tick had been wrong. As long as Pagel could remember, Zecke had always been right. He had never been wrong in his judgment of a teacher. He had almost had a premonition of what kind of questions would be asked, what topics would be covered in the exam paper. During the war, he had been the first to set up a great leave system for the distribution of Salvarsan in the Balkans, in Turkey. And when that business started to get lazy, he had again been the first, before giving it up altogether, to fill the salvarsan packs with some crud, a mixture of sand and disc honey probably. Then he had exported chanteuses and diseuses of the eighth order to the Bosporus. A lovely plant, all in all, on the one hand stupid as a horn, on the other hand of a razor-sharp cunning. After the war he had laid on yarn - heaven knows what he was trading now! It didn't matter to him - he would push with bull elephants if there was money to be made!

Actually, thought about this man and so-called good friend Zecke exactly, was not to see why he should give you money - Pagel suddenly admitted it to himself. He had also never tried to pump him before. But there was the other feeling in Wolfgang Pagel's chest, the feeling that Zecke was now 'ripe', that he would absolutely do it. A player compass, so to speak, a signal that was suddenly pulled, the executioner knew why. Absolutely he would give money. There were such moments in life. Suddenly you did what you would not have done yesterday at any price. And from what one had done, something else followed all by itself, for example, one won a huge sum tonight - and now suddenly everything changed! Life continued at an angle to the previous trajectory. You could buy twenty tenement houses in the city (the stalls were available for dirt) or open a giant bar (eighty girls behind the bar table) - not a bad idea yet! - or once you didn't have to do anything at all, you could also sit down and twiddle your thumbs, have a real rest, eat and drink well and enjoy Peter. Or better yet, buy a car and drive Peter around the world! Show her everything, churches, pictures, just everything, the girl had opportunities for development - but of course. Did anyone deny that -?! Not him, anyway, a great girl, never uncomfortable. (Or almost never.)

Fahnenjunker a. D. Wolfgang Pagel got off at Podbielskiallee and strolled down the few streets to Zecke's Villa. So really lazy and leisurely in the heat. Now he stands in front of the house, that is, in front of the front garden, of course, the garden, the plant, the park. And not directly in front of it, of course, there is a forged lattice and some carved stone, set up in column form, say shell limestone. There is also a very small brass sign that says nothing more than 'von Zecke' and a brass bell button. Well cleaned. You can't see much of the house, it's hidden behind bushes and trees, you only have an idea of large, reflecting panes and a not too high, slightly articulated facade.

Pagel looks at the presents, he has time. Then he turns around and looks at the villas across the street. Pompous - so here live the gentlemen who could not live at any price in a backyard near Alexanderplatz. Wolfgang Pagel considers himself capable of doing both, sometimes Dahlem, sometimes Alex, it doesn't matter to him. But perhaps because it doesn't matter to him, he doesn't live in Dahlem, but on Georgenkirchstrasse.

He turns back and looks at the sign, button, flower beds, greenery, facade. It remains a mystery why Tick is bothered with such stuff. Because that kind of thing is a burden. Having a house, a huge mansion, half a palace, forever demanding something from you: pay taxes, have it cleaned; electric light line fails, coke has to be bought - anyway, Tick must have changed. In the past, he would also have thought: it's a burden. The last time he saw him, Zecke had two highly elegant bachelor rooms on Kurfürstendamm (with girlfriend, telephone connection and bathroom) - that suited Zecke.

Not this. But he was probably married. Any nonsense experienced with a man was explained by the fact that he was married. That a woman was there. Well, they would probably get to see her, and of course she would immediately guess that this old friend of her husband's wanted to pump money. In response, she would treat him half irritably, half contemptuously. But she was happy to do that for his sake, who went out for robbery in the evening as a pari-panther was completely immune to women's whims.

Pagel is already about to press the bell button - you have to do it once, as pleasant as it is to stand here lazily in the sun and think of all the nice money he is about to take from the tick. But he remembers just in time that he still has almost 100,000 marks in his pocket. Now there is the sentence that money wants to money, but in this form the sentence is not correct. It should read: a lot of money wants too much money. But what Pagel is carrying in his pocket is out of the question. Under these circumstances, it is much better, he is completely blank before tick. Absolutely, you represent a loan request more convincingly if you don't even have the fare home in your pocket. For this hundred thousand you will get about two cognacs, and these two cognacs will give further weight to his loan request!

Pagel has turned around and is strolling back down the street. He goes right, then left, right again, back and forth - but it proves difficult to convert the money into alcohol. There seem to be neither stores nor pubs in this piquant villa neighborhood. Of course, such people everything is brought to the house, wine and liquor they keep by the cellar.

Pagel only finds a newspaper man, but he doesn't like to invest the money in newspapers. No, thank you, he has nothing to do with that kind of thing. When he already reads the headline 'Lifting the border barrier to the occupied territory' - it's none of his business, do what you want, it's a slice!

Next he meets a flower woman, she is standing at a bus stop, hawking roses. The thought of going under the nose of Herr von Zecke, who has a whole garden full of roses, with a bouquet of roses is so beautiful that Pagel almost buys. But then he shrugs and moves on. He is not entirely sure that Tick is taking his pumping attempt lightly and humorously.

But the money has to come out of the pocket - that much is certain. Pagel would prefer to give it to a beggar, that always brings good luck. But there are not even beggars here in Dahlem. They prefer to sit down at Alexanderplatz with the poor people. They still tend to have a little money left over.

For a while, Wolfgang then walked behind an older, skinny lady who, in her gray-looking jacket with shot purple lapels and some jangle of black melting beads, gave him the impression of a 'bashful poor'. But then he refrained from putting the money in her hand. For it would have been of the very worst forethought not to get rid of the money right away, but to get it back first.

Eventually Pagel got on the dog. Quietly amused, he sat on a bench and whistled and nuzzled a stroming, white, brown-spotted fox. The animal was filled with a fantastic lust for life, barking defiantly, challengingly at the flatterer, then suddenly being affectionate, laying its head on its side examiningly and wagging the stump of its tail. Almost Wolf had him tight, he was already chasing again, barking up merrily, over in the plants, while one a maid with swung leash, desperately Schnaps! Schnapps! shouting, hurrying after him.

Faced with a choice between the calmly smoking man and the excited girl, Fox chose the man. He nudged Pagel's leg with his muzzle in a prompting manner, and there was a clear request in his eyes to start a new game. Wolf had just slipped the bills tightly under his collar, when the girl came, heated and indignant, and breathlessly exclaimed: "Let go of our dog!

Oh, Fräulein, said Wolfgang. For liquor, we men are all now. - And ... he added, because in the freshly washed dress was a pleasing girl, and for love.

Oh, you! said the girl, and her annoyed face changed so suddenly that Wolfgang had to smile, too. You have no idea, she said, trying to put the prancing, yowling Fox on a leash, what kind of trouble I'm in with the dog. And always address a gentleman. - What is it? she asked in surprise, because she had felt the paper under the collar.

A letter, Pagel said as he walked away. A letter for you. You must have noticed, I have been following you every morning for a week. But read it later when you're alone, it's all in there. Goodbye!

And he hurriedly went around the corner, for her face shone too brightly for him to witness the discovery of the truth. Around a corner again, and now he could probably slow down, now he was safe from her. He was also sweating again; in fact, he had been sweating the whole time since he got off at Podbielskiallee. As slow as he had gone. And suddenly it came over him that it wasn't the sunburn that made him so warm, not just the sunburn. No, no, it was something else, something else: he was excited, he was scared!

With a jerk, he stopped and looked around. Silently, in the midday glow, the villas stood between the screens of pines. Somewhere a vacuum cleaner was humming. Everything he had done so far to delay pressing the bell button had been entered by fear. And it had started much earlier: he would not have bought a Lucky Strike, but a breakfast for them both - if he had not been afraid. Without the fear, he would not have left the things to the uncle either.

Yes, he said, and went on slowly, it is drifting towards the end. He suddenly saw both of their situations as they really were: in debt, without any prospect for the next day, Petra almost naked in the stinking cave, him here in the rich man's neighborhood with his scraped, field-gray skirt, not even the fare in his pocket.

'I must persuade him to give us money,' he thought. 'Even if it's very little.'

But it was idiocy, it was complete madness to expect a loan from Zecke! Nothing he knew about Zecke warranted the expectation that he would lend money - with a minimum chance of getting it back. But then what if he said 'no' -? (And he would say 'No' of course, Wolfgang could calmly spare himself any question).

The long, rather wide avenue, at the end of which lies Zecke's villa, opens up in front of Pagel. He begins to walk down it, rather slowly at first. Then faster and faster, as if it were driving him down a mountainside, toward his fate.

'He has to say yes,' Wolfgang Pagel thinks once again, 'even if he gives so little. Then I'll stop playing. I can still become a cab driver - Gottschalk has promised me his second car. Then Petra gets it easier, too.'

Now he is already very close to the villa. He sees again shell limestone and iron grille, brass sign and bell button. Hesitating anew, he crosses the street.

'But of course he says no. - Oh, damn, damn!!!' When he looks around, he sees a girl coming from the end of the street; the yelping Fox tugging at the leash already gives away what kind of girl she is. And between argument here and request there, hunted and hunter, he presses the doorbell button, and only breathes a sigh of relief when the door lock whirs softly. Without a glance at the approaching woman, he enters, carefully pulls the door shut, and breathes a sigh of relief when a bend in the path leads him between covering bushes.

After all, Tick can only say 'no', but this service bolt there can make an inhuman racket - Wolfgang hates racket with women. It always gets so rampant right away.

7

So there you really are, Pagel, said Herr von Zecke. Half and half I expected you. And when Wolfgang made a move: Not exactly today - but you were due, weren't you?

And Tick smiles superiorly, but Wolfgang Pagel is annoyed. It occurs to him that Zecke has always loved this pompous secrecy, that he has always had that superior smile, and that he, Pagel, has always been annoyed by it. Tick smiled like that when he felt particularly smart.

Well, I'm just saying, so Tick grinned. After all, you really are sitting here with me - you probably won't want to deny that. Well, leave it. I know what I know. Let's have a schnabus, have a cigarette and look at my paintings, huh?

Pagel has long since seen the pictures. They sit in a large, very decently furnished garden room. A few doors to the sun-drenched terrace are open, you can see sun and greenery, but it's still pleasantly cool in here. A beautiful light coming through the greenish blinds in front of the windows, light and dark at the same time and above all cool.

They sit in beautiful armchairs, not those awful, slick, cold leather ones you see everywhere now, but deep, roomy cases covered in some flowery English fabric - chintz, probably. Books up to a third of the height of the wall,

Hans Fallada   Wolf among Wolves

above them pictures, good modern pictures, Pagel saw it right away. But he does not react to Zecke's question, he has already noticed that the atmosphere is not at all unfavorable to him, that his visit somehow suits the gentleman from Zecke. Of course, Tick wants something from him, and so you can calmly wait and be a little stroppy. ('I'll get my money already!')

Pagel points to the books: Fine books. You read a lot -?

But von Zecke is not that stupid. He laughs heartily. Me and read -?! Still the little teaser? You want me to say 'yes', and then you bore me with what Nietzsche says! Suddenly his face changes, it becomes thoughtful. I think it's a pretty good capital investment. Full leather binding. You have to make sure that you invest your money in a way that keeps its value. I don't know anything about books - Salvarsan is easier. But I have this little student who advises me ... He thinks for a moment, probably about whether the little student is worth the money he is paying him. Then he asks again: Well - and the pictures?

But Pagel just won't. He points to a few sculptures standing there: Figures of apostles, a Madonna and Child, a crucifix, two lamentations. Do you collect medieval wooden sculpture too?

Tick makes a sorrowful face. Do not collect, no. Invest money. But I don't know how it comes, I suddenly enjoy it too. Look here, this fellow here with the key, Peter, right. I got it from Würzburg. I don't know, I don't understand anything about it, it really doesn't look much, not at all pompous and all that - but I like it. And this candlestick angel - the arm is certainly supplemented, do you think that I am swindled -?

Wolfgang Pagel looks at von Zecke with a scrutinizing eye. Tick is a small man, despite his four or twenty-five years, he is already getting roundish and his forehead high due to hair loss. It is also dark - and Wolfgang dislikes all this. He also dislikes the fact that von Zecke takes a liking to wooden sculptures and that his paintings seem to cause him real concern. Tick is a raw slider, nothing more, and so he has to stay. Interest in art with him seems ridiculous and outrageous. Most of all, however, Wolf is outraged that he should approach this transformed tick for money. He is able and gives it out of decency -! No, Tick has to be and remain a racketeer, and if he lends money, he has to take usurious interest, otherwise Wolfgang may have nothing to do with him. From a tick he does not want money as a gift!

So Pagel says, and looks disapprovingly at the candlestick angel: So now it's candlestick angels - you don't deal with vaudeville hookers anymore -?

Pagel immediately sees from Zecke's reaction that he has pushed it too far, that he has made a crucial mistake. You are no longer at school, where you had to endure clumsy confidences, where they were downright sport. Tick's nose turns white, Pagel remembers this from earlier, while his face remains very red.

But if von Zecke still has not learned to read books, to control himself he has learned (and in this point is far ahead of Pagel). He doesn't seem to have heard anything. Slowly he sits the candelabra angel down again, strokes once more thoughtfully over the probably completed arm and says: "Yes, yes, the pictures. You must also have some beautiful ones at home - from your father.

'Aha! So that's what you want!' Pagel thinks, deeply satisfied. And aloud he says: Yes, but some very good things are still there.

I know, says Tick, pours another schnapps, first into Pagel's glass, then into his glass. He sits down comfortably. So if you ever need money - you see, I buy pictures ...

That was a blow, the first response to the insolence, but Pagel doesn't let on. I don't think we are selling now.

You're not quite taught there, Tick smiles at him amiably. Just last month your mother sold trees to England to the gallery in Glasgow in the fall. Well, cheers! He drinks, then leans back contentedly and says harmlessly:

Well, after all, what is the old woman supposed to live on? What papers she had are just dirt today.

Tick is not grinning, but Pagel has the strong feeling that the term 'good friend', which he used for him this morning, is exaggerated. Pagel has two blows away, and the third will hardly be long in coming. Right, a poisonous toad had always been from tick, a bad enemy. So it's already better to meet him halfway - then at least the matter is done and over with. He says, and tries to say it as lightly as he can: I'm in a bit of a pickle, tick. Could you help me out with some money?

What do you call a little money? asks Tick, looking at his bellhop.

Well, really not much, a little something for you, Pagel says. What do you think about a hundred million?

A hundred million, says Tick, dreamily. I didn't earn that much from all the variety hookers ...

Third strike, and this time it seems to have been Knockout. But Wolfgang Pagel is not so easily beaten down. He starts laughing, laughing quite heartily and unconcernedly. Then he says: You're right, tick! Great! And I am the camel. Talk big, and yet want to pump me money from you. Get stroppy. But you know, it kind of pissed me off right away how I came in here .... I don't know if you understand ... I live in a cave on the Alex... Tick nods as if he knows ... Have nothing at all ... and then here so rin in the splendor! Not at all like Neureichs and Raffkes, really nice - and I don't even think that the arm is supplemented ...

He breaks off and looks searchingly at Tick. That's all he can do, that's all he can bring himself to do. But when Tick does not move even now, he says: All right, don't give me any money either, tick. I deserved that, stupid as I was.

I'm not saying no, Tick explains. I just want to hear it like this. Money is money, and you do not want it as a gift -?

No, as soon as I can, you'll get it back.

And when can you?

Possibly, if things go well, as early as tomorrow.

So, says Tick, not particularly enthusiastic. Well, let's have another schnapps. - And what do you need the money for?

Ah, says Pagel, getting embarrassed and starting to get angry. I have some debts to my landlady, small things actually - you know, a hundred million sounds a lot, but in the end it's not much more than a hundred dollars, nothing that outstanding ...

So debts to the landlady, says Tick quite unmoved and looks at the friend attentively from dark eyes. And what else?

Yes, says Pagel peevishly, I also pawned something at my uncle's ...

At the same moment it occurs to him that this is really not true. But he did not think at the moment that sold is not transferred, and so he leaves it at that. After all, it really doesn't matter that much ...

So, transferred to the uncle, says von Zecke and continues to look dark and scrutinizing. You know, Pagel, he then says. I have to ask you one more thing - excuse me. Money is money, after all, and even very little money (a hundred dollars, for example) is a lot of money to some people - to you, for example.

Pagel has decided not to pay attention to these stings anymore, after all, the main thing is that he gets his money. He says sullenly: So ask already.

And what are you doing? asks Tick. I mean, what do you do for a living? Do you have a position that pays you? Agent for commission? Employee with salary?

Right now, I don't have anything, Pagel says. But I can enter at any moment as a cab driver.

Yes, then of course! says Tick and seems quite satisfied. If you like another Schnabus, please! I have enough for the morning. - So cab driver ... he starts drilling again, this carrion, this racketeer, this human abuser, this criminal. (Sand instead of Salvarsan!) Taxi driver - certainly a nice bread, adequate earnings ... (How he sneers, that vicious monkey!) ... But surely not so adequate that you could give me my money back tomorrow. You remember, you said, if it goes well, already tomorrow?! Driving a cab isn't that good after all?

My dear tick, says Wolfgang and stands up. You want to torture me a little, huh? But the money is not that important to me after all.

He is almost trembling with anger.

But Pagel! - Tick calls out and is quite startled. I torture you -?! How do I get to that? Look, you specifically didn't ask me for a gift - you'd have had the few bills by now. You want a loan after all, have given details about the repayment - so I ask about it, inquire how you think - and you scold?!!! I don't understand.

I can, Pagel says, just put it that way earlier. In reality, I could only pay you back in weekly installments, like two million weekly ....

Doesn't matter, old boy! shouts von Zecke cheerfully. Doesn't matter at all among us old friends, does it? The main thing is that you don't gamble the money away again, right, Pagel?

The two look at each other.

It's no use, Pagel, Tick then says hurriedly and quietly, that you're screaming. I get yelled at so often, it doesn't bother me at all. If you want to get violent, you have to do it very quickly - Look, now I've already pressed the bell button - Oh yes, Reimers, this gentleman wishes to leave. You show him the way, yes? Goodbye, Pagel, old friend, and if you ever want to sell a picture of your father, I am always available for you, always ... Are you crazy?" Tick suddenly interrupts himself.

For Pagel has started to laugh, lightly and completely amused he laughs.

God, what a wonderful pig you've become, Tick! exclaims Pagel with a laugh. That must have hurt you, what I said about the vaudeville whores, that you then give all your dirt from you. - He used to deal in vaudeville whores, your boss, he says to the man behind him. (A cross between a man and a gentleman.) He doesn't want to know anymore, but it still hurts him when you talk about it. But, Tick, says Pagel suddenly quite expertly serious, I do tend that the arm of this candlestick angel is supplemented, and badly. I would do it this way ...

And before Tick and his man could stop him, the angel is without an arm. Von Zecke screams as if he feels the pain of amputation. The man Reimers wants to penetrate Pagel, but he is, despite inadequate nutrition, still a strong young man. With one hand he fends off the man, in the other he holds the amputated arm with the light spout. I would like to keep this crude forgery in memory of you, old friend Tick, says Wolfgang gleefully. You know: the light went out - and so. Goodbye and a prosperous lunch to all. Pagel leaves, amused and satisfied, because if von Zecke really wants to be happy that he didn't give him any money, he will have to think of the arm of the candelabra angel stuck in Pagel's pocket. And the pain will prevail.

8

Unchallenged, Pagel reaches the gate of Zecke's villa. When he pulls it open, there is a girl standing in front of it, a girl with a pushing Fox on a leash, her face very red.

God, are you still standing there, Miss?! he exclaims in horror. I had not thought of you at all.

Listen! she says, and her anger has lost none of its heat from waiting in the sun. Listen! she says and holds out the bills to him. If you think I'm one of those, thank you, yikes! Take your money!

And so little at that! says Pagel, completely unconcerned. You can't even buy a pair of silk stockings for that ... No, he says quickly. I don't want to tease you anymore, listen, I even want to ask you for advice ...

She stands there staring at him, the bills in one hand, the leash with the tugging fox in the other, completely taken aback by his change in tone. Listen -! she says again, but the threat is only weak.

Shall we go this way? suggests Pagel. Let's go! Don't be silly, come with me for a bit, Lina, Trina, Stina. I can't do anything to you here on the open road, and I'm not crazy either ...

I don't have time, she says. I should be home by now. The madam ...

Tell the madam, liquor ran out, and now listen. I was just in there with the fine guy in the villa, schoolmate of mine, wanted to pump me money ...

And there you put your money my dog ...

Don't be a goose, kitty!

Liesbeth.

Listen, Liesbeth! Of course I didn't get anything - because you were at the door with my money! Because you don't get money as long as you still have some, and that's why I had put it in your dog's collar. Got it -?

But with her, it's considerably slower. So you haven't been following me around for a week and you haven't put a letter in it either? I thought the dog had lost it ...

No, no, Liesbeth," Pagel grins cheekily, but he still feels miserable. No letter - and with the money I didn't want to buy your purity. But the question I want you to answer now is: what should I do now? Not a penny more. A pad at the Alex, for which the rent is not paid. My little one sits in it as a pawn, dressed only in my summer paletot. All the things I sold to come here.

Seriously? asks the girl Liesbeth. No more bullshit?

No more bullshit! Completely serious!

She looks at him. She looks incredibly freshly washed and clean - despite the heat - it smells like sunlight soap around her, so to speak. Maybe she's not quite as young as he first thought, plus she has quite an energetic chin.

She knows now that it is really serious. She looks at him, then at the money in her hand.

'Is she giving it back to me now?" he ponders. 'Then I have to go to Peter and I have to do something. But what to do, I really don't know. I don't feel like doing anything anymore. No, let her tell me what to do ...'

She smoothed out the money and put it in her pocket.

So, she says, now come with me first. Home I must go now - and you also look to me like you could use some lunch in our kitchen. All green and yellow you look. The cook says nothing and the madam also agrees. But to think that your girlfriend sits in your summer overcoat on your pad, and 'ne cuddly landlady possibly in addition, and perhaps nothing in the stomach - and such a thing puts dogs money in the collar and wants to flirt immediately again from fresh - shit bastards are you men yet!

She talked faster and faster, tugged the dog, walked more hurriedly, but not for a moment was she unsure whether he was also walking with her.

And he really went along, Wolfgang Pagel, son of a not unknown painter, Fahnenjunker a. D. and player at the end.

9

With the second order at eleven the letter carrier had already brought the letter. But at that time, Mrs. Pagel was still out running errands. So Minna had placed it on the console table under the mirror in the forecourt. There it was, a gray envelope, some hammered, rather pompous handmade paper, the address painted on steeply and very large with quite a written-out hand, and every free space in the front as well as in the back was pasted full with the thousand-value stamps, although it was only a city letter.

Hans Fallada   -111-   Wolf among Wolves

When Mrs. Pagel returned from town a little late and quite heated, she only glanced at the letter. 'Oh, from Cousin Betty!' she thought. 'Now I have to see to my dinner first. What the old clap wants, I'll hear soon enough.'

It was only when she was sitting at the table that she remembered the letter. She sent Minna after her, Minna who, as always, stood behind her in the doorway, while, as always, the place setting for Wolfgang lay unused at the other end of the table. From Frau von Anklam, she said over her shoulder to Minna, tearing open the letter.

God, that wouldn't have been so urgent either, madam, that your food has to get cold because of it.

But from the silence, from the rigid posture of the madam, from the motionlessness with which she stared at the letter, she guessed that it had been important after all.

Minna waited for a long time, silently, without movement. Then she cleared her throat, finally saying admonishingly: "The food is getting cold, madam!

How -?! Mrs. Pagel almost shouted, wheeled around and stared at Minna as if she were completely unknown to her. I see ... she reflected. It's just ... Minna, Frau von Anklam writes it to me ... It's just - our young master is getting married today!

And there it was over. The head with the white hair lay on the edge of the table; the straight back, which the will had tightened again and again, was crooked - the old woman was crying.

God! Minna said. God!

She stepped closer. Although she didn't find so much bad in this marriage, but she understood grievance, pain, abandonment of the mistress. Carefully she put her processed hand on her back and said, "It doesn't have to be true yet, madam. It was far from all true what Mrs. von Anklam told.

This time it's true, whispered Mrs. Pagel. Someone read the notice when it was posted and told her about it. Today at half past twelve.

She raised her head, looking searchingly along the walls. Then she reflected, and her eyes found the watch she was looking for on her arm. Half past two already! she cried. And the letter has been lying outside for so long, I could have known in time ...

True suffering finds nourishment in everything, even in the absurd. The fact that she had not known in time, that she had not been able to think at half past twelve: 'Now they will be married' - that only increased Frau Pagel's grief. With tears streaming, her lip quivering, she sat there, looked at her Minna and said: "Now we don't need to set a place, now Wolf is completely gone, Minna. Oh, that horrible woman - and now she's called Frau Pagel, just like me!

She considered the path she had walked under that name; the rushing, hurrying flower path first. Then the long, the endless years at the side of the paralyzed man, who, becoming more and more strange, calmly and kindly painted pictures, while she hunted for him a health for which he seemed to ask nothing more. Finally, she remembered the awakening, the resurrected one with the white temples, who, entangled in the silliest of mischiefs, was carried into her house shamefully dead ...

Every step of this long way had been so laboriously walked by her, not a year without sorrow; sorrow had been her bedfellow, and her shadow was called sorrow. But over it she had become a Pagel, from the fair deceptions of young flesh the firm woman had risen, who was called now and forever Frau Pagel. Still in heaven she would be a pagel; it was totally impossible that God would ever let her be anything but a pagel. But all this hard-fought, this transformation, which had been a painful growing into its destiny, that fell into the lap of this young thing as if it were nothing. Songlike, as they had come together, they bound themselves to each other. Where you go, I will go; where you stay, I will stay. Your people are my people, and your God is my

God. Where you die, I also die; there I also want to be buried. The Lord do this to me and that; death must separate me and you!' - Yes, that was what they said, but they knew nothing about it. Mrs. Pagel, that was not a name, that was a destiny! But they made a notice, had half past one written in - and that was it!

Minna also said it just now, to comfort her, but it was right: It will only be a registry office, madam, not a church.

The madam straightened up a little, she asked more eagerly: "Don't you think so, Minna? Wolfgang didn't really think it over, he only does it because this girl forces him. He also does not consider the registry office to be full. He doesn't give me the grief.

It is probably, explained the incorruptible Minna, because registry office must be, church not. He will be short of money, the young gentleman.

Yes, said Mrs. Pagel and heard only what was right for her. And what has run together in this way also runs apart again just as easily.

The young gentleman, Minna thought, has always had it too easy. He has no idea how a poor person earns money. First you made everything easy for him, madam - and now the girl does. Some men are like that - all their life they need a nanny - and it's funny, they always find one.

Money, the old woman repeated. They will hardly have any money. A young thing is vain, likes to dress pretty - if we gave her money, Minna?

She would only give it to him, madam. And he would gamble it away.

Minna! exclaimed Frau Pagel in horror. What you think! He's not going to play now that he's married! Children can come after all -

They could come before, madam, it has nothing to do with gambling.

The madam would not hear it, she stared across the table at the empty seat. Just cover up, Minna! she called. I can't watch this stuff anymore. I'm eating squab here - and he got married! The sobbing came again. Oh, Minna, what are we going to do?! I can't continue to sit here, in my rooms, as if nothing had happened! We have to do something!

If we went there once? Minna asked cautiously.

Go there? We? And he doesn't come to us?! And he does not even write to me that he is getting married?! No, that is quite impossible!

You don't have to pretend to know anything!

I lie to the wolf -?! No, Minna, I'm not going to start that again! It's bad enough that I realize he doesn't care about lying to me - no!

And what if I go there alone? Minna asks again cautiously. They're used to me, and I'm not too fussy about a little fibbing either!

Bad enough, Minna, says Frau Pagel sharply. Very ugly of you! - Well, I'm going to lie down for a bit, I have a terrible headache. Why don't you bring me a glass of water for the pills?

And she went into her husband's room. For a while she stood silently in front of the young woman's picture, perhaps thinking: 'She can never love Edmund the way I do. They can also go apart again, very, very quickly.'

She hears Minna going back and forth over there clearing the table, she ponders angrily, 'She's an old cross-head.' She was supposed to bring me a glass of water, no, she has to clear up first. I don't even think about doing her will! The day after tomorrow she has her afternoon off, she can do what she wants. If she goes today, the young thing realizes right away, she comes just for that. You know how calculating these young girls are! Wolf is a sheep, I will tell him that too. He thinks she takes it because of him. But she has seen the apartment and the pictures, of course she knows about the prices long ago. Also that this picture actually belongs to him. It's funny that he's never asked me to do it before, but that's the way Wolf is, never calculating ...'

She hears the water pipe running in the kitchen. Minna wants to bring her probably quite cold water. Quickly she goes to the sofa and lies down. She pulls a blanket over herself.

You could have brought me the water five minutes ago, Minna! You know I'm lying here with my horrible headache ....

She gives Minna a nasty look. But Minna has her old, wrinkled wooden face, there's nothing to look at her when she doesn't want to.

All right then, Minna! And be very quiet in the kitchen - I want to get some sleep. When you have washed everything off, you can go. Take your afternoon off today. Leave the window cleaning for tomorrow, you can't pull yourself together and be quiet! They always rumble with the buckets, and then nothing happens to my sleep. So farewell, Minna.

Adieu, madam, Minna says and leaves. She closes the door very gently, not at all rudely.

'Stupid woman!' thinks Mrs. Pagel. 'How she just stared at me again - like an old owl! I want to pay attention when she leaves. Then I quickly run to Betty. Maybe she was at the registry office or sent someone - no one is more curious than Betty. And I'll be back before Minna - she doesn't need to know everything now either!'

Mrs. Pagel looks again at the picture on the wall. The woman in the window looks away from her. Seen from here, the dark shadows behind the woman's head are shifting apart, clearing up - it almost looks as if a man's head is approaching his mouth to the woman's neck. Mrs. Pagel has seen it many times before, this time it annoys her.

'This damned sensuality!' she thinks. 'It spoils everything for young people. Forever they fall for it.'

Then she reflects that now that the two have married, the young woman's picture actually belongs to half of it. Isn't that how it is?

'But let her come to me only! She should only come! She's already got one backs off - but I've got more ...'

Almost smiling, she turns over and is asleep in a minute.

Chapter 04

- Afternoon sultriness over city and country -

04 01

Listen, said Director Dr. Klotzsche to the reporter Kastner, who had come to Meienburg Penitentiary today, of all days, on his tour of Prussia's solid houses. Listen! You don't have to give a damn about what they gossip about us in the little town below. If ten prisoners are a little loud, it resounds in this house of cement and iron as if a thousand were roaring.

After all, you called for Reichswehr, noted reporter Kastner.

It's outrageous ... Director Klotzsche wanted to break loose and get excited about press espionage, which extended to his long-distance calls. But at the right time he remembered that this Mr. Kastner carried a recommendation of the Minister of Justice in his pocket. In addition, the Reich Chancellor's name was probably Cuno, but he was already supposed to be shaky again, and with the SPD, whose press Mr. Kastner represented, it was therefore not to be messed with. It is outrageous, he continued, much more moderately, how in this gossip nest a big deal is made out of the simple fulfillment of an official regulation. If there is a threat of unrest in the penitentiary, I have to notify the police and the Reichswehr as a precaution. After five minutes, I was already able to cancel the alarm. You see, doctor -!

But even the doctor did not pull with this man. He asked: After all, in your opinion, there was also a threat of unrest. Why -?

The director was disgracefully annoyed - but what good did it do? - It was because of the bread, he said slowly. It was not good enough for one, he screamed. And when they heard the shouting, immediately twenty shouted with ...

Twenty, not ten, said the reporter.

A hundred, if you like," shouted the director, who was overcome with bile. For my sake, my lord, a thousand, all -! I can't help it, the bread is not good - but what can I do? Our food rates lag behind monetary devaluation by four weeks. I can't buy wholemeal flour - what should I do!

Provide decent bread. Why don't you raise a ruckus at the ministry? Make debts for the administration of justice, all things equal - people are to be fed sufficiently according to regulations.

Yes," said the director bitterly, "I'm risking my neck and neck so that my gentlemen can eat well. And outside the unpunished people are starving, eh?!

But Mr. Kastner was not amenable to irony and bitterness. He had seen a man in penitentiary clothes polishing the corridor; he called out, suddenly quite friendly: You, listen, you there! Your name please?

Liebschner.

Listen, Mr. Liebschner, tell me honestly: how is the food? Especially the bread?

The prisoner looked with quick eyes from the director to the dark gentleman in civilian clothes, still unsure of what was to be heard. You couldn't know, the stranger could be from the prosecutor's office, and if you tore open the flap, you were sitting in it. He decided to be careful: the food? I like it. Oh, Mr. Liebschner, said the reporter, who was not talking to a prisoner for the first time, I am the press, you don't have to be embarrassed in front of me. You will not have any disadvantages if you speak openly. We will keep an eye on you. So what was that about the bread this morning?

I beg your pardon! shouted the director, pale with rage. This borders on incitement ...

Don't make a fool of yourself! barked Mr. Kastner. If I ask the man to tell the truth, is that incitement? Feel free to talk off the cuff - I'm Kastner from the Social Democratic Press Group. You can always write to me ...

But the prisoner had already made up his mind. Some people always have to grumble, he said, looking the reporter faithfully in the eye. The bread is what it is, and I like to eat it. Those who scream the loudest in here are usually hungry outside and don't have a pair of pants on their butt.

So, said the reporter Kastner with a furrowed brow, visibly dissatisfied, while the director breathed easier. Like this! - What are you punished for?

Imposture, replied Mr. Liebschner. And then, yes, harvest commandos are supposed to go out now, tobacco and meat, as much as you want ...

Thank you! said the reporter briefly, and turned to the director: Shall we go further? I would have liked to see another cell. You also know what to make of the chatter of the calf factors, they are all afraid for their posts. And then imposture - impostors and pimps, that is the most untrustworthy rabble of the world!

At first, however, you seemed to care a lot about the testimony of this impostor, Mr. Kastner. - The director smiled behind his blond beard.

The reporter did not see and did not hear. And then harvest commandos! Do the big agrarians their dirty work, for which even the pollacks are too good! And for shop wages! Is this an invention of yours?

Not at all, said the director kindly. Don't. A decree of your party comrade in the Prussian Ministry of Justice, Mr. Kastner ...

04 02

Mrs. Thumann, Petra said in her landlady's kitchen, had her shabby summer paletot buttoned tightly from top to bottom and paid no attention at all to her room visavis, the racy but boozy Ida from the Alex, who sat at the kitchen table dipping beautiful glazed snails in latte - Mrs. Thumann, don't you have a little something for me to do?

Jotte doch, Mächen! groaned the Pottmadamm at the sink. What do you think you have to do with wat again? Do you want to check the clock to see if he's coming, or are you hungry?

Allet beedet, said Ida in her deep voice, scratchy from the schnapps, and sipped her coffee over a piece of sugar in her mouth.

The green herrings have already been removed and scaled, and the potato salad isn't made the way Willem wants it - and what else?

She looked around, but couldn't think of anything.

Da ha'ck nu jespannt und jejachtert, dat ick noch rechtzeitig zu de pikfeine Trauung unter de Kirchentür stehe, und nu ist es ein Uhr vierzig, und wat de Braut ist, die läuft noch in 'nem Herrenpaletot mit nackje Beene. Imma you get hammered!

Petra sat down on a chair. She really felt a little very weak in the stomach, a pulling sensation with a faint hint of coming pain, weakness in the knees, and always a break of sweat that could not have come from the stifling sultriness alone. But their mood was still quite good. A great, happiness-inducing certainty was within her. She could let them talk calmly, there was no longer the pride and no longer the shame of before. She knew where the path was going. The important thing was that it led to the destination, not that it was difficult.

Just sit down slowly on the chair, my lady! sneered the racy Ida again: Otherwise it won't hold until the bride's jamm comes to fetch you to the wedding ceremony.

Don't make it too bad with her in my kitchen, Ida, admonished the Pottmadamm at the sink table. So far he has paid for everything, and paying guests are supposed to be nice.

It's over for once, Thumann," said Ida wisely. I have an eye for the men, I know when Marie is getting thin, and he wants to move back - hers is moved today.

Don't you dare, Ida! complained Mrs. Thumann tearfully. What should we do with the girl with nothing but a paletot and bare legs? - Oh God? she screamed loudly and threw a pot so that it rattled, everything is going wrong for me, I can cook her another dress every week, just to get rid of her!

A Kleed koofen! said Ida contemptuously. Too stupid dresses ooch not pretty, Thumann! Then you sar to the next Sipo so-and-so - there's one living in the front building - and you vastehnse and fraud and off with her to the police station and uff den Alex. They'll put something on you, Miss, what do you think, a blue hussar and a headscarf, do you see?!

You don't have to scare me, Petra said peacefully and a little weakly. She has probably also been dumped once. She had not wanted to say it, but whose heart is full, his mouth overflows - and so she had said it!

Ida stopped breathing, as if someone had pushed her roughly in front of her chest.

He's gone, girl! Thumann giggled.

Eener, Fräulein?" said Ida with a raised voice. Eener - saren Se?! A hundred should sar! There are not enough hundred times, det I me ice legs and thick knees stand, and the Seejer uff de Normaluhr jeht and jeht, until I dußlijet Aas finally realize: mir hat wieda eena vasetzt! But, she went from the wistful memories to the attack, "because someone who doesn't even have anything to wear on her wedding day doesn't have to hold it against me for a long time! Eene who only kiekt me with Jieroojen the snails in the mouth and counts de coffee swallowers. So eene like ...

Firm, firm! rejoiced the Thumann.

And anyway! Is it then a thing for a decent girl, that she comes in such a distressed laje snooty in a foreign kitchen and asks like Jräfin Hochkotz:

Hamm Se wat for me to do?! If you don't have, you have to go begging, my dad already wrote that on my back with a log, and you would have thought so: Ida, I'm hungry, give me a snail, you would have had one long ago! And anyway, Mrs. Thumann! I'll pay you a dollar a day for your bug hutch and not even a night light on the stairs, where the gentlemen always complain about it - that's when you have to laugh and shout: you've lost him, girl! So you have to protect me, and if someone like that gets married and sleeps with her boyfriend for nothing, to the Vajniejen, and the Thumann can see where she gets the pink, we don't work, We don't go on the line and don't create - we're too good for that - no, Thumann, I have to wonder a lot about you, and if you're the cheeky bastard who accuses me of not always being lucky with the gentlemen, if you don't throw them out on the spot - then I'll draw!

The racy Ida stood there red with rage, she still had a snail in her hand, she was bright red and became even redder the more she realized how badly she had been insulted. The Thumanns and Petra looked quite stunned at this storm that had arisen; no one knew from where or why. (And the racy Ida, if she could only have thought, was surely as surprised at the conclusion of her speech as the other two).

Petra would have loved to get up and slip into her room, lock the door and throw herself onto the bed - oh, the good bed! But it became weaker and weaker to her, it sometimes roared in her ears and before her eyes it spun, then the angry voice spoke very far away. But suddenly it came close again, it screamed directly into her ears, and before her eyes it spun anew. Then fire ran down her neck, down her back, debilitating sweat broke out ... If she did the math, she hadn't eaten anything real for a long time; only when Wolf had money, a bockwurst with salad, or rolls and liverwurst on the edge of the bed. And since yesterday morning nothing at all, where it was so important that she fed well -! She had to try to get into her room quickly, and then lock it, especially lock it tightly; even if they knocked with police, don't open it; only open it again when Wolfgang came ...

Jotte doch! she heard the Thumann whining in the distance, what a stink you're giving me with your cheeky mouth, girl! Those who don't have anything don't have to yak the bread off the table, and Ida is a fine lady who comes every day with her dollar - you don't have anything to reproach her for, you know! And now make sure you get out of my kitchen, and a bit quick, otherwise something will shake ...

No! Ida screamed unbearably sharply. That's not true, Thumann! Either she goes or I go! Beleidijen let ick me nich of such a - raus with her from de apartment or ick pull this minute.

But, girl, Ida, child of the heart! wailed the Thumann. You can see how she is: spit on a lime wall, and nothing on a body and nothing in the body - I can't let her tower like that ...

Can't you, Thumann? No, you can't? So - let's see - you can look me right in your front door, Mrs. Thumann -!

Little girl, Ida, Thumann begged, just wait until her guy comes back, make love to me! - Then they should both have to walk the same minute! - Make sure you get out of her room, you stupid Jans, you! she whispered excitedly to Petra. If she just doesn't see you anymore, she'll rest!

I'm going, Petra whispered and stood up. Suddenly she could stand and she also saw well the black hole of the open kitchen door into the dark hallway, but she did not see the faces of the women. She walked slowly, they said something else, faster and faster, louder and louder, but she didn't hear it clearly, so she couldn't understand it either ...

But she could walk for that, and she walked slowly out of the bright, hot sultriness toward the black hole. Behind it came the almost dark hallway with 'her' door; she only had to enter, lock it - and then the bed ...

But she passed, it was like in a dream, her limbs went differently than the head thought it out. She took one more look at the room as she passed - 'I should have made the bed after all,' she thought, and she was gone. Already the front door was there, and she opened it, took a step over the threshold, and pulled it shut again behind her.

The light on the right and left were faces of female neighbors.

What's the noise with you? one of them asked.

You threw them out, miss?

Jotte does! Like a warmed up corpse!

But Petra only quietly moved her head in denial. She was not allowed to speak or she would wake up and sit in the kitchen again, and they would argue and yell at her.... Quietly, only quietly, otherwise the dream fades away ... She carefully grasped the railing, she stepped down a step - and she really did get lower. It was a real dream staircase, you got lower on it, not higher.

Then she descended further.

She had to hurry. Upstairs they had opened the door again, they shouted something behind her: Mächen, mach doch keene Zicken! Where do you want to go, so naked? Come back, the Ida will show you too...

Petra made a negating motion with her hand and went lower. She climbed and climbed - to the bottom of a well. But below was a bright gate - like in a fairy tale. There was such a fairy tale, Wolfgang had told her. And now she went out through the bright gate into the sun, through corridors, across sunny courtyards ... and now there was the street, an almost empty, very sunny street -

Petra looked up and down them - where was Wolf?

04 03

Field inspector Meier - Negermeier - has been out in the sugar beet field right after the start of work at one o'clock. It was exactly as he had thought: the bailiff Kowalewski, in his limpness, had let the women scrape only so on top, half of the weeds still sat firmly in the earth.

Immediately, little Meier had puffed himself up, turned red and started to rant: damn mess, standing around and poussing with the women instead of opening his eyes, miserable wimp - and so on, up and down the whole scale already known and repeated at every irregularity.

People's bailiff Kowalewski had let the furious torrent pass over him without a word of protest, lowering his gray, already almost white head, and in the process had picked one or two miserable weeds out of the dusty, solid earth with his own paws.

You should not grab, but watch out! Meier had shouted. But you prefer grabbing, of course!

A completely groundless suspicion of the old man. But Meier had his laugh with the people and hit the spruces. There, his turkey blush immediately changed to his usual face color - a healthy reddish brown - and he laughed so hard his belly shook. That's who he had given it to, the old fool! At least the next three days this beating would last again! You had to have learned that, to roar with rage without being even the slightest bit angry, otherwise you made yourself dead with people.

The cavalry captain, though an old officer and a recruit referee, could not. He was annoyed that he became snow-white, that he turned as red as a turkey, and after each such outburst he was completely exhausted for twenty-four hours. Strange nut, big man, really!

One could be curious what kind of people he came back with today, if he brought any at all. If he brought some, they were of course excellent, because he, the Herr Rittmeister, had engaged them - and he, Meier, had to see how he got along with them. Lawsuits excluded.

Well, it would be all right. He, the little Meier, still got along with all the big men, the main thing remained that there were a few nice girls around. Amanda was quite good so far, but such a Polish Madka still had a completely different breed and fire, and - above all - she never set her mind to anything. Negermeier sang to himself obliviously: Because the rose and the girl wants to be shitty!

Young man - you are not alone! said a booming voice - and driving together, Field Inspector Meier saw the father-in-law of his employer, the Privy Economist von Teschow, standing under a spruce by the road.

Underneath, the old gentleman, especially for such an oppressively hot summer day, was dressed quite adequately, namely with high top boots and green loden bustle. From the waist up, however, which was a monstrous belly of pain, he wore only a hunter's shirt with a colored pique insert, which stood wide open and let the gray-red chest, covered with beads of sweat, be seen. Then further up came wool again, namely a reddish, grayish, whitish, yellowish, woolly full beard. A red bulbous nose, two cunning and amused sparkling little eyes, and on top a green loden hat with a chamois beard. The whole of the Geheime Ökonomierat Horst-Heinz von Teschow, owner of two manors and eight thousand acres of forest, called 'the old man' for short.

And, of course, the old man had a couple of stout clubs in his paw again - his hunting car was sure to stop somewhere around the corner. Field Inspector Meier knew the old gentleman was not averse to his son-in-law's official, for he hated all ducking and subtlety. Therefore Meier said quite undaunted: "Have you seen some firewood, Mr. Privy Councillor?

In his old age, Herr von Teschow had leased both estates - Neulohe to his son-in-law, Birnbaum to his son. For himself he had kept only the 'few spruces', as he called his eight thousand acres of forest. And just as he took the highest possible rent from his son and son-in-law ('stupid gang, if they let me cheat them'), he was also, like the devil after the poor soul, after the use of his forest. Nothing was allowed to perish; every time he went out, he packed his hunting wagon full of dead firewood with his own hands. 'Am not as fine a bone as my Lord son-in-law. Don't buy me firewood, not even from my own spruces, find it for me, Army law - huh-huh-huh!'

For this time, however, he was not inclined to make known his views on firewood acquisition. The clubs in his hands, he thoughtfully looked at the young man who reached up to the armpit of the bearded old man. Almost worried, he asked: "You've been bitching again, haven't you, young man? My Lady is on the move! Is the fucking rose now at least the backs -?

Artfully and politely, like a good son, the little farmer answered: "Mr. Privy Councillor, we really only went through the poultry bills.

Suddenly, the old man turned purple: What's my poultry bill to you, sir!!! What do you care about my mamsel, what!!! You are an official with my son-in-law, not with my mamsel, understand? Not even with me!!

Yes, Privy Councillor! says the little Meier obediently and peacefully.

Does it have to be my wife's mamsel, Meier, Jüngling, Apoll! the old man complained again. There are so many girls after all -!!! Be considerate of an old man! And if it has to be - do you have to do it just so that she sees it?! I understand everything, I was young once too, I didn't sweat it through my ribs either - but do I have to have the trouble now because you're such a Casanova?! You want me to kick you out! I can't, I tell her, it's not my official, I can't kick him out. You throw your mamsel out. - No, she can't, she's just seduced, she says, and besides, she's so capable. Good poultry midwives are in short supply; field officers are a dime a dozen. - Now she's mucking with me, and as soon as my son-in-law is back, she'll be tooting his ears off - there you see!

We have only gone through poultry bills, insists the little Meier just in case, because 'Don't confess anything' is the slogan of all little criminals. Fräulein Backs is so bad at adding up - so I helped her.

Well, laughed the old man, she'll learn it from you, my son, the arithmetic, eh? And he laughed uproariously. By the way, my son-in-law called, he got people.

Thank God! Meier said hopefully.

But they slipped through his fingers again, he must have commanded a bit too much! I don't know, I don't understand, my granddaughter, Violet, was on the line. He is stuck in Fürstenwalde - do you understand that!!! When did Fürstenwalde become Berlin?

May I ask you, Mr. Privy Councillor," said little Meier with all the politeness he always had ready for superiors and higher-ups, "should I send wagons to the railroad this evening or not?

I don't know! said the old man. I'm going to talk you into your economy, I think you'd like that, son. That you will say later, when you make a mistake, that I ordered it! No - ask the Violet! She knows. Or doesn't know either. With your economy, you never know!

Yes, Privy Councillor! said the well-behaved Meier.

('You have to get along with the old man. Who knows how long the Rittmeister will make it on the lease - and maybe the old man will take me on as an official.')

The old gentleman whistled shrilly on two fingers for his car. You can still give me the cudgels on the cart, he said graciously. And how are your sugar beets doing? I guess you're just hacking now? Do not grow, how? You heroes must have forgotten all about the sulfuric acid ammonia, eh? I wait and wait, no one spreads fertilizer, I think, well let them, a clever child knows everything by itself. And laugh my ass off. Tomorrow, my lord!

04 04

The sweltering heat at Alexanderplatz Police Headquarters could knock you over. The hallways reeked of fermented urine, rotten fruit, unventilated, damp clothes. People stood around everywhere, gray figures with gray, wrinkled faces, eyes extinguished or flickering wildly. The tired policemen were dull or irritable. Rittmeister von Prackwitz, flaming with rage, had had to ask twenty people, walk dozens of corridors, climb up and down endless flights of stairs, until finally, half an hour later, he was sitting in a large, unclean, smelly office. Over there, barely a few meters away, the light rail rattled outside the window, you heard it more than you saw it through the gray dusty windows.

Von Prackwitz was not alone with the official. At an adjacent table, another plainclothes officer was asking a pale-faced, big-nosed kid about some pickpocketing. At another table, in the background, four men put their heads together and muttered to each other without a break. It was impossible to tell if there were any 'criminals' among them, because they were all in shirtsleeves.

The cavalry captain had made his report, at first briefly, precisely, repressing his anger, then quite vividly and almost loudly, when anger at his incursion had overwhelmed him again after all. The officer, a pale, haggard-looking civilian, had listened with lowered eyes, without an interjection. Or maybe he wasn't listening, but in any case he had been eagerly trying to place three matches next to each other in such a way that they didn't fall over.

Now that the cavalryman was finished, the man looked up. Colorless eyes, colorless face, short mustache, everything a bit sad, almost dusty, but not unsympathetic.

And what should we do about it? he asked.

It gave the cavalry captain a jolt. Catch the guys! he shouted.

Why?

Because he didn't honor his contract.

But you hadn't signed a contract with him, had you?

Yes, it does! Orally!

He will deny that. Do you have any witnesses? The gentleman from the exchange will hardly confirm your claims, will he?

No. But the guy, the Vorschnitter cheated me out of thirty dollars!

I'd rather not hear that, the officer said quietly.

How -?!

Do you have a bank certificate confirming the legal acquisition of the foreign currency? Were you allowed to buy them? Were you allowed to pass them on?

The cavalry captain sat there, quite white, chewing his lips. So this was the help that the state gave him! He had been cheated - and he was threatened! They all had foreign currency instead of the dirty money - he could have bet the gray man there in front of him carried some in his pocket, too!

Let the man go, Herr von Prackwitz, the officer said benevolently. What good does it do you for us to get the man and plug him in? The money is then long gone and people get you thereby also not! Cases upon cases, day after day, hour after hour. A wanted sheet daily sooo long - there is no point, believe me! Suddenly, however, quite on duty: Of course, if you wish, there is the matter of the fare ... You file a criminal complaint - I then create a file ...

Von Prackwitz shrugged, finally saying, "And I have my crop outside. Understand, bread about bread! Enough bread for hundreds! After all, I didn't give him the foreign exchange for my own pleasure, simply because there are no people to get ...

Yes, of course, said the other. I get it. So let's drop the matter. There are enough intermediaries around the Schlesischer Bahnhof - you're sure to get people. And do not pay anything in advance. Not even to the intermediary.

Fine, said the cavalry captain. So I want to try again.

At the next table, the big-nosed thief was now crying. He looked repulsive, I'm sure he was just crying because he didn't know any more lies.

So, thank you, said von Prackwitz, almost against his will. And suddenly, half aloud to the other, almost comradely, as to a fellow sufferer: Do you still find your way through - here - with everything like this? He made a vague hand gesture.

The other shrugged his shoulders and dropped them hopelessly again. He put on, hesitated, finally he said: since noon the dollar stands 760 thousand. What are people supposed to do there? Hunger hurts.

The cavalry captain also shrugged hopelessly and walked wordlessly to the door.

04 05

In one hour or another of his life, the active man, having reached a turning point in his existence, is overwhelmed by the feeling of his powerlessness and drops his hands. Defenseless, without the thought of even fighting back, he lets himself be pushed and shoved - not even retracting his neck before the blow that threatens him. Drift away, man, leaf on the stream of life! On hasty waves it carries you under a bank of still water; but already a new eddy seizes you, and nothing remains for you but to let yourself whirl, to perish or to linger anew - do you know it?

Petra Ledig, the half-naked expelled, would have conjured up the storm of the two women in the kitchen with a few words - it was all not so bad, if only she had spoken. Words change everything, they sand off the sharp edges - already everything is completely different; how was it just now? Just not this rigid silence that could hide arrogance like despair, hunger like contempt.

Nothing forced Petra Ledig to walk past the open door of her room. Enter and turn the key, she could, but she did not. The wave of life lifted the leaf, lifted it, lifted it. For too long it had lain in the quiet corner of the bank, only sometimes trembling softly under the last spurs of eddies. Now the wave washed the will-less out, into the complete uncertainty - out onto the street.

It was afternoon, maybe three, maybe already half past three - the workers were not yet back from the factories, the women were not yet going to their errands. Behind the store windows, even in the dark, musty-smelling back rooms of the stores, the shopkeepers sat, nodded and dozed. Not a customer in sight. It was so hot -!

A cat lay blinking on a stair stone; from across the street, a dog peered. But then it was not worth it to him, he opened wide the soft rose-colored throat and yawned.

The sun, whose light was probably still blinding, was only visible behind haze like a reddish ball of embers boiling over its edges. Whatever it might be, house walls or tree bark, shop window or pavement, piece of laundry on the balcony lattice or urine residue from a horse on the road embankment - everything breathed, groaned, sweated, smelled. Hot. Blazing hot. To the girl standing quietly, it was as if she heard a buzzing through the city, a low, monotonous sound, always humming away - as if the whole city was boiling.

Petra Ledig waited, blinking her eyes wearily against the light, waiting for some impetus to drive the page forward, wherever, anywhere. The city hummed with heat. For a while she stared strained at the dog, as if some impulse could come from it. The dog stared back - then dropped down, stretched all fours, groaning with heat, and fell asleep. Petra Ledig stood, stood; no, she did not pull in her neck, even a blow would have been redemption now - but nothing happened. The city hummed with heat. -

And as she stood waiting for something on the overheated Georgenkirchstrasse, her lover, Wolfgang Pagel, sat waiting in a strange house, in a strange kitchen - waiting for what? His guide, Liesbeth, so freshly washed, had disappeared inside the house. At the snow-white stove with the chrome fittings was another young girl, whom Liesbeth had told with a few whispered words. A pot rattled on the griddle, boiling busily. Wolfgang sat, waiting, barely waiting, elbow propped on one knee, chin in hand.

He had not yet seen such a kitchen. Large as a dance hall, white, silver, copper-red, the dull, grainy black of the electric pots - and running through the middle of them was a railing, waist-high, made of white wood, bordering a kind of podium, separating the workroom from the lounge. There were two steps; downstairs were stove, kitchen table, pots, cupboards. But upstairs, where Pagel sat, was a long dining table, snow-white, comfortable white chairs. Yes, even a fireplace was here, made of beautiful, red-burnt stones with clean white joints.

Wolfgang was sitting upstairs, while the strange girl was managing the stove downstairs.

He looked equanimously, bluntly through the high, bright panes, in front of which vine leaves hung, into the sunlit garden - admittedly, there were bars in front of the panes. And', he had to think absentmindedly, 'just as crime is kept behind bars, so wealth also takes refuge behind bars, only feels safe there - behind the bars of the banks, the steel walls of the safes, the wrought-iron ornaments, which are nevertheless also bars, the steel roller blinds and alarm devices of his villas. Strange resemblance - not so strange actually, but I'm so tired ...'

He yawned. Just then the girl looked at him from the stove. He nodded, smiling softly, not without emphasized seriousness. So one more girl, also not unsympathetic - ah, girls enough, and nods everywhere, compassion! -'But what on earth am I supposed to do?! I can't just sit here like this... What am I waiting for? But not on this Liesbeth, what should she tell me?! Pray and work, morning hour has gold in the mouth, work and diligence, these are the wings, work is the citizen's adornment, work makes life sweet. But neither does labor disgrace, and every laborer is worthy of his wages, therefore let him also be a laborer in the vineyard, working and not despairing ...'

Oh', Wolfgang thought again and smiled very faintly, almost as if he were a little disgusted, 'what slogans people have made up just to convince themselves that they have to work and that work is something good. They would all prefer to sit here like me, doing nothing, waiting for something, I don't know what myself. Only in the evening at the gaming table do I know when the ball purrs and rattles and is about to fall into the hole - that's when I know what I'm waiting for. But then when it has fallen into the hole, whether the desired one or another, it doesn't matter - then I don't know again.'

He stares in front of him, he doesn't have a bad head, no, thoughts are stirring in it. But he is rotten and lazy, he doesn't like to think anything through. Why also -? This is who I am and this is who I will remain. Wolfgang Pagel for ever! He has quite senselessly sold their last belongings, just to visit Tick, to borrow money. But having reached Zecke, he has just as senselessly, just for the sake of a spiteful word, destroyed all prospects of making money. And again senselessly he went along with the first person who then crossed his path and now sits there - in the murky, shallow, dead water, the will-less leaf, epitome of all will-less leaves. Limp, not without gifts, not even without kindness, not even unloving - but really just as old Minna said: now a nanny would have to come again, take him by the hand and tell him what to do. Really nothing more than a flag boy (ret.) for about five years now.

The news of his being here is probably spread around the house by Liesbeth. Now a chubby woman comes in, not a lady, a woman. She casts a quick, almost embarrassed glance at Wolf and then says aloud at the kitchen stove, "The gentleman just called. We eat punctually at half past three.

Good! says the girl at the stove, and the woman leaves again, not without having taken a second look at Wolfgang.

'Silly gawking! I'll be out of here in a minute!'

The door opens again. A servant in livery comes in, the valet. He doesn't need any excuse like the fat woman, he walks across the kitchen, climbs the two steps and joins Wolfgang at the table. The servant is already an older man, but with a freshly colored, friendly face.

He reaches out his hand to Wolfgang, without any embarrassment, and says: My name is Hoffmann.

Pagel, says Wolfgang, after a moment's hesitation.

It's very humid today, the servant says kindly, in a soft but very clear, trained voice. May I perhaps bring you something cool - a bottle of beer?

Wolfgang thinks for a moment, then: If I could ask for a glass of water?

Beer makes you flabby, says the other in agreement. And get a glass of water. The glass is on a plate, and there is even ice floating in the water, everything as it should be.

Yes, that feels good, says Wolfgang, drinking greedily.

Take your time, says the other, always with the same friendly seriousness. They do not drink us all the water. -

Nor the ice, he adds after a pause, and wrinkles appear in the corners of his eyes. But he gets a second glass.

Thank you very much, says Wolfgang.

Miss Liesbeth is busy at the moment, says the servant. But it will come soon.

Yes, says Wolfgang slowly. And, giving himself a jolt: I'd better go now, I'm all fresh again.

Fräulein Liesbeth, says the other kindly, is a very good girl, very good and very capable.

Sure, agrees Wolfgang politely. Only the thought of his money in this Fräulein Liesbeth's clothes pocket keeps him here. These few bills, so despised just now, would quickly bring him to Alexanderplatz. There are a lot of good girls, he says approvingly.

No, says the other firmly. Forgive me for contradicting you: the kind of good girl I mean is rare.

Yes? asks Wolfgang.

Yes, says the other. You don't have to do the good just because you enjoy it, but always because you love the good. He looks at Wolfgang again, not quite as friendly as before. ('Putzige Kruke', thinks Wolfgang.) The servant says in conclusion: So it won't be long now.

He walks out of the kitchen again, just as gently, just as prudently as before. Wolfgang has the feeling that this servant does not take a good impression of him, although he hardly said anything.

Now he has to move something: the girl from the stove comes with a tablecloth, then with a tray and starts to set the table. Sit still, she says. They do not interfere.

She also has a pleasant voice, the people in this house have a good way of speaking, it catches Wolfgang's eye. They speak very purely, very clearly.

This is your place setting, the girl says as Wolfgang stares thoughtlessly at the paper napkin in front of him. Today at lunch you will eat here.

Wolfgang makes a thoughtless but defensive movement. Something is starting to bother him. It is a house not far from Zecke's palazzo, but very far away. But they should not talk to him as if he were a sick person, no, as if he were someone who had done a bad deed in delusion, with whom one still speaks gently so as not to wake him up quickly.

The girl says: You won't disappoint Liesbeth, will you? And after a pause: The madam agrees.

She sets the table, jingles a little with the cutlery - very little, everything goes quickly and quietly from her hand. Wolfgang sits motionless, it must be some kind of paralysis, of course the heat does that. So a kind of beggar, coming in from the street, is hungry, with the permission of the lordship a midday meal is served. His mother had Minna make some sandwiches, the beggar was not allowed in the kitchen. In the highest case, a plate of soup was passed through the door and had to be spooned out on the landing.

Well, here in Dahlem people were more refined, but for the beggar it made little difference, beggar was beggar, in front of the door as in the kitchen, from now on until all eternity. Amen!

He hated himself for not going. He didn't want food, what did he care about food? He could eat at his mother's, Minna had told, there was always a place setting for him. Not that he was ashamed, but they shouldn't talk to him as if he were a sick person to be spared - he wasn't sick! Just that damn money! Why hadn't he taken those pathetic rags out of her hand earlier?! He would already be sitting in the subway ...

In his nervousness he has preferred a cigarette, he is already about to light it when the girl says: Please, if you can stand it at all, not now. Immediately after I send the food up. The Lord tastes so delicate ...

The door opens and in comes a little girl, daughter of the house, ten years or twelve, bright, cheerful, light. She certainly doesn't know about the evil gray, smelly city outside! Will take a look at the beggar, beggars really seem a rare item in Dahlem!

Daddy is already on his way, Trudchen, the child says to the girl at the stove. In fifteen minutes we can eat. - What is it, Trudchen?

Potted creeper! laughs the girl and lifts a lid. Steam rises, the child sniffs eagerly. Then it says: Oh, just old pods! No, really say, Trudchen.

Soup, meat and pods, Trudchen says hypocritically.

And -? the child asks urgently.

And, said Mr. Rund - then the dog bit him! the girl half laughs singing.

'That still exists,' Wolfgang thinks, half smiling, half despairing. 'So all of that still exists. I just didn't get to see it anymore, in my cave Georgenkirchstraße, so I forgot about it. But real children, innocence, unspoiled, ignorant innocence also still exists. The question of sweet food an importance, as a hundred thousand may not ask the question of daily bread at all! Looting in Gliwice and Breslau, food riots in Frankfurt am Main and Neuruppin, Eisleben and Dramburg ...'

He looks at the child dismissively. 'It's bogus, after all,' he continues to think, 'an artificial innocence, a fearfully protected innocence - just like they have bars in front of their windows.' Life is coming after all - what will be left of this innocence in two or three years?'

Hello! the child says to him. It noticed him only now, perhaps because he moved the chair to get up and leave. He takes the hand that the child holds out to him. It has dark eyes under a clear, beautiful forehead, it looks at him seriously. You are the gentleman who came with our Liesbeth? it asks insistently.

Yes, he says, trying to smile against so much seriousness. How old are you?

Eleven years, she says politely. And your wife has nothing but a paletot?

Right, he says, still trying to smile and act light. But it is a cursed thing to meet one's deeds in the mouths of others, and now even of children. And she didn't eat anything either - and is unlikely to get anything, not even food with macaroons.

But she doesn't even realize that he wanted to hurt her. Mom has so many things, she says thoughtfully. Most of it doesn't attract them at all.

Right, perfectly fine, he says again, and yet feels so shabby with his cheap brashness. That's just life. You haven't had that in school yet? How?!

More and more pitiful, more and more miserable, especially in front of those serious eyes that look at him - almost sad.

I don't go to school, says the child with a little pompous seriousness. Because I am blind. Again the look, then: Dad is also blind. But Dad used to be able to see. I have never been able to see.

She stands in front of him - and the one so quickly punished for his cheap mockery feels more and more as if she is looking at him. No, not with the eyes, but perhaps with the clear forehead, the boldly curved, a little pale mouth. As if this blind child saw more of him than his seeing Petra.

There she tells: Mom can see. But she says she'd rather not see either, she never knows how dad and I are going to feel. But we don't allow her to.

No, agrees Wolfgang. I don't think you want that.

Fräulein and Liesbeth and Trudchen and Herr Hoffmann can also tell us what they see. But when mom tells it, it's different.

Because it's Mama, isn't it? Wolfgang asks cautiously.

Yes, said the child. Dad and I, we are both mom's kids. Dad too.

He is silent, but the child does not expect an answer, these things he speaks of are probably natural to him, there is also nothing to say about them. Now it means: Does your wife also have a mommy - or does she have no one?

Wolfgang stands there, a very thin smile around his mouth. No, no one, he says firmly. And thinks: 'Away! Go ahead!' Knockout beaten in its unkindness, in its halfness by a child.

Dad will surely give you money, the child thinks. And mom wants to go to your wife's house this afternoon. Where is it?

Georgenkirchstrasse 17, he says. Second yard, he says. With Ms. Thumann, he says.

Something welled up in him: if only she was helped! She should be helped! She is worth any help!

Slipping world in which you drifted, poor man, entangled and entangling. Suddenly, as you feel her detach from you, you realize how precious she was to you. Driven out into the darkness, in the distance still the clear light - and now it goes out. You are alone - and whether you can and will return - you do not know! We had good hours, but they ran into the sand. Sometimes still a taste on the lip, fleeting, sweet - and over! And there! Poor Petra ...! Beggar truly, now that the turn comes, maybe help, he feels that help cannot help him because he is hollow, burnt out, empty. Gone! Gone!

I'm leaving now, he said through the kitchen. He shook the child's hand, nodded, asked: You know the address? and left. Went into the sultriness, into the narrow, raging, chasing city, once again to pass the fight for money and bread, for what, for whom -?

He did not know, still not, not for a long time.

04 06

What people called 'the castle' in Neulohe was the old man's house. Rittmeister von Prackwitz lived a good five hundred meters away, already between the fields, outside the estate, in a small villa. Six rooms, modern masonry style, a shoddy, already flaking building from the first inflation period. The castle, from which the old man had not wanted to move, if only to stay near his beloved spruces and - by the way - to watch the son-in-law a little bit - the castle was also only a yellow box, but with three times as many rooms as with the young people, and at least with a real staircase, a garden room with doors made of glass down to the ground, called the 'hall', and a park.

Negermeier passed by the castle. He had nothing to look for there and he did not want to look for anything for this time - because of the angry madam. In a moment, uncomfortably close, because too much under supervision, came the official house, where the office was and his room (everything else was empty because of the cavalryman's saving methods - but the cavalryman is a great man). Since Meier wanted to inquire with the madam about the telephone conversation with his father, he first went to his room and washed his hands and face. Then he poured a perfume 'Russian Juchten' extensively on his chest - it was absolutely the right perfume for the country. As the ad had said: 'tart, masculine, racy'.

Afterwards he looked at himself in the mirror. The time when he had considered his smallness, the bulging lips, the indented nose, the protruding eyes a disgrace was, of course, long gone. His success with women had taught him that beauty did not matter. On the contrary, a bit of distinctive appearance attracted the girls like the salt lick attracts the game.

Of course, it was not as easy with Violet as with any Amanda Backs or Sophie Kowalewski. However, the little meier - once again deviating from his employer, the cavalry captain - considered it certain that little Weio, despite her fifteen years, was already a hussy. Those looks, that young, eagerly marked chest, those phrases, cheeky, and the second after that bluest innocence - there was no mistaking it for such an experienced woman hunter as he! It was also clear: already from the bedroom of the then still unmarried mother, the old gentleman von Teschow should have put out a lover, with the whip, which afterwards also got to taste the mama. Told people - well, the world was big and possible in it everything. The apple does not fall far from the tree. It would be a bit of an exaggeration to call the little field inspector Meier a schemer and a roguish seducer because of his thoughts in front of the mirror. These were not plans, they were youthful drivel, vanity - pipe dreams. Like a young dog, he had an enormous appetite, he would have loved to gnaw everything - and the Violet was really very pretty!

But just like a young dog, his fear was at least as great as his appetite - just don't get a beating! He would never be able to be as cheeky as he was to the Amanda without an attachment to this Weio, behind whom stood an irascible father. If in his dreams he had done everything up to the kidnapping and secret wedding in the best possible way - he was still dreading the return home to his father-in-law. He couldn't even come up with the homecoming conversation with him; the young woman handled that best. There was no need to fear or respect her: once you've slept with one, you're no better than the one she slept with, and even the noble lineage - mysterious, yet awe-inspiring - had then come off like the polish from a piece of factory furniture - all just common spruce!

Negermeier grins at himself in the mirror. He remembers, as if to confirm his self-assessment, that the lieutenant spoke to him this morning in a completely different, much more comradely tone than he did to the old sneak, forester Kniebusch.

Meier greets himself with his hand in the mirror, he waves to himself in a friendly way: 'Good luck on your way, son of luck!' And marches off to Violet von Prackwitz.

In the office, Mrs. Hartig cleans up, a coachman's wife, still quite capable; would like to be, but after twenty-five, women are ancient. The good Hartig, about twenty-seven, no less than eight children, today tightly clenched her mouth. The eyes sparkle angrily, the forehead is full of wrinkles, Meier doesn't care, but just as he wants to pass her, the cast-iron floor lamp falls from the desk with a threatening crash, and the green lampshade shatters into a hundred shards.

Meier has to stop and put in his two cents.

Well, he says with a grin. Shards bring luck - is that true for you or is it true for me? And when she only looks at him silently, but glaring wickedly: What's the matter with you? Thunderstorm? It's humid enough for that.

And he automatically looks at the barometer, which has been falling slowly but steadily since noon.

With me you leave your messes! says the Hartig shrill and angry. Think, I'll clean up your mess longer! And she goes into her apron pocket, opens her hand - she has three hairpins in it. (In 1923, the bob had not yet conquered the flat land.) They were lying in your bed! she almost shrieks. Bastard, miserable! But I'm not cleaning it up anymore, I'll show the madam!

Which one, Mrs. Hartig? laughs Meier. The old one knows it - and already prays for me; but the young one thinks so too and laughs all the more!

He looks at her superiorly, mockingly.

What a mean woman! Hartig shrieks. Can't you look in bed before she takes off? But no, I'm supposed to clean up after her, me the poultry mistress! No shame has such 'n beast!

Yes, yes, Mrs. Hartig, most certainly! says Negermeier seriously. And again he grins: But your youngest has such beautiful red hair? Just like the feed master. Should he become a coachman like his father or a forage master like his stepfather?

And with that, Meier marches off, chuckling to himself, wonderfully satisfied, while inside, still angry, but half already appeased, Frau Hartig stares at the three hairpins in her hand. 'He's a carrion, after all, but with a whistle, small as he is!'

She looks at the hairpins again, shakes them so that they rattle, and resolutely puts them into her own hair.

'I'll get you yet,' she thinks. 'Amanda won't rule forever either!'

She clears away the shards of the lampshade, very amused suddenly, because she is firmly convinced that they will bring her happiness.

Meier also thinks about the shards and the happiness they will bring him right now. He arrives at the captain's villa in the best of moods. First he peers into the garden - for he would prefer not to meet Weio within earshot of her mother - but she is not in the garden. This is not difficult to determine, because although the garden is not quite small, it can be overlooked at a glance, this occasional creation of the gracious lady, stomped out of the bare field a few years ago and half dried up again.

Nothing can better symbolize the firmness of the position in Neulohe and the distance between owner and tenant than the observation of Teschow's castle park and Prackwitz's garden: there hundred-year-old large trees, in all abundance, bursting with leaves and sap, here a few dozen bare poles, with few, already yellowed leaves. There wide lawns, dark green; here sparse grass, hard, yellow, in hopeless struggle with the field pansies, couch grass, horsetail, advancing again. There a not quite small pond with rowing boat and swan; here a so-called paddling pool, probably made of Solnhofen slabs, but filled with a green slurry. There inherited growth, coming from the time for the time; here something hardly born, already dying again, nevertheless: the cavalry captain is a great man.

Field Inspector Meier was already about to press the bell button when he gets a call from the side. On the flat roof of the kitchen annex (mere tar paper) are a deck chair and a large garden umbrella, a ladder leans against the annex. From up there it called: Mr. Meier.

Meier gives himself the necessary official jolt: Yes?

Ungracious voice from above: What is it? Mom is all worn out from the heat, wants to sleep - just don't disturb her!

I just wanted to ask, madam ... The Herr von Teschow told me that the Herr Rittmeister had telephoned ... A little annoying: it is because of the cars ... Should I send to the track tonight or not?

Don't shout like that! shouts the voice from above. I'm not one of your yard-walker girls after all! Mom wants peace, I told you!

Meier looks up at the flat roof in despair. But it's too high, and he's standing too low: he can't see anything of the abducted and married woman in the dream, only a piece of deck chair and a slightly larger piece of mushroom umbrella. He decides to whisper - as loud as he can: Whether I should send wagons - tonight - to the railroad -?

Pause. Silence. Wait.

Then from above: Did you say something? I always understand station!

Ha-ha-ha! Meier dutifully laughs at the most common idiom of the time. Then he repeats his request a little louder.

You are not supposed to shout! he immediately has his rebuke away.

He stands there, knowing full well, of course, that she just wants to tweak him. He's just dad's field officer. Has to do what he is told. Has to stand and wait for the madam to deign. Just you wait, my dear, one day you will have to stand and wait - but for me!

Now, however, he seems to have waited long enough, because she calls from above (amazingly loudly, by the way, for such a considerate daughter): Mr. Meier! You don't say anything anymore?! Are you even still there -?!

Yes, madam.

I was beginning to think you had melted in the sun. Butter you need to have enough on your head for this.

('Knows already, of course. But it doesn't do any harm - it just whets her appetite.')

Mr. Meier.

Yes, madam -?

So if you've been down long enough, maybe you'll notice that there's a ladder, and you'll tell me up here what you actually want.

Once again: Yes, madam! and up the ladder.

'Jawohl, gnädiges Fräulein' is always good, flatters her, costs nothing, emphasizes distance and allows everything. You can look her in the neckline and say 'Jawohl, gnädiges Fräulein' with humility, you can even say it and give her a kiss - 'Jawohl, gnädiges Fräulein' is chivalrous, cavalier, dashing - like the officers in Ostade, Negermeier thinks.

He now stands at the foot of her deck chair and looks obediently and yet cheekily blinking at his young mistress who is lying there in front of him dressed in nothing but a very short bathing suit. Violet von Prackwitz, fifteen years old, is already a bit full, too full with the heavy chest, the fleshy hips, the strong buttocks, considering the years. She has the soft flesh, the too white skin of the lymphatic girls, plus a little protruding eyes like the mother.

They are blue, pale blue, sleepy blue. The good, innocent child has raised her naked arms, she stretches a little, it doesn't look bad at all, the slut is pretty and - golly! - what a body! That has to nestle in your arm.

Sleepily, blinking pleasurably through almost closed lids, she watches the inspector's face. Well, what are you looking at? she then asks challengingly. I don't wear anything else in the family bathroom either. Just don't make a fuss. She studies his face. Then: Well, mom should see us both here like this ...

He fights with himself. The sun burns insanely hot, it flickers, now it stretches again. He takes a step ...: I ... Weio, o Weio ...

Oh my! Oh my! she laughs. No, no, Mr. Meier, you'd better get back up there by the ladder. Suddenly quite mistress: You are funny! You must be imagining things. I only need to call out once and mom is at her window!

Then, when she sees that he is parrying again: Today you do not need to send to the railroad. Probably tomorrow morning for the first train. Dad makes another call.

Understood everything earlier quite well, the naughty bitch! Just wanted to show off to him, to torture him! But wait, I'll get you yet!

Why don't you let us drive in? asks the young girl, the one to be kidnapped, the one to be secretly married.

Because people have to bind and put on. - Quite grumpy.

And if there's a thunderstorm and everything gets wet, Dad will make you a huge noise.

And when there's no thunderstorm and I've let it roll in, it makes noise for me, too.

But there is a thunderstorm.

There's no way to know that for sure.

I know it though.

Hans Fallada   -146-   Wolf among Wolves

So, madam, do you want me to drive in?

I don't even think about it! She laughs uproariously, her strong chest literally bouncing in her swimsuit. That you blame me afterwards when it's not right for dad! No, do your stupid things alone!

She looks at him sympathetically. This brat of fifteen years is so cheeky -! Why cheeky -? Because she happens to be a born von Prackwitz, heiress of Neulohe - just because of that cheeky!

Then I can go, madam? asks Negermeier.

Yes. Take care of the economy for a bit. She rolled onto her side, looking at him once again with a sneer. He is already going.

Heh, Mr. Meier! she calls.

Yes, madam? - It doesn't help, he has to.

Is manure actually driven?

No, madam ...

Why do you smell funny?

It takes him quite a while to realize that she means his perfume. Then, wordlessly but furiously, he turns around and climbs down the ladder as fast as he can.

'What a carrion! You shouldn't even bother with such a carrion! The Reds are quite right: up against the wall with all this cheeky baggage! Nobility! Damn it! Insolence, most impudent insolence ... Nothing like big-headed manners ...'

He is off the ladder, he is marching off, his short legs kicking the earth furiously. There comes again the voice from above, the voice from heaven, the voice of the mistress: Mr. Meier!

He is driving together. Full of rage - and again it can't be helped, full of rage he shouts: Yes, madam?

Very ungraciously it comes from above: I have already told you three times not to shout like that. Mom is sleeping! And impatient: come up again!

Meier climbs the ladder again, his belly full of rage: 'Yep, as your tree frog up and down the ladder as you do the weather. Well, wait a minute, I've got you first, I'll leave you for sure, with child, without a penny ...'

And yet again in a tight posture: Please, madam ...?

She doesn't think about showing him her body now, she thinks about it, but she has already decided the matter with herself. She's just unsure how to tell him. Finally, she explains as harmlessly as possible: "You have to get me a letter, Mr. Meier.

Yes, madam.

Suddenly she has it in her hands, mysteriously from where, an oblong envelope made of bluish paper; as far as can be seen from Meier's point of view, without any inscription ...

You are still going to the village tonight -?

He is completely surprised and quite unsure. Is she just saying that or does she know something? But that's impossible!

I don't know, maybe. If you wish, madam, in any case!

You will be asked about the letter from a gentleman. Then hand it over.

Which gentleman? I don't understand ...

She suddenly becomes angry, irritated. You don't need to understand anything either. I just want you to do what I tell you to do. A gentleman will ask for the letter and you will give it to him. That is quite simple!

Yes, madam, he says. It sounds a bit weak though, he's too much in thought.

So, she says. That will be all, Mr. Meier.

He gets the letter in his hand. He doesn't want to believe it yet, but now he has the letter in his hand, this weapon against them!

'Wait, my little sheep! Are you going to get stupid on me one more time!'

He pulls himself together: Everything will be done in the best way, madam!

And he climbs down the ladder.

That's what I meant, too! her voice sounds quite challenging to him from above. Otherwise I'll tell grandpa and dad who burned the forest!

The voice falls silent. Meier stopped in the middle of the ladder so as not to say a word.

'So! So. There I have it! That's how it is! Baked on, she says. Right to the heart. Bravo! For fifteen years excellent. You can become something! Nah, you can stay like that!'

And the lieutenant can't take a joke either, the voice says - and now he hears her rolling on her side with her fat, rotten meat. The deck chair groans. Fräulein Violet von Prackwitz yawns comfortably up there, and Herr Feldinspektor Meier is allowed to go about his work downstairs - that's right, it's all right, the stuff.

But Meier, little Meier, Negermeier is not going to his work yet. Very slowly, deep in senses, he trots the way to his pad. He has the letter in the outside pocket of his reed-lined jacket, and over its smooth surface he has placed his hand so that he can always feel it. He must feel that he really has the letter, that it is there. This letter he is about to read. She said little enough, that sly little minx, but she said enough for him. Long enough! So she knows the lieutenant, this enigmatic, somewhat torn, but quite dashing gentleman who calls nightly meetings at the schoolmaster's house and stands at attention in front of the forester Kniebusch. And she met this lieutenant today between twelve and three, otherwise she could not know about the fire.

But if this lieutenant nodded so comradely to Field Inspector Meier, it was not because he thought that Negermeier was so much more capable than old Kniebusch, but because he already knew: Meier was destined to be the secret letter carrier! The lieutenant already knew quite well about Neulohe! Longer, clandestine agreement.

'You've come plenty far already, you two! I can think of everything. And once I read the letter - stupid you are, you haughty, silly goose! You think I'm going to pass the letter and not look at what's in it! I want to know, and then I'll see what I'm doing. Maybe tell the cavalry captain everything - what's a bit of forest fire against that? That doesn't mean you have me on the line by a long shot. But I don't think I'll say anything at all to the cavalry captain. Because you are still so stupid that you don't even realize that such a guy as the lieutenant will naturally abandon you. You only have to look at him once to know that. But then I'm there - no, my child, I don't mind. I don't get offended by that kind of thing. Breaking in young horses is not much fun and a lot of effort - it's better if they know every step and gait! But then you shall pay me, for every insolent, haughty word, for every yes, madam - and for this letter above all! - How do you open such a letter in the first place? I heard with steam - but where do I get steam on my pad in a hurry? Oh well, I'll just try to get the flap off with a knife, and if the envelope breaks, I'll use one of my own. Yellow or blue - after that he will hardly see ...' He arrived at the office. Without even taking off his cap, he sinks into the desk chair. He places the letter in front of him on the faded, inky green felt. Stare. He is wet with sweat, his limbs are hanging off him, and his mouth is dry. He is completely exhausted. He hears the chickens clucking on the farm, the Swiss rattling buckets and milk cans in the cow barn. ('Was going to ask for it too - high time to milk it!')

The letter is in front of him. The flies buzz and buzz monotonously, it is unbearably humid. He wants to take a look at the barometer on the wall ('Maybe a thunderstorm is coming after all?'), but he doesn't look up: 'It doesn't matter!'

Hans Fallada   -150-   Wolf among Wolves

The letter, the bluish-white pure rectangle on the stained green felt! Your letter!

Casually, half-playfully, he reaches for the paper knife, pulls the letter closer, and puts both down again. He first wipes his sweaty hands dry on his jacket. Then he takes the paper knife and slowly, with relish, he inserts the blunt tip into the small opening at the top between the cover flap and the envelope. His eyes are fixed, a slight, satisfied smile plays around his thick lips. Yes, he opens the letter. Carefully pushing, lifting, prodding, pressing, he released the carelessly taped flap. Now he already sees a corner of the letter, there are little glasses that don't want to comply, like little hairs - but at the same time he sees them, he sees Weio, as he has just seen her, on the deck chair ... She stretches her body, her white, full flesh trembles a little ... she throws up her arms and in her armpits it shimmers brightly, ripples ...

Oh! moans Negermeier. Oh! He was staring at the letter all the time, he opened it while doing so - but he was away below, five hundred meters from here, on the flat, sun-sweating cardboard roof - flesh by flesh, skin by skin, hair by hair -: O you! You.

The wave becomes flatter. Shining once more in the colors of beautiful, living flesh, as if irradiated by an evening glow, it fades into the sand. Negermeier breathes a sigh of relief. 'No, something like that!' he now wonders after all. 'This beast must have made me all crazy! But the heat does something to it too!'

The letter has opened impeccably. The flap does not even need to be freshly gummed afterwards, so carelessly did Fräulein Violet von Prackwitz tape it shut. So, let's read ... But before that, he wipes his hands on the yo-yo again, they are already wet with sweat.

Then he really pulls the sheet out of the envelope, opens it. It is not very long, the letter, but it has it in it. He reads:

Dearest! Dearest!! Only one!!! You've just left and I'm already wild about you again! I am flying all over and it is humming inside me that I have to close my eyes all the time! Then I see you! I love you sooo much! Dad is definitely not coming today, so I'll be waiting for you between eleven and twelve at the pond near the swan house. See that the stupid assembly is certainly all gone by then. I long for you terribly!

100 000 000 kisses and much more! I press you to my heart, which beats very hard for your Violet.

God! says little Meier, staring at the letterhead. She really loves him: so dear with three o's and yours underlined. Such a little pim-girl - he's going to fool her nicely. Well, so much the better!

He types the letter on his typewriter, carefully counting the zeros in the kiss number ('Pure inflation - it goes along with it!'), and sticks it shut again. He puts the copy of the letter in the 1900 volume of the official county gazette, and puts the letter back in his yoke pocket. And now he is completely satisfied. And completely ready for the economy. He looks at the barometer. It fell again a little bit.

'I wonder if there will be a thunderstorm after all? I wonder if I will run it in after all? Oh, nonsense, she's just talking nonsense!'

He goes off to his mowing machine.

04 07

I thought you would come and see me today, my dear, my poor Mathilde!

Frau von Anklam, widowed Major General, over seventy, snow-white, unformally fat, has laboriously emerged from her deep armchair where she was taking her afternoon nap. She holds the visitor's hand with both hands and looks into her face with her big brown, still beautiful eyes. For the time being, it speaks only carried - as in the case of a death. But she also knows another key, that of the government commander, who kept all the ladies of the regiment in discipline, order and decorum.

We are getting old, but our burden is not getting lighter. Our children, while they are young, step on our laps. Then later on our heart.

(Mrs. von Anklam has never had children. She could never stand kids either).

Come sit here on the sofa, Mathilde. I ring the bell - Miss is about to bring coffee and cake. I sent for the cake from Hilbrich today, he always has the best after all. Only it's not really worth it for me alone - forty thousand marks fare, you see, forty thousand! Robbers they are! - Yes, Miss, pastries and coffee, quite strong, my cousin has received sad news. - Yes, dear Mathilde, I was just sitting there in my chair thinking. Miss thinks I'm asleep, but of course I'm not. I hear every noise in the kitchen, and if a plate is broken while I'm doing the dishes, I'm right there! Does your Minna also break so much -? There is still the old Nymphenburg porcelain that Grandfather Kuno received from the Most Blessed Lord for his Diamond Wedding Anniversary - God, there is enough for me old woman, but still, one must also think of one's heirs! I had actually promised Irene, but I have been wavering again lately, Irene has such strange views on child rearing - straight up, how shall I say, revolutionary!

And the news is certainly correct, Betty? asks Mrs. Pagel, just straightened up, skinny - and no close relative, no matter how sympathetic, could see that she had cried tears.

The message? What message? Oh, the message! But dear Mathilde, I must say, where I wrote it to you specially -! This quite as commanding, but now again sympathetically: No, of course right - the good boy, the Eitel-Fritz had to do there. He read it with his own eyes, the posse is called. I don't know what he had to do there, though. I was so excited that I didn't ask him about it. But you know Eitel-Fritz, he is so original, he goes to the strangest places - Attention! La Servante!

'The Miss' appears with the coffee set, with the tray, with the Nymphenburg from the diamond grandfather. The ladies fall silent, and silently Fräulein, an elderly, mousy creature, sets the table.

It is always just 'Fräulein' - all these frequently changing figures in Frau Generalmajor von Anklam are nameless. Miss covers and Miss stuffs, Miss reads and Miss tells something, and above all: Miss listens! Fräulein listens from morning till night, stories of regimental ladies, long dead and forgotten ('I tell her: dear child, what tact means, I decide!'); stories of children, long in possession of their own children ('And there says this sweet angel child to me ...'); tales of relatives, long since pledged; tales of blue letters and promotions; tales of decorations; tales of wounds; tales of marital aberrations and of divorces - clutter and junk of a life spent entirely in gossip, Intima, Intimissima!

Miss, colorless, mouse gray, listens, says yes, oh no!, something like that!, heavenly! - but when there is a visitor at Excellency's, she hears nothing, Frau Generalmajor whispers with the last remnant of her Lausanne pension French: Attention! La Servante!, and the ladies fall silent. If there is a visitor - Fräulein becomes air, that's the way it should be. (Only when the visit is gone again, everything is told to her).

But after the first silence, Ms. von Anklam does not remain silent, which is not appropriate either. She talks about the weather, it's so humid today, maybe there will be a thunderstorm, maybe yes, maybe no. She once had a lady who got tearing in her big toe before thunderstorms - very strange, huh? -

It was always true, and once, when Fräulein was just on vacation, we still had the estate then, you know, we got the thunderstorm with the heavy hailstorm that smashed the whole harvest together - if Fräulein hadn't had a vacation now, we would have known that beforehand, and that would have been sooo good, wouldn't it, dear Mathilde? But of course, just then Fräulein had to be on vacation! -

Yes, it's all right, miss, thank you. You can still flatten the lace ruffles on my black taffeta dress now. You are already flattened, I know, Miss. There is no need for you to tell me. But they are not flattened as I am used to, they must be like a breath ... Miss! Like a breath! So you do that, miss!

And no sooner has the door closed behind Fräulein than Frau von Anklam turns again quite sympathetically to Frau Pagel. I have thought about it back and forth, dear Mathilde, but the fact remains: she is simply a person!

Mrs. Pagel shrinks, looks anxiously at the door: Miss?

But Mathilde, concentrate a little! What are we talking about? From the marriage of your son! If I wanted to be so unfocused! I have always told my ladies ...

Mrs. Pagel still has the hope to experience something positive, she doesn't really know what. She succeeds in inserting it: The girl may not be all bad after all ...

Mathilde. One person! Only one person!!

She loves Wolfgang - in her way ...

I don't want to hear about that! Indecency, no, not in my home ...

But Wolfgang plays, Betty, plays everything ...

Mrs. von Anklam laughs. Seeing your face, best Mathilde! The boy jeuts a bit - you don't have to say 'play', 'play' sounds so common - all young people jeut a bit. I remember how we had the regiment in Stolp at that time, there was also a lot of jeut among the young people. Excellency von Bardenwiek said to me: 'What are we going to do, Madam von Anklam? We have to do something about it.' 'Your Excellency,' I said, 'we're not going to do anything.' As long as the young people play, they do not do anything else stupid. And he immediately agreed with me ... Come in!

There was a soft and careful knock at the door. Now Miss sticks her head in: Ernst is back, Excellency.

Serious -? What does he want -? What are these new fashions, miss?! You know I have a visitor! Serious - unbelievable!

Despite this thunderstorm, the young lady still dares to say something, she chirps like a mouse in a trap: He was at the registry office, Excellency.

Frau von Anklam transfigures: Oh, of course, he should come in as soon as he has washed his hands. What long stories you make of everything, missy! - Miss, just a moment, don't always run away so headlong - please wait for my instructions. First give him a few splashes of cologne, yes, of the wash cologne! It is not known who he was with there.

Alone again with the cousin: I wanted to know how the wedding ceremony went. I thought long and hard about who I could send to something like this. I sent our Ernst. Well, now we will hear ...

And her eye lights up, she moves the heavy corpulence back and forth in the armchair, all expectation. She'll hear something new, something for the junk room again - oh God, great!

The servant Ernst enters, an older man, about sixty, a male, long since, a lifetime already with Frau von Anklam.

Under the door! she calls. Stop under the door, Ernst!

I know, Your Excellency!

Right after you bathe, change your clothes, who knows what bacteria are on you, Ernst! - Come on, tell us: how was the wedding ceremony?

It was not at all, Your Excellency!

You see, Mathilde - what do I always tell you? You don't get excited about anything! What did I tell you just three minutes ago: an ordinary person! She dumped him!

Mrs. Pagel weakly: If I could question Ernst, dear Betty -?

Hans Fallada   -156-   Wolf among Wolves

But of course, dear Mathilde. - Ernst, I don't understand you, you stand there like a stick, you hear, Mrs. Pagel wants to know everything! Tell, talk - she dumped him, of course! Now further - what did he say about it?

Hold to Grace, Your Excellency! I think the young gentleman has them - did not come ...

You see, Mathilde, exactly what I told you! The boy is quite all right, the little 'jeu' does not hurt him, on the contrary - completely reasonable, such a person you do not marry!

Finally, Mrs. Pagel gets through: Seriously, is it safe too? Surely it was not a wedding ceremony? Maybe you came a little too late?

No, madam, certainly not. I was there in time and waited until the end and also asked the official: they both did not come.

You see, Mathilde ...

But why do you think, Ernst, that it was my son? You get the idea ...

I wanted to be sure, madam, something could have happened. At the registry office I learned the apartment. So I went there, madam ....

Seriously, be sure to bathe immediately and completely fresh laundry -!

At your command, Your Excellency! - The young gentleman has not been seen there since this morning. And the girl was put out because the rent was not paid. It was still under the door. I have them ...

Mrs. Pagel stands up with a jerk. Suddenly she is again all determination, dark, energetic, rigid neck.

Thank you, Ernst. They put my mind at ease a lot. I am sorry, dear Betty, to go so informally, but I must go home at once. I have the definite feeling that Wolfgang is sitting there, desperately waiting for me. Something must have happened. Oh God, and Minna is gone too! Well, he still has his keys to the apartment. Sorry, I'm all mixed up, dear Betty ....

Shape! Shape, attitude, dear Mathilde! Attitude in every situation in life. Of course you should have stayed home on such an afternoon, of course he is waiting for you. Of course, I would not have left the house on such a day. And one thing above all - please, Mathilde, just a moment, you can't just run off like that - be tough with him! No false softness! Above all, do not give him money, not a penny! Apartment, food, clothes - good! But no money, he's just blowing it! Mathilde -! Mathilde. Away! No shape! - Listen, Ernst ...

The thumanness of the upper ten thousand continues to speak, on and on ...

04 08

The dog was still asleep, the cat was also asleep, nor was the Georgenkirchstraße asleep.

The girl Petra Ledig stood in the gateway to the backyards of the house in the shade. In front of her, the street flickered with white, merciless heat; the glare hurt her eyes; what she saw lost outline, seemed to melt away. Then she closed her eyelids, and now blackness came into her head, blackness with sudden flares of aching crimson. Darein heard them strike clocks - it was good, so time passed. At first she had thought she had to go somewhere, do something. But when she felt time passing in the moments of half twilight, she knew that all she had to do was stand here and wait. He had to come, he had to come at any moment, he brought money. Then they would go, around the corner was a bakery store, next to it the butcher. She feels herself biting into the fresh roll, it cracks, the yellowish-brown exterior, its crispy shell shattering, small, flat, pointed splinters remaining at the edge. The interior is whitish loose.

Now something reddish pushes itself in between again, she tries to recognize it with closed eyes, she can do that, too, because it is not outside her, it is in her, in her brain: circular, small, reddish spots. What can it be -? And suddenly she knows: they are strawberries! Of course, they've moved on, she's not even standing in the bakery store anymore, she's in a vegetable store. In a chip basket are the strawberries. They smell fresh, she smells it - oh, how she smells it! The strawberries are on green leaves, which are also fresh ... It's all very mild and very fresh - now also runs water, very clear and cool ...

With difficulty she tears herself away from her dream image, but the water runs so insistently, it ripples as if it has something to tell her. Slowly her eyes open, slowly she recognizes again the gateway in which she is still standing, the glistening street - finally the man in front of her who says something to her, an elderly man with a yellow, scrawny face and yellow-gray sideburns, a stiff black hat on his head.

How -? she asked with effort, and had to ask it again, for the first time there was only a small, unintelligible sound in the scrawny, withered mouth.

Many a person has passed it by in the time it has stood here. If he really saw the figure in the gateway, shadowed by the open gate wing, he only walked faster. It is poor region and anemic misery time, everywhere, at every hour of the day the miserable figures of women, girls, widows, hunger and misery in the faces, the most impossible rags pulled on the body, which - the very last resort - should still find a buyer. The widows of war, deprived of their pensions, the workers' wives, to whom the weekly wage of even the most sober, the most industrious man is listed out of their hands with every devaluation of the dollar, girls, almost still children, who can no longer look at the misery of their childish brothers and sisters - every day, every hour, every minute they slam the door of their caves, where hunger was their companion, worry their bedfellow - they slam the door definitively behind them and say: 'Now I do it! Store it for what? For an even greater misery? For the next flu? For poor man's doctor and poor man's coffin? Everything flees, rushes, hurries, changes - and I am supposed to preserve myself?'

There they stand, in every nook and cranny, at all times, insolent or frightened, talkative or wordless, asking, begging: Oh, just a cup of coffee and a roll ...

It's poor neighborhood, Georgenkirchstraße. The cashier of the gas company, the intermediate foreman of the ready-made clothing, the letter carrier - they walked just a little faster when they saw the girl. They didn't pull a face, not a naughty word, not a joke, not a thought of antics. Only quickly onward and past, lest a word, a plea, a plea yet to the heart, seduce that heart into a gift that must not be given. Because the same worry is waiting for everyone at home, the evil gnome is crouching on everyone's neck - who knows when my wife, my daughter, my girl will be standing like this, in the shadow of the gate wing the first day, but soon on the bright street! Nothing seen and past, no murmur reaches our ears. Alone are you, alone am I, alone we all die - save yourself, who can!

But now one has just stopped in front of Petra, an elderly gentleman with a bowler hat, yellowish owl face and yellowish owl eyes.

How -? she finally asked quite clearly.

Well, miss! He shakes his head a little disapprovingly. I wonder if Pagels live here?

Pagels -? So he doesn't want something like that, he's asking for Pagels. Pagels, multiple Pagels, at least two. She wants to understand who is what he wants, maybe it is important for Wolfgang ... Yes -? She tries to pull herself together, this gentleman wants something from them. He must not know that she belongs to Wolfgang, she who is so in the way of the gate. Pagels -? she asks again to gain time.

Yes, Pagels! Well, you probably don't know! A little drunk, huh? He winks his eyes, he seems to be quite a good-natured man. You don't have to do it, miss, during the day. In the evening, if you like. But during the day it is unhealthy.

Yes, Pagels live here, she says. But they are not there. Have both gone away. (Because he is not allowed to go up to the Thumann - what would he get to hear there, it could hurt Wolfgang!)

Like this? Both gone? Probably for the wedding ceremony, huh? But then they must have come too late. The registry office is already closed.

He knows that too! Who could it possibly be? Wolfgang always said he had no more acquaintances.

When did they leave? the gentleman asks again.

Half an hour ago. No, already an hour ago! she says hastily. And they told me they weren't coming back today.

(He must not go up to the Thumann! Just not!)

So, did they tell you that, Miss? asks the gentleman, suddenly suspicious. You must be friends with Pagels?

No! No! she protests hastily. They only know me by sight. It's just because I'm always standing here that they told me.

So ... says the gentleman thoughtfully. Well, thank you very much. And he walks slowly through the gateway to the first courtyard.

Oh, please! she calls out in a weak voice, even walking a few steps behind him.

What else? he asks, turning around but not going back. (He definitely wants to go up there!)

Please! she said pleadingly. Those up there are such bad people! Don't believe what Mr. Pagel's tell you. Mr. Pagel is a very fine, a very decent man - I, I have never had anything to do with him, I really only know him by sight ...

The man is standing in the middle of the bright sunshine in the courtyard. He looks sharply back at Petra, but he certainly can't see her clearly, standing there in the dim doorway, a slight, weak figure, her head bent forward a little, her lips half open, looking anxiously for the effect of her words, her hands placed pleadingly on her chest.

He rubs his yellow-gray beard thoughtfully between his thumb and forefinger; after a long deliberation, he says, "Don't worry, miss. I don't believe everything people tell me either.

It doesn't sound biting, maybe it's not aimed at her at all, it even sounds friendly.

I know the young gentleman quite well. I knew him when he was so small ...

And it shows an improbably tiny distance from Earth. But that's enough - he nods once more to Petra and finally disappears into the passageway to the second courtyard.

Petra, however, slides back into her protective corner behind the gate wing. Of course, she already knows now, she did everything wrong, she should not have had to give this old gentleman, who had known Wolfgang since he was a child, any information at all, no, she should have said: I do not know if Pagels live here ...

But she is too tired, too battered, too sick to think about it any further. She just wants to stop here and wait for him to come back. Then she will read the information received from his face. She will tell him what a wonderful person Wolfgang is, who never does anything bad, never harms anyone ... And while she lays her head against the cool wall, closes her eyes and this time almost unwillingly feels the blackness coming, which means being far away from her ego and her worries - while she tries to accompany the old gentleman on his way across the backyard. Then up the stairs to Mrs. Thumann's door. She thinks she hears him ring the bell, and now she wants to think about his conversation with Mrs. Thumann ... She'll talk, the woman, oh, she'll talk, dig it all up, throw mud at them both, whine about the lost money....

But suddenly their two rooms appear, this ugly cave is gilded with the glow of their love ... Further and further the voice of Pottmadamm fades away, here they both laughed, slept, talked, read ... He stood brushing his teeth at the washstand, she said something ...

Now I don't understand anything! he shouted. Red louder!

She did.

He cleaned. Louder! - Do not understand a word, even louder!

She did it, he cleaned, lathered.

Louder, I say!

She did it, they laughed ...

Here they had been together, together, she had been allowed to wait for him, never in vain ...

And suddenly, in a rapid, aching blink, she saw the road, knew she was going on ... Fairy tale fountain ... Hermannspark ... on and on, still city ... And now land, endless land, with fields and forests, bridges, bushes ... And again cities full of houses with gateways and again land and water, immense seas ... and again countries and country and city, incomprehensible ... And the possibility of going out, leaving everything behind, the thousand possibilities of life, on every corner, in every village ... 'All this, however,' it tangled in her brain, 'I will surrender and adore you if you give me our room again and the waiting for him in it ...'

Slowly it turned black. Everything erased, the world became indistinct. The wisps of blackness flew over it, obscuring it ... For a moment she thought she could still see the curtains of the room, yellowish-gray, hanging limp and motionless in the immense sultriness - then that too went out for the night.

But even the night held no peace for her, now it glowed red within her, with a glowing, evil red ... ah, the dog from over there was up. Growing larger and larger, he came across the street toward them. His yawning maw with sharp, pointed canines was already above her head. Evil red the eyes, evil red the threatening fangs, and now with tremendous weight he put his paw on her shoulder, she screamed in fear, but no sound reached her ear. It sinks down ...

The servant Ernst, his hand on her shoulder, says admonishingly: Miss, please! Miss!!

Petra saw him coming from far away and asked immediately, as if the question had been urgently waiting in her since his departure: What did they say?

The servant moved his shoulders doubtfully. Then: Where has the young gentleman gone? He sees her hesitate, he says reassuringly: "You don't have to be embarrassed in front of me, I'm just his aunt's servant. I won't tell you anything I don't want to.

And they, since he can not experience worse than he will have already heard above: Fort. Get money.

And did not come back?

No. Not yet. Waiting.

They both stood there in silence for a while, she patiently waiting to see what fate and perhaps this man had in store for her, he undecided whether he could leave so easily to report to his mistress. It was not difficult to guess what Frau Generalmajor von Anklam thought about this girl, what she would say about active help. After all ...

The servant Ernst stepped slowly out of the gateway onto the street, looked indecisively up and down, the expected person was not to be seen ... For a moment he had the thought of just walking away. He thought he knew exactly that this girl would not stop him with a word. It was the simplest solution, any other could cause him trouble with excellence. Or else it cost him money - and the more worthless the small capital saved by the servant Ernst in one human age became, the more firmly he clung to these bills with the nonsensical numbers. At home in his small chamber, he filled one tinny tea packet after another with them ...

Nevertheless ...

He looked up and down the street again: nothing. Hesitantly, a little reluctant about his own actions, he went back into the doorway and asked, just as reluctantly, "And if the young gentleman doesn't bring any money now?

She just looked at him, with a slight movement of the head - already the vague prospect in these words that Wolfgang might come after all, even if without money, invigorated her.

And if he doesn't come back at all, what do you do?

Her head sank forward a little, her eyelids closed - without a word being uttered, it was clear enough how indifferent everything was to her then.

Miss, he said hesitantly, a servant does not earn much. And then, yes, I lost all my savings, but if you want to take this ....

He tries to slip a bill into her hand. He chose it from the worn, thin wallet: Fifty thousand. And as she withdraws her hand, more urgently: No, no, you can take this. After all, it's just the fare to get you home. He pauses, considers. You can't keep standing here like this! Surely you have some relative to whom you can go first.

Again he breaks off. It occurred to him that she couldn't possibly get on an electric in this getup, legs naked to above the knees, wearing only represented slippers, with a pathetic man's paletot that shows too much chest.

He stands there, embarrassed, almost angry. He wants to help, but Jesus! - how do you help?! He can't take her with him, dress her up - and finally: what then?!

Oh God, Miss! he suddenly says sadly. How could the young gentleman have let it get this far?!

Petra, however, understood only one thing: So you also think that he will not come back?

The servant moves his shoulders. How do I know? Did you have a fight? I thought you were getting married today?

Get married - right! The word still reaches her, she didn't even think about it anymore. We are getting married today, yes ... she says and smiles vaguely. She remembers that today she was to lose the name 'Ledig', which had always been something of a stigma. She remembers how she woke up and did not dare to look for his purse, and yet she was still sure: today it would be! Then the first doubts had come, his indecisive attitude when she urged him, then demanded, then asked ... And as she had felt, when slamming the door already: today it will not be after all!

But suddenly then (and incomprehensibly, yet happened: the hunger had made her burning brain forget even that) - suddenly in front of the mirror the realization had come over her, the knowledge that he had probably gone, but still remained with her, eternally unloseable in her. What had happened then: the begging squatting in Thumann's kitchen with the squinting at Ida's snails, the expulsion, the idle waiting here in the passage - that had only been done by hunger, guileful enemy in body and brain, which had made her forget what should never be forgotten: this in her.

What was wrong with her? Was she bewitched and enchanted?! She had still made it in her life, the mother had been with her as raw as she could be - a few tears, but on! The amiable cavaliers with the razor-sharp creases on the girl hunt might be so mean and stingy afterwards - teeth together, but on! Wolfgang liked to come back or not come back - bad, sad, evil ... But for twenty-two years she had eaten every dirt only for her own sake - and now she was to stand here, idle, ordered and not picked up - since for the first time in her life another was dependent on her, on her all alone, and no other woman in the world could replace her - simply ridiculous!

An abundance of thoughts floods into her, she can't grasp it all that quickly. After the hunger has sunk her poor head into blackness and vague dreams for a while, it now makes it survive, all awake and clear: but it's all very simple. She has to take care of someone, and since that someone is in her, she has to take care of herself first - nothing is more self-evident. Everything else will be found.

And while she is thinking this, she is also thinking other things in her head. She makes plans about what to do, later, but also right now. And that is why she suddenly says quite clearly and firmly: Yes, it is nice of you to want to give me the money. I can use it very well. Thank you!

The servant looks at her, puzzled. Only a fraction of a minute has passed since he reminded her that she was getting married today. The servant Ernst cannot guess what thoughts this one sentence has awakened in her brain, what all she experienced and planned in those few seconds. He only sees the change in her face, which is suddenly no longer slack, which is full of life, it has even gained color. He suddenly hears an energetic tone, almost a command, instead of the hesitant, half-loud speech. Without even thinking, he put the money in her hand.

Well, Miss, he says, surprised and again quietly annoyed, suddenly you are so lively! Why? The registry office is already closed. I really think you have one sitting.

No, she replies. I just suddenly thought of something good. And the fact that I seem so funny to you is not because of drinking. But I haven't eaten anything, for quite a long time, and it makes you feel so funny in your head ....

Ernst, the servant, who has always eaten his meal at the appointed hour all his life, is really indignant. Nothing to eat! But the young gentleman should really not do something like that!

She looks at him, with a half, lost smile. She knows what is going on in his head, what he is thinking and feeling full of indignation, and she has to smile at him. For this time, when the good, well-bred servant Ernst, grayed in his dealings with the first circles, really takes a stand for her and against the young master, this time she really feels how far people live from each other. The young master would have been allowed to treat her badly, he would have been allowed to cheat on her, he would have been allowed to abandon her - all this would not have outraged the good servant Ernst (and most of his fellow men) so much. But that he gave her nothing to eat -! No, you really didn't do anything like that!!!

He looks at her with a furrowed brow, she can see how big decisions he is facing, she makes it easy for him. If you would just get me some rolls! she says. Here just around the corner is a bakery store. And then you don't have to worry about me anymore. Once I've eaten a little bit, I'll be fine. I have a plan ... Of course I'm going to get some ribs, he says eagerly. And maybe something else, something to drink, milk, yes?

He hurries away, he goes to three, four stores: butter, bread, rolls, sausage, a few tomatoes ... He no longer thinks about his money, the savings ... The fact that a person is hungry but has nothing to eat has him all confused. 'The young gentleman shouldn't have done something like that,' he keeps thinking. 'She may be as she likes, but starve her - no!'

He ran, rushing himself and the sleepy shopkeepers, everything had to be done in a hurry, quickly. He would have preferred to say: 'Please, because it is for a person who is starving ...' - But now that he comes back, he stands even more confused: she is not there. Not on the gate way, not on the street, not even in the yard. She is gone!

Hesitantly, he decides to go up to the Thumann once again, certainly not very gladly, for this uninhibited chatterbox bore a resemblance to Her Excellency, Major General Bettina von Anklam that was all too fatal for him. But he only got to see Ida, half already commercially, half still domestically dressed, which rather frightened him. And this young lady inquired very ungraciously with him whether it probably beeped in his brain box, because:

The bitch won't get back in! If she just rings the bell, she already has a bell! Nah, wat such people imagine everything -!

Servant Ernst descends the stairs again, crosses the courtyards again, comes back into the doorway.

No one is standing in the shadow of the doorway. Shaking his head, he walks down the street: nothing. Those bags and packets of food, that bottle full of milk, he can't take that to his dominion. Miss would surely see it, and surely Miss would tell Her Excellency.

He turns back again, sets up his errands in the deepest, darkest corner behind the doorway and leaves for good, not without looking around frequently. Only when he sits in the underground, he no longer thinks back, he can think ahead again.

'What am I saying Excellency -?!'

After careful consideration, he decides to say as little as possible.

Chapter 05

- The thunderstorm breaks loose -

05 01

Leo Gubalke, the head constable of the police force, had returned to his apartment on Georgenkirchstraße from his allotment close to the Rummelsburg railway station at around three o'clock. He had ample time to wash thoroughly and change for duty. But he didn't have time to take another nap, as he had wanted to. For his rather strenuous service went from four o'clock in the afternoon until two o'clock in the morning, and it was always good to have a little rest on the ear beforehand. It benefited the service, and especially the nerves on duty.

Chief Constable Leo Gubalke is all alone in his two-room apartment. The woman has been at the allotment (North Pole Colony) since morning, and the two brats went straight there from school. The policeman has taken the large zinc tub that his wife usually uses for laundry into the kitchen and is slowly and carefully scrubbing down from the top.

It's an old argument between him and his wife about how best to wash whole. He does it from the top: head, neck, shoulders, chest, and so on, until he gets down to the feet. This is really neat and clean, because nothing already cleaned will be touched again by washing the next part of the body. In addition, it is economical, because the abundant water running from above, mixed with soap, already softens the parts of the body to be cleaned later.

Ms. Gubalke does not want to realize this, or, if she does realize it, she does not. She washes herself quite systemlessly, now her back, then her feet, now her chest, now her thighs. Chief Constable Leo Gubalke, who has to deal with excited women almost every day on duty, is firmly convinced that

Hans Fallada   -170-   Wolf among Wolves

women can have brains, too. But in any case, a very different kind of mind than men, and it is completely useless to try to convince them of something they may not be convinced of.

Mrs. Gubalke is a fabulously tidy woman, the kitchen just sparkles, and Gubalke knows that in every carefully closed drawer, behind every reliably locked cabinet door, every item is in order, but system in her personal hygiene is impossible to get. That's just the way it is with women, and if it's like that, you shouldn't try to change it, otherwise they get angry easily. But at least the father had the triumph that the two children, two girls, washed according to his method.

Chief Constable Gubalke is a man in his early forties, reddish-blond, already a bit fat, a very tidy man, not without benevolence, if only it was possible. He no longer felt any particular enthusiasm for his profession, although it actually corresponded to his inclination for order. Whether he was reprimanding chauffeurs for driving against the rules, taking a rowdy drunk to the police station, or directing a prostitute out of the forbidden Königstraße - he kept the city of Berlin in order, he made sure that everything on the street was in order. Of course, public order could never reach the rank of private order, such as in his home. Perhaps this was what spoiled his enjoyment of his job.

He would rather have sat in the typing pool, kept registers, kept card indexes in order. There, with paper, pen, and possibly even a typewriter, something could be achieved that most closely corresponded to his ideal image of the world. But his superiors wouldn't take him off the street. This calm, level-headed, perhaps a touch slow man was hard to replace, especially in these difficult, confused times.

While Leo Gubalke is scrubbing his somewhat rosy fat so that it turns red, he is once again thinking about how he should give the matter a twist, which it now apparently has to have, so that his so often expressed wish for a transfer to internal service is fulfilled. To achieve this transfer, even if the superiors do not want it, there are many means. For example, cowardice - but cowardice, of course, is out of the question. Or excitement, losing one's nerve - but Chief Constable Gubalke, of course, can't lose his nerve in front of everyone on the street. You could also get too dashing, report every dirt, drag everything to the guard - but that would be uncollegial again. Or one would have to make a mistake, a gross, fat mistake, which would compromise the police and about which some newspapers are so pleased - that would certainly make him impossible on the street - but for that he is too fond of this uniform, is too fond of the term 'police', to which he has now belonged for so long.

The chief constable sighs. Looking at the case more closely, it is really amazing how much the world is disguised for a man who looks at order. A hundred things that a less conscientious person does every day are impossible for him. On the other hand, you constantly have the feeling, without which you would not want to live, that you are not only keeping the world in order, no, that you are also in order with it.

Gubalke carefully wipes out the zinc tub until every last drop of water is absorbed, then hangs it on its hook in the toilet. In the kitchen, the floor is wiped again, although the few splashes would dry anyway in the frightening sultriness. Now it is strapped on and finally the chako is put on. As always, Leo Gubalke first tries it in front of the kitchen mirror, which is hardly more than the size of a hand. As always, he finds that it is not possible to see exactly whether the chako fits properly here. So into the dark hallway in front of the big mirror. It is annoying to have to turn on the electric light for such a short moment (power consumption is supposed to be highest at the moment of turning it on), but it doesn't help.

Now everything is ready, twenty minutes to four - one minute to four Chief Constable Leo Gubalke will be at the station. He descends the stairs, one white glove he has put on, the other he holds loosely in his hand - this is how he approaches the gateway and the girl Petra Ledig.

The girl leans against the wall again with her eyes closed. Just as she was asking Ernst the servant for some rolls when he went off to fetch them, she was overcome by such a vivid imagination of the pastry that was now very near ... She thought she smelled it, something of the fresh, nourishing taste had suddenly entered the stale, felt mouth - she had to swallow. Then it choked her.

It went black in her head again, her limbs gave way as if there was no support in them at all, her knees were soft, and a constant trembling and pounding sat in her arms and shoulders. Oh, come on! Please, come on! But she does not know whom she whispers, all alone in her hunger hell - the servant or the lover.

The chief constable of the Schupo Leo Gubalke has of course stopped, he looks at this first. He knows the girl by sight, as she lives in the same house with him, albeit in the back. Something unfavorable about them is not known to him by service. After all, she lives with a woman who occasionally hosts prostitutes, and lives, without being married, with a young man who seems to be just playing. Professional player - if you can give something on the gossip of women. So, all in all, there is no reason for either special severity or leniency - the official observes and considers.

Of course, she has had too much to drink - but she is close to her apartment and will make it up the stairs. Besides, his shift doesn't start until four o'clock. He does not need to have seen anything, which is all the more likely since this is not his district and since she has not yet noticed him. Gubalke already wants to leave, when a new, violent choking attack throws her upper body forward, Gubalke looks directly into the coat neckline - and looks away.

This is not possible after all. This he cannot overlook; a whole, neat, orderly life stands up against it. The chief constable approaches the girl, taps the closed-eyed strangler on the shoulder with his gloved finger and says: Well - Miss?!

His profession, which makes the policeman skeptical of all fellow human beings, also leaves his trust in his own perceptions intact. Up to this point, Chief Constable Leo Gubalke had believed that the girl was completely drunk, and her suit or proper getup could only confirm this belief. No girl who cared a little bit about order in herself and around herself went out on the street like that.

But that look that met him from the girl's eyes when he put his hand on her shoulder, that flaming yet clear gaze, tormented creature, yet disregarding her torment - that look dispelled any thought of alcohol. In a completely different tone, he asked: Are you sick?

She was leaning against the wall. The uniform, the chako, the rosy, full face with the reddish-blond, tousled beard were only vaguely before her eyes. It was unclear to her who was asking her, whom she should answer, what she should say in response. But perhaps no one understands as well as a tidy person, who has to deal with all the disorder in the world every day, what extent this disorder can take. From a few questions, laborious answers, Chief Constable Gubalke had quickly built up a picture of the facts of the case, he also already knew that only a few rolls should be waited for, that the girl then intended to go around the corner to the 'uncle', who would certainly help her out with a dress, that any friends or relatives of the man should then be visited (she had the fare in her hand) - in short, that the nuisance would in all probability be eliminated in a few minutes.

The chief constable learned all this, knew it now, and was already about to say: 'All right, miss, I'll let you have it this once', and to go to guard and duty, when he was embarrassed by the thought of when he would actually arrive at the guard -? A glance at his wristwatch taught him that it was three minutes to four. Under no circumstances would he be able to be at the station before four fifteen. Missed fifteen minutes of duty - and with what excuse -?! That he had chatted away this quarter of an hour with a rather indecently clothed wench without proceeding to any official act! Impossible - everyone would think: 'The Gubalke just missed out!'

Impossible, Miss, he said officiously. I can't possibly let you go out on the street like that. First of all, you have to come with me.

Gently, yet firmly, he placed his gloved hand on her upper arm, holding her gently, yet firmly, he walked her out into the street where he could not possibly let her go. (Order often brings with it such absurdities).

Nothing will happen to you, miss, he said comfortingly. After all, you haven't done anything wrong. But if I let you out on the street like that, it could be public nuisance and worse, and then you'd be up to no good.

The girl walks beside him willingly. The man who leads them like this, not without care, has nothing about him that could make one uneasy, even though he wears a uniform. Petra Ledig, who, not so long ago, was still nonsensically afraid of every policeman, back when she went out on the streets a little without permission, Petra realizes that policemen need not have anything frightening about them, they even have something fatherly about them. We're not equipped for that at the station, he says, but I'll see that you get something to eat right away. Those in the registration department are usually not that hungry, so I'll grab a sandwich. He laughs. Such a foreign sandwich, a little dried and in crumpled wrapping paper, is just something nice. When I bring my brats something like this, they are always crazy about it. Rabbit bread is what they call it. Do you also say so for it?

Yes, says Petra. And when Mr. Pagel brought me a piece of rabbit bread, I was always happy.

At the mention of Herr Pagel, Oberwachtmeister Leo Gubalke makes his most officious face. Although men must always stand by each other, and especially against women, he does not agree at all with this young gentleman, who is supposed to be a gambler to boot. He won't say anything to the young girl, but he does plan to take a closer look at this master's lifestyle. This Mr. Pagel has hardly behaved very decently, and it is only good that such an airhead realizes that he is being watched.

Hans Fallada   -175-   Wolf among Wolves

The chief constable has fallen silent, striding out faster. The girl goes along willingly, it is only good if she quickly gets away from this gawking. So the two of them disappear, towards the guard - and for nothing the servant Ernst comes with his rolls, for nothing the girl Minna of the Mrs. legation attaché Pagel will inquire about her, for nothing the opulent Maybach drives off in Dahlem, in which a lady sits with a blind child.

At this time Wolfgang Pagel falls out with his mother for good.

Petra Ledig has been removed from all civilian influence for the time being.

05 02

Wolfgang Pagel has walked the long way from the villas of the rich in Dahlem through the crowded streets of Schöneberg to the old west of Berlin, step by step, without any particular hurry, but also without stopping once. He passed through many streets where hardly anyone walked except him, through empty, deserted streets, as if burned bare by the sun. And again, he walked other paths that were rushed by traffic, teeming with the teeming, drifting aimlessly among the aiming.

Above him hung the haze of sultriness and breath of the city. As Pagel walked between the tree-lined avenues of Dahlem, he still cast a clear, sharp shadow. But the deeper he got lost in the city, the more the shadow faded, blending into the gray of the granite slabs on the sidewalk. Not only the fellow swarmers extinguished him, not only the house walls towering ever steeper and narrower above him, no, the haze grew thicker, the sun paler. The heat that constantly flung them into the overheated city extinguished them.

There were still no clouds to be seen. Perhaps they were already lurking behind the rows of houses, crouched along the hidden horizon, ready to rise up, to pour themselves out with fire, thunder and pouring wetness, vain intrusion of nature into an artificial world.

Wolfgang Pagel does not go any faster because of this. At first, he left without a specific goal, only out of the feeling that he was not allowed to sit in that ruler's kitchen anymore. Then, when suddenly the goal of his march was clear to him, he did not go faster because of it. He has always been a leisurely man, with knowledge and consciousness he was slow, he liked to make a gesture with his hand before giving an answer to a question: this postponed the answer a little.

Even now he goes slowly; it postpones the decision a little! In the kitchen, during the conversation with the blind child, he had still thought that he had to leave the care of Petra to other people. He had thought that he could not help Petra. Help for a girl without clothes, without food, with debts could only mean money, but he had no money. But then it occurred to him that he did have money, or if not money, then something that was worth as much as money. To be precise, von Zecke had given him the idea: he possessed a picture. This picture, young woman at the window, undeniably belonged to him. He probably remembered how his mother, when he went into the field, had said: This picture is now yours, Wolf. Always remember in the field: Father's most beautiful picture is waiting for you here.

He didn't think it was very pretty, but it would have its market price. He wouldn't do the favor for Tick, but there were enough art dealers who would gladly take a Pagel. Wolfgang decided to go to a large art dealer on Bellevue Street. There, they would certainly disdain to overreach him; a pagel was a business even without overreach.

There would be an outrageous sum numerically for it, hundreds of millions probably (a billion?!), but he would not touch any of the money, not one bill was to be exchanged! He would even walk to Georgenkirchstraße - if one has walked from Dahlem to the city, this last bit of walking can also mean nothing. No, no bill was exchanged - with the whole tremendous sum he will overwhelm the waiting!

Pagel walks along through the glowing city of Berlin, without hurrying and without stopping. He thinks through his plans many times, there are many things to consider. But what he likes best is the moment when he lays a huge sum of money on her table, or even better: lets it rain down on the woman lying in bed, so that she disappears completely in the money, is covered with money in the cave of dirt. He often dreamed this moment. Earlier, he had thought it would be the game winner. Now it will be other money, from the sale of a paternal painting. Money earned, snatched from the three birds of prey, so to speak - that would have been even nicer, of course. Well, the thought is finally over, 'it' is no longer thought of!

So he goes along, Wolfgang Pagel, Fahnenjunker a. D., Spieler a. D., Liebhaber a. D. He has once again done nothing, he just goes, goes from here to there, from there to here. In the morning he was still driving, he had plans then too, but only these now are the right ones. He has the most excellent intentions, he goes without haste. He is gentle, in balance with himself, completely satisfied with himself. He will sell a picture, make money, he will bring the money to Peter - great! Not for a moment does it occur to him that his Peter might not care about the money at all. He brings her money, lots of money, more money than she has ever had in her life - can you do more for your girl?! The world is hunting, the dollar is rising, the girl is starving - he walks leisurely, because what he is going to do is as good as done. He is in no hurry, everything has its time, we still managed!

And now he turns into Tannenstraße, which is just a dead end. He walks the few steps, unlocks the front door and climbs the old stairs to his mother's apartment. The old porcelain sign with the legation attaché on the door, older than himself, with the chipped corner that he once, endlessly long ago, knocked off with his skate. The old smell in the hallway with its dark chests, oak cupboards, the old, moody grandfather clock, and the father's hurried, large sketches high on the walls that seemed to float bright as clouds over the dark world.

But what is new are the two large festive bouquets of asters on the old-fashioned mirrored table, and when Wolfgang looks at them, he finds a note from his mother between the two China blue vases. 'Good day, Wolf!' he reads. 'Coffee is in your room. Make yourself comfortable, I just have to go away again quickly.'

For a moment he stands undecided before this greeting. He knows from Minna's reports that his mother expects him every day, every hour - but this is too much for him. He thought of this waiting differently, not so purposefully, more casually. The thought occurs to him to leave the coffee in his own room undrunk, pick up the picture and leave. But he does not like that again, like a thief in the night - no! He shrugs, the pale man across from him in the greenish mirror does the same, and smiles almost sheepishly to himself. Then he crumples up the note and puts it in his pocket. Now the mother guesses from the absence of the note: he is there - and is looking for him. The sooner, the better.

He goes to his room.

There are flowers there too, this time gladioli. He darkly remembers once telling his mother he liked gladioli. Of course she kept it and put some for him, but now he should like it again. But also feel: how your mother loves you that she thinks of all this -!

Yes, she was great in that: she reckoned in love: if I do this, he has to feel that way. He did not even think about it, the gladioli were not beautiful! They were stiff and artificial with their thin colors - brushed wax! Peter would never calculate in love -!

'Why am I suddenly thinking about Mom in such an irritable way?" he muses as he pours himself the really still hot coffee. (She must have just put it down. It's a wonder they hadn't run into each other on stairs or on the street!) 'I'm directly angry with her. Whether it's the house, the old smell, all the memories -? I've only really known since I've been at home with Peter how she has always bullied and patronized me ... Anything she wanted was good;

any boyfriend I chose was no good. And now this intrusive reception ... Yes, I saw it a long time ago: there's another piece of paper on the desk. And above the chair hangs the freshly ironed civilian suit and laundry. A silk overshirt, in which of course she has already put the buttons ...'

He prepares his third roll, it tastes excellent. The coffee is strong and mild at the same time, its full flavor gently fills the whole oral cavity. Something other than the slack and yet caustic brew of the Pottmadamm. (I wonder if Peter drinks coffee now, too? Of course, she has long since left it behind! Maybe afternoon coffee!)

While Wolfgang Pagel stretches out comfortably on the chaise longue, he tries to guess what the note might say. Of course, something like, 'You'll have to pick out the tie yourself, they hang on the inside of the closet door.' Or: 'Bath water is hot.'

Of course, something like that will be on it, and as he looks now after all, he reads that the bath oven is heated. Annoyed, he pushes one crumpled piece of paper to the other. That he guessed the mother so well does not please him, it only makes him angrier.

'Of course,' he thinks, 'I can guess them so well because I know them so well. Ownership Seizure. Paternalism. Whenever I came out of school, I had to wash my hands immediately and put on a fresh collar. I had been together with the others - but we were different, better! It is an outright insolence against me, but especially against Peter, which the mama has thought up there again! This time her changing is not enough, I have to take a bath too! I've been with someone like that, who was smacked by mom! Insolence - but I will not put up with this now!'

He stares angrily at his youthful room with its yellow-birch desk, its birch bookshelves, in front of which half hangs a dark green silk curtain. The birch bed shimmers like silver and gold. Light, joy - there are trees outside the window, old trees. Everything is so tidy, so clean, so fresh - when you think of Thumann's Cave, you immediately discover why this is all kept so neat and ready. The Lord Son shall compare: so you have it with this girl, but here your faithful loving mother cares for you! Outright insolence and challenge!

'Stop!' he says again, trying to slow himself down. 'Stop! You run away with yourself. The horses go through you. Some things are true, flowers and notes are disgusting, but the room has never looked different. So why am I so angry? Because I had to think about Mama slapping Peter? I wo, you don't have to take something like that tragically with Mom, and Peter didn't take it tragically for a moment either. It must be something else ...'

He steps to the window. Furthermore, the neighboring houses, you can see the sky here. And really, piled high on the horizon are black, crouching clouds. The light is pale, no wind stirs, no leaf moves on the tree. On the mansard roof over there he sees a couple of sparrows sitting, the belligerent fellows squatting puffed up, motionless there, they too already crouched under the near threat of the sky.

'I must quickly see that I get on,' he thinks. 'Walking through a thunderstorm with the picture under your arm would not be pleasant ...'

And suddenly he knows. He sees himself walking through the streets to the art dealer with the painting wrapped in some already soiled wrapping paper. He can't even afford a cab. An object worth millions, maybe billions, but tucked under the arm like a thief! Secretly, like a drunkard carries his wife's beds secretly from the house to his uncle.

'But it's my property,' he interjects. 'I have nothing to be ashamed of!'

'I'm ashamed of myself,' he says. 'It's not right.'

'Why is it not right? She gave it to me!'

'You know exactly how attached she is to that picture. That's why she gave it to you, she wanted to bind you even tighter to her. You will mortally wound her, take it away.'

'Then she just didn't have to give it to me. Now I can do what I want with it.'

'You've had it bad before. You've thought about this sale before, and yet you never did it.'

'Cause we've never had it so bad. Now is the time.'

'So, is that it? How do others find out who don't have something like that in reserve?'

Others would not have let it get this far. Others would not have let everything drift indifferently until it went quite badly. Others would not have hurt the mother as a last resort to give bread to the beloved. Others would not have played without hesitation - without hesitation because the picture was there as a reserve. Others would have looked for work in time and earned money. Others would not have indifferently transferred, pumped and begged. Others would not have just taken and taken from a girl without ever thinking: what are you giving?

The sky is now black higher up. Maybe it's already weather-lit back there, you can't see it through the haze. Maybe thunder is rumbling in the distance, but you can't hear it. It thunders, hisses and screams even louder the city.

'You are cowardly,' it says. 'Poor you are, withered at twenty-three. Everything was there for you, love and gentle care, but you ran away. Certainly, certainly, you are young. Youth is restless, youth is afraid of happiness, it does not want happiness at all. Because happiness means rest, and youth is restless. But where did you run to? Did you run to the youth? No, precisely where the old sit, who no longer feel the sting of the flesh, who no longer have hunger ... into the smoldering, dry sandy desert of artificial passions, you ran - smoldering, dry, artificial - unyoung!'

'Coward you are! Now I want you to make up your mind for once. Already you stand and dither. You don't want to hurt the mother and yet help Peter. Oh, what you would like most is for your mother to ask you, implore you, with your hands up, to sell the painting. But she won't do that, she won't make the decision for you, you yourself are the man! There is no middle ground, no way out, no compromise, no pinching. You've let it drift too long, now decide - one or the other!'

The cloud rises higher and higher. Wolfgang Pagel is still standing at the window, irresolute. He is good to look at, with narrow hips and broad shoulders, a fighter figure. But he is not a fighter. He has an open face, with a good forehead, a strong, straight nose - but he is not open, he is not straight. Many thoughts come and go in him, all of them unpleasant, embarrassing. They all demand something from him, he is angry that he has to think such thoughts.

'Others have it better,' he thinks. 'They do what suits them and don't give it a second thought.' Everything is difficult with me. I'll have to think about it again. Is there no way out - mother or Peter?'

For a while he stands his ground, he makes an effort, this time he does not want to avoid responsibility. But gradually, as he finds no way out, as everything keeps demanding the decision from him, he gets tired. He lights a cigarette, he takes another sip of coffee. He quietly opens the door to the room and listens into the apartment. Everything is quiet, mother is not back yet.

He has blond, curly hair, his chin is not very strong - he is soft, he is floppy. He smiles, he has made his decision. Once again, he dodged the decision. He will use the absence of the mother and leave without dealing with the image. He smiles, suddenly he is completely satisfied with himself, the tormenting thoughts are gone.

He walks straight across the hall, toward Dad's room. He has no time to lose, the thunderstorm is about to break loose, Mom may return at any moment.

He opens the door to his father's room, and there, just in front of him, in the big armchair, sits black, stiff, upright his mother -!

Hello, Wolfgang! she says. I am glad!

05 03

He is not happy at all, on the contrary: he feels like a caught house thief.

I thought you were running errands, Mom, he says sheepishly, limply shaking her hand, which she squeezes energetically and with meaning.

She smiles. I wanted to give you time to feel at home again, didn't want to ambush you right away. Well, sit down, Wolfgang, don't stand around so indecisive ... You don't have any plans now, you're not here for a visit, you're at home...

Obediently he sits down, immediately son again, under maternal command and guardianship. But on visit! Just for a jump, he probably mumbles, but she overhears that, whether willingly or really, he will find out later.

The coffee was still hot, yes? Good. I had just brewed it when you came in. You haven't bathed and changed yet? Well, there's time for that. I understand you wanted to see our home first. It is your world after all. Ours, she adds toning down, as she watches his face.

Mama, he starts, because this emphasis on the world here, the insinuation that the Thumann cave is Petra's world, annoys him. Mom, you are very wrong ...

But she interrupts him. Wolfgang, she says in another, much warmer tone, Wolfgang, you don't have to tell me anything, explain anything. I know a lot, but I don't need to know everything. But in order not to leave anything unclear from the beginning, I would like to explain to you for this one time that I did not behave quite right against your friend. I regret many things I have said, even more one thing I have done. You understand me. Is that enough for you, Wolfgang? Come on, give me your hand, boy!

Wolfgang looks his mother in the face. He doesn't want to believe it at first, but there is no doubt, he knows his mother, knows her face, she means it sincerely. She regrets, she repents. She has made her peace with him and Peter - so she is reconciled, heaven knows how that came about. Maybe the waiting time has made them soft.

It's almost hard to believe. He holds her hand, he doesn't want to play hide and seek now either, he says: Mom, that's very nice of you. But surely you do not know yet, we were going to get married today. It's just ...

She interrupts him again - what willingness, what concession, she makes everything easy for him! It's good, Wolfgang. After all, it's all done now. I am so happy that you are sitting here again ...

A feeling of immense relief comes over him. A moment ago he was standing at the window of his room, tormented by doubts as to whom he should hurt: Mother or Petra. There seemed to be no way out, only these two options. And already everything had changed: the mother had realized her mistake, the way to this orderly home was open to them both.

He has stood up, looking down at the white, fine-threaded crown of his mother's head, one hair lying like the other, clean, clear. Suddenly something like emotion seizes him. He swallows, he wants to say something, almost shouts: I wish life was a little different! No, I wish I were different, then I would have run it differently!

The old woman sits at the table with a wooden, stiff face. She doesn't look at her son, but she raps her knuckles sharply on the table. It sounds wooden.

Oh, Wolfgang, she says. Please, don't be a child. When you were sitting down for Easter, you also used to shout: I wanted to ... And if your locomotive was broken, you regretted it too, afterwards, how you had dealt with it. But that is useless, and you are no longer a child. Regret backwards doesn't help at all - boy, learn at last: it goes on, always on. You can't change the past, but you can change yourself - for the future!

Yes, certainly, Mama, he says dutifully. After all, I only wanted to ...

But he does not speak further. Outside it has closed, hurried, overhasty. Now come quick steps across the aisle ...

It's just Minna, his mother says to him, explaining.

The door opens without knocking, it flies open, in it stands the elderly Minna, yellowish, gray, dry.

Thank you, Minna, says Mrs. Pagel quickly, because she does not want any message from Georgenkirchstrasse at the moment; she has everything that interested her there now here. Thank you, Minna, she says as sternly as possible. Please prepare dinner immediately.

But Minna is not the obedient servant this time, she stands in the doorway with evil, suspicious eyes, her yellow-grey, wrinkled cheeks wearing red spots. She does not pay attention to the madam at all, she stares angrily at the otherwise so beloved young gentleman.

Yikes! she then says breathlessly. Fie, Wolfgang, so here you sit ...

Are you just twisted, Minna?" exclaims Mrs. Pagel indignantly, for she has never experienced anything like this with her Minna in twenty years of being together. You are disturbing! Go now ...

But it is not heard at all. Wolfgang immediately understood that something had happened 'there', a foreboding came over him, he saw Peter in front of him, as she had said to him: Take care, Wolf, and he went to his uncle with the suitcase. She gave him another kiss ...

He grabs Minna by the shoulders. Minna, were you there? What's going on? Say quickly ...

You don't say a word, Minna! exclaims Frau Pagel. Or you're fired on the spot!

You don't have to dismiss me, madam, says Minna, suddenly outwardly calm. I'm going the same way. Do you think I stay here, where the mother persuades the son to do bad things, and the son does it. Oh, Wolfi, that you did that! That you could be so mean!

Minna, how dare you?! What do you allow yourself, you ...

Just call me a wench or a goose again, I'm used to it, madam. But I always thought you were just saying it for fun. But now I know that you really mean it, that we are different, I'm one of those from the kitchen and you're a fine lady ...

Minna! shouts Wolfgang and shakes the old, completely out of control girl vigorously. Minna, tell me, what happened to Peter? Is she ...?

So? Do you really still care, Wolfi? Where you ran away from her, just on the wedding day, and sold all her things from her body, and she had nothing left but the old, worn summer paletot - the one from the madam still, madam! -, no piece underneath, no stockings, nothing ... And so the police took them away. But what has been the worst and what I never and never forgive you, Wolfi, completely starved she was! She kept choking, and on the stairs she almost fell down ...

But why the police? cries Wolfgang desperately and shakes Minna as hard as he can. What does the police have to do with it -?!

Do I know that?" Minna cries against it and tries to tear herself away from the young gentleman, who involuntarily holds her tighter and tighter. Do I know what you got her into, Wolfi -?! Because Petra certainly didn't do anything bad on her own, I know her far too well for that. And the mean person who still lives on the floor said that it serves Petra right, because she feels much too fine to go on the street. I have but one gelangt -! Minna stands there triumphantly for a moment, but immediately she says again, very sullenly: God bless her that she didn't, even though you and all you man-boys certainly didn't deserve it for her.

Wolfgang lets go of Minna so suddenly that she almost falls. And immediately she falls silent.

Mom, he says excitedly, Mom, I really have no idea what could have happened. I can't imagine it either. I left around noon, wanting to get some money. It is true that I sold Petra's things, we also had debts to the landlady. And maybe she really has been eating very little lately, I have to confess, I haven't really been paying attention. I was away a lot - from there. But what the police have to do with all this ...

He spoke more and more softly. It would have been much easier to tell Minna all this than to tell Mama, who sits there so woodenly, so hard, just under that conscious picture, by the way - now over, that's done, no longer necessary.

Well, whatever's going on with the police, I'll fix it right away. It is quite certain, mama, that nothing real can be there - we have done nothing, no. I'll go there right away. It must be a mistake. Just, Mom...

It becomes more and more difficult to speak to the dark woman, who sits there completely motionless, distant, strange, completely dismissive ... Only, Mama, it is unfortunate that I am completely without money at the moment. I need some fare, maybe I have to pay the debt to the landlady right away; a deposit, what do I know, stuff for Petra, food ...

He stares urgently at his mother. He's in such a hurry, she has to get free, he has to leave - why doesn't she go to her writing cabinet and get the money already?

You're excited now, Wolfgang, says Mrs. Pagel, but that's not why we want to act haphazardly. I completely agree with you that something must be done immediately for the girl. But I don't think that you, especially in your present condition, are the man for it. There may be lengthy arguments with the police - you're a bit short-tempered, Wolfgang. I think we'll call Justice Thomas right now. He knows about this kind of stuff, he does it much faster and smoother than you do.

Wolfgang looked so intently at his mother's mouth, as if he not only had to hear every word, but also read it from her lips. Now he runs his hand over his face. He has a dry feeling there, the skin should actually rustle. But the hand has become wet.

Mom! he asks. It is impossible for me to have this matter settled by your judicial councilor and in the meantime sit here quietly, bathe and eat supper. I ask you to help me this one time the way I want. I have to do this alone, help Peter alone, get her out alone, talk to her myself....

That's what I thought, says Frau Pagel, once again rapping her knuckles hard on the table, making it sound wooden. Then more calmly: I must unfortunately remind you, Wolfgang, that you have already asked me a hundred times in your life to do your will for once in this single matter. If I did, it was always wrong ...

Mom, you can't compare this case with some childish trifle!

Dear boy, when you wanted something, everything else was always a small thing to you. And this time I will not give in at all, because these efforts and negotiations would bring you back together with the girl. Be glad you are rid of her, don't start with her again because of some mistake of the police and some silly stair talk. A sharp glance was shot to Minna, who, yellow and dry, stands motionless under the door - in her usual place. You finally broke away from her today, you renounced this ridiculous marriage. You had come back to me and I accepted you without a question, without a reproach. And now I'm supposed to witness it, yes, I'm supposed to make it possible for you to get back together with the girl? No, Wolfgang, not at all!

She sits straight and lean. She looks at him with flaming eyes. There is no inkling of doubt in her, her resolve is ironclad. Had she ever been light and buoyant? Had she ever once laughed, ever once felt love for a man?

Hans Fallada   -189-   Wolf among Wolves

There! There! The father despised her advice, but that did not stop her, she went on her way - should she now submit to the son? Do something she doesn't think is right? Never!

Wolfgang looks at her. He too, just like the mother by the way, has now pushed his lower jaw forward a little, his eyes are shimmering, he asks very gently: What was that just now, Mom? I finally broke away from Peter today?

She makes a gruff gesture. Let's not talk about it. I am not asking for explanations. You are here, that is enough for me.

And he almost more gently: I have renounced this ridiculous marriage?

Now she is already getting sharper, she smells danger, but that doesn't make her more cautious, that makes her aggressive. She says: If the young husband does not come to the registry office, it will probably be allowed to be taken that way.

Mama, says Wolfgang, sitting down on the other side of the table and leaning far over the table, you seem to be very well informed about my comings and goings. So you should know that the bride did not come either.

Outside it has become completely dark. A first gust of wind rumbles through the treetops, a few yellow leaves swirl into the window. Under the door stands the girl Minna, gaunt and motionless, forgotten by her mother as well as by her son. Now it lights up once pale yellow, from the twilight emerge tense, white faces and sink into even deeper twilight. Long reverberating rolls a still distant thunder.

The elements want to break loose, but Mrs. Pagel tries to catch herself once again. Wolfgang, she says almost pleadingly, do we want to argue about how far you had already detached yourself from Petra? I am firmly convinced that if this incident with the police had not happened, you would hardly have thought about the girl. Leave this matter to an attorney. I ask you, Wolfgang, and I have never asked you like this before: do my will this one time!

The son hears the mother asking, just as he asked her a few minutes before. But he doesn't notice that at all. In the deep twilight, he has the mother's face darkly before him. The sky behind the head lights up sulfur yellow, sinks into blackness and lights up anew.

Mama, says Wolfgang, and his will is increasingly inflamed by her resistance. You are in a crucial error. I didn't come here because I had detached, in whole or in part, from Petra. I came here because I wanted to get the money for this ridiculous wedding ....

The mother sits motionless for a moment, not answering. But even though the blow may have hit her hard, she doesn't let it show. She says bitterly, "Well, my son, I can tell you that your way was in vain. You won't get a penny for that here.

Her voice is very soft, but it doesn't waver a bit. Almost more quietly and without a trace of warmth, he replies, "Knowing you, I never expected any other answer from you. You love only those people who want to be blessed according to your liking, although one must actually say that you yourself have not become overly blessed in your life....

Oh ... the woman moans deeply, struck to death, in her whole life, in her whole marriage, in her whole motherhood, by her own son.

But this one sound of pain only excites him even more. As it has been brewing outside since the early hours of the morning from haze, sultriness and stench, now close to breaking loose - so it has been brewing in his own life from paternalism, hectoring, knowing better, ruthless exploitation of the mother position, the cashier. And what makes his anger most dangerous is not even this, it is not even the mother's contempt for Petra (who, after all, does not mean so much to him without this contempt). But out of his own weakness, out of his own cowardice, the strongest fury smolders. That he has given in to her a hundred times, he must avenge that. That he was afraid of this confrontation is what makes him so fearful. The fact that he secretly wanted to take the picture away makes him shameless in his anger.

Oh ...! moaned the mother, but in him it only triggers a deep joy. It's hungry time, wolf time. The sons have turned against their own parents, the hungry pack of wolves bared their teeth at each other - he who is strong, live! But he who is weak, let him die! And he dies under my bite!

Oh ...!

And I also have to tell you, Mom, when I came into the room so quietly just now, I really thought you were gone. Because I secretly wanted to get the picture, the picture, you know which one, the picture you gave me....

Very fast, but with an unmistakable tremor in his voice: I never gave you a picture!

Wolfgang hears this well. But he continues to speak. He is drunk with vindictiveness. He no longer knows shame.

I wanted to sell it secretly. Get a lot of money for it, nice money, a lot of money, foreign exchange, dollars, pounds, Danish crowns - and all the money I wanted to bring to my dear, good Petra ... He mocks them, but he also mocks himself. He is a fool. Oh - this is almost better than playing, it excites, it drives wild. Speaking into the darkness, and the lightning to it, and the now almost non-stop distant threat and rumble of thunder. From the primordial depths of all human existence, freed from evil time, rises the primal hatred of children against parents, the hatred of youth against age, of storming courage against slow reflection, of blossoming flesh against withering ...

I wanted to get it secretly, but that was nonsense, of course. It's quite good that I can finally tell you everything, everything, everything ... And when I have said it, I take the picture ...

I'm not giving it away! she shouts. No! And she jumps up and stands in front of the picture.

I'll take it, he says, unperturbed, and remains seated. I carry it away in front of you and sell it, and all the money goes to Petra, all the money ...

Hans Fallada   -192-   Wolf among Wolves

You will not take it from me by force ... she says quickly, but it sounds like fear in her voice.

I will take it by force too, he shouts, because I want it. And you will be reasonable. You know I want it, and then I'll get it ...

I'm calling the police! she says threateningly, wavering between the telephone and the picture.

You don't call the police! he laughs. Because you know well, you gave me the picture!

Look at him, Minna! exclaims Frau Pagel, and now even she has forgotten that it is the son who is standing there. But it is the man, the man who always acts contrary, the counterpart of the woman, the enemy from the very beginning.

Just look at him, how he can't wait to get to his beloved girl! To redeem them from the police! It's all lies and theater, the girl is as indifferent to him as anything in the world - it's all about the money!

She mimics him: nice money, lots of money, dollars, pounds - but not for dear, beautiful, good Petra in the pokey, the Fräulein Ledig, no, for the gambling table ...

She takes two steps, releases the picture, stands at the table, lets her knuckles rattle woodenly on it. There, take the picture. I'm doing you the worst thing I can do, I'm leaving you the picture. Sell it, get money for it, lots of money. But I, your stupid, stubborn, opinionated mother will be right once again - you won't make the girl happy with that. You will gamble away the money as you have gambled away everything: love, decency, passion, ambition, labor.

She stands there, breathless, eyes blazing.

Anyway, thank you, Mama, says Wolfgang, suddenly very tired, tired of all the arguing, tired of all the talking. Now we are done with that, how? And with everything else, too. I will send for my things tonight, I don't want to burden you with them any longer. But as far as your prophecies are concerned ...

Take everything! she screams louder and, trembling in all her limbs, sees him take the picture from the wall. Would you also like some of the silver for the young woman's outfit? Take it! Oh, I know you Pagels! she exclaims and is suddenly the young girl again, long, long before nuptials and marriage. - Friendly and gentle on the outside, but greedy and dry on the inside. Go, just go quickly! I don't like to see you anymore, I sacrificed a whole life for you, and in the end you threw dirt at me, father like son, one like the other.... Yes, just go like that, without a word, without a look. Your father did it the same way, he was too distinguished for arguments, but when he had a guilty conscience at night, he would sneak out of the room on stockings.

Wolfgang is already going, the picture under his arm. He had looked around, he had wanted to ask Minna for wrapping paper and string, but she stood so rigidly under the door. And always that voice was there, that jelly, pitiless voice, like an ugly-sounding bell of iron, tinny but indestructible, indestructible since his childhood days.

He tucks the picture, such as it is, under his arm. Just away, just quickly - it's not raining yet.

But as he crosses the threshold of the room, always that wild, raging voice behind him, says the old girl, that silly goose, who, of course, you can never please either: Fie! Says to him, almost in his face, hard, angry: Fie!

He merely shrugs his shoulders. He did it for Petra after all, he should do something for Petra, even in her opinion. But anyway, let them talk.

Now he is out of the apartment, the door slams shut, from the porcelain sign once hit a corner. Now he descends the stairs.

'How much do you think I'll get for the picture -?'

On this July 26, 1923, the divorced Countess Mutzbauer, a born Fräulein Fischmann, wanted to drive across country with her current boyfriend, a Berlin cattle dealer named Quarkus, to visit farms.

The cattle dealer, a man in his late forties, stocky, with curly, dark and already somewhat thinning hair, with a wrinkled forehead and an equally wrinkled neck of flab, a long-time, almost silver spouse and father of five children - this cattle dealer, then, had first watched with pleasure as inflation made him richer and richer. A few months had turned him from a man with a weekly turnover of one wagon of pigs and two dozen head of cattle into a wholesaler whose buyers traveled as far as southern Germany and even into Holland. Before the bought and paid cattle arrived in Berlin, even before they were loaded, they had increased in value by double, even by triple, quintuple, and Quarkus had still been right when he had said to his masters, "Pay what the people demand - it is always too little!

At first, therefore, this money-raking had made Mr. Quarkus pure joy. Two months had been enough to put him off the Schultheißkneipen, the Bötzowbraustübl and the Aschingerquellen. It had become a generous, even popular, patron of all the bars in the old Friedrichstadt and the new West, and claimed with conviction that there were only three places in Berlin where one could really eat decently. And when it happened to him that a real countess took him in her arms, he thought that no earthly wish was still unfulfilled for him.

Gradually, however, the richer he became, the less money mattered, the more thoughtful Quarkus the cattle dealer became. His unhesitating optimism, which had made him count on the fall of the mark without any thought of the future, was darkened by the leaps he saw the mark make around the dollar, leaps that would have carried a flea away over Ulm Cathedral.

What's too much is too much, he muttered when he learned that his pigs had brought him twenty times the purchase price. And at a time when hundreds of thousands did not know where to get the money for a piece of bread, the thought of where he should actually go with his money made him sleepless.

The word 'material assets', murmured from many sides, had also reached Quarkus' ear. No one can get away from their youth. The boy Emil (the name Quarkus had acquired meaning for his environment only from his twenty-fifth year), the boy Emil had had to drive a cow along many German country roads, to herd three pigs. He had been a drover before becoming a cattle dealer. The lanky, always hungry boy had looked with longing eyes at the farmhouses along the country road, from whose doors it smelled so temptingly of fried potatoes with bacon. When the wind was blowing, when rain or snow was driving, when it was freezing, the farms always lay comfortably crouched along the path, their broad thatched or tiled roofs promised protection, warmth, comfort. Even the ox that Emil Quarkus was driving noticed this: in the rain, stretching its tail stiffly, it lifted its mouth and roared longingly at the farms.

What had been the epitome of all security and comfort for the boy Emil remained a solid castle for the man Quarkus. In the days of the bouncing, jumping, tumbling Mark, nothing could be safer than a farm - five or ten farms at most. And Quarkus was determined to buy it.

The Countess Mutzbauer, born Fräulein Fischmann (which she admittedly did not tell her friend Quarkus), had, however, been more in favor of a manor with a castle, grand staircase and racing stables. But this time Quarkus was ironclad. I have bought enough cattle on knights' estates, he said. I will not buy worries after all!

He was sure, if he came to a farm with a handbag, better still with a suitcase full of money, demanded to buy a cow, bought ten, threw the money, bragged about the money, lured with the money - no owner would be able to resist! To the ten cows he bought the cowshed, the straw, the land where the straw grew, the whole farm finally. And if he then told the owner that he could stay, continue to manage, do what he wanted with the proceeds - he would think he was out of his mind, would bring him other sellers, more than he wanted. Until, of course, one day the day would come when the mark - yes, how it would be with the mark on that day, no one could even imagine. But in any case, then the farm was there. No, the farms.

These were roughly the Quarkusian considerations as he often and frequently presented them to the Countess Mutzbauer. Since the manor was rejected, she was actually quite uninterested in the whole story. But that Countess Mutzbauer, in her disinterest, would have gone so far as to let her friend go alone, she was again too clever for that. It was always better to stay close by, there were mean women enough everywhere, for whom money was what dung was for the dung beetle. And finally: if he bought ten farms, maybe an eleventh fell off for her, and even if the thought of owning a farm was about the same as owning a locomotive - you could sell it again anyway, you could sell anything. (Countess Mutzbauer had already resold three cars she had received from her boyfriend, one after the other, and fobbed Quarkus off with the nice explanation: You are far too much of a gentleman, Quarkus, to subject me to such an outdated, unfashionable car. And he was really too cavalier - besides, he hardly cared).

This idea of the eleventh farm, however, had reminded the countess that her maid Sophie was from the countryside. So when she had slept off around noon, she rang her maid and had the following conversation with her:

Sophie, you're from the countryside, aren't you?

Yes, I do, Countess, but I don't like the country at all.

Are you from a farm?

But no, Countess, I am from a manor.

You see, Sophie, I also told Mr. Quarkus to buy a manor. But he says he just wants a farm.

Yes, Countess, my Hans was like that. When he had money for Habel and partridges, he was quite willing to go to Aschinger for spoon peas with bacon. That's just the way men are.

But you also think, Sophie, that a manor is much better?

But of course, Countess. After all, a manor is much bigger, and if you own it, you don't need to work, you have your people for it.

And on a farm you have to work?

Terrible, Countess, and nothing but work that spoils the skin.

Hastily, the countess decided to forego the eleventh farm and instead prefer to take a diamond ring as a gift. This, however, removed any interest of her own in the trip, any interest in making a good purchase, and thus any reason to take Sophie along on the trip as an advisor.

Listen, Sophie, if Mr. Quarkus should ask you too, don't tell him that. There is no point in talking him out of it, it only spoils his mood, and he buys after all!

Just like my Hans! Sophie said with a sigh, and she thought sadly that the police would never have caught Hans Liebschner if he had followed their advice.

Beautiful, Sophie. Then everything is in order. I knew you knew about the countryside. Mr. Quarkus is taking me farm shopping today, and actually I wanted to buy one too. That's where I would have taken you as a consultant. But if it looks so bad with the farms ...

Sophie realized too late that she had spoken too quickly. A cross-country car ride with rich Quarkus wouldn't have been so bad. She tried again: Well, Countess, of course there are different types of farms ...

No, no, said the former Miss Fishman. They explained everything to me quite excellently. I do not buy.

Since nothing could be saved here, Sophie looked for her advantage on the other side. I guess the Countess will be gone for a while?

Yes, Countess Mutzbauer would hardly be back before tomorrow evening.

Oh, if the Countess would be so good ... My aunt in Neukölln is so seriously ill, and I've been supposed to come there for days ... If I could have this afternoon off -? And maybe until tomorrow at noon?

Well, Sophie, said her mistress graciously, although she judged the ailing aunt in Neukölln just as correctly as Sophie judged the Countess's contemplated 'acquisition' of a farm. Actually, it's probably Mathilde's turn to go out. But since you advised me so well earlier .... But that there are no quarrels with Mathilde -!

I wo, Countess, if I give her a cinema ticket, she will be quite happy. She's so stingy! The other day the cobbler said to her: "Miss, you're not going out at all? Their soles are now holding for the second year. - But that's really how she is ...

Perhaps the cook Mathilde, in terms of avarice, output, cinema, was really like that. Perhaps Sophie Kowalewski had reported quite rightly. But in this, at any rate, Sophie had miscalculated how Mathilde would take this free afternoon out of the line. Sophie had talked quite contemptuously about a shoddy movie ticket that would easily appease Mathilde, but nothing of the sort, nothing at all like that! The cook Mathilde rages. How will she put up with that! She, the thrifty, solid one, should stand back in free days behind such a whore, who goes along with every tango cavalier for three shots! Sophie immediately renounces this tricked exit, or Mathilde immediately goes to the countess, and what she then gets to hear, Sophie alone can imagine! You don't put such filth in your mouth twice without need!

Whereupon she immediately puts it in her mouth in front of her colleague.

Oh, the fat, chubby, comfortable Mathilde - Sophie doesn't understand at all why she's actually raving like this. She has already let herself be passed over ten times during the days off, has voluntarily and involuntarily gone without, and if she has really grumbled once, a box of confectionery or a movie ticket have always appeased her. Has this sultry heat driven the old woman crazy?

For a moment, Sophie considers whether she might not give in. If Mathilde brings all her nonsense before the Countess, there can be quite a stink. Although Sophie is not afraid of that either. She has yet to deal with any belligerent drunk, and they can certainly be almost as bad as a belligerent woman.

So Sophie thinks for a moment ... But then she says quite viciously calmly: I don't even know what you have, Mathilde. What do you want to go out for? You don't have anything to wear.

Oh, how this gentle oil fizzes up, how the flame beats higher and higher! Nothing to wear, admittedly, if you use like others of the gracious closet -!

You would too, Mathilde. Only nothing fits you. You're straight up fat.

Already in 1923 it is a serious insult for a woman to be called fat - and now even fat! Mathilde promptly bursts into tears, shouting in rage: Whore! Whoremonger! The whore! and falls down to the lady, with whom Mr. Quarkus has also just made his entrance. Because now it's off to the countryside.

Sophie remains behind, shrugging. She should not care what comes. Actually, life here has them plenty over, all of a sudden. The minute before she didn't know about it, she wouldn't have liked to go. But that's often the case now, nothing lasts. What was valid a moment ago is already invalid again. Never before has the gas tap been turned on so often and so surprisingly as in these times.

Suddenly Sophie feels how dog-tired, how exhausted she is. The thought of a few weeks of vacation with her parents in Neulohe surfaces in her mind. That would be really nice - sleep in, do nothing, drink nothing - and above all, no cavaliers for a change. To show herself to the envious schoolmates of former times as an accomplished lady from the city, just now, when they have to work themselves to death in the harvest! And finally and most importantly, very close to Neulohe is the small town of Meienburg. There stands a solid house, viewed with creepy shivers by little Sophie on rare trips to town, but now Hans lives in it. Suddenly she feels an insane, completely physical longing for her friend - her whole body trembles for him, she gets hot and cold. She must go to him, she must live near him, she must feel him once again - at least she must see him! Surely she will manage to get in touch with him ... Prison guards are also just men ...

Sophie has long since stopped cleaning silver - what's the point of doing anything else? She's leaving today after all, break up in this Bumms! Smiling with satisfaction, she hears Mathilde's palatable, howling voice from the front, in between the Countess's somewhat sharp, ever-so-slightly irritated one, and rarely Mr. Quarkus's spit-roarse, hoarse one. Dis shall only come and reproach her even one - she will unpack, oh, how she will unpack! They should have no choice but to put them on the street - but not without their wages until the end of the day! And the tramp, the Mathilde, can see where her day off remains - all work she will be allowed to do alone, the -!

Only reluctantly does the Countess Mutzbauer send her friend Quarkus into the kitchen to call Sophie. She does not at all wish to quarrel with her maid, even more so in front of her boyfriend's ears. There was a somewhat strange burglary in the apartment some time ago. Mr. Quarkus had generously replaced the lost jewelry, but at that time already wanted to contact the police. It would not be pleasant if Sophie clarified the context of this theft. However, it would be even more embarrassing if she told about certain bedroom visits.

Countess Mutzbauer was convinced that the cavalier Quarkus was not joking about this, and even if she knew that one should not weep for a lost lover, because there are more oxen to be milked everywhere than Father Brehm could have dreamed of - she was downright cowardly afraid of a brutal beating.

But what was to be done? Mathilde had given such a detailed account of the use of not only the clothes closet, no, also the linen closet, by mistress and maid (which had long been known to the mistress), before Herr Quarkus' ears, she had also given such a detailed account of an 'orje', which had taken place during a two-day absence of the mistress in the Mutzbauer rooms, an orgy in which not only 'foreign Louis and hookers' but also very own Mutzbauer cigarettes, liqueurs, champagne and - here Mr. Quarkus jumped up and screamed hoarse: Ow damn! -, in which unfortunately the Mutzbauer bed also played a role.

The Countess hoped against all sense and reason that Sophie would be reasonable. In any case, nothing would happen from their side to push things to the extreme.

Whereupon the said things came to a head in the first three minutes, to plunge from there into a dizzying abyss, where it stank infernally! The cattle trader Emil Quarkus was certainly not a spoiled child, and he had had to digest a lot of dirt in his life, and time was not conducive to breeding sensitivities ... but what these three women threw at each other shrilly for minutes stank as unspeakably as the dung heaps of all his future farms could never stink!

Quarkus also screamed and raved. He threw each of the three out single-handedly and then, howling with rage, brought them back in for questioning and vindication. He pushed them together with their heads, and he tore the claw-staring ones apart again; he phoned for the police and promptly undid the phone call; he revised Sophie's suitcases and already had to rush back into the count's bedroom, where a manslaughter seemed to be in progress; he took his hat and marched off with the contemptuous exclamation: Women, dammit, kiss my ass, all of you! from the apartment, descended the stairs and got into his car, but immediately had the car stopped again, because it had occurred to him that he would by no means leave 'his jewelry' to this mean woman....

In the end, he sat on a couch, completely exhausted, unable to do anything. Still with reddened cheeks and flashing eyes, the Countess Mutzbauer walked up and down and mixed her Emil a fortifying potion.

Such mean women - all of course fabricated and lied. It's good that you dismissed them both right away, Quarkus! (He had done nothing of the sort.) You are quite right not to have called the police (he would have loved to), after all, your wife would have found out about it, and you know how she is ....

Mathilde is still sitting on her locking basket in the kitchen; quietly sniffing through her nose, she waits for the parcel drive that has been called to fetch the basket. Then she will go with the underground to her brother-in-law, who lives at the Warsaw Bridge. Although the sister will not be very enthusiastic about this robbery, the salary of a streetcar conductor is not enough as it is. But in possession of a handsome pile of foreign exchange, which Quarkus, bribed by her cooking, has gradually procured for her, she feels armed against any sisterly displeasure. In fact, Mathilde's dismissal is just what she needs: now she really has time to take care of her illegitimate offspring, fifteen-year-old Hans-Günther, whom she read about in the newspaper this morning as the leader of a revolt in the Berlin reformatory. That was the only reason she had gone so wild that Sophie had stolen her day off. So now she had her day off. She is satisfied.

Sophie Kowalewski, however, is the most satisfied. The car cab drives with her through the increasingly strong thunderstorm towards the Christian

Hospice in Krausenstraße. (Accompanied by men, Sophie has nothing against the sleaziest flophouse hotel, but as a young lady traveling alone, she knows only the Christian Hospice). She is going on summer vacation, her suitcases are full to bursting with the most beautiful things from the count's property, she has received her monthly wage and also has sufficient money, and she will come into contact with Hans, perhaps even see him. Sophie is very pleased!

Only Mr. Quarkus is not quite as satisfied as the three women. But he is not really aware of it, now he has to buy farms in a hurry, the Mark is chasing him harder than the women.

05 05

Forester Kniebusch walks slowly through the village of Neulohe, the pointing dog on a leash. You never know what's coming, anyway most people are incomprehensibly more afraid of a dog than a human.

Old Kniebusch has always been reluctant to go to the village - the forester's lodge is a bit off the beaten track, on the edge of the forest - but today he is particularly disgruntled. He delayed the ordered gathering of the people at ten o'clock at the schoolmaster's house as long as possible. But now that the thunderstorm is already pitch black covering the whole western sky - it comes from the Berlin area, of course, what good can come from Berlin?! -, now he just had to go. It doesn't help, he must, he mustn't spoil it with anyone.

The village of Altlohe can be left to the left of Kniebusch (figuratively speaking, it is on the right of his way), there is no one living in Altlohe who could be considered for such a secret military matter. In Altlohe live only miners and industrial workers, that is Spartacists and communists, that is field thieves, wood thieves, poachers, says Mr. Kniebusch.

Forester Kniebusch knew quite well why he had not seen the wood thieves this morning - they had been Altloher. The people of Altloh became slightly angry, openly proclaiming something like a right to steal. Forester Kniebusch also knew exactly why he had left the shotgun in the house, but had taken the dog with him: a weapon only irritated people and made them even more vicious. But a dog could bring a torn trouser leg, and pants were a precious thing!

Depressed and slow, the forester creeps through the village under the increasingly threatening thunderstorm. I would like to die peacefully in my bed, he had just said again to his wife, who was almost paralyzed by rheumatism. She nodded and spoke: We are all in God's hands.

Oh you!" he would have liked to answer, because he is sure for a long time that God cannot have anything to do with all this horrible confusion. But with a glance at the colorful supper on the wall, he prefers to remain silent. For a long time now, you can't even tell your own wife what you're thinking.

He thought of his age a little differently, the forester Kniebusch. If it hadn't been for the war and that ten times damned inflation, he would have been sitting in his own little house in Meienburg long ago, letting service be service and wood thieves be wood thieves, and taking care only of his bees. But that can calculate itself probably each humans easily, how excellently can be starved in these times of an age pension. And the savings book still lies, carefully hidden from thieves, between the sheets in his wife's linen closet, but the final sum, a little over 7,000 marks, scraped together mark by mark in forty long years of service, you don't even want to look at it anymore, otherwise tears will come to your eyes immediately. That would have been a cottage in Meienburg, clean as a doll! And for living one would have had the interest from the mortgage, first mortgage, good mortgage on the farm of Schulzen Haase here in Neulohe, punctual interest payer, 4%, 10,000 Marks capital, a little inheritance and again a lot of savings - 400 Marks in the year yield, that would have been a nice addition to the pension!

Over and out! Inconceivable off and over! The tired, worn-out old man has to keep running, working, paying attention, weaving his way between people's assaults and the boss's admonitions. Now the one in need of rest fears nothing more than that he will be put to rest - what then saves them both old people from starvation -?! The two sons were killed in the war and the daughter, married to a railroad secretary in Landsberg, does not know how to feed her children. She only writes to parents when slaughter is imminent to remind them of the fat package.

So he has to run on, the old man, has to endear himself, ingratiate himself, be humble - in this way prevent the impending dismissal. And when such a snooty lieutenant beckons, you just put your heels together and say obediently: "At your command, Lieutenant! Do you know if the boss does not want that?

It is a gloomy tour of the village. All the men the forester should talk to are still in the field, although it is already six o'clock and feeding time. Or they rush past the forester, sweating, barely waving their hand. They have no time, because before the impending thunderstorm, everything that can possibly get in must get in.

So the forester has to place his order with the women, and of course they don't mince their words: he must have gone crazy to order the men to the schoolmaster at ten o'clock at night in the most urgent harvest time? Of course, he has it good, he doesn't feel his bones, he goes for a walk while others work themselves to death. He gets up at six in the morning, but her men at half past two! They do not even think about ordering such nonsense, he may look for more stupid! - Hands clasped at your sides: see, there you have it!

The forester has to coax and beg, and when he finally leaves the farm, he is still not sure that they will actually place the order.

Some women, however, stifle their mouths angrily, they listen to the forester's order silently, with evil eyes that have grown small. Then they turn around and walk away, but the forester hears them still murmuring: whether an old man is not ashamed at all to still take part in such things?! Hadn't

Hans Fallada Wolf among Wolves

there been enough deaths in the world war already? Secret plots by an old geezer who had better think of his own peaceful death -!

The forester's face becomes more and more worried, almost grim, the further he gets. He mumbles heavily into his white-gray beard. Somehow he has to express his anger, he has gotten into the habit of talking to himself. Otherwise, he has no one with whom he can vent his heart, the woman has only Bible verses in her mouth for everything. It is like a fainting rage that he bites there between the grinding, almost toothless jaws - that he is so faint only makes him hurt more!

Now he comes to the village square, where Schulzenhof, Krämerei, inn, school and parish are located. He has nothing to do with any of them: Krämer and Krüger are far too cautious to get involved in anything that might spoil things for one of their customers. Cantor Friedemann is too old and Pastor Lehnich always pretends that he is not quite of this world, even though he is very good at arithmetic. Schulze Haase, however, surely already knows, otherwise the meeting would not have been ordered to him.

Nevertheless, Forester Kniebusch stands hesitantly in the square, does not go any further, but looks over to the Schulzenhof. It wouldn't be bad to get up close and personal with the Schulzen and talk to him about interest and mortgages. But before he has come to a decision, a window in the jar flies open. The ugly head of little Negermeier comes out with sparkling glasses and quite reddened. Meier yells: Well, Kniebusch, old water hen, come over here and toast with me to my farewell to Neulohe!

Actually, the forester doesn't feel like drinking, and he knows that the drunken Negermeier is as vicious as an old bull, but this shout sounds too much like news, and news is hard for the forester to resist. He must know everything in order to be able to adjust to everything. So he steps into the jug, the dog crawls under the table with all canine surrender to his fate and is ready to endure silently now, be it half an hour or four. The forester knocks on the table and says warningly: But I don't have any money with me!

Neither do I! grins Negermeier, who has already made a strong showing. But that's why I'm inviting you, Kniebusch. And with pleasure! They're all out in the field, so I got a bottle of cognac from the buffet, and I can pour you some beer, too, if you'd rather.

The forester is afraid of the consequences of this unauthorized self-service. Embarrassed, he says: Nah, thanks, Meier, I'd rather not drink.

Immediately, Field Inspector Meier's face turns even redder. Oh, you mean I steal?! Oh, you think I don't pay for what I take?! I resent that, Kniebusch! Say a single time where I stole something ... Or -!

'Or' remains unclear, because the forester immediately assures that everything is fine, and that he would like a cognac.

A cognac is nothing! shouts little Meier and despite gentle objections he also artfully pours a glass of beer and fetches the box of cigars. For himself he brings a pack of cigarettes.

Cheers, Kniebusch! That our children will have long necks!

The forester furrows his bushy brow at this toast, for he must think of his two fallen sons. But there is no point in protesting to someone like Negermeier, so he prefers to ask: What has happened since noon today that you are celebrating your departure so suddenly?

Immediately, Meier is darkened. The storm happened, he grumbles. This miserable Berlin shit storm! We never get thunderstorms when the wind blows from the west. But today we get it!

Yes, in ten minutes it's going to be puddling, says Kniebusch and looks at the dark window. Have not run in -? The whole village drives in!

I can see that, too, you big brute! cries Meier irritably. And it's really hard not to notice it: just now another cartload chases across the village square and disappears in the Haase yard.

But it is not yet certain that the captain will throw you out, Kniebusch consoles. Of course, if I were you, I would have preferred to run it in.

If you were me, you would have eaten your dirt because you were so smart! Negermeier shouts angrily. He drinks hastily, drinks again and then says more calmly: Afterwards, all the stupid ones are smart. Why didn't you tell me at lunch today that you were going to run in, heh, what? He smiles superiorly, then yawns and drinks again. Now he looks at the forester with narrowed eyes mysteriously winking and says forcedly: By the way, the cavalry captain doesn't kick me out just because of that.

No? says the forester and asks: By the way, have you seen if the Schulze is in his yard?

Yes, it does, says Negermeier. Came in earlier with the lieutenant.

This does not suit Kniebusch at all. If the lieutenant is in, there is no point in going to the Schulzen and talking to him about the mortgage. And it would be necessary after all. In five days, the half-yearly interest is due once again, and he can't have two hundred marks worth of paper shoved into his hand!

Are you stupid on both ears, forester?! Meier shouted. I ask you how old the weio is!

The madam -? She turned fifteen in May.

Oh my! O wei! marks Meier. The cavalry captain will kick me out for sure!

Why? Kniebusch does not understand, but the ever-awake curiosity of the informer and informer already pricks him. What do you think?

Oh, leave it! Meier makes a grand, throwaway gesture. You'll find out everything soon enough. He drinks and looks at the forester again through his narrowed eyelids, impudently smirking. But a great chest the girl has, I can tell you, Kniebusch, old bon vivant!

What girl -? asks the forester, puzzled. He does not want to believe this after all.

Well, the little crab, the Weio! says Negermeier carelessly. A cute doll, I tell you. The way she greeted me in her recliner earlier. On the kitchen extension, I tell you, only in a bathing suit. And then she undid the underarm bands like this and then - well, let's not talk about it, cavalier remains cavalier!

You're crazy, Meier! says the forester Kniebusch indignantly. You're sohlst yes! You're drunk!

Of course I do," says Negermeier with feigned indifference. Of course I am drunk. But if anyone asks you, Kniebusch, you can order from me that the Weio there - he points to the chest, quite deep below the armpit - has a small brown birthmark, and a sweet hickey it is, Kniebusch, I can whisper to you ...

Meier looks at the forester expectantly.

He muses aloud: That you saw her in a bathing suit, Meier, I'll take your word for it. She has already lain like this on the kitchen extension a couple of times, and the madam doesn't like it at all, I know that from the cook Armgard. But that she otherwise with you ... No, Meier, I don't buy it, you have to tell it to someone more stupid than the forester Kniebusch!

The forester grins, now he feels superior. He pushes back the half-full shot glass and stands up: Come, Caesar!

You don't believe me?! Negermeier shouts and also jumps up. You have no idea, Kniebusch, how crazy the women are about me. I can have them all, all of them! And the little Weio ...

No, no, Meier, says Kniebusch, grinning contemptuously, and with this statement makes little Meier his eternal mortal enemy. You might have enough for a stable maid or a poultry maid. But the lady, no, Meier, you're just drunk.

Shall I prove it to you?! Meier literally shouts. He is completely out of his mind with alcohol, anger, humiliation. Shall I show you in black and white?! There, can you read, you stupid bitch? There, your madam has written me the letter! He rips the letter out of his pocket, shreds it open. Can you read -? Your Violet! 'Yours' underlined, see that, goggle-eye?! There, read: Dearest! Dearest!! Only one!!! - See the exclamation points? There - no, you don't need to read everything - there this: I love you sooo much! He repeats it: Sooo - well, is that love? What do you say now?!

He stands there triumphantly. His thick lips tremble, his eyes sparkle. The face is reddened.

But the effect of his words is different than he expected. Forester Kniebusch stepped away from him, towards the door of the tavern. - No, Meier, he says. You shouldn't have done that, shown me the letter and told me all that. What a pig you are, Meier! Nah, I don't want to have seen that, I don't know anything about that, that could cost me my head and neck. No, Meier, says Kniebusch, looking at him in a blatantly hostile way with his old, somewhat pale eyes. If I were you, I would pack my suitcase on the spot and leave, without signing out, as far away as possible. Because if the cavalry captain finds out -

Don't be like that, you old coward," Meier says grumpily, but stuffs the letter back into his pocket. The cavalry captain will not find out after all. If you shut up ...

I'll keep my mouth shut already, says the forester, and this time I really want to. I don't like to burn it at all. But you, you will not hold it ... Nah, Meier, do something sensible for once and leave. And very quickly. - So, that's where it really starts ...

They stopped paying attention to the weather outside. Darker and darker the sky has become. A moment ago, it was shining brightly into the guest room, then it rattled deafeningly, and now it bursts out of a thousand celestial sources, roaring and pattering.

Hans Fallada   -211-   Wolf among Wolves

You're not going to run into the storm! Meier says involuntarily.

Yes, it is! says the forester. I quickly run over to the Schulzen. I do not want here ... And it is already running.

Negermeier sees him disappear behind the thick curtain of rain. In the pub it smells of alcohol, sour beer, dirt. Slowly, Meier opens one window after the other. He passes the table where they were sitting. Involuntarily, he reaches for the bottle.

But when he has it to his mouth, he shudders at the smell of the alcohol, takes the bottle and lets it chug empty in the village square. Then he goes back to the table and lights a cigarette. He reaches into his pocket, pulls out the letter. The torn open envelope is finally spoiled and the letter - he puts it on the table with the slow, careful movements of the half-drunk - and the letter is completely crumpled. He tries to smooth out the wrinkles by hand. As he does so, he thinks exhaustedly, 'What am I doing? What am I doing?'

He notices that it is slowly getting damp under the smoothing hand. He looks. He put the letter in a pool of cognac, all smeared.

'What am I going to do?" he thinks anew.

He stuffs the scrawl into his pocket. Then he takes his stick and goes out into the pouring rain. He wants to go to bed first, sleep it off.

05 06

The old forester Kniebusch ran as fast as he could through the increasingly heavy rain to the Haase homestead. As unpleasant as it was for an old man to get wet to the skin - it was still ten times better than sitting with that guy, the Negermeier, and listening to his smut -!

In the rain shadow of the Haase barn Kniebusch stopped: as he was now, he could not go in to the Schulzen. He puffed and awkwardly dried his face and tried to untangle the soaking wet strands of his beard. But while he was doing all this quite mechanically, he kept thinking, just like the negermeier over at the tavern: 'What am I doing? What am I doing?'

Once again, he was saddened by the fact that he had no soul to pour out his heart to; if only he could have told one person about this great thing, it would have been so much easier for him! But what he heard already burned and stung him so much that it was almost unbearable. It was like a sore spot on your finger that you kept bumping into; it was like an itchy eczema that you had to scratch - even if it cost you blood.

Forester Kniebusch knew well - from many a bitter experience - how dangerous this ever-increasing chattiness and gossip was for him. He had already caused the worst stories with it, had had the most unpleasant appearances. As he leans there, quite sheltered, against the boarded gable of the Haase barn and keeps wiping and drying himself, he eagerly tries to take away the fuel of his old age talk: he has nothing to tell! It was all just drunken talk from that womanizing guy, the little Meier!

But when he is ready, when he prepares to go into the Schulzen's parlor, completely calm and without any dangerous charge in him, then a bolt of lightning falls from the sky: Inspector Meier stands in the parlor, tears the letter out of his pocket, shreds it open, shreds it open, reads it....

Forester Kniebusch whistles very high and long, although it actually takes his breath away. The dog on his leg, shivering from the wet cold, pulls up and stands there, front foot high, as if scenting game. Forester Kniebusch, however, is already further along than his dog: he has spotted the black boar, the bristling pig, the damned boar in his wallow and put the bullet on his blade: Negermeier lied after all!!!

'After all, there's no other way,' groans Kniebusch, the forester, with relief. 'That negro with the beaded lips and our gracious lady! I could not eat that. And it wasn't my grub either! Such a stupid braggart and liar, think I do not come to him on it. Tear open the letter before my eyes and yet already know what's inside! Says he has just been with Miss Violet, and has a letter from her in his pocket! Of course, she just gave him the letter to get, and the guy snooped through it on the sly. Oh, I still have to think through this matter today in peace and devotion. I should be surprised if I didn't get everything out clearly, and most of all I should be surprised if I couldn't make a rope out of you, Meierchen! You shall not be allowed to call me scaredy-cat and goggle-eyed for much longer - we'll see who gets it with the fear and goggles!'

Kniebusch turns around and takes front after the inn. But it is not yet visible again, the rain veils are too thick.

'It's better that way,' Kniebusch thinks. 'Just don't do anything rash now! This must all be carefully considered, because it is clear that I must turn the matter in such a way that I get a stone in the board of the madam. It can still be very useful to me one day.'

With that, Kniebusch piercingly whistles the signal: 'To the attack, march, march!' and marches off, straight into the Schulzenstube. He does not even leave the dog on the brick floor of the kitchen as usual, but allows him to kick dirt circles on the waxed floorboards with his wet paws. That's how confident of victory he is.

In the parlor, however, it gives him a jolt, because there sits not only the long Schulze Haase, but in the middle of the settled canapé squats the lieutenant! His old field cap lies on the crocheted schooner of the canapé backrest, and there he sits, gruff, shaggy, yet always on his toes. With a large cup of coffee he eats fried eggs with bacon, and in the fat he cuts himself bread cubes, completely rural shameful. And only the hour, six o'clock in the afternoon, is actually not quite right for fried eggs.

Order executed! the forester reports and pulls his bones together, as he does in front of everyone he believes has some commanding power in them.

At ease! orders the lieutenant. But then quite friendly, a fat shred of egg on the tin fork: Well, forester Kniebusch, still lively on the old legs? Everything ordered and aligned? All encountered?

That's just it," says the forester, suddenly very sad again, and tells what he experienced earlier on his order tour in the village and what Mrs. Pieplow and Mrs. Päplow said.

Old sheep's head! says the lieutenant and continues to eat calmly. Then you'll have to go around the whole town again when the guys are home, got it?! To tell the women something like that - I always say it, the oiliest are the stupidest!

And he quietly gets back to his food.

The forester dutifully said Zu Befehl, Herr Leutnant! and did not let on how angry he was. He could ask this young snob what right he has to yap at him and why he is giving him orders here - but it's not worth it, he prefers not to.

For this, Kniebusch turns to the Schulzen, who has sat long and wrinkled, silent, as he usually is, in his ear chair and listened to the Knaatsch without making a face. He doesn't ask him nicely at all: "Oh, Schulze, now that I'm here, I wanted to ask you, how is it with us and with my interest? They're due in five days, and I need to know now how you're going to do it.

Don't you know that? asks the Schulze, looking over warily at the lieutenant. He, however, continues to eat calmly and cares for nothing but his fried eggs and the flakes of bread he drifts across his plate. It's all in the mortgage note, isn't it?

But Schulze, says the forester almost pleadingly, we don't want to anger each other, old people as we both are.

How can we be angry, Kniebusch? asks the Schulze in amazement. You get what's written, and by the way, I'm nowhere near as old as you are.

My ten thousand marks, says the forester in a trembling voice, which I gave you to your farm, were good peace money - I saved for over twenty years before I had it together. And on the last interest day you gave me such a rag - it still lies at home in the drawer, not a stamp, not a nail have I been able to buy for it ....

Kniebusch can't help himself, and this time it's not just feeble old age, it's honest grief that brings tears to his eyes. So he looks at Schulzen Haase, who slowly rubs his hands between his knees and is just about to answer when the sharp voice from the sofa commands: "Forester!

The forester drives around, abruptly torn from his grief and from his pleading. At your command, Lieutenant?

Give me a light, forester!

The lieutenant has finished eating. He has dried the last trace of grease from his plate, drunk the last of the coffee - now he lies, comfortably stretched out, with his dirty boots on the Haase canapé, his eyes closed, but a cigarette between his lips, and demands a light.

The forester gives it to him. As the lieutenant draws in the first smoke, he opens his eyelids and looks straight into the forester's watery eye. Well, what?! says the lieutenant. I even think you're crying, Kniebusch?

It's just the smoke, Herr Leutnant, Kniebusch replies sheepishly.

Well, that's all right then, says the lieutenant, closing his eyes again and throwing himself onto his side.

I don't really know why I listen to your constant grumbling, Kniebusch, says the Schulze when the forester comes back to him. You have to get two hundred marks according to the mortgage deed. And the last time I gave you a thousand mark bill, and because you couldn't give it to me, I left it all for you....

I couldn't buy one nail for it! the forester repeats grimly.

And this time I don't want to be like that either. I already have a ten thousand ready for you, and I don't want to be like that again: you shouldn't have to give me anything either, yet ten thousand is as much as your whole mortgage ....

But Schulze! shouts the forester. It's all just mockery and ridicule! You know quite well that this ten thousand is still much less than the thousand half a year ago! And I gave you my good money ... The grief almost breaks his heart.

But what is that to me! Schulze Haase now also shouts angrily. Did I badmouth your good money? You'll have to turn to the gentlemen in Berlin, it's not my fault! Written is written ...

But justice must be done, Schulze," the forester asks. I can't have saved for twenty years and indulged in nothing that you now give me an ass-whoop for it!

So?" says the schoolman venomously. Is that what you're saying, Kniebusch? And how was it in the drought year back then, when I couldn't get the money together - who said: written is written?! And how was it, when the fat pigs cost eighteen marks a hundredweight, and I said: The money is too expensive, you have to let up a little, Kniebusch! - Who answered me there: Money is money, and if you don't pay, Schulze, I'll have it seized. - Who said that! Was it you, Kniebusch, or was it someone else?

But that was something completely different, Schulze, says the forester rather meekly. At that time they were small differences, but now it's like you don't want to give me anything at all. I am not asking you to reimburse me for the full value, but if instead of the two hundred marks you wanted to give me twenty hundredweight of rye.

Twenty hundredweight of rye! Haase bursts out laughing. I think, Kniebusch, you've gone crazy! Twenty hundredweight of rye, that's over twenty million marks ...

And are still not nearly what you would have to pay me, Schulze, Kniebusch insists. In peacetime, it was usually thirty hundredweight.

Yes, in peace! says the Schulze quite upset, because he notices that the forester does not simply let himself be fobbed off, but seriously wants to get at his bag. But now we don't have peace, we have the In-Fla-Ti-On - and everybody has to take care of himself. And now I want to tell you that I am fed up with your eternal grumbling, Kniebusch. In the village you also gossip about us forever, and the other day at the bakery you said why the Schulze can eat roast goose when he does not pay his interest honestly. (Don't talk, Kniebusch, you said that, I'll learn everything.) But now I'll cycle to Meienburg tomorrow and with the lawyer I'll send you the interest, exactly two hundred marks, as it has to be, and you'll get the notice of the mortgage in addition, and on New Year's Eve you'll get your money back, exactly ten thousand marks - and how much you can then buy for it, that shouldn't matter to me. Yes, I do, Kniebusch, because I'm tired of you, your eternal whining about your savings. I do it and I do it ...

You won't do that, Schulze Haase, came a sharp voice from the sofa. And it will go the same way.

The lieutenant sat upright again, fully awake, the still-smoking cigarette in the corner of his mouth.

You will give the forester his twenty hundredweight of rye at the last, and we will draw up a paper now that you will continue, as long as this dirty money circulates, to undertake to make the same payment ...

No, Herr Leutnant, I won't write that, says Schulze resolutely. You can't order me to do something like that. Otherwise yes, but not this.

If I tell that to the Major ... he gives you a kick in the butt and kicks you out. Or even puts you up against the wall as a traitor, it's all possible, Schulze. - God's man! the lieutenant shouted more vividly, jumped up, went to the Schulzen and grabbed him by the button of his skirt. You know what it's all about, and you veteran man want to profit from the messes of the brothers in Berlin before the end of the day! Shame on you, Schulze! He turned around, went to the table, took a new cigarette. He commanded: Fire, forester!

Kniebusch, a thousandfold relieved, slavishly grateful, rushed over. He whispered, while serving the lieutenant with fire: It should also be written that the mortgage may not be canceled. Otherwise, he'll pay me off with the dirty money now - and it's all my savings after all!

The pity for himself overwhelmed him, the joy over the unexpected savior made him even softer: Forester Kniebusch was crying again.

Disgusted, the lieutenant saw it. Kniebusch, old washerwoman, he said. Get out of here - or I won't say another word. Do you think I care about you?! You and your felty toads - I don't care about you soo much. It's for the sake of it, the thing has to be clean.

The forester walked into the window corner, embarrassed - wasn't his right as clear as day? Why did he have to be snapped at?

The lieutenant turned to the Schulzen. Well, how is it, Haase? he asked, fuming.

Herr Leutnant, said the almost pleadingly. Why should I be worse off than the others? Everybody around here is now pushing off their mortgages. And the Kniebusch is really not one to be taken into consideration.

This time the lieutenant said, "It's not about the Kniebusch, it's about you, Haase. You can't make your cut through the frauds of the Berliners and want to overthrow them because of those frauds. That's as clear as day, every child understands that, you understand that too, Haase - and in there, he tapped him lightly on the vest, and uneasily the Schulze withdrew, in there you also know quite well that you're wrong.

The Schulze Haase was in a difficult fight. He had learned to hold on in a long, busy life; he had not learned to give away. At last he said slowly: I will write that I will not cancel his mortgage and that I will pay him every half year the value of ten hundredweight of rye ... That's all the yard will bear, Lieutnant, these are bad times ...

Fie, Schulze! said the lieutenant quietly and looked at the old man very seriously. You don't trust your conscience with the whole mess, but the little one will digest it, eh? - Look at me, man! I'm really not worthy of boasting about otherwise, but on this point ... I have nothing, Schulze, for five years I have had nothing but what I wear on my body. Sometimes I get pay, sometimes I don't. It also does not matter. Either you believe in something, then you give everything for it, or you don't believe in it - well, and if that's the case, Schulze, then you and I don't have much more to talk about.

The Schulze Haase was silent for a long time. Finally he said sullenly: You are a young man, and I am an old one. I have a yard, Herr Leutnant, I have to fit on the yard. We Haases have been sitting here for an infinitely long time, I don't want to be seen in front of my father and grandfather when I'm loosing the farm.

But if you get it through a scam - it doesn't matter, does it, Schulze?

It is not a fraud! shouted the Schulze again heatedly. Everybody does it. And besides, Herr Leutnant, he said, gently smiling with the wrinkles around his eyes, we are all human and not angels. The father also once sold a horse as draughtproof, which it was not. We are cheated, and we also cheat sometimes - I think that God can also forgive, is not only on paper from the Bible.

The lieutenant was already on to the next cigarette. What the Schulze thought about God did not interest him. It was important to him that things first got better in this world. Fire, forester! he ordered, and the forester, who had been playing with the pom-poms on the curtains, jumped.

Back to cover! the lieutenant ordered, and Kniebusch jumped back into the curtains.

If you don't do what I tell you, the lieutenant declared grimly - for he could be at least as hard-headed as an old peasant Schulze - if you don't do what is the simple duty of every decent fellow, then I can't use you in our cause either, Schulze.

I always thought you needed us, said the Schulze, unmoved.

And if you didn't go along with our cause, Schulze, the lieutenant continued, completely unperturbed, and we are then the masters in four weeks or two months - do you think it will look very favorable for you then? How?

God, said the Schulze Haase leisurely, if you want to punish all those who did not participate, Herr Leutnant - that will give a howl of woe through all the villages. And, he scoffed, you're not exactly going to become the Minister of Agriculture, Lieutenant.

Nice! said the lieutenant briefly and fished his cap off the canapé. So you don't want to, Schulze?

I said what I want, the Schulze repeated stubbornly. Do not quit and ten hundredweight of rye value.

You and I are through with each other, Schulze, the lieutenant said. Come on, forester, I'll tell you where the meeting is today. Not here, anyway.

Schulze Haase would have liked to say something else, but he pinched his thin lips tightly together. The lieutenant was not a trader, he would not be bargained with, he demanded all or nothing. Since the Schulze did not want to approve everything, he preferred to keep silent.

The lieutenant stood in the doorway of the Schulzenhaus and looked out onto the courtyard. Behind him stood silently the forester Kniebusch and his dog. It looked as if the lieutenant was afraid to step out into the thundershower, which was falling weaker but still hard enough. But he wasn't thinking about the rain at all, he was lost in thought, looking at the open barn, where they quickly unloaded the last rye barrel salvaged from the storm before closing time.

Herr Leutnant, said the forester Kniebusch cautiously, one could perhaps hold the meeting at farmer Bentzien's ...

Bentzien, jawohl, Bentzien ... said the lieutenant thoughtfully and continued to watch the unloading of the cartload. The crackling dry straw rustled over to him. The lieutenant had not been in the field, he was too young for that, but also in the Baltic, also in Upper Silesia one could learn that in the end the greater tenacity decided. The lieutenant had said to the Schulzen that they were both finished with each other, but even if Haase wanted to believe that, the lieutenant was not yet finished with the Schulzen. Grade not. Gasoline ... he muttered again, and then gruffly: You wait here, forester!

With that, the lieutenant turns around and goes back into the house.

Barely five minutes later, the forester is also called in. The Schulze sits at the table and writes his confirmation that he waives termination of the mortgage and commits himself to an interest payment of forty hundredweight of rye, payable in two semi-annual installments. You don't see anything on the Schulzen, and you don't see anything on the Leutnant. The forester wants to howl with happiness, but he can't, or the thing might go back again. So he bites his feelings and makes a face like a red-painted nutcracker.

So, loading is fine, says the lieutenant and also signs 'as a witness' with a scribble. And now order the people, Kniebusch. Here, of course here. Farmer Bentzien? Gasoline is out of the question here!

And he laughs, a little maliciously, while the Schulze remains silent.

+++

The conversation between the lieutenant and the Schulzen had been very brief.

Hans Fallada   -222-   Wolf among Wolves

Tell me, Schulze, the lieutenant had asked, sauntering in, what had just occurred to me: what about the fire insurance?

With the fire insurance? the Schulze had asked, puzzled.

Well, yes! the lieutenant had said impatiently, as if a child had to understand that. How are you insured?

Forty thousand, said the schoolman.

Paper mark, huh?

Yesss... Very long stretched.

I think that's about forty pounds of rye, huh?

Yesss...

Isn't that friggin' reckless? Now that you have the barn full of the dry hay and straw, how?

But there is no other insurance! the Schulze had exclaimed in despair.

Yes, Schulze, yes, the lieutenant had said. Namely, if you now call in the forester Kniebusch and write what I tell you.

Whereupon the forester Kniebusch was called in.

05 07

That afternoon, the hotel's receptionist, retired Lieutenant von Studmann, had a rather unpleasant experience. About three o'clock in the afternoon, at a time when no passengers were coming from the trains, a rather tall, strongly built gentleman had appeared in the entrance hall, impeccably dressed in English cloth, a pigskin trunk in his hand.

One-bed room with bathroom without telephone on the second floor, the gentleman had requested.

He was told that all the rooms in the hotel had telephones. The gentleman, a thirty-something, with sharply cut, but yellowish pale face, could twitch extraordinarily frightening with this his face. He did so now and spread such terror that the porter drove back.

Studmann stepped closer. If desired, the phone could of course be removed from the room. After all ...

It is desired! the stranger suddenly shouted abruptly. And without transition, he quite peacefully demanded that the bell buttons in his room be put out of action as well. I don't want all this modern technology, he had said frowning.

Von Studmann had bowed silently. He waited for the removal of electric light to be requested next, but either the gentleman did not count electric light as modern technology, or he had forgotten this point. He climbed the stairs muttering, a boy with the pigskin case behind him, the room waiter with the message pad in front of him.

Von Studmann has now been a receptionist in a big-city caravanserai long enough to be too surprised by guests' requests. From the South American woman traveling alone who screamed for a room toilet for her monkey, to the soigné elderly gentleman who showed up at two in the morning in his pajamas and whispered immediately - but please immediately! - (Don't make such a fuss! We're all men!) -, almost nothing could still confuse Studmann's composure.

Still, there was something about this new guest that made him wary. On average, hotels are visited by the average, and the average would rather read scandals in the newspaper than witness them. Something in the receptionist's chest warned him. It was not so much the silly wishes, but rather the grimacing, the sudden shouting, the restless, soon cheeky, soon rushed look in the guest's eyes that had disturbed him.

At least the reports that von Studmann received within a short time were satisfactory. The Boy had been tipped an entire American paper dollar; the guest's purse had been exceptionally well filled. The room waiter brought the registration form. The gentleman had registered himself as 'Reichsfreiherr Baron von Bergen'.

The cautious waiter Süskind had also asked to see the stranger's passport, which he was entitled to do according to a regulation of the police chief. The passport - a domestic passport issued by the Amtshauptmannschaft in Wurzen - had undoubtedly been in order. Gotha, who was consulted immediately, proved that there were indeed imperial barons of Bergen, they were located in Saxony.

So everything's fine, Süskind, said von Studmann and folded the Gotha shut again.

Süskind cradled his head uncertainly. I don't know, he said. Funny is the Lord.

Why funny? Impostor? If he pays, we can't care, Süskind.

Impostor? No thought! But I think he's nuts.

Nuts -? asked von Studmann, annoyed that Süskind also had the same impression as himself. Nonsense, Süskind! Maybe a little nervous. Or drunk.

Nervous? Drunk? No thought! He's crazy ...

But why, Süskind? Did he act funny upstairs in any way -

Not at all! Süskind readily admitted. The little bit of face-cutting and shenanigans doesn't mean anything. Some people think they're impressing us with something like that.

So -?

You get the feeling, Mr. Director. How half a year ago the jersey uncle hung himself on 43, I've also had it in the feeling ...

For God's sake, Süskind! Don't paint the devil on the wall! - Well, I have to go now. Keep me informed and always keep an eye on the Lord ...

Von Studmann had a very busy afternoon. The new dollar exchange rate had not only made it necessary to re-label all prices, no, the entire budget had to be recalculated. Studmann was sitting like on coals in the boardroom of the directorate. In an infinitely long-winded manner, General Director Vogel explained that it was necessary to consider whether, as a precaution against further dollar increases, a certain surcharge on the current exchange rate should not be calculated in order to avoid being 'blown out'.

We must preserve the substance, gentlemen! The substance! And he disclosed that, for example, our supply of alabaster soft soap had dropped from 17 to half a hundredweight in the last year.

Despite the disapproving looks of his superior, Studmann kept running out into the hall. After the fourth hour, the flow of travelers had started very strongly, in the reception all the employees were feverishly busy, and the stream of arrivals was jammed against those who had suddenly decided to leave.

Studmann only nodded his head fleetingly when Süskind whispered to him that the gentleman on 37 had taken a bath, then gone to bed and sent for a bottle of cognac and a bottle of champagne.

'So a drunk after all,' he thought rushedly. 'If he starts rioting, I'll send the hotel doctor to give him a sleeping pill.'

And he hurried on.

Studmann had just come out of the meeting room again, where General Manager Vogel was now in the process of explaining that lime eggs were the ruin of the hotel industry. - After all, under today's circumstances, it should be considered whether a certain stock ... since the supply of fresh eggs ... and there unfortunately also the cold storage eggs ...

'Idiot!' thought von Studmann as he rushed away. And wondered: 'Why am I so irritable? I've known this nölerei but forever ... The storm must be in my bones ...'

The room waiter Süskind stopped him. Here we go, Mr. Director, he said with his face distorted by the grayness of his black tailcoat.

What's going on? Say what you want quickly, Süskind. I do not have time.

But Herr von 37 did, Herr Direktor! Süskind said reproachfully. He says there's a snail in the champagne!

A snail -? Von Studmann had to laugh. Nonsense, Süskind, don't let yourself be dragged through the mud! How are snails supposed to get into the champagne! Never heard anything like it.

But there is one in there, Süskind insisted sorrowfully. I have seen them with my own eyes. A large black nudibranch ...

You have -? Suddenly Studmann had become serious, he was thinking. It was completely impossible that there were snails in the champagne of his house! Here, they did not sell candy-striped sparkling wine! That's how he stuck it in, to play a joke on us, he decided. Bring him another bottle without calculation. Here - for the cellar master.

He wrote out the receipt with a flying hand.

And pay close attention, Süskind. That he does not make the fun again!

Süskind cradled his head quite brokenly. Wouldn't you rather go to him yourself for once? I'm afraid ...

Nonsense, Süskind. I don't have time for such jokes. If you can't fix it yourself, take the cellar master with you as a witness or whoever you want ...

Studmann was already running. In the hall the well-known iron magnate Brachwede shouted that he had rented the rooms for ten million a day, and here on the bill were fifteen ... He had to inform the magnate about what he had known for a long time, namely about the increased dollar, he had to coax here, to smile there, to give an angry wave to a boy that he

Hans Fallada   -227-   Wolf among Wolves

should pay a little better attention, to supervise the transport of a paralyzed lady into the elevator, to reject three telephone calls ...

When the saddened Süskind was already standing behind him again.

Director. Oh, please, Herr Direktor! he whispered, a true old-style stage intriguer whispering on the nerves.

What's the matter now, Süskind?!

The gentleman at 37, Mr. Director ...

What? What?! Another snail in the champagne?

Mr. Tuchmann (this was the cellar master) just opened the eleventh bottle - there are snails in all of them!

In all! von Studmann literally shouted. And more quietly, when he felt the glances of the guests on him: Have you gone crazy now, too, Süskind?

Süskind nodded sadly. The Lord cries out. Black slugs he resents, he shouts ...

Go! Studmann shouted and was already racing up the stairs to the second floor, completely disregarding the dignified posture that the receptionist and sub-director of such a distinguished establishment must maintain in every situation. The grief-stricken Süskind raced behind.

They splashed through the stunned guests - and the rumor immediately spread, uncontrollably from where: the coloratura singer Contessa Vagenza, who was to perform tonight in the Kammersäle, had just given birth.

They arrived at the same time before number 37. In view of the reports received, von Studmann felt he could dispense with all time-consuming pleasantries. He knocked only briefly and entered without waiting for anyone to come in. He was followed by the waiter Süskind, who carefully closed the padded double door to keep the noise of the coming argument away from the other guests.

The electric light was on in the rather large room. The curtains of the two windows were tightly closed. Likewise, the door to the adjoining bathroom was closed - as it would soon turn out, it was also locked. The key had been removed.

In the wide, quite modern metal bed made of chrome steel lay the guest. The yellow of his face, which Studmann had already noticed in the hall, looked even more morbid against the white pillows. In addition, the guest wore purple pajamas made of what appeared to be a very precious brocade fabric - the yellow, thick embroidery of these pajamas looked sallow against the bilious face. One hand, a strong hand with a strikingly beautiful signet ring, the guest held open on the blue silk quilt. The other was under the blanket.

Studmann saw all this at a glance, he also saw the table pushed up against the bed, the myriad of cognac and champagne bottles on it amazed him. Much more must have been brought up than the eleven bottles mentioned by Süskind.

Annoyed, von Studmann noticed at the same time that the overanxious Süskind had not been content with the cellar master's testimony; a bellboy, the chambermaid, an elevator boy, and some gray female who had presumably been busy cleaning rooms on a temporary basis were also standing near the table, a small, very anxious and embarrassed group.

For a moment Studmann wondered whether he should first throw these witnesses to a possible scandal out the door, but a glance at the guest's horribly twitching face taught him that haste was in order. So he approached the bed with a bow, gave his name and stood waiting.

Immediately the gentleman's face lay still. Not pleasant! he mumbled in that arrogant lieutenant's tone that von Studmann had thought had long since died out. Exceptionally unpleasant for - you! Snails in champagne - insane mess!

I don't see any snails, von Studmann said with a quick glance at champagne goblets and bottles. What deeply disturbed him was not this silly complaint, but the look of boundless hatred from the guest's dark eyes, these eyes that were bold and cowardly at the same time, eyes such as Studmann had never seen before.

But they're inside! the guest shouted so suddenly that everyone jolted. He was sitting up in bed now, one hand clawed into the quilt, another under it.

('Attention! Attention!' said von Studmann to himself. 'He's up to something!')

All have seen the snails. Take the bottle, no, that!

Indifferently, Studmann took the bottle in his hand, holding it against the light. He was completely convinced that the champagne was just fine - and that the guest knew that as well as he did. With some trick he had taken the simple-minded waiter and cellar master by surprise - out of an intention that Studmann did not yet know, but would probably soon learn.

Attention, Mr. Director! shouted the room waiter Süskind - and Studmann wheeled around. But it was already too late. Engrossed in contemplating the bottle, Studmann had taken his eyes off the guest. He had slipped out of bed and to the door, locked it - and now he was standing there, the key in one hand, a pistol raised in the other.

Von Studmann had been in the field for many a year, a gun pointed at him could not particularly upset him. What frightened him was the expression of hatred and bleak despair that was on the face of the mysterious stranger. At the same time, this face was now quite calm, nothing more of grimaces, rather a smile, a very mocking smile though.

What's the point? Studmann asked briefly.

That means, said the guest quietly but very clearly, that the parlor now listens to my command. Whoever does not parry will be shot.

Do you have intentions on our money? The loot will hardly be worth it. Aren't you the Baron von Bergen?

Waiter! said the stranger. Magnificently he stood there, in his purple pajamas embroidered with yellow, too magnificent for the yellow, sick face above. Waiter, now pour in seven champagne goblets of cognac. - I count to three, and whoever hasn't finished their drink by then gets a shot. - Well, will it?!

With a pleading look at Herr von Studmann, Süskind had set about pouring the ordered drink.

What are these jokes about? von Studmann asked reluctantly.

Let them drink! said the host guest. One - two - three -! Drink!! Will it?! You shall drink!

Now he was screaming again.

The others looked at Studmann - Studmann hesitated ...

The stranger shouted once again: Drink! Drink up! And shot. Not only the women screamed. Alone, von Studmann would have dared to fight with the man, but consideration for the faceless people in the room, the reputation of the hotel ordered him to exercise restraint.

He turned, calmly said: So drink! smiled encouragingly at the anxious faces and drank himself.

There were several very large gulps of cognac in the champagne glass, Studmann quickly conquered them, but behind him he heard the others choking and snorting.

It must be drunk up, said the stranger quarrelsomely. Anyone who does not finish his drink will be shot.

Von Studmann was not allowed to turn around, he had to keep an eye on the guest; still he hoped that the guest would not pay attention for a moment and thus allow him to take away the weapon.

Hans Fallada   Wolf among Wolves

They shot into the ceiling, he said politely. Thank you for your consideration. May I now know why we are supposed to get drunk here?

I don't care about shooting you, though I don't care about that. I care that you get drunk. No one leaves this room alive until every drop of alcohol is drunk. - Waiter, pour champagne now.

Exactly, said von Studmann, who was keen to keep a conversation going. I had already understood that. I would now be interested to know why we should get drunk.

Because I want to have my fun. - Now drinking.

A hand had pushed a champagne goblet into von Studmann's hand from behind, he drank. Then he said, "Because you enjoy it, that is. And as indifferent as possible: I suppose you know that you are mentally ill?

I am, said the other just as equanimously, already incapacitated for six years and placed in a hinged box. - Waiter, now again, say, a bowl of cognac. Explaining: I do not want to rush, the pleasure should last longer. And again equanimously reporting: I couldn't stand shooting in the field, everyone was always shooting at me. Since then I have been shooting alone. - Drink.

Von Studmann drank. He felt the alcohol rising cloudily in his brain like a fine mist for the time being. Out of the corner of his eye, without turning his head, he saw the waiter Süskind appear at the other end of the room and creep toward the bathroom door. But the baron had also seen him. Unfortunately completed, he said with a smile, and Süskind disappeared from the receptionist's field of vision again, with a regretful movement of his shoulders.

Then von Studmann heard a woman screeching softly behind him and whispering from the men. 'Attention, Lieutenant! Attention!' it spoke in him, and his head was quite clear again.

I understand, he said. But how do we get the honor of drinking with you in this hotel, since you are interned in an institution?

The baron laughed briefly. They are so stupid. The old Privy Councillor will swear nicely when he comes for me again. I did a few nice things in the meantime, not to mention the guard, who I hit on the head. - It's going too slow, he suddenly muttered sullenly. Much too slow. Another cognac, waiter. The whole cup!

I would ask for champagne, Studmann tried.

But it was wrong.

Cognac! the guest shouted all the more wildly. Cognac! - Anyone who does not drink cognac will be shot! - I don't care! he shouted with meaning to Studmann. I have the paragraph 51, nothing happens to me. I am the Baron of Bergen. No policeman is allowed to touch me. I am mentally ill. - Drink.

'This has to go wrong,' thought von Studmann in despair as the oily stuff slowly trickled down his throat. 'The chicks in the back are already laughing and giggling. In five minutes, he'll have me as far as he wants us to go, too, and he'll see the sane crawling like mad animals before the insane man. I have to see ...' But there was nothing to see. With an unflinching alertness, the fool stood under the door, pistol in hand, finger on the trigger - giving no quarter.

Pour! he just ordered again. A whole goblet of champagne, that the mouth becomes fresh again.

Right, master, you are right! someone shouted, it was probably a boy, but the others laughed in agreement.

You are cavalier, Studmann tried again. I suggest that we at least let the two ladies out of the room. None of the rest of us is trying to get out in the meantime, I give you my word of honor ....

Ladies out - is not! it bawled from behind. Right, Miezeken? So fine and so noble we do not get it every day ...

You listen! smiled the baron with a sneer. And: Drink! - Now cognac again. And sit down already! There, right, on the sofa. Always go, even on the bed! You will also sit down, my director! Go! Do you think I'm kidding? I shoot! There! It banged. They shouted. So - drink again first. And now make yourselves comfortable. Skirts off, collar off, girl there, tie off the apron. Yes, go ahead and take off your blouses ...

Baron! says von Studmann bitterly. We are not in a brothel here. I refuse to ...

And yet he felt how, under the influence of alcohol, will and deed no longer ran parallel: his frock coat was already hanging over the back of his chair, he was fiddling with his bandage.

I refuse to ... he called out weakly once again.

Drink! shouted the other. And sneer: in five minutes you will no longer refuse. - Now sparkling wine!

There was a crash, clang of broken glass. The waiter Süskind had fallen across the table, then to the ground. Now he lay there, gasping, visibly unconscious ...

The cellar master, his thick paw firmly on the girl's chest, sat on the bed laughing. The elderly Reinmache woman held one of the boys in each arm; bright red, she no longer seemed to notice anything of the world around her.

You shall drink! shouted the madman. You, Lord, pour now! Sparkling wine!

'I'll be lost in three minutes,' Studmann thought, reaching for the champagne bottle. In three minutes I'll be as far as the others ...'

He felt the end of the bottle cool and firm in his hand, suddenly his head was clear.

'It's all very easy ...' he thought.

The champagne bottle had become a hand grenade. He pulled off and threw it at the redcoat's head. He jumped behind.

The baron had dropped his key and pistol, he had fallen down, he shouted: You must not harm me! I am insane! I have the paragraph 51! Don't hit me, please don't, you're liable to prosecution! I have the hunting license!

And while von Studmann kept hitting the wailing creature in drunken rage, he thought angrily: 'Did I fall for him after all! That's just a coward, how they filled their pants in the field with every drum fire! I should have punched him in the face in the first minute!'

Then he was disgusted to continue beating into that soft, cowardly whine, he saw the key on the ground beside him, took it, stood up staggering, locked and stepped out into the hallway.

+++

The guests, who had sought shelter in great numbers from the descending thundershower in the large hotel lobby, were startled to see a staggering man in torn shirt sleeves with a bleeding face appear at the top of the broad, red-runnered parade staircase to the second floor. At first, only a few noticed him, but a waiting silence arose among them. Already others were looking around, staring as if they couldn't believe it.

The gentleman, the man stood balancing at the top of the first step, he stared down into the teeming hall, he didn't seem to know what this was, where he was. He muttered something. You couldn't understand it, but it was getting quieter downstairs. The musicians' violins now sounded clearly from the café.

Rittmeister von Prackwitz had risen from his chair, staring in disbelief at the apparition.

The hotel staff looked up, staring, wanting to do something, but not knowing what ...

Fools! shouted the drunk up there now. Insane! Think they have the hunting license, but I thresh them ...!

Weaker shouted once again to those staring from below: I'm flailing you idiots!

He lost his footing. He shouted merrily: "Oops!" He managed six steps upright. Then he fell forward, and so he fell down the stairs, at the feet of the retreating guests.

There he lay, motionless, unconscious.

Where do we take him? asked Rittmeister von Prackwitz hastily, already grasping him under the armpits.

Suddenly, employees swarmed around the fallen man. The guests were pushed back. Under the stairs, in the corridor to the utility rooms, the porters disappeared - with Studmann and Prackwitz. The first news circulated: young German-American. Not used to alcohol, prohibition, dollar billionaire, drunk as a skunk ...

Everything was back to normal three minutes later: chatting, bored, asking for mail, talking on the phone, checking the rain.

05 08

When Wolfgang Pagel stepped out of the art store on Bellevuestraße between six and seven o'clock in the evening, it was still raining, albeit more gently. Doubting, he looked up and down the street. Car cabs stopped at both the Esplanade Hotel and the Rolandsbrunnen, they would have taken him to Petra quickly enough. But a stubborn obstinacy forbade him to attack this money intended solely for his girl.

He tightened his old field cap and went off - in half an hour he could well be with Peter. Earlier, without money, he had arrived very nicely at Potsdamer Platz by electric train, although the picture made him conspicuous to every conductor. But the evening rush on the railroads, increased by the storm, had made it possible for him to ride in black despite all this. Now, with inconceivable millions in his pocket, it was impossible to dare such an illegal trip - if he was caught, he would have lost his millions.

Pagel whistles contentedly to himself as he walks along the endless garden wall of the Reich Chancellor's Palace. He knows very well that all these considerations about fare or no fare are sheer nonsense, that it would be much more important (and also more decent) to bring help to Peter quickly - but he shrugs his shoulders.

Once again, he is the player. He had resolved to bet only red all evening, come what may - and he will bet only red, the devil take him, the odds may be against him as they may! Red wins after all! Thus, if he only carries out his resolution to put the 760 million into Petra's hands intact, their cause will come to a good end. But if only ten thousand, only one thousand marks of the money are missing, the black consequences are not to be foreseen at all!

Maybe stupid, certainly superstitious - but can you know? This life is so tricky, always comes around from behind, thwarts all logic, every exact calculation - isn't there the greatest chance to get to the bottom of it with superstition, with stupid calculation, with absurdity and lack of understanding? Well then, Wolfgang, it is all right, and if it is not right, it is still so! Whether one calculates wrongly with logic or with lack of understanding is the private property of each individual - he, Wolfgang Pagel, is for lack of understanding.

Thus I am, thus I remain, for eternity, Amen!

Seven hundred and sixty million! Round thousand dollars! Four thousand two hundred peace marks!!! A pretty penny in the evening hour for one who at noon still had to beg his uncle for a single dollar! For which two rolls and a - very worn - enamel pot with mixed coffee in the morning hour were everything possible except the range!

Pagel has arrived under the Brandenburg Gate, he wants to catch his breath here for a moment before the rain that is forever pouring down, to dry his face. But it is not possible - under the archway crowds of beggars, peddlers, war wounded. All of them - from the entrances of the Tiergarten, from Pariser Platz - have been shooed into this shelter by the rain, and when Pagel places himself among them, his inability to say 'no' endangers the inviolability of his sacred cash transport. So he escapes himself and the beggars' pleas - hard like many people out of weakness, not hardness - and goes back out into the rain.

He holds his hands carefully over the pockets of his tunic - this posture is a bit forced. Not in the trouser pockets, not even in the inside pockets, but in these outside pockets his money is at risk of getting wet. He does not forget for a second (whatever he may think) that he is carrying this sum: 760 million. Among them a quarter, or $250, in good American Federal Reserve paper, splendid paper dollars, the most desirable thing in Berlin today ...

I can make the city dance for it tonight! thinks Wolfgang and whistles contentedly. The rest - 570 million - is German paper, some in incredibly small amounts.

But how it had also come together! It had been hard enough to snatch this sum from the art critic this evening! There is not so much money left in the house, you can't send to the banks either, they are already closed. A deposit, yes, and the rest tomorrow morning, 9:30 a.m. by messenger to any spot in Berlin that Herr Pagel would wish. He would be good to Mr. Pagel for this sum, eh?

And at that, the merchant, a heavy, massive man, quite red-faced, and with it an Assyrian beard, black, had looked along his walls. With a loving pride.

Wolfgang had followed this look with his eyes. So far he was now, after all, his father's son, he had understood the pride, and also the love of this heavy man, who actually did not look like art at all, for his paintings.

Over there, two blocks away, on Potsdamer Strasse, they also sold pictures in the 'Sturm'. There one had sometimes stood for a long time with Peter and looked at these Marcs, Kampendoncks, Klees, Noldes. Sometimes one had to laugh or shake one's head or scold, because much was simply pompous impudence - these were the times of Cubism, Futurism, Expressionism. They glued newsprint into their pictures and broke the world into triangles that you wanted to put back together like a jigsaw puzzle. But sometimes one had also stood there, jolted by something. A feeling stirred, something moved one, a chord sounded: this is something, isn't it? Is something alive born out of this rotten time after all?

But here, with this rich man who bought paintings only if he liked them, who cared little about selling what he had bought - here one did not see such experiments, no tentative attempts. Here, already in the reception room, there was a Corot, some pond, completely bathed in reddish light, and redder still was the cap of the lonely ferryman, who pushed the barge off the shore with the oar pole. There was a glorious van Gogh: the endless expanse of greening and yellowing fields, with the much wider blue of the sky above, already beginning to turn black from the rising thunderstorm. There was a Gauguin, with the soft-brown, beautiful-breasted girls; yes, also a pointillist like Signac, a childishly awkward man like Rousseau, a quiet animal piece by Zügel, red-sunned pines by Leistikow ... But all this had long since been removed from the experiment - understanding had tested it and found it worthy of love, and now all this was loved. This man could be trusted.

But even if Wolfgang Pagel saw and understood all this, he knew just as well that he could demand whatever he wanted here, even something impossible, like scraping together the sum of 760 million after six o'clock, when there is no more money in the house. Already when he had entered, dripping wet like a bathed cat, and had pulled out from under his tunic the picture which he had protected there from the thundershower as well as he could - when he had shown this picture to the somewhat plummy gentleman who received him and when he had said matter-of-factly, but with a suspicious look at him: Certainly, a pagel. - From his first time. - You sell on behalf of -? - Already then he had felt that this picture would be bought here under all circumstances, that he could make the conditions.

Then the plum soft - on Pagel's answer had: I sell on my own behalf - called the owner, and he had, without even making a fuss about the man in the tunic (in those days, the most unlikely wretches sold the most unlikely treasures) - the latter had said only briefly: Put it there once. - Of course I know that, Doctor Mainz. Family owned. A very unusually good Pagel - sometimes he just got ahead of himself. Not often three - or four times ... Most of the time, it's too pretty for me. Smooth, licked - how?

He had suddenly turned to Wolfgang: But you don't know anything about that? How? You just want the money, huh? As much as possible, yes?

Under this sudden attack Pagel had collapsed. He felt blush slowly rising in his cheeks.

I am the son, he said as calmly as possible.

It had been perfectly sufficient.

Sorry a thousand times, the dealer had said. I admit that I am an ass. I should have seen it in the eyes - if in nothing, then in the eyes. Your father often sat here. Yes. Came in his wheelchair, wanted to see pictures. He liked to see pictures. - You like to see pictures too?

Again, this abrupt, sudden - this too was actually an attack. At least that's how Wolfgang felt about it. He had never thought about whether this picture he had taken away from his mother was a beautiful picture. Basically, this picture man had guessed quite correctly: even if he was the 'son', for him it had only been about money - albeit money for Peter.

Annoyance, mixed with a little sadness that he really was as he was judged, rose in Wolfgang.

Yes, yes, with pleasure, he said sullenly.

It's a beautiful picture, the dealer said thoughtfully. I've seen it two, no, three times. Her wife mother didn't like it when I looked at it. - She agrees with this sale?

Again, an attack. Pagel became so angry. God, what a circumstance around a picture, barely half a square meter of painted canvas. A picture was something you could look at if you wanted to; you didn't have to, it wasn't at all necessary. You could live without pictures, but not without money.

No, he said crossly. My mother does not agree at all with this sale.

The merchant looked at him politely, waited wordlessly.

She gave this (with feigned indifference) thing to me once, like you give things in the family, you know. Since I needed money right now, I remembered it. I sell, he said emphatically, against the will of my mother.

The merchant had listened in silence, then aimlessly, but noticeably cooler Yes, yes. I understand. Said naturally.

The plum soft, who had disappeared unnoticed, the doctor Mainz, appeared again. The merchant looked at his art history assistant, the assistant returned the look and nodded briefly. Anyway, the dealer said, your wife mother does not object to the sale. At a questioning look Pagels: I just made a phone call. Please, please, this is not mistrust. I am a businessman, a careful businessman. I do not like difficulties ...

And you pay? Pagel asked briefly and annoyed.

His mother could have stopped the sale with one word on the phone. She hadn't done it - Wolfgang felt the break was final. Let him go his way, it was now and forever his way alone. She was without interest.

I give, said the dealer, a thousand dollars, which is 760 million marks. - Let me have the painting on commission, that I hang it here and sell it on your behalf, it is possible that I will get a much higher price. But if I understand correctly, you need the money immediately?

Immediately. This hour.

Well, let's say tomorrow morning, smiled the merchant. This is also very fast. I will send it to you with a messenger wherever you want.

Now! said Pagel. This hour! I have to ... He broke off.

The merchant looked at him attentively. We have already sent our cash to the bank, he said kindly, as if explaining something to a child. I never keep money in the house overnight. But tomorrow morning ...

Now! Pagel said and put his hand on the frame of the picture. Or nothing can come of the sale.

Oh, Pagel! had grasped the situation correctly! Although the dealer disapproved of this sale of an insubordinate son who took away his mother's most beloved picture, although he had lowered the temperature of conversation to cool since he learned of this, nevertheless he would not hesitate for a moment to take advantage of this constellation despite all disapproval and to buy the picture. This tall, secure, rich man with the black Assyrian beard just had his rotten spot too - like all of them. There was not the slightest reason to be ashamed of him - on the contrary! He, Pagel, had to sell; but the big man did not have to buy at all.

I must, Pagel said calmly, have the whole amount in half an hour. I need the money tonight, not tomorrow morning. There are other buyers ...

The art dealer made a throwing away hand gesture, at least for this painting other dealers were out of the question. The money will be raised. I don't know how yet. But it is being procured.

He whispered a moment with his adlatus Mainz, who nodded and left.

Please come with me, Mr. Pagel. But yes - you can leave the picture here, I bought it.

Pagel was led into the man's study, a large, almost gloomy room; only large-engraved charcoal drawings by some unknown artist hung on the wall.

Please, sit down. Maybe there. Here are cigarettes. I'll put whiskey and the soda bottle within reach. It will ... quiet mockery ... perhaps also take thirty-five minutes. So make yourself comfortable. Come in!

They came in one after the other, the employees of the house - from the academically educated art historians to the completely unacademic cleaning ladies of the house, who had already begun their evening work. Doctor Mainz had told them, they approached their master's desk without a word, pulled out their belongings from pockets of clothes, vest pockets, purses, wallets, counted up, and the boss wrote: Doctor Mainz: one million, four hundred and thirty-five thousand. Miss Sieber: two hundred and sixty thousand, Miss Plosch: seven hundred and thirty-three thousand. Thank you, Miss Plosch ... There must have been a good bond between boss and employee in this house, everyone gave without a word, with a matter-of-factness that seemed good. They might have given up something they had planned for this evening, these typists, accountants, gallery attendants. Sometimes a glance from them fell on the gentleman in the armchair, who was drinking whiskey soda and smoking; it was not a hostile glance, it was a very strange glance.

They did not care what this man in the shabby tunic was in such a hurry to get the money for that they had to give up their evening pleasures; they did not care if a picture the boss wished to buy was carried out of the house again. The handing over, listing, noting down of the money happened so naturally on both sides - also on the part of the merchant without any eager thanks, without cheap joke, without embarrassed explanation - that just this matter of course almost caused Pagel to say explanatorily, apologetically: 'I really still need the money tonight. Because my girl is in jail and I have to ...'

Yes, what did he have to -? Anyway, immediately have money, a lot of money.

Wolfgang Pagel said nothing.

Stop, Fräulein Bierla, said the merchant. I see another fifty thousand in your wallet - excuse me, but we have to scrape together every mark tonight....

Embarrassed, the brownish beauty mumbled something about fare.

Of course, you do not need a fare. Doctor Mainz ordered a couple of cabs to the door at closing time. The chauffeurs will drive you wherever you want.

Slowly, the pile of paper bills on the desk grew. Dissatisfied, the merchant, rummaging in his own wallet, emptying it, said to Doctor Mainz: "If you read the newspapers, listen to people, everything is swimming in money. It sits in all pockets, rustles in all hands. Here lies what twenty-seven people, including you and me, were carrying. It is not yet seven hundred marks, according to peace rate. A ridiculously hyped-up affair, this time. Once people realize how few digits precede so many zeros, they wouldn't be so charmed.

Doctor Mainz whispered something half-loud, hasty.

Well of course, make a phone call right from here. In the meantime, I'm going to see my wife. I'm sure I'll find money there.

While Doctor Mainz was on the phone with some Director Nolte, who was supposed to get 250 paper dollars this evening, but now had to wait until tomorrow morning, Pagel was thinking about the unusual disorder his request had brought into the company. But - he noted in amazement - how neatly unwound even such disorder! Quietly, of course - cars were waiting outside the door, each employee still gets where he wants to go; on a piece of paper neatly write the individual amounts ... While the mess is being created, everything is already being done to get rid of it after the shortest possible span.

'I,' Pagel thinks gloomily, 'have also allowed messes to develop, but never thought of cleaning them up.' It has grown bigger and bigger, taking hold of districts I had never thought of. Now everything is disorder with me, there is nothing orderly with me!'

For a moment he remembers that he often asked Petra to get dressed in the morning before the Thumann brought the coffee.

'I was pretending to myself and especially to her. Disorder does not become order when you put a blanket over it. On the contrary, it becomes a disorder that one no longer dares to represent. To a lying, cowardly disorder. I wonder if Peter understood any of that -? What she was thinking -? Is that why she wanted us to marry each other so much? Was it also with her the desire for order? Always she did what I suggested without a word. Basically, I don't know anything about what she was thinking ...'

The merchant comes back laughing, brandishing a thick wad of paper money.

Tonight everything stays at home with me. My wife is blessed, she was going to some gruesome premiere, with subsequent celebration of the poet already swollen into a bullfrog. She is glad that we cannot go there now. She is already on the phone enthusing all the world that we are completely without a penny - tomorrow I will read my suspension of payments in the newspaper. - And you, doctor?

It turned out that Doctor Mainz had also been successful: Director Nolte wanted to wait for his 250 dollars until tomorrow morning.

Please, Mr. Pagel, said the dealer. One thousand dollars - seven hundred and sixty million. It took, though, he pulled the clock, thirty-eight minutes; I apologize for the eight minutes.

'Why is he actually mocking me?" thought Pagel bitterly. 'He'd better ask me what I need the money for! You can get into a situation where you need money right away, can't you?' A voice inside him said that one could very well get into such a situation, but that there was still something like a question of guilt ... 'Can I be held responsible for the stupidity of the police -?!' he bitched....

It is a bit much paper, according to the course of time, smiled the art dealer. Would you like me to have you make a package out of it? You prefer to put it in your pockets? It is raining very hard outside. Well, you probably take a car ... Just to the right as you come out our door, in front of the Hotel Esplanade ... Or should I have one called for you?

No, thank you, Pagel had said sullenly, squeezing the paper into his pockets. I go ...

And now he was already walking through Königstraße, quite soaked, his hands protectively spread over the two outside pockets. They might get angry with him like the mother, or sneer like that picture guy, they might also get into trouble like the Peter - he did exactly what he wanted, with his head through the wall. He did not touch the money, he did not think of taking a car, and if his pockets burst with money -! If he did not want to, neither rain nor hardship forced him.

He did not go directly to the police station where Petra was sitting; he first went to Thumann's - on reconnaissance. He was still convinced that everything in life had time. He was a mule: the more you beat him, the more stubborn he became.

Or else - was he perhaps simply afraid of what he would learn at the station? Was he afraid of the shame he would have to feel when he saw Petra again in this pitiful position?

Whistling, he crosses Alexanderplatz and turns into Landsberger Straße. He thinks hard about what would give Petra more pleasure: a cigar store or a flower store? Or even better an ice cream parlor -?

05 09

The police sergeant Leo Gubalke was certainly not a man who - on or off duty - was prone to assaults, petty nastiness, harassment. That most dangerous temptation for every man, in whose mouth the word of power is put: 'Obey or perish!' - she never tempted him. If, at home or in the service, he was occasionally guilty of those little vulgarities that no man's sense of self is spared, it was always his exaggerated sense of order and punctuality that seduced him.

It was this sense that had made him take the girl Petra Ledig out of the gateway in Georgenkirchstraße, and it was this same sense that made him answer the reproachful question of his precinct commander: "But Gubalke, man, you of all people are going twenty minutes behind? - had tightly reported: Had an arrest. Girls - has to do with players.

This epilogue, which he would never have said if he had not been late - for nothing was further from his mind than to do evil to Petra Ledig - was for a few hours provisionally the only thing the guard learned about this arrest. Chief Constable Gubalke had only wanted to get the half-naked girl off the street. He had intended to sit her on a bench in the guardhouse, get her something to eat. Then, in the course of the evening, one would have seen what was actually up with this girl, would have chased off some clothes from some welfare association and, after a serious argument about order and licentiousness, would have released the little girl back out into life.

Instead of carrying out these good intentions, Mr. Gubalke reported: Has to do with players. A tardiness excused only with a good heart, only by pity remained a tardiness; this sentence from the players turned the tardiness into a necessary official act. Up to the second, when this sentence, not recoverable, escaped from his tongue, Gubalke had not thought even in his dreams of conceding to the girl Petra any complicity in her friend's passion for gambling, known to him even only through women's gossip. But man is a weak creature and in most - men as well as women - the tongue of weakness is the weakest point. In the need to apologize, Petra's fate became mixed up with that of a player, and to make it just right, the player became players.

It is quite certain that Oberwachtmeister Leo Gubalke at that moment did not even realize the implications of what he inflicted on Petra Ledig with that one sentence. He hastily strapped on the pistol, hooked the rubber shillelagh, and thought only of the fact that he had to join his comrades in Kleine Frankfurter Strasse at top speed, who had got into a scramble there with some rival ring clubs. He was in such a hurry that he didn't even give the girl on guard a glance as he ran away. If he thought of her again, it was certainly without a trace of bad conscience. Anyway, for now she was off the streets and safe at the station. He would be back in two hours at the latest to set the story straight.

Unfortunately, however, only two hours later Oberwachtmeister Leo Gubalke lay dying in a hospital bed at Friedrichshain, his intestines torn apart by a sneaky assassin's bullet, dying hour after hour very painfully and very laboriously the messiest, dirtiest death that can do such a neat, orderly man in. The Petra Ledig case was removed from his influence.

If the dying also continued to influence him. The two hours until the news of Gubalke's murder reached the guard and aroused, Petra Ledig had spent still quite composed and unmolested. Except for a minor incident, nothing worth mentioning had happened to her. Some indifferent uniformed man - neither good nor bad - had pushed her into a small cell, almost like an animal cage in the zoo, with three solid walls and a fourth open to the guard room, secured with bars. At her request to bring her something to eat, no matter what, the policeman had promised her, the indifferent man had first grumbled: They are not equipped for that here, she would have to wait until she got to the Alex. - After a while, however, he had appeared with a strong edge of dry bread and a mug of coffee. He had handed both to her through the rather wide bars without unlocking them.

Nothing more appropriate could have been given to the half-starved Petra as first food. The old, very hard bread edge forced them to bite off very small pieces that had to be chewed for a long time. At first, when she ate slowly, she was overcome by waves of nausea; the stomach refused to accept the food, to start its activity again. Squatting on the seat board, her head pressed into the corner of the cell with her eyes closed, rushed from one sweat of weakness to the next, Petra heroically fought this nausea. Again and again she forced the food back into her stomach.

'I have to eat,' she thought dully, boundlessly exhausted, but without any indulgence. 'It's not like I'm eating just for me!'

For example, Petra took almost half an hour to finish this piece of bread, which a three-year-old child would have managed in five minutes. But when she had consumed it completely, a physical feeling of warmth filled her that was very close to the mental feeling of happiness.

While she had not noticed anything of the environment during this time, she now, almost fully recovered, watched the life in the guard room with interest. This world was without any horror for them. Whoever came from where they had been at home, neither greed nor meanness, neither vice nor drunkenness were frightening for him - all this belonged to human life, was an expression of this life, just as Wolfgang's smile and embrace, joy at a new dress, the window of a flower store belonged to life.

Nothing special happened in the next half hour that should have frightened them. A pointy-nosed, starved-looking boy was brought in who, it emerged from the semi-loud interrogation, had tried to steal a pair of shoes from a department store. A pretty drunk carouser. An unhappy looking woman in a shawl who appeared to be renting furnished rooms commercially, with the sole intention of taking something. A man who sold doublé watches as heavy gold and found buyers enough, pretending that this unique opportunity came from a pickpocket.

All this flotsam and jetsam, washed into the guardroom by the wave of the day going to the desert, let the interrogation pass with calm composure and wandered humbly into its cage, whose door the uniformed man indifferently locked.

Then it got loud. Two guards brought a raving, completely drunk woman. They wore it rather than it went between them. They listened to the foulest insults with an almost friendly composure and made the report that this girl had 'pulled' the wallet of her equally drunken cavalier.

A third guard brought the pale, dim-witted cavalier, who visibly understood little of what was going on around him, being much more preoccupied with what was happening inside. Because he was very sick.

The girl thwarted every protocol recording with her drunken screeching; the yellowish, only half-loud secretary could not force her to be quiet. Again and again she drove with her long, lacquer-red, but dirty claws after the faces of the policemen, the secretary, also her cavalier.

Petra Ledig saw this girl with hot fright. It reminded her of a time in her life that she thought had sunk in and of which she was still ashamed today. She knew this girl, though not by name, but nevertheless from his activity in the better West, Tauentzienstraße, Kurfürstendamm, after closing time also in Augsburger Straße. She was called only the 'hen harrier' there in her hunting grounds, probably because of her thin, crooked nose and because of her irrepressible hatred of any competition.

In those bad days, when Petra had not yet asked Wolfgang to take her with him; when she was still, when the lack of money became too frightening, going on the hunt for a paying gentleman herself (rarely enough), she had also had two or three run-ins with the hen harrier. The girl had probably just been put under control and from that hour on had persecuted all those who did not belong to the 'professionals' with a flaming, loud hatred that spared no vulgarity. Thus, if she discovered a girl poaching in her 'territory', addressing a gentleman, yes, just glancing, she first tried to interest the police in the case. If she did not succeed or if there was no policeman around, she did not shy away from belittling the 'stranger' to the cavalier, whereby she escalated from one bad allegation to the worse: first merely that she was stealing, then soon that she was sexually ill, had scabies, and so on and so forth.

Even then, the last weapon of the hen's nest had been a howling shriek, a hysterical scream of rage, heightened to the point of incomprehensibility by cocaine and alcohol - every cavalier looked the other way when she started it.

Petra had always had the feeling that she was particularly disliked by the chicken consecration and was pursued by her with an even increased hatred. Once she had escaped a physical attack by a panic-stricken flight through the night streets down to Viktoria Luise Square, where she finally found a hiding place behind the semicircle of columns. Another time, however, she had not been so lucky: the hen harrier had retrieved her from a car cab she had gotten into with a gentleman, and there had been a fight between the two (the gentleman had escaped in the car) in which Petra had had a dress torn and an umbrella broken.

This was all a very long time ago, almost a year - or already more than a year? -, Petra had learned an infinite amount after that. The gate of another world had opened for her since then, and yet she looked with the old fear at the enemy of that time. It had also changed since then, but for the worse. If the transfer of the hunting ground from the rich West to the poor East already said enough about the diminishing charms of the consecration of the chicken, in the main the intoxicants - cocaine and alcohol - had probably done their work in the young creature. The then still soft, round cheek had become gaunt and wrinkled, the soft red mouth cracked and dry, every movement erratic, as if in error.

She screamed, she splashed all the drool, she nagged breathlessly - then the yellowish secretary asked something, and she started again, as if, mysteriously, the dirt was constantly renewing itself inside her. Finally the secretary made a movement to the two policemen, they turned the girl away from the negotiating table to the cells, and one of them said calmly: Well, come on, little one, sleep off your drunkenness.

She was about to start ranting again when her gaze fell through the bars to Petra. With a jerk, she stopped and shouted triumphantly, "Have you finally got the carrion?! Thank God, that fucking whore - is she under control yet?! Such a pig - takes away all the cavaliers from a decent girl and still makes her sick, this whore, this miserable! She's still on the street, officer, and still - and she's got all the diseases in her body, such a dirty pig, like that -!

Come, come, girl, the policeman said calmly, releasing her hand finger by finger from the bars in front of Petra's cell, which she clutched. Get some sleep!

The secretary had gotten up from behind his desk and stepped closer. Better get them in the back, he said. Otherwise you won't understand your own word here. Coke - once it's gone, she'll collapse like a wet washcloth.

The policemen nodded, between their firm figures the girl fluttered, held upright only by nonsensical rage that ignited at everything. Still over her shoulder, then already invisible, she shouted insults against Petra.

The secretary slowly turned his dark, tired and sickly gaze (the whites of his eyes were also bile yellow) on Petra and asked half aloud: Is what she says true? Did you go on the hustle?

Petra nodded, curtly: Yes. Earlier, a year ago. Not for a long time now.

The secretary also nodded, very indifferently. He went back to his table. But stopped once again, turned and asked: Are you really sick?

Petra shook her head vigorously: No. Never been.

Again the secretary nodded, went fully to the table and set about his interrupted writing.

Life in the guardroom went on, perhaps some of the arrested were in fear, in restlessness and worry, perhaps dreams tormented the drunkards - outwardly everything was smooth, calm, apathetic.

Until shortly after six o'clock, when the telephone message arrived that Senior Constable Leo Gubalke was lying hopelessly shot in the stomach. He would probably die before midnight. From then on, the face of the precinct changed completely. Doors rattled constantly, plainclothes officers in uniform were always coming and going. Whispered to each other; a third joined in, one cursed. At half past six the comrades of Gubalke arrived, in whose fight with the two wrestling clubs he had just wanted to intervene, when the murderer's bullet hit him. (The only shot that had ever been fired.)

The whispering, the whispering intensified. There was banging on the table; a policeman stood gloomily in a corner, bobbing his rubber shillelagh incessantly; the glances that grazed the prisoners were no longer indifferent, they were sinister.

But the glances that remained fixed on Petra Ledig were particularly emphatic. Everyone was told by the secretary that this was 'Leo's last official act'. Because he had arrested this girl, Gubalke was twenty minutes late. If he had been punctual, united with the others, the murderer's bullet might not have hit him - no, definitely not! - hit!

The heavy and agonizing dying man was now perhaps thinking of his wife and children. And perhaps it pleased him in the hell of his pain that at least his girls washed like him. He left a trace of his being in this world, a small sign of what he had thought was order. Or he thought, overshadowed by the premonition of death, that he would now never in his life sit on a clean office and keep proper lists. Or to his deciduous garden. Or whether they would pay enough from the death and burial fund to pay for a decent burial, given the current devaluation of money. The dying man could think of many things - but the probability that he thought of his 'last official act' Petra Ledig was very low.

And yet the dying man seized this case, he set it apart from all others. The eyes of colleagues no longer saw a trivial young girl sitting there on the bench - not for nothing could the dying man be twenty minutes late because of her! Gubalke's last official act must have been important.

The heavy, tall, sad-looking precinct commander with the gray constable's mustache came into the room, stood next to the secretary's table, and, pointing with his eyes, asked: "That's her -?

That's her! the secretary confirmed half aloud.

He just told me that it had to do with players. Nothing more.

I haven't heard them yet, whispered the secretary. I wanted to wait until - he would come back.

Interrogate them, said the precinct commander.

The drunk earlier who made such a racket recognized her. She has been on the line, admitted it to me too, claims though, not lately.

Yes, he had a sharp eye. He saw everything that was not quite right. I will miss him very much.

All of us. Mighty hardworking and a good comrade, not a nerd at all.

Yes - all of us. - Hear them. Remember that the only thing he said was something about players.

I'm already thinking about that. How can I forget?! I'm going to get a firm grip on them.

Petra was led to the table. If she had not already noticed from the frequent glances, from the stopping at her cell, that something was going on - the way the yellowish secretary now spoke to her must have told her that the mood had changed, and to her disadvantage. Something must have happened that made people think ill of her - could it be related to Wolf? This uncertainty made them anxious and self-conscious. Once or twice she appealed to the friendly constable 'who lives in our house,' but the grim silence which both precinct-master and secretary had on this appeal frightened her still more.

As long as the interrogation concerned her alone, as long as she could stick to the truth, it was still okay. But when the question of her friend's sources of livelihood came up, when the word 'gambler' came up, she got into bad distress and confusion.

She had admitted without hesitation that she had several times - about eight or ten times, I don't remember exactly - approached gentlemen on the street, had gone with them and had been given money for it. But she didn't want to admit that Wolfgang was a gambler, playing for money, that this game had been her main occupation for a long time.

She wasn't even quite sure if it was forbidden, since Wolfgang had made no secret of it at all. But rather she was careful and lied. Alas, the dying man had done her a disservice on this point as well. The word 'player' means something quite different in the east of Berlin than in the west. A dubious girl who went on the hustle and had a steady boyfriend, in addition 'had to do with gamblers', that could only be the girlfriend of a cardsharp in the East, a peasant catcher with the caraway leaf. In the eyes of the two police officers, she was a girl who used her boyfriend as a decoy to net the victims to be plucked.

At a security station in western Berlin, this reference to players would have had a very different ring to it. In the West - as everyone there knew - there was a huge number of gambling clubs. Almost half the living world and certainly all the half-world went to these clubs. The police gambling department must have hunted tirelessly for these clubs night after night, but it was a Sisyphean task: for ten closed clubs, twenty new ones stepped in. They didn't punish the gamblers involved either - that would have depopulated half the West - they just arrested the entrepreneurs and croupiers and confiscated all the money they found.

If Petra had confessed that her boyfriend was going to a gambling club in the West, the matter would have lost all further interest for the police in the East. Instead, she made excuses, feigned ignorance, lied, was caught two or three times in her lies, and now, out of helplessness, kept silent altogether.

If the dying man had not invisibly still had the case in his hands, it would probably have been lost. There could not have been much behind it; a girl who lied so clumsily, and blushed and promised herself at every lie, could hardly be the instigator of a cunning pawn, and not at all the helper of a heavy boy. So, however, still the possibility remained that something unknown, heavy was behind it. Petra was yelled at, admonished paternally, told of the dire consequences - and when all that failed to get her to speak openly, returned to her cell.

With the transport at seven to the Alex, decided the precinct commander. Call attention to the importance of the case in the minutes.

The secretary whispered something.

Certainly, we can see that we still catch the guy. But he will have long since made off. But in any case, I'll send a man to Georgenkirchstraße right away.

When the police's green collection van stopped in front of the station at seven o'clock, Petra was also invited along. It was raining. She came to sit in a place next to the enemy, the hen harrier, but the secretary was right: the cocaine rush had faded and the girl had completely collapsed. Petra had to support and hold her during the ride so she wouldn't fall off the seat.

05 10

From Landsberger Straße he turns into Gollnowstraße. On the right remains Weinstraße, on the left Landwehrstraße. Now on the right comes Fliederstraße, which with its few houses is just a little street, at its corner is a 'large distillery', where Pagel has never been.

Slowly and deliberately, he climbs the steps, goes to the bar and asks for a vermouth. The vermouth costs seventy thousand marks, it tastes fuzzy. Pagel pays, he goes to the door, then he remembers that he has no more cigarettes. He turns back and asks for a pack of Lucky Strike. But they don't have Lucky Strike, they have Camel instead. 'not bad either,' Pagel thinks, takes Camel, lights one and asks for another vermouth.

He stands in front of the bar for a while, shivering a bit in his wet clothes, the fuzzy vermouth not helping either. So he takes another double cognac, two sticks high, but it tastes awfully of gasoline. But now a slight warmth rises from his stomach and slowly spreads through him. It is only a physical warmth that does not belong to him, it does not convey that feeling of serene happiness that Petra felt after eating the edge of the bread.

Pagel stands casually, looking indifferently through the smelly taproom with its rowdy characters. A boundless despair has suddenly seized him; he is convinced that even now, before he has taken another step for Petra, everything will fail. It no longer matters in the slightest that this carefully guarded money has now been touched. Yes, he would rather it flow, scatter - if possible, without him having to do anything - because what can money do? But if money doesn't help - what does?! Oh, does help always have to be given at all?! After all, nothing really matters!

That's how it stands. He would prefer to stand there like this forever; every step he takes brings him closer to a decision that he does not want to grasp, that he wants to delay until the last possible moment. It occurs to him that he has actually done nothing but procrastinate all day. Once he had money, then he wanted to do something, then he would go off, so big -! Now he had money - and stood calmly waiting at a counter.

A young boy, his slouched cap crooked in one ear, approaches him, sniffs the smoke and begs for a cigarette: "Give me one, I'm wild about the sweet English. Don't be like that, at least give me your cigarette!

Wolfgang quietly shakes his head without a word, smiling, and the fellow's face suddenly darkens. He turns around and leaves. Wolfgang reaches into his pocket, takes a cigarette out of the packet in his pocket, calls out sharply "Catch!" and throws the cigarette to the fellow. He catches them, nods briefly, and immediately three or four brats are around Pagel, begging for cigarettes too. He pays quickly at the counter, sees the eyes of the boys on his thick money pack, and jostles the one who tries to push him hard with his shoulder on his way out.

He only has three minutes to his apartment, and this time he really only needs three minutes to get there. He rings the bell at the Pottmadamm. As the bell rattles, he suddenly feels that the small revival that had risen from the clash in the distillery has already evaporated - the boundless sadness has seized him anew. It seems to spread heavy and weighty inside him like the dark thundercloud in the sky this afternoon.

He hears the disgusting shuffling step of the Pottmadamm in the hallway, their slimy, fat coughing. These sounds are already changing the cloud of sadness in him again, something is tightening. He feels he will do something else to this woman, he will punish her for what happened - no matter what happened.

The door opens cautiously just a crack, but from a push of Pagel's foot it flies open completely, standing tall before the startled woman.

Jotte doch, Herr Pajel, what a fright you gave me! she whines.

He stands in front of her without a sound, perhaps waiting for her to say something, to start from what happened. But he must have really scared her, she can't get a word out, she just keeps running her hands over her apron.

Suddenly - Pagel himself did not know the second before that he would do this - he steps into the dark hallway, jostles the shrieking woman with his shoulder as he did earlier in the distillery, and walks without hesitation into the dark hallway toward his room.

Mrs. Thumann, who shrieked, dashes in behind him. Mr. Pajel! Mr. Pajel! Please, just for a moment! she whispers excitedly.

Well? he asks, and with a quick turn he stops in front of her so suddenly that she is startled all over again.

Jott, what have you got there, Mr. Pajel?! Ick versteh Se nich! And quickly, as he wants to go off again: It's just that I've rented your place again. To a friend of Ida's. She is in now, not alone. Se vastehn already! - What are you looking at?! You're trying to scare me, aren't you? You don't need to, I'm scared enough as it is! If only Willem wanted to come! Whereas you have no things in there and your little one is taken away by the police ...

It is once again underway, the Pottmadamm. But Pagel no longer listens. He pushes open the door to his room - if it had been locked, he would have broken it open, but it's not - and steps into the room.

On the bed sits half-naked a wench, a hooker of course - it is the same narrow iron bed in which he was still lying with Petra that morning. There is a young man in the room, some indifferent, lanky pickled herring, who is just unbuttoning his suspenders.

Out! says Pagel to the people driving together.

And the Thumanns lamenting under the door: "Mr. Pajel, I must ask you very much, but now the Krajen bursts! Ick call the police. That's my room, and where you haven't paid, I need my dough too. - No, Lotte, don't talk, the man is crazy, they took his little girl with them to the station, his bird is out today ...

Shut up! Pagel says sharply and shoves the young man in the back with his fist. Will it soon?! Get out of my room! But hurry up!

I beg your pardon ... says the young man and puffs himself up, but only tentatively.

I ... says Pagel quietly, but very clearly, "I'm just in the mood to spank you very badly. If you are not out of the room in a minute with the whore ...

Suddenly he realizes that he can no longer speak. He is trembling with rage all over his body. True, he never thought with a thought of claiming this cursed shithole for himself. But now it would be all right with him if that damned store boy would only contradict with one word -! But he doesn't dare. Without a word, with a cowardly haste, he buttoned the straps, fished for the vest and jacket ...

At the door, the Pottmadamm whines despondently: Mr. Pajel! Mr. Pajel!! Ick vastehe nich! You as a jebüldeter! Where we always got along so well with each other! Where today I wanted to give the girl a snail and a pot of coffee, only that Ida didn't like it ... Everything came from Ida anyway, I never had anything against you! - Jotte but - nu he still pokes me the apartment!

Pagel, ignoring the chatter, stood at the window. He watched attentively, thoughtlessly, as the girl on the bed put on her blouse with flying haste. Then he remembered that he no longer smoked. He took a cigarette, lit it, thoughtfully looked at the burning match in his hand. Right next to it was the curtain, the disgusting yellow-gray curtain he had always hated. He guided the burning match to it. The lined edge browned, then curved. Now a bright flame ran out of it.

The Thumanns, the girl screamed. The man took a step toward him, stopped again hesitantly.

So! said Pagel then, crumpled up the curtain and thereby extinguished the flame. Because this is my room. What do you get, Ms. Thumann? I pay up to the first. Here ... He gave her money, anything, a few bills, it didn't matter. He was about to put the pack back in his pocket when he saw the girl's sadly adoring look on it. 'If you guessed,' he thought, yet somehow satisfied by this thought, 'that this is only one of six money packs and the most worthless ...'

There! he said to the girl and held it out to her.

She looked at the money, then at him. He understood that she did not believe him. So don't! he said equanimously and put the money back in his pocket. Beautifully stupid you are. If you had grabbed it, you would have had it. Now nothing.

He goes against the door again.

I'm going to the police now, Mrs. Thumann, he says. I'll be back here in an hour with my wife. Make sure there is something for dinner.

Will do, Mr. Pajel, she says. But the Jardine, they still have to pay Se. - A quarter of an hour ago, one of the police was there after you. Ick have him azählt, Se are abjehauen ...

Good, good, says Pagel. I'm going there now.

Hans Fallada   -260-   Wolf among Wolves

And, Mr. Pajel, she hurries behind him, don't hold it against me, you'll hear it on the watch after all. I only said one word, that you are still a bit behind, I'll have to sign something in a minute. But I take it back, Mr. Pajel, I didn't mean to. I'll go straight to the police station and take it back, I haven't wanted it yet because of the criminal charges for fraud, that's what the policeman said. I'll be there in a minute, but first the girl from the apartment. Such a smart girl, she never brings the rent, and what a gentleman she is, did you see her, Mr. Pajel, with the board in front of her chest on a knob ...

Pagel is already descending the stairs; the last one to bite is the dog, and so it is also quite right that Mrs. Thumann has filed a criminal complaint for fraud. It's not him, it's just Petra...

He turns around again, climbs up once more and says to Pottmadamm, who on the landing first tells a neighbor about the events: If you're not at the station in twenty minutes, it's thunder, Mrs. Thumann! -

The yellowish secretary on the police office has a bad day. It really became a bilious attack, as he feared already in the morning when getting up; the dull pressure in the bilious region, a quiet nausea had warned him. He knows quite well, and the doctor has told him often enough, that he should call in sick, that he needs a cure. But what married person today can hand over his family to sickness benefits that lag behind devaluation?

Now the excitement over the Gubalke case has given him a real bile colic. He barely managed to finish the papers for the seven o'clock transport to the Alex, then he sat hunched over on the toilet while they were already calling for him again outside. He could have roared in pain. Of course, you can go home if you are sick, no precinct commander, and this one especially, will say anything against it, but you can't abandon your service so suddenly, not just now. Now, at this hour, the closing of business throws thousands of employees and merchants into the streets, the lights of a thousand restaurants light up, the frenzy of amusement, fever and fear sweeps the people away, and the main work of the police begins. He'll be fine until he's relieved at ten!

He is now sitting behind his table again. Concerned, he notices that the attack of bile with its pain has ceased, but that instead a state of extreme irritability has remained in him. It all annoys him, and almost with hatred he looks into the pale, spongy face of a street vendor who sells toilet soaps of dark origin from a carry-on suitcase without a business license and started ruckus when the constable told him not to. 'I have to pull myself together,' the secretary thinks. 'I can't let myself go, I can't look at him like that ...'

It is forbidden to hawk goods on the street without an itinerant trade license ... he says for the tenth time, as gently as possible.

Everything is forbidden here! shouts the merchant. You ruin everything! With you is only allowed to die of hunger!

I do not make the laws! says the secretary.

But you get paid to enforce the fucking laws, bacon hunter, damn you! screams the man.

Behind the man on the half-left is a young, good-looking fellow in a field-gray uniform. The fellow has an open, quite intelligent face. He gives the secretary the strength to endure such abuse without outburst. Where did you get the soap? asks the secretary.

Smell your own filth! the merchant shouts. Must you brothers interfere in everything?! You just want to ruin ours, you corpse worms! When we're all dead, you'll be fat!

He continues to shout insults while a Schupo pushes him by the shoulders against the cell corridor. The secretary bleakly slams the lid of the soap case and places it on the table. Please! he says to the young man in the field-gray uniform.

The young man watched with a furrowed brow and advanced chin as the rampaging merchant was carried away. Now the secretary realizes that this face is not as open as he thought, there is defiance in it and a stubborn obstinacy. Also, the Secretary knows this spasmodic expression; some men have it when they see a uniformed man use force against a civilian. Such men - the born Löcker against the sting - then see red, especially when they have drunk a little.

But this young lad has a pretty good grip on himself. Almost with a sigh of relief, he turns his gaze away from the removal as soon as the iron door to the rear cell corridor is closed again. He jerks one shoulder in the slightly too tight tunic, approaches the table and says, a little defiantly, a touch defiantly, but perfectly decently: My name is Pagel. Wolfgang Pagel.

The secretary waits, but nothing further comes. Yes, says the secretary then, and you wish?

I'm probably expected here, the young man replies almost angrily. Pagel. Pagel from Georgenkirch Street.

I see, says the secretary. Right. We have sent a man to you. We would have liked to talk to you, Mr. Pagel.

And your husband forced my landlady to sign a criminal complaint against me!

Not forced. Hardly compelled, the secretary improves. And in the firm determination to get along with the young man on good terms: We have no particular interest in punitive applications. We are suffocating.

Nevertheless, you arrested my wife for no reason at all, the young man says fiercely.

Not your wife, the secretary improved again. A single girl - Petra Ledig, right?

We were supposed to get married at noon today, Pagel says, blushing a little. Our bid hangs on the registry office.

The arrest was made just this evening, wasn't it? And so at noon you did not get married?

No, Pagel said. But it will be made up quickly. I just didn't have any money this morning.

I understand, said the secretary slowly. But his biliousness still made him say: So a single girl after all, isn't she?

He was silent, looking at the green, inky felt in front of him. Then he reached for the pile of paper on the left, pulled out a sheet and looked at it. He avoided looking at the young man, but now he could not refrain from saying again: And also not arrested for no reason. No.

If you mean the landlady's fraud charge - I just paid the bill. The landlady will be here within ten minutes and withdraw the criminal complaint.

So tonight you have money, was the surprising answer of the secretary.

Pagel felt like asking this bile-yellow man what business it was of his, but he didn't. Instead, he asked, "If the criminal complaint is withdrawn, there is nothing standing in the way of Miss Ledig's dismissal, is there?

I think so, said the secretary.

He was very tired, tired of all these things, and above all he was afraid of quarrels. He would have liked to lie in his bed, the hot water bottle on his stomach; his wife would read him today's novel sequel from the newspaper. Instead, there would absolutely be arguments with this young man who was agitated; his voice was becoming more and more dashing. Stronger, however, than the sick secretary's need for rest would be the irritation that seeped incessantly from his bile and poisoned his blood.

But he still held to himself; of all his arguments, he chose the weakest so as not to upset this Herr Pagel even more: When she was arrested, she was homeless and dressed only in a man's overcoat. He watched the effect of his words on Pagel's face. He declared: excitation of public nuisance.

The young man had turned very red. He hurriedly said: The room is already rented and paid again. So she has a shelter. - And as for her clothes, in half an hour, in a quarter of an hour, I can buy her as many dresses and linen as desired.

So you have money for that too? Quite a lot of money?

The secretary was enough of a criminalist to immediately nail down anything an interviewee admitted in passing.

Enough! Enough for that! Wolfgang said fiercely. So she is then dismissed.

The stores are closed now, replied the secretary.

Never mind! exclaimed Pagel. I'll get the clothes anyway! And almost asking: You dismiss Miss Ledig?

As I said, Mr. Pagel, the Secretary replied, we would have liked to have spoken to you once, even independently of this story. That's why we sent an official by to see you.

The secretary whispered a moment with a uniform. The uniform nodded briefly and disappeared.

But you are still standing, please, take a chair.

I don't want a chair! I demand that my friend be released immediately!!! yelled Pagel.

But he pulled himself together at the same moment.

Excuse me, he said more quietly. This will not happen again. I am very worried, Miss Ledig is a very good girl. I alone am to blame for everything that can be blamed on her. I did not pay the rent, I sold her clothes. Please, release them!

Please, sit down, replied the secretary.

Pagel was about to flare up, but he reconsidered and sat down.

There is a type of interrogation by criminalists that completely demoralizes almost everyone, and certainly everyone who is inexperienced. It is far from any mildness, from any humanity. Nor can it be otherwise. The interrogator, who in most cases is supposed to discover a fact that the interrogated person does not want to admit at any price, must deprive the interviewee of sense and reason so that this fact slips out against his will.

The secretary had before him a man who, according to a vague accusation, was making his money by professional racketeering. The man would never admit the veracity of this accusation in a calm, level-headed state. To make him rash, you had to irritate him. It is often difficult to find something that irritates an accused so much that he loses his senses over it. Here the secretary had immediately found what he needed: this man seemed to be in real, unflattering concern for his girl. This had to become the lever with which to open the door to a confession. But such a lever was not to be used with delicacy; one does not rid peasants from the East of a caraway-leaf player by gentle consideration. One had to touch this young man particularly strongly, he had self-control, he had just not raved, he had sat down on the chair.

I would have to ask you about a few things, the secretary said.

Gladly, Pagel replied. According to what you want. If you would first confirm for me that Miss Ledig will still be released tonight.

We can still talk about that, the secretary said.

Why don't you tell me now, Pagel asked. I am restless. Be, he said, do not be inhuman. Don't torture me. Say yes.

I am not inhuman, replied the secretary. I am a civil servant.

Pagel leaned back, discouraged, irritated.

Through the door came a tall, heavy uniformed man, he had a gray-black constable's mustache and looked sad, with thick, puffy bags under large eyes. The man stepped behind the secretary's chair, he took his cigar out of his mouth and asked: Is that him?

The secretary put his head back, looked up at his superior and said, whispering quite audibly: That's him!

The precinct commander nodded slowly, gave Pagel a long scrutinizing look, and said, "Go ahead! He continued to smoke.

Now to our questions ... the secretary began.

But Pagel interrupted him. Do you mind if I light a cigarette?

The secretary tapped his hand on the table. Smoking is prohibited in the service rooms - for the public.

The precinct commander took a big drag on his cigar. Annoyed, no, furious, Pagel put his cigarettes back in his pocket.

Now to our questions ... the secretary began again.

One moment, the precinct commander interrupted and put his big hand on the secretary's shoulder. Do you hear the man in his own cause or in that of the girl?

So I also have my own thing here? Pagel asked in amazement.

We will see then, said the secretary. And to his superior, again in that silly, audible whisper: in his own business.

'They're playing a trick on you here,' Pagel thought bitterly. And immediately: 'But I won't be teased. The main thing is that I still get Petra out tonight.' And again: 'Mama was perhaps right after all, I should have a lawyer here. Then the brothers would be more careful.'

He sat there attentively and outwardly calm. But inside him it was restless. Since he had gone to that distillery, the feeling of sad despair did not leave him, as if everything was in vain after all.

Now to our questions ... he heard the persistent secretary say again.

And now it really started.

Your name?

Hans Fallada   -267-   Wolf among Wolves

Pagel said.

Born when?

Pagel said.

Where.

He said.

Occupation?

He was without a profession.

Apartment?

Pagel said.

Do you have identification papers?

Pagel had it.

Let me see it!

Pagel showed them here.

The secretary looked at her. The precinct commander also looked at her. The precinct commander showed something to the secretary, and the secretary nodded. He did not give Pagel the papers back, but laid them on the table in front of him.

So, the secretary said, leaning back and looking at Pagel.

Now to our questions ... Pagel said.

How?! asked the secretary.

I said: now to our questions ... Pagel replied politely.

Right, said the secretary. Now to our questions ...

It could not be determined whether Pagel's irony had made an impression on the two officers.

Your mother lives in Berlin?

As shown in the papers, Pagel replied. And thought:

'Stupid they want to make me. Or they are stupid. By the way, they are certainly stupid!'

You do not live with your mother?

My registration is for Georgenkirchstraße.

And you don't live with your mother?

But in the Georgenkirchstraße.

Isn't it more pleasant to live on Tannenstrasse?

That is a matter of taste.

Are you at enmity with your mother?

Hardly. (A whole lie became Pagel heavy, for it this thing was not important enough now nevertheless. But telling the truth was impossible: the truth would have evoked a never-ending chain of questions).

I don't suppose your mother would like you to live with her?

I live with my girlfriend.

And your mother does not wish that?

It is my girlfriend.

So not your mother's? So your mother disapproves of the proposed marriage?

The secretary looked at the precinct commander, and the precinct commander looked at the secretary.

'How proud they are that they put that out there,' Pagel thought. 'But they are not stupid. No, not at all. I want to know how they start it, but they get it out. I need to pay better attention.'

Your mother has assets? the secretary started again.

Who has assets now in the inflation? Pagel asked in contrast.

So you support your mother then? the secretary asked.

No, Pagel said angrily.

So she has to live?

Sure!

And maybe supports you?

No, Pagel said again.

Do you earn your own living?

Yes.

And your girlfriend's?

Also.

With what?

'Stop, stop!" thought Pagel. 'They want to catch me. You heard something ringing. Certainly nothing can happen to me, playing is not punished. But better I do not even start from it. Peter certainly didn't give anything away.'

I sell things.

What kind of stuff do you sell?

For example, those of my girlfriend.

To whom do you sell?

For example, to the pawnbroker Feld in Gollnowstraße.

And if there is nothing left to sell?

There is still something there.

The officer thought for a moment, looking up at the supervisor. The provost nodded slightly.

The secretary took a pencil, put it on the tip, looked at it thoughtfully and let it fall down. Lightly he asked: Your girlfriend does not sell anything?

Nothing!

I bet she doesn't sell anything?

Nothing at all!

You know that it is possible to sell other than just things?

'What on earth,' Pagel thought, dumbfounded, 'could Peter have sold that they would ask such a stupid question?!'

Aloud he said, "By things, too, I meant not only clothes and such.

But for example?

Images.

Pictures -?

Yes, pictures!

What kind of pictures in the world?!

For example, oil paintings.

Oil paintings ... Yes, are you a painter?

Not me - but I am the son of a painter.

So, said the secretary very dissatisfied. So you sell oil paintings of your father. Well, we will talk about that later. Now only once again the confirmation: Miss Ledig does not sell anything?

Nothing. Everything that is sold, I sell.

It could be, said the secretary, and his bilious pains plagued him again very much - this young brat even acted too superior. It could also be that Fräulein Ledig sold something behind your back - without you needing to know?

Pagel thought. He pushed back all the anxiety, all the dark apprehension that kept gathering inside him. He admitted: "Theoretically, that would be possible.

And practically -?

Practically not. He smiled. After all, we do not own so much, I would immediately notice the absence of even the slightest little thing.

So ... so ... said the secretary. He looked back at the precinct commander, the commander returned the look - Pagel felt as if the shadow of a smile appeared in the corners of their eyes. His restlessness, his suspicion became stronger and stronger. The secretary lowered his eyelids: And we agreed that you can sell not only things, pictures, tangible things, but - also other things?

Again the dark threat, barely hidden. What on earth could Petra have sold?!

For example -? Wolfgang asked crossly. Because I can't get an idea of the intangible things my friend seems to have sold!

For example ... the secretary began and looked up at the precinct commander again.

The precinct commander closed his eyes, moving his sad face once from right to left, in denial. Pagel saw it clearly. The secretary smiled. It wasn't quite there yet, but it was almost there.

For example - we will see in a moment, said the secretary. First, back to our questions. So you admit to making a living by selling pictures ...

Gentlemen! said Pagel, standing up and standing behind his chair. He gripped the backrest in front of him tightly with both hands. He looked down at those hands: the knuckles stood out white through the reddened skin. Gentlemen! he said resolutely. They play cat and mouse with me for some reason I don't know. I'm not going along with this any longer! If, as it seems, Fräulein Ledig has committed any stupidity, I alone bear the responsibility. I didn't take care of her enough, I never gave her money, probably not even enough to eat. I stand up for everything. And as far as damage has occurred, I can compensate the damage. Here is money ... He tore at his pockets, he threw the packages, one by one, on the table. I want to pay what damage has been done, but finally tell me what has happened ....

Money, a lot of money ... said the secretary, scowling at the nonsensical, ever-increasing pile.

The precinct commander closed his eyes as if he wanted to look away from it, as if he could not bear the sight.

Here's another $250! Pagel shouted, himself overwhelmed anew by the amount of money. He threw the pack on the table last. I cannot think of any damage that could not be paid for with it today. I want to give everything away, he said stubbornly, but let Fräulein Ledig go free tonight!

He, too, stared at the money, the drab white or brownish of the German ones, the rainbow colors of the American bills.

Through the door the uniformed man let in Mrs. Thumann, the Pottmadamm. Her sloppy fullness slouched in drooping robes. The hem of the skirt, worn down of course, still went up to the heels of the shoes, at a time when women no longer wore skirts to the knee. Her gray, flabby, wrinkled face trembled, her lower lip drooped and had the inside turned inside out.

Jotte doch, det ick noch zurechtkommen, Her Pajel! Wat bin ick jeloofen! Wat ha ick for een Schiß jehabt, Se kokeln mir die Bude noch noch an, wie Sie jed bedroht haben! I came on time, but as I'm in Gollnowstraße and I'm thinking of you and how to get along, a car runs into a horse. I can't go any further! Det janze Jedärme outside, and I think to myself: Aujuste, bekiek you that! They always say that you shouldn't compare humans and animals, but inside there must be quite a resemblance, and I thought to myself, since you always have to deal with your bladder, and a bladder has such a Hafamotoa as well...

So Mr. Pagel threatened to burn your apartment if you didn't come here immediately and withdraw the charges?

But you can't take Mrs. Thumann for a fool; she talks a lot, but she won't let herself be pinned down to anything. She saw the money on the table, realized the situation, and already she starts talking: Who says dat?! You say he threatened mia?! I didn't say that, I'll put it in the minutes, Lieutenant, you'd better blame yourself for those words! We are threatened, since he is such an affable, kind gentleman, Mr. Pajel! And I wouldn't have signed the charges against him and the girl if your man hadn't told me about the sense and nonsense. It's jesetz, he says - and how can it be jesetz, I ask you, when I have all my money, and there's no question of cheating! Nah, my Anzeije want ick again, before I make you liable ...

Silence now! thunders the precinct commander, for the secretary's timid attempts to interrupt do not succeed against this stream of words. Please step outside the door for a moment, Mr. Pagel. We would like to talk to your landlady alone ...

Pagel looks at them for a moment, then at the money and papers on the table. He bows silently and steps out into the hallway. Opposite him is now the door to the registration office, a little further towards the street, directly at the exit door, the guard room. He sees people walking on the street through the open door outside. It seems to have stopped raining, a cool breeze comes in and fights the stale air of the hallway.

Pagel leans against the wall and lights the long-awaited cigarette. The first, deeply inhaled puffs are a relief. But then he immediately forgets that he smokes.

'They haven't arrested me yet,' he thinks. 'Otherwise they wouldn't have sent me out the door so alone.'

Inside, the voice of the Thumanns goes again, but more tearful. In between, the voice of the precinct commander barks - funny how well the sad man can snap. 'But he must be able to do it, that's what you have to be able to do in your profession.' - By the way, it doesn't prove anything that they sent me out the door. All my money is in there on the table, they know quite well, no one runs away from so much money so easily. But why would they actually arrest me? And what about Petra? What can Petra have sold?'

He muses. Again and again he gets the idea that she might have sold something from the Thumann. Bedding or something to buy food. 'But that's nonsense! The Pottmadamm would have talked that out long ago. And otherwise Peter has no opportunity to get anything at all!'

In his mind he goes to the exit door, the air in the corridor gives him a headache, also the voices in the secretary's room disturb him.

He is standing on the street. The asphalt is as smooth as glass. 'Tough day for the cab drivers,' he thinks as the cars pass him so carefully, groping as it were. 'No, I don't want to be a cab driver.' But what on earth do I want to be? I'm not good for anything anymore. I've been doing nothing but nonsense all day, and even now I won't be able to get Peter out. I feel it. What could Peter have done?'

He stops, at the edge of the roadway. The lights are reflected in the rain-soaked asphalt, no light shines on him. Then someone bumps into him, and of course it's the Pottmadamm.

Jotte doch, Mr. Pajel, good that I see you standing here! I thought you'd been stormed. Just don't do it, get your nice money. Wat wem Se det den Brüdern lassen?! I don't understand and I don't know what the authorities want to be, with a criminalistic sharpness of vision and all that, and so each horse has given them something to look forward to. Se are een Bauernfänger mit Kümmelblättchen. They know where to put the card and throw it over the table, and the other one has to guess where the card is ... So stupid! A fine man like you! Ick have them but de ears ausjeputzt, da is de skin with det Schmalz wegjegangen! Allet solidet Jlücksspiel ha ick jesacht, fein mit Bank und die Herren im Frack, aba nur was die Herren sind, die det Jeld innehmen, Sie natürlich nicht, wie ick allens oft durch die Tür jehert habe, wie Se et dem Peter erzählt haben ...

And what about the Peter?

Yes, you know, Mr. Pajel, I don't know what's wrong with her. They don't make a sound, it stinks with Petra! But because of the fraud display and so on, it's no longer there - they had to give it back to me, and I tore it up in front of the yellow-eyed man's quince. And with the Jardine, I also thought it was a joke from you, and if you wanted to give me something now for the new Jardine ...

First I have to get my money back, Mrs. Thumann, says Pagel and goes back into the back room.

The secretary is there alone now, the precinct commander is no longer there. Yes, interest has waned, it now seems after all, the dying man was wrong. It's not an important thing, it's just a trifle. This is not a time for trivia. The secretary has no more desire to work with criminalistic tricks, the last official act of Leo Gubalke has withered away before the dying man has taken his last breath.

Indifferently, the secretary checks the copy of the art dealer's purchase confirmation, it will be correct. He doesn't even call there anymore - after all, it's too unlikely that someone with caraway leaves will win a thousand dollars in a few afternoon hours.

But you're not allowed to play in gambling clubs, he says boredly and gives Pagel back the purchase confirmation. Gambling is prohibited by law.

Certainly, says Pagel politely. I'm not playing again either. - May I perhaps post bail for Miss Ledig?

It's no longer here, says the secretary, and for him it really doesn't exist at all. It's already in the Alexanderplatz police prison.

But why?! cries Pagel. Just tell me why!!!

Because she fornicates without being under control, the secretary says deadpan. By the way, she is also said to be sexually ill.

It is good that the chair is still there. Pagel grabs him so tightly that he thinks he must break. That's impossible, he says wearily at last.

She has been recognized, the secretary explains, and now finally wants to get to his work, by another girl of the same trade here. By the way, she also admitted it.

She admitted it?!

She admitted it ...

Thank you, says Pagel, lets go of the chair and goes against the door.

Your money, your papers! the secretary calls impatiently.

Pagel makes a dismissive movement, but then comes to his senses and stuffs everything back into his pockets.

You will lose your money, says the secretary indifferently.

Pagel again makes a move of defense and marches out the door.

Only five minutes later, in the middle of a mechanical typing session, does it occur to the secretary that he has given Mr. Pagel incorrect, or at least misleading, information. Petra Ledig only admitted that she had fornicated in a few, few instances about a year ago. Venereal disease she has not admitted at all.

The secretary thinks for a moment. 'Maybe that's not a bad thing,' he muses. 'Maybe he won't marry her now. You should not marry such girls. No, never!'

And he returns to his writing. Finally sinks for him the case Ledig ... the last official act of the police chief constable Leo Gubalke.

Chapter 06

- The thunderstorm is over, but it remains humid -

06 01

After the first rush of low- and high-ranking employees of the hotel, it had become quiet around the pair of friends Prackwitz and Studmann. The receptionist was asleep on an old, rather holey chaise longue in a basement room of the hotel. He slept the leaden and ugly sleep of the drunk, with drooping chin, wet mouth, and a bloated face whose skin suddenly looked stubbly, as if it had not been shaved for a long time. A red scrape ran across his forehead from the fall down the stairs.

Von Prackwitz looked at his friend, then at the cellar room. It was not a welcoming chamber to which they had carried their receptionist. A large electric reel took up most of the space. Empty washing baskets were arranged in the corner, two ironing boards leaned against the wall.

When a waiter peeked in - everything seemed to believe itself in the right to look in without any circumstance, to make unabashed remarks at the door, even to laugh - Rittmeister von Prackwitz asked quite angrily: Herr von Studmann must have his own room here in the hotel. Why hasn't he been taken to his room?

The waiter shrugged and said with a curious look at the sleeping man: How am I supposed to know that? I didn't drag him here after all!

Von Prackwitz defeated himself. Send me - please - someone from the line.

The waiter disappeared. Prackwitz was waiting.

But no one came. No one came for a long time. The cavalry captain leaned back on the kitchen chair, crossed his legs and yawned. He was tired and weary. He felt he had experienced plenty since his train, coming from Ostade, had pulled into Silesian Station this morning. Too much, actually, for a simple country dweller who was alienated from big-city excitement.

The cavalry captain lit a cigarette, perhaps it would freshen him up a bit. No, still no one came. Word must have gotten around to the management of the hotel that the receptionist and sub-director had fallen down the stairs in view of the crowded hotel lobby - after some confused speeches. Nevertheless, none of the gentlemen made an effort. The cavalry captain frowned unwillingly. There was no doubt: something about this was not right. It had not been a simple fall from the stairs, as it can happen once - by the deceitfulness of the object - even to the best behaved. The intrusiveness of the lower staff, the absence of the upper hotel staff, the breath of the sleeper revealed it sufficiently: First Lieutenant von Studmann had been drunk, senselessly drunk. Still was.

Von Prackwitz wondered if Studmann had perhaps become a drunk? It was possible. Anything was possible in these cursed times. But the cavalry captain immediately dismissed the idea of habitual drinking anyway. On the one hand, a habitual drinker does not fall down stairs - such a thing happens only to dilettantes in drinking; on the other hand, the management of no great hotel keeps a drinker in its service.

No - and Rittmeister von Prackwitz got up and started pacing up and down the rolling chamber -, this Studmann case was different. Something quite unexpected had happened, something that would already be known, but about which it was pointless to rack one's brains now. The only thing that mattered was what consequences this thing would have for Studmann. From the behavior of the staff, Prackwitz concluded that these consequences would be very unpleasant. He was determined to defend the friend, as long as he was not capable of negotiating himself - with teeth and claws!

'With teeth and claws!' the cavalry captain repeated to himself, very pleased with this warlike formulation.

'But if,' he continued to think to himself, 'everything doesn't help (and you know those cold moneybags), maybe that's not so bad either. I might be able to persuade him ...'

Now the cavalry captain thinks of his lonely way through the Lange Straße to the reaper's agency. He thinks of how many paths he has marched lonely since his military days, always that one conscious imaginary point before his eyes. He remembers how often he missed a comrade. In the cadet school, at the draft, in the war - there had always been comrades with whom one could chat, guys of the same mind, of the same interests, of the same honor. Since the war, all that was over, everyone was on his own; there was no more cohesion, no more togetherness.

'But he wouldn't like to come as a guest,' the cavalry captain reflects and thinks further. Why should he fool himself? Today

early on the reaper's agency he made a mistake, and when he gave the reaper the dollars at the Silesian station, he made another mistake. His behavior at police headquarters may not have been quite right either, and when an hour ago, after endless running and talking, he let a mediator talk him into sixty people whom he is not supposed to see until tomorrow morning at all, just to finally bring this disgusting story to a conclusion, that may not have been very wise either.

He's just too hot-tempered, rash, on it and off it, rents from the bush - but then suddenly bored, disgusted with everything. Besides: he doesn't understand a lot of things well enough"; his father-in-law, the old Privy Councillor von Teschow, may be right: he will never become a real businessman!

The cavalry captain throws his extinguished stub into a corner and lights a new cigarette. Yep, he's putting deprivation on himself, smoking this junk instead of his favorite brand. He also picks fights with his wife when she has once again bought two pairs of silk stockings. But when the cattle dealer is there and bargains with him for the fat oxen, and talks for an hour and bargains for the second hour, and has them sent away and is there again, and sticks and is humble when he is yelled at - finally then the Herr Rittergutspächter von Prackwitz gives in. He has grown soft, or bored, or disgusted, and now sells the beautiful oxen at a price that makes the old Privy Councillor, just hearing him, whoop softly. To which he of course immediately says: Excuse me, Joachim. Of course, I'm not talking you into your economy. Only - I never had money enough to throw out the window!

No, he would have no difficulty in convincing Studmann that he would be a very necessary, very useful, not at all highly enough paid helper on Neulohe, not to mention comradely. It wouldn't work with Meier in the long run. What Violet had said on the phone earlier (when he phoned about the cars tomorrow morning), that Meier didn't let them drive in, but had drunk himself silly in the early afternoon, in the middle of his shift, was beyond him!

The cavalry captain's blood is inflamed by the idea of a field inspector Meier who is drunk on duty: 'I'll throw the brother out tomorrow morning with an octagon! Much too good-natured I am always with the guys! Octagonal he flies -!'

Until his eyes fall on his sleeping friend and his sense of justice reminds him that he, too, has gotten drunk on duty.

'With Studmann, of course, it's a completely different matter!' The captain wants to talk himself into it. 'There must be special circumstances in his case.'

But after all, nothing stands in the way of the assumption that special circumstances also existed in the case of Field Inspector Meier - even his habit of getting drunk on duty had not existed up to that point.

Of course, it's only because I'm out of town," the captain says to himself angrily, but that doesn't quite catch on either, because he's been out of town many times before without anything similar happening. And so he loses himself again in assumptions about the Studmann case on the one hand and the Meier case on the other, when there is a knock on the door and a darkly dressed, older gentleman enters and introduces himself with a bow as Doctor Zetsche, hotel doctor.

Von Prackwitz also gives his name and explains that he is a friend of Mr. Studmann, an old regimental comrade.

I happened to be in the hall when the accident happened.

The accident, yes, said the doctor and, rubbing his nose thoughtfully with one finger, looked at the cavalry captain. So you're calling it an accident?

When someone falls down a flight of stairs, doesn't he? said the cavalry captain, waiting.

The doctor diagnosed von Studmann with drunkenness. Complete drunkenness. Alcohol intoxication. The scratch on his forehead means nothing.

You know -? the cavalry captain began cautiously.

The doctor prescribed some Eumed or aspirin or pyramidone - whatever was at hand when he woke up.

Here, said the cavalry captain with a glance through the rolling room, there should be nothing to hand. Can't you arrange for my friend to be taken to his room? It was a bad case.

It's a bad case! the doctor shouted emphatically. Six people upstairs - equally drunk - all hotel employees. An orgy - under the direction of your friend. And the only non-drunk participant, the guest of the hotel, Herr Reichsfreiherr Baron von Bergen - knocked down by your friend!

But I don't understand ... said the cavalry captain, quite bewildered by these fairy-tale revelations.

I don't understand it either! said the doctor firmly. And I don't even want to understand it!

But explain to me ... asked the cavalry captain.

Hans Fallada   -282-   Wolf among Wolves

There is no explanation! said the doctor steadfastly. The guest, an imperial baron - knocked down by the drunken receptionist!

There must have been, exclaimed the Rittmeister hitziger, special circumstances. I have known Mr. von Studmann for a long time; he has always done his duty, even under the most difficult circumstances.

Undoubtedly, said the doctor politely and retreated from the excited against the door.

When he had the door handle in his hand, he cried out, suddenly also excited: The one woman was half-naked - in the presence of the Imperial Baron!

I demand, the cavalry captain shouted in a strong voice, that Herr von Studmann be taken to a humane prison!

He hurried after the fleeing doctor.

I hold you responsible, doctor!

I refuse, the doctor shouted over his shoulder, I refuse any responsibility for this orgy and its participants!

And he crashed into a side passage.

The cavalry captain rushed after him.

He is sick, doctor!

The doctor had achieved his goal. Easily the old gentleman jumped into the open paternoster elevator.

He's drunk, he shouted, already with his feet at the belly level of the onrushing opponent. He would have liked to force him to perform his duties - in vain, the next elevator cell appeared in front of him, and the doctor, oblivious to his duties, had finally escaped his gaze.

Von Prackwitz, who with all his zeal had achieved nothing - except the petty decree of Pyramidon - for his friend, uttered a curse and made his way back to the Rollstube. But the confusion of the white corridors with the same doors made him perplexed. On the hunt for the doctor he had not paid attention to which hooks this hare had hit, he went searching, uncertainly back and forth - once he must have examined all the gears. If he only persevered, he also found the door, he remembered exactly having left it open.

He went and he went. White doors, white corridors. His sense of place wanted to tell him that he was getting farther and farther away from his destination, but eventually the basements of even a large hotel must come to an end. But there were now the stairs. Had he passed a staircase earlier? Up or down? He descended, convinced that this was wrong, and encountered an elderly female, with a stern look behind a klemmer, arranging laundry in cupboards in complete solitude.

The young lady turned at the sound of his footsteps and seriously eyed the stranger.

Von Prackwitz, aware of wandering here quite unauthorized, greeted very politely. The laundry keeper bowed her head seriously without a word. Von Prackwitz decided: "Oh, please, how do I get to the roller room here?

His polite smile did nothing to soften the lady's seriousness. She seemed to ponder, then made a sweeping hand gesture: We have so many wheelhouses here ...

Prackwitz tried to describe his to her without having to mention Studmann. There are laundry baskets in the corner, he described. Oh right! And a chaise longue with blue floral upholstery. Quite torn, he added, not without bitterness.

Again she thought. Finally, she said dismissively, "I don't think we have a faulty chaise longue. With us, everything is always repaired right away.

Now this was not actually the science that Prackwitz had wanted in response to his questions. But he had always dealt with people in his former as well as in his present profession, and so he was well acquainted with this species, which never knows how to answer a question exactly.

Nevertheless, he tried again. Where do you think the hotel lobby is, he asked.

Promptly came the answer: The guests from the hotel are completely forbidden to enter the service rooms.

Goose, said the cavalry captain seriously.

How -?! she almost shouted and completely lost rigor and poise, got something chicken-like shooed.

Completely or better yet strictly forbidden, improved the cavalryman. Not entirely. - Good evening then and thank you very much!

He greeted with dignity, as if she were the commander of the regiment and he a young lieutenant. He departed. Completely or totally confused, she was left behind.

The cavalry captain was walking more calmly now, the little incident had refreshed him. Again, he had achieved nothing for his friend, as he noted with regret, but at least something like that did him good. Moreover, he was now walking on carpets, and if perhaps he was getting farther and farther away from Studmann, he was possibly approaching inhabited areas of the hotel.

Suddenly he was standing in front of a long row of doors made of matt waxed oak, solid doors that inspired confidence.

'Cash register I' he read. 'Cash register II' he read. He went on. There came the company treasury, purchasing A and purchasing B, employee issues, in-house counsel, doctor.

The cavalry captain looked disapprovingly at the doctor's sign, then shrugged and went on his way.

'Secretariat'.

'Higher up,' the cavalry captain decided.

'Director Hasse'.

He reflected. No. Next. Even further.

'Director Kainz'. 'Director Lange'. 'Director Niedergesäß'.

'Very attractive, no doubt.'

He considered. There had to be something attractive about a director Niedergesäß - a person who became a director in spite of such names was necessarily eminently capable.

But then the cavalry captain remembered that he really wanted to show it to the people, and he went one more door. He had done right, on this door hung a sign 'Generaldirektor Vogel'.

'Let this bird sing to me,' thought the cavalryman, knocking shortly and entering.

Behind the desk sat a gray, sallow, tall, bulky man dictating something into the machine to a very pretty young secretary. He barely looked up when the cavalry captain introduced himself.

Pleaseangenehmbittenehmensieplatz ... he said hastily, with the distracted, insubstantial politeness of men who have to meet new people all the time for their jobs. One moment please. - How far were we, miss? - Smoke, please, help yourself!

The phone rang.

Very quietly he spoke into the machine, but very clearly: bird. - Yes, bird itself. - His doctor comes? - What is his name? How -? Spell! What is his name? Schröck? Privy Councillor Schröck? - When is he coming? In five minutes? Fine, immediately to me. - Yes, yes, it can be done. - I just have something to dictate and a short meeting - he looked at the Rittmeister thoughtfully, absentmindedly over the phone ... three minutes. - Beautiful. So by no means up to 37, but to me. Thank you.

The receiver was hung up hastily, but carefully.

How far were we, miss?

The Miss mumbled something, the General Manager started dictating again.

'Three minutes you give me,' the cavalry captain thought angrily. 'Well, wait, you're supposed to be wrong! I will show you ...'

His chain of thought snapped. He heard a name, paused, listened more closely ...

The director dictated hurriedly, tonelessly: We are extremely sorry that Mr. von Studmann, whose human and professional qualities we have come to appreciate so much during his one and a half years of work in our company ...

The general manager caught his breath ...

One moment! exclaimed the cavalry captain briskly and stood up.

One moment! said the director tonelessly. I'll be ready in a moment. - How far were we, Miss -?

No, Miss, protested the cavalry captain. Please - if I understood correctly, are you dictating a testimonial for Mr. von Studmann? Mr. von Studmann is my friend.

Excellent, said the director gray. This is how you will take care of him. We were embarrassed ...

Herr von Studmann is lying on a torn chaise longue in a platted room, the cavalry captain complained bitterly. Not a soul cares about him.

Very unfortunate, the director politely admitted. An oversight that I apologize for due to the momentary disarray created by the event. - Miss, call. Mr. von Studmann is to be taken inconspicuously to his room. Inconspicuous, Miss, please, inconspicuous!

They want to kick Mr. von Studmann out! the cavalry captain shouted indignantly and pointed to the shorthand pad. You don't convict a defendant without hearing him.

The young lady was on the phone. The general manager said calmly, grayly: "Mr. von Studmann will be taken to his room immediately.

You may not dismiss him without further ado! exclaimed von Prackwitz.

We are not dismissing him, the general manager objected.

Von Prackwitz had the impression that this gray colossus could not be reached by any excitement, any request, any human feeling.

We grant Mr. von Studmann an extended leave of absence.

Herr von Studmann doesn't need a vacation! assured the cavalry captain, clueless but vehement. But he already felt his anger melting before this unassailable, passionless gray.

Mr. von Studmann needs a vacation, the other insisted. His nerves are under attack.

You condemn him without hearing, the cavalry captain shouted more weakly.

In the room occupied by Baron von Bergen, the general manager said monotonously, as if reading a protocol, we found nineteen champagne bottles, fifteen of them emptied. Four bottles of cognac - empty. Two boys of the hotel - completely drunk. Two other male, but adult employees of the hotel - completely drunk. A poorly dressed maid of the hotel - completely drunk. A cleaning lady employed on a temporary basis - completely drunk.

The guest, Baron von Bergen - completely sober, but with his eye beaten blue, but almost senseless as a result of several brutal blows over the head. You probably know where we found your friend Mr. von Studmann.

But somewhat embarrassed, Rittmeister von Prackwitz bowed his head.

On the one hand, said the general manager no longer quite so colorless, honors you friend loyalty. On the other hand, I ask you: does an educated person with healthy nerves participate in such bacchanal?

But there must have been a special cause! exclaimed von Prackwitz in despair. Without that, Mr. von Studmann would never ...

Can you think of any particular cause for which you would participate in such an orgy, Herr von ...?

Prackwitz, helped from Prackwitz.

Mr. von Prackwitz. It must be understandable to you that we cannot continue to employ such a compromised man in our company. Already because of the employees ...

There was a short, warlike knock.

The door flew open, and in rushed a small, saber-legged old man with a high, beautiful forehead, sparkling blue eyes, and a yellowing full beard that must have once been bright red. He was followed more slowly by a stocky, stout man whose jacket sat taut over his shoulders like a prizefighter.

Do you still have it?! the reddened old man shouted in a crowing voice. Where do you have it?! For God's sake, don't let him get away! Turk, take care! Frolic!!! Do not let him go! Run! - For twenty-four hours I've been racing all over Berlin after this fellow! I don't think there's a hooker joint in this miserable town that I haven't stuck my woebegone nose into! Damn!!

He had grasped the said nose with his hand and looked breathlessly at those frozen in the circle. Behind him still kept, without cavorting, the four-haired man in the too tight jacket, presumably therefore Mr. Turk.

The general manager was the first to emerge from his torpor - probably his profession had hardened him against the wildest spawns of human species.

Bird, he introduced himself. Presumably I am speaking to Privy Councillor Schröck?

No, I am talking to you! cried the old man. He let go of his nose. The transition from calm to the strongest outburst was so sudden that everyone - except the imperturbable Mr. Turk - was startled. There must have been an irrepressible temper in this saber-legged old man. I've been asking you for three minutes if this guy is still here!

If you mean the Reichsfreiherr Baron von Bergen, gray and lost the general manager started again, so he is to my knowledge in room 37 ...

Turk! shouted the Privy Councillor Schröck, did you hear it: Room 37 -? Go upstairs, bring me down the infamous brat as he walks and stands. Watch out, you know his antics! Remember that he locked your colleague in his room ...

The four-haired man nodded grumpily: I already can't get him out. He shouldn't have done something like that with me, Mr. Privy Councillor ...

He slowly pushed his way out the door.

An excellent lunatic nurse! muttered the Privy Councillor. A man without a trace of sentimentality! And with suddenly newly awakened concern: Surely he won't have run away again -?

No, no, the general manager carefully reassured the mad doctor. He cannot leave. Unfortunately, some things have happened ... With a glance at the cavalry captain: I'll report to you immediately when I see this gentleman ...

With a relieved sigh, Geheimrat Schröck let himself sink into an armchair. He dried his forehead. So he can't leave. Thank God! Something has happened. Wherever the fellow goes, something falls forward. With a sigh of surrender: Police? Prosecutor?

No, no, hurried the general manager Vogel, that will not be necessary. The Lord will surely make amends. With a nasty, hurried look at the cavalry captain, "We'll make up for any damage. One of our employees unfortunately forgot himself to the point of beating the Baron.

The old man jumped up from his chair. Where is he? Who is it? Towards the cavalry captain: Is it you?

He apparently threw a champagne bottle at his head! complained the general manager in pale but noncommittal sadness.

Excellent! cried the old man. A champagne bottle - great! You do not -? Your friend? Let me see your friend! I have to thank him. It does not work? Why is it not possible?

Your fosterling seems to have gotten my friend - and half a dozen others - mysteriously drunk.

There you go, said Privy Councillor Schröck. So the usual mess! He sat down surrendered. I will fix this, no one shall be harmed. You there, my dear Director General, seem to be still blinded by the title 'Reichsfreiherr' and so on. Let me tell you, this Reichsfreiherr is the windiest, most depraved, meanest, most sadistic brat in the world! And cowardly too!!!

Privy Councillor! the General Director asked formally.

It is so! sparkled the Privy Councillor. He imagines that because he has been incapacitated for extravagance, and because he was once acquitted in a wicked matter on the §51, he can now do as he pleases. Lazy and without respect, without a trace of human feeling ... It flared up anew. In the morning and in the evening he would have to be beaten, he would have to be put in prison, at least in a state insane asylum ... his jokes would be driven out of him!

But he is in your sanatorium - a poor sick man! pleaded the general manager.

Alas! scolded the privy councilor. Unfortunately still. I offer him to my colleagues like sour beer, but no one wants him, despite him being my highest paying patient. Come on, patient -! Simply a vicious monkey! - If I now take him back to my asylum, of course to the closed ward, behind bars and secure doors, he'll keep quiet for four weeks, he'll keep quiet for eight weeks - especially if your friend has beaten him up properly ...

A quarter of an hour ago, he was almost out of his mind, said the general manager, who swung in.

Excellent! - But then the oats sting him again. He tortures defenseless patients to the point of blood, steals cigarettes, irritates all the nurses, drives me and my assistants crazy ... And then he's not stupid, he's devilishly clever, then he breaks out again. We can pay attention as much as we want, he always finds a fool to dupe ... He pumps himself money, he steals it ... And I can't do anything, the old man gritted. I can't get rid of him. The law for him is: not in full possession of his mental powers ...

He suddenly sat there old and quite exhausted: "For twenty-four hours I have been chasing after him in my car. The Privy Council looked around the circle, tired. If only I could get rid of him! he moaned again in despair. But possibly he will then come to freedom - no, I cannot justify it. He reflected: let's at least try the last one, the cost. Maybe his mother - he only has one mother, unfortunately - will be able to pay for him one day. Mr. Director, may I ask for a bill, a statement ...

Yes, said the director hesitantly, there has been plenty of alcohol consumed, champagne, cognac ...

Nonsense, the Privy Councillor said angrily. These are trifles. Sparkling wine! Cognac!!! No, every injured party is entitled to compensation. I hear of half a dozen people he got drunk .... Your friend, for example -?

Hans Fallada   -292-   Wolf among Wolves

I don't know if my friend ... von Prackwitz began hesitantly.

For heaven's sake!" the Privy Councilor was furious. Don't be a fool! Forgive me, of course I shouldn't say that, but really don't be a fool. The more costs are incurred, the more likely it is that the mother will really lock the boy up in a mental institution one day. You are doing a service to humanity ...

The Rittmeister looked first at the general manager, then at the typewriter with the discharge certificate still clamped in it.

However, my friend, sub-director and receptionist here, is to be fired by the hotel management here for getting drunk on duty ... he said hesitantly.

Excellent! shouted the Privy Councillor, but this time the General Director interrupted.

I'm afraid I have to disagree with Herr von Prackwitz, he said hurriedly. We grant Mr. von Studmann a longer leave, say a quarter, say even half a year. During this time, Mr. von Studmann will easily find another position given his efficiency. We dismiss him, spoke the general director energetically, but gray, not for drunkenness on duty. We ask him to look for another job, because a hotel man must not attract attention under any circumstances. Mr. von Studmann unfortunately attracted a lot of attention when he fell down the hall stairs in front of many employees and even more guests, poorly dressed and completely drunk.

There is no doubt, said the Privy Councillor with satisfaction, that apart from compensation for a lost position, compensation for pain and suffering is also an option. I am sincerely glad, I see light. I should not be surprised if this would first give the boy Bergen the rest. How do I reach your friend? With you? Thank you. I'll make a note of your address. You will hear from me in two to three days. Really excellent. By the way, we naturally pay stable value. - I assure you, there can not be enough costs. - Oh, don't worry about it! Do you think I'm embarrassed?! I am embarrassed the deubel! Does not hurt anyone, unfortunately.

The cavalry captain stood up. Strange was this life. Here, someone had really fallen down the stairs once and thus got rid of his worries. Herr von Studmann could come to Neulohe, a carefree man, because of him paying guest, he was no longer alone.

He said goodbye; once again the Privy Councillor regretted not being able to shake his friend's hand for his excellent report.

When von Prackwitz wanted to leave the door, it opened, and in staggered, half supported by the orderly Türke, half led away, a red, yellow flamed being, pitiful to look at with the blue beaten eye, the swollen face. To look at contemptuously with the cowardly creeping look.

Bergen! crowed the voice of the privy councillor as garish as cockcrow. Bergen, come here a minute!

The coward crumpled; in his pajamas, resplendent and wailing, he fell to his knees.

Privy Councilor! he pleaded. Do not hurt me, do not send me to a lunatic asylum, I did not do anything, they were quite happy to drink the champagne ...

Bergen! declared the Privy Council. First, you will be deprived of your cigarettes.

Privy Councillor, please, don't do that! You know I can't stand it. I can not live without smoking! And I also just shot into the ceiling when the gentleman did not want to drink ...

Von Prackwitz quietly pulled the door closed behind him. It was a double, a padded door, the wailing of the miserable guy, this wailing of a child without the purity and innocence of the child, had died away.

'If only I were back in Neulohe!' thought von Prackwitz. 'I think Berlin sucks. 'No, it's not just the banknote machine gone great,' he continued to think, looking down the clean hallway with its dark, neat, oak doors. 'It all still looks like neat, clean living, but it's rotten.' Pissed off. I wonder if it's still the war that's in their bones. I don't know. And anyway, I don't understand it.'

He walked slowly down the hall, came into the hall, asked for the friend's room. An elevator took him up to the roof. Von Studmann sat on the edge of the bed, his head in his hands.

I have a disgusting buzzing head, Prackwitz, he said looking up. Do you have time to walk with me for half an hour in the fresh air?

I have all the time in the world, the cavalry captain suddenly said cheerfully. For you and for fresh air. Allow me to tie a collar around you first ...

06 02

The little field inspector Meier, his head thick and stupid from intoxication, had thrown himself on his bed just as he was: in dirt-spattered shoes, his clothes wet with rain. Outside the open window it was still rushing from the sky. From the cowshed, from the pigsty sounded scolding, Meier half listened, he liked or not.

'What are they doing?" he thought. 'What do they have? Come on, I want to sleep. I have to sleep, forget; when I wake up, it's all not true.'

He put his hand in front of his eyes, now it became dark around him. Oh, it was good, this darkness! Darkness was black, black was nothingness; where nothingness is, nothing has been, nothing has happened, nothing has screwed up.

But the dark becomes gray, and the gray becomes lighter. Out of the lighter it comes off: there stands the table, there stands the bottle, there stand the glasses ... there lies the letter!

'Oh God, what am I going to do?' thinks little Meier, pressing his hand tighter against his eyes. Yes, it's going black again. But out of the black turn luminous wheels. In many colors they rotate, circling faster and faster. He gets dizzy, nauseous.

Now he sits half in bed and stares across the still daylit room. It disgusts him, he knows it far too well, from the ever-smelling toilet bucket next to the vanity to the over-seen nude photos of girls around the mirror, cut out from all sorts of magazines and pinned into the wallpaper.

His room disgusts him, his condition disgusts him as much as what happened; he wants to do something, to get out of his present situation, to be something completely different. But he sits there now, motionless, with a puffy face, a hanging, wet lower lip and bulging eyes - he can't do anything. Everything will come over him, he just has to keep still, wait - and he didn't mean any harm after all! If only he could at least sleep -!

Thankfully - as a desired little change - there is a knock on the door of the adjoining office. He roars hoarsely, "Come in!" and when the knocker hesitates, he shouts even louder: "Come in, you ox!

Immediately, however, he gets a fright: perhaps it is someone he is not allowed to call 'ox', the privy council or the madam, then he has already buttered it up again - ouch!

But it is only the old people's bailiff Kowalewski.

What's wrong?" Meier yells at him, glad to have found someone to vent his anger on.

I just wanted to ask, Inspector, says the old man humbly, his cap in his hand. We have received a telegram from our daughter in Berlin, she is coming tomorrow morning on the ten o'clock train ...

So that's what you wanted to ask, Kowalewski, Meier says with a sneer. Well, now you've asked it, now you can go again.

It is only because of the luggage, says the people's bailiff. Do you think a car will go to the railroad tomorrow?

Sure, sure, says Meier. Tomorrow, a whole lot of cars are going to the railroad. In Ostade and in Meienburg and in Frankfurt for sure.

I only mean, Kowalewski insistently explains, whether one of our wagons is going to the railroad, which can take their luggage?

Oh, that's what you mean! Meier scoffs. You are a mighty fine toff, Vogt, to talk about 'our wagons'!

The old people's bailiff does not give up courage yet. He has seen generations of inspectors, this one is certainly the worst of them all. But a poor man has to ask a hundred times before a mighty one says yes once, and sometimes the little Meier is different. That's just the way he is, he likes to have fun with people, you can't hold that against him.

It's only because of the suitcase, Inspector, he asks. Walking doesn't bother Sophie at all, she likes to walk.

And she'd rather lie down for a long time, wouldn't you, Kowalewski? grins Meier.

The old man stands there calmly, he does not contort his face. Maybe one of the farmers is also going to the railroad, he thinks to himself half aloud.

But now Meier is satisfied. He vented his anger a bit, he felt that he was not completely without power.

Well, get out of here, Kowalewski, he says graciously. The reapers and the cavalry captain will arrive with the ten o'clock train, so there will be room for your Sophinka. - Get lost, old raven, you stink! he suddenly shouts again, and with a murmured thank you and good evening the bailiff leaves.

Meier, Negermeier, is again alone with himself and with his thoughts, and immediately his mood falls. 'If only I could at least sleep!' he grumbles to himself again. 'Any carrion can sleep when it has drunk so much, but not me, I'm always unlucky, of course!'

The thought occurs to him that perhaps he has not drunk enough. When he warbled off in the inn, he was actually quite pretty dhn, only now it's all faded away. He could go to the jug again, but he's too lazy to do it. In addition, he would then have to pay for everything he has taken, and he dreads the offsetting. Well, the Amanda can certainly be seen again tonight, then she can run and get him another bottle of schnapps. At least she has something to do, he can't smell women today. He's fed up with them nowadays - if the Weio hadn't been so scared of him, he would never have done all those stupid things! But something like that must drive a guy crazy!

Meier has risen ponderously from the soiled, damp bed and lurches giddily around the parlor. Many things go through his mind. For example, that the forester told him to pack his bags and make him go away.

The suitcases are on top of the closet. He has two carry-on cases, an ordinary break-thing made of pasted cardboard and a snazzy leather case he took from the last position. He was standing there like that on the floor. Meier puts his head back and squints complacently up at the suitcase: he is always happy about this cheap acquisition.

When you see suitcases, you think of travel. And when you think of travel, travel money comes to mind. All by himself, without even glancing through the ajar office door, Meier remembers the safe next door, a massive, green-painted block whose gilded arabesques have turned a dirty yellow over the years.

Usually the cavalry captain has the key to this safe and only hands over the necessary money before each payment or other expenditure. Meier is completely reliable in money matters, but the Rittmeister is a big man and suspicious. It would serve him right if he were to fall in thoroughly with his mistrust for once!

Meier pushes open the door to the office with his shoulder and plants himself thoughtfully in front of the money cabinet. Last night, the cavalry captain counted out the stock for him, even twice - there is quite a nice lump of money in the cupboard, more than Inspector Meier can earn in three years. Meier fingers the key to the safe in his pocket. But - he doesn't take it out. But - he does not unlock the cabinet.

Nah, so stupid! thinks Meier.

What he does otherwise is all well and good, he may get kicked out for it, but he won't go to jail for it. Fly out, it doesn't matter. After a while, you always get a new position; no boss ever writes what got you fired in your report card. But Meier has a lively antipathy toward Kittchen.

I'll only get the money in a week or a fortnight," Meier thinks to himself, "and then I'll be broke and won't be able to take on a new job because they'll be looking for me. Nah, I'd rather not -!'

Nevertheless, he remains standing in front of the safe for a long time - it fascinates him after all.

'Get out of all this muck!' he thinks. 'They kitschen long not all. In Berlin you should be able to get false papers cheaply. I just want to know where. I wonder how long it will take before the lieutenant finds out I didn't deliver the letter -? Well, tonight the two miss each other for the time being. Will you have to go to bed hungry, dear Weio -!'

He grins gleefully.

There is another knock, and Meier quickly steps away from the safe and leans as casually as possible against the wall before he calls in - this time in a mannerly manner. But the circumstance would not have been necessary at all, it is also this time nobody right, but merely the waiting, the coachwoman with the seven brats, the Hartig, who comes in.

Dinner, inspector, she says.

Meier doesn't want her to see the dirty bed in his room (Amanda can fix it up later!), he doesn't want to make a stink. Put it on the desk there, he says. What's up?

I don't know what the women have with you, says Hartig and takes a lid off the bowl. Now the Armgard from over there also starts ... Freshly roasted meat and red cabbage in the evening for the inspector ...

Shame! says Meier. I would prefer a herring. - Äx - all that fat! - Because I have lifted one.

You can see that, confirms Hartig. That you men can not stop drinking! What if we women did the same? - Was the Amanda with you?

I wo! I don't need them to drink! He laughs. Suddenly, he's all perky and chipper. What's it like, Hartig? Do you like the grub? I'm not eating today.

Hartig beams. My old man will laugh! I'll quickly cook us some potatoes, then it's enough for him and me!

Nah! says Meier stretched from his wall. This is for you, Hartig, not for your ole boy. Do you think I'm feeding this to forces?! So blue! Nah, if you want the grub, you'll have to eat it here. And in a moment!

He stares at her.

Here -? asks Hartig, staring at Negermeier again.

Their voices have both become different, almost quiet.

Here! replies Negermeier.

Then I want to close the windows and draw the curtains a little," says Hartig more quietly. If anyone sees me eating here ...

Meier does not answer her, but he follows her with his eyes as she closes the two windows and carefully draws the curtains. Lock it, too! he says softly.

She looks at him, then does it. She sits down in front of the tray that is on the desk. Well, I'm supposed to like it! she says with made cheerfulness.

He does not answer again. He watches her carefully as she puts the meat on the plate, then potatoes, then red cabbage. Now she spoons the sauce over it ...

Hartig, listen! he says softly.

She asks the same question and doesn't look up, seemingly preoccupied with her food.

What I wanted to say ... he says stretched. Yes, you - is your blouse actually front or back buttoning?

In front, she says quietly, does not look up, but begins to cut the meat. Want to see?

Yes, he says. And impatiently: Just get going!

You have to do it yourself, she replies. Otherwise, my food will get cold. - Oh you ... ah ... Yes, you sweet ... the beautiful food ... yes ... yes ...

3

Weio von Prackwitz sits with her mother at dinner.

The servant Räder stands at the sideboard with a serious attitude. Wheels, although little over twenty, belongs to the serious servant type. He is completely imbued with the feeling that his master will one day move out of this 'hovel' into the castle of the old people over there, that he will then no longer be the servant there, but the 'butler', with an apprentice servant under him. Therefore, he also sees the old Privy Councillor and his wife - in spite of impeccably observed external forms - as people who withhold from his rule something that is actually due to it. But above all, he hates old Elias over there, who commands the family silver - how to be called Elias! The servant Räder is called Hubert - and that's how his master calls him.

Hubert has one eye on the table to see if they need anything there, and both ears on the conversation. Despite the fact that he does not make a fuss about his somewhat wrinkled face, he is filled with great joy at the way in which the madam is swindling the madam. Hubert has little to do in the small household besides the cook Armgard and the girl Lotte, so he has made an occupation out of experiencing everything, seeing everything, knowing everything. Hubert knows a lot - for example, he knows exactly how the madam spent her afternoon. What the madam does not know.

Did you also check on Grandpa's geese this afternoon? Hubert hears Frau von Prackwitz ask.

Frau Eva von Prackwitz is a very good-looking woman, perhaps a touch too full, but you don't notice that until she's standing next to the long, lean Rittmeister. She has all the sensual appeal of a woman who likes to be a woman, who is happy to be a woman, who, moreover, loves country life and for whom the land seems to thank this love with inexhaustible freshness.

Weio makes a reproachful face: "But Mom, there was a thunderstorm this afternoon!

Hubert understands: Miss Violet is playing the very little girl tonight; she likes to do that, especially when she's done something particularly adult. That way, their parents don't get the wrong - means right - ideas.

You're really doing me a favor, Violet, says Frau von Prackwitz, if you fit in well with Grandpa's geese. You know Dad gets so annoyed when the geese go into his vetches. And the thunderstorm didn't start until six!

If I were a goose, I wouldn't want to be in Grandpa's old, damp park with the sour grass either, explains Weio, still with a pout. I think the park stinks!

Servant Hubert, knowing how often and with pleasure the madam secretly stays in the secret council park, is highly enthusiastic about the precautionary naivety of this answer.

But Weio - stink and at the table! Her gaze passes (with smiling calm) to the servant Räder, who makes an irreproachable, if already completely unyoung and wrinkled face.

Hans Fallada   -302-   Wolf among Wolves

Well, mom, I'm not going in, I think he st ... smells like corpses ...

No, Weio! The madam taps the table very vigorously with her fork handle. But now it is enough. Sometimes I really think you could be a bit more grown up.

Yes, Mom? Were you more grown up when you were as grown up as I am?

At this question, Weio makes a completely radiant, completely innocent face - nevertheless, the servant Räder considers whether this little simpleton has perhaps heard something ringing of the youthful pranks of Mrs. Mama. There is a rumor about the old privy councillor who beat a peasant boy out of his daughter's bedroom window. Maybe this rumor is even true, in any case Hubert thinks that the next question of the madam fits very well to this rumor.

It's: What did you have to talk about with Inspector Meier for so long this afternoon?

Och! says Weio throwing away and makes another scoop. The old negermeier! Suddenly she laughs. Just think, Mom, all the girls and women here in the village are supposed to run after him - and yet he is as ugly as ... ah, I don't know how ol' Abraham -! (Abraham is the goat kept in the horse stable, which according to old cavalryman beliefs is supposed to drive out all diseases).

The dessert, Hubert! admonishes the madam calmly, but with quite dangerously twinkling eyes.

Wheels marches out of the room, though not without regret. Miss Weio slipped, now she's sure to get her head washed. She has laid it on a bit thick in her exuberance, but the madam is not completely foolish.

Hubert liked to hear what the madam was saying now, and especially what the Fraulein was answering. But Hubert doesn't listen at doors, he marches straight into the kitchen. If you have a manly brain, there are many ways to learn something, you don't have to shake the trust of the rulers in an exemplary servant by such eavesdropping.

In the kitchen, the old forester Kniebusch sits waiting at the kitchen table.

Good evening, Mr. Räder, he says very politely. For the silent servant Räder, who lives completely for himself, is taken for a power. Is dinner over already?

Dessert, Armgard! Räder says and starts to arrange the dishes on the tray. Good evening, Mr. Kniebusch. Who do you want to talk to? The Herr Rittmeister will not be back until tomorrow.

I wanted the madam once, says forester Kniebusch cautiously. After much deliberation, he came to the conclusion that he would better utilize his science with the older generation. The madam is really too young to be of any use to such an old man.

I will report you, Mr. Kniebusch, Räder says.

Mr. Wheels! Kniebusch asks cautiously. If it could be done in such a way that Miss Weio would not be there -?

The wrinkled face of Rader becomes even more wrinkled. To buy time, he drives the cook: Why don't you close it, Armgard? A hundred times I've told you to garnish the cheese platter before I get there!

In this heat! sneers the cook, who hates the servant. All those butter globules would stick together!

You take the butter out of the freezer at the last moment! But if you just now cut the cheese -! And to the forester half loudly: Why shouldn't the lady be there?

The forester becomes visibly embarrassed: Yes, you know ... i thought so ... It's not all for young girls after all ...

Räder looks at the embarrassed man with idolatrous seriousness. What is not yet for young girls, Mr. Kniebusch? he asks, but without all noticeable curiosity.

Kniebusch blushes with the effort of inventing a lie. Well, Mr. Räder, you understand, when you're so young, and then there's the rut....

Wheels feast on his embarrassment. Now there is no rut! he says contemptuously. Well, I get it. Thank you. Uniform - U-ni-form is the watchword!

He looks at the shattered and confused forester with his expressionless, fishy eye. Then he turns to the cook: Well, finally, Armgard! - But if the madam scolds, I'll tell her whose fault it is. - Please do not address me! I am not talking to you at all!

He walks out of the kitchen, serving board in hand, serious, unyoung, rather mysterious.

We'll talk later, Mr. Kniebusch, he nods and disappears, leaving the requested registration completely in the dark.

What a monkey imagines!" scolds Armgard, the cook, behind him. Just don't get involved with him, Mr. Kniebusch! He just eavesdrops on you - and afterwards he gossips everything to the cavalry captain.

Is he always like this with you? the forester inquires.

Always! she shouts indignantly. Never a kind word to Lotte or me! Herr Rittmeister is nowhere near as fine as the monkey. Do you think he'll eat at the same table with us?! She stares at the forester, who mumbles something unintelligible in embarrassment. Nah, plate in hand he goes to his chamber! I think Mr. Kniebusch, she whispers mysteriously, is different at all. He has nothing at all in mind with women. This one is ...

Yes -? the forester asks expectantly.

No, I don't want to have anything to do with something like that, Armgard declares energetically. Do you think he even goes for the Rittmeister's cigarettes?

Yes, he does? says the forester full of hope. That's what all servants do! Elias also always smokes the old man's cigars. I smell that because sometimes the Privy Council gives me one.

What?! You know about the Elias?! I'll rub that in the old geezer's face! So much for stealing cigars from the lordship - and mobbing me because I didn't properly kick off my shoes at the castle entrance -!

For God's sake, Armgard! No, no, don't tell him anything! I could be wrong! The old man is getting ahead of himself in his fears. It is certainly a very different cigar, and you also said that the cavalry captain's Hubert smokes cigarettes ...

I did not say that! Just the opposite I said! That he doesn't smoke and that he doesn't drink, and that he doesn't listen at the doors, that he thinks he's too good for that, the stupid rascal ...

Thank you very much! it buzzes, and the two of them look deeply shocked into the face of the servant Räder ('Olles Froschgesicht!' thinks Armgard angrily). So I am a stupid rascal. It's good to know that, how people think about you. - Go to the madam now, Armgard, she wants to talk to you. Not that I would have slapped you for your cheese plate, you are far too stupid for that! But you can tell her that I am a stupid rascal in your eyes .... Come on, Mr. Kniebusch!

And obediently, but very depressed by all the complications of daily life, the forester follows him, squinting sheepishly at the cook Armgard, who is high red with tears.

The chamber of the servant Räder is only a narrow towel, in the basement of the villa, between the coal cellar and the laundry room. This in itself is a reason for the servant Räder to resent the servant Elias, because

Elias has a real, big, two-floored room on the upper floor of the castle, very comfortably furnished with old furniture. The servant Hubert's chamber, however, has only an iron cot, an iron wash stand, an iron old folding chair from the garden and an old, rickety cupboard made of spruce. Nothing reveals that a human being lives in this chamber. No article of clothing is visible, no small object of use of the resident; not even soap and towel can be seen at the wash stand, because Hubert Räder washes himself in the bathroom.

So, says the servant Räder, but only leans the door. So - you can still sit on the chair now until she comes. Then stand up and make room for her.

Who is coming -? Kniebusch asks, confused.

You shouldn't quack so much, Mr. Kniebusch, the servant explains with serious disapproval. A man does not quack - especially not with females.

I didn't say anything, the forester defends himself.

Now, of course, she has to wash her face first because she was crying, says the wrinkled idol. But then when she is with the gracious lady, she comes.

Who is coming, who is with the madam? asks the forester, completely confused.

A uniform is a uniform, the servant instructs him. My livery does not apply, of course, and neither does your green one, because you are merely a private forester. If you were a state forester, that would be different again.

Kniebusch says forlornly: Yes, of course, he still hopes that he will eventually understand something of Räder's riddles.

A civilian should not mix with the uniforms, the servant announces sternly. He thinks for a long time, his forehead in many wrinkles. Then he pushes the door open a little.

He listens. Now he nods, walks across the chamber toward the forester, and says quietly, full of reproach, "You are a civilian, Mr. Kniebusch, and you wanted to mingle with the uniforms.

But no, exclaims the forester in horror.

You haven't noticed that yet, Mr. Kniebusch, says the servant, and has returned to his listening post by the ajar door, which the Privy Councillor likes best?

No. Why? wonders the forester. I don't know at all what you actually want, Mr. Räder.

Do you really not know?

No. However, I believe its Forst.

The servant nods. Yes, he doesn't want to give them away before he dies. - And then to whom does he bequeath them?

He looks expectantly at the forester.

There is the old madam, says the forester thoughtfully, and then there is the son in Birnbaum. And here is the Herr Rittmeister ...

He considers the case.

Well, who is he going to give the forest to? the servant asks patronizingly, like one asks a retarded schoolchild for something very easy. Or does he have it divided, into two pieces or three?

Share - his forest?! The knee bush is completely contempt. No, you're not imagining things, Mr. Räder! I think he would still come out of the grave and tear out the boundary stones if they divided the forest after his death. But he will have already written down how the forest is to be.

And what will he have written down, Mr. Kniebusch? the servant persistently continues to probe. About the old madam?

Excluded! Whereas she always says she doesn't go into the woods because of snakes. No, Mr. Wheels, out of the question at all.

Or the Birnbaumer?

I don't think so either, says the forester. He always scolds him because he's too refined and is forever coming after money - and now he's bought himself a racing car ... 'That he can run away from his debts!' the old man scolded.

So the old man already knows about the racing car," says Räder thoughtfully. I'm sure you told him that, Mr. Kniebusch.

The old man wants to protest in high red, but Hubert doesn't even pay attention. He concludes: "Then the forest is inherited by the lady up here. And he points to the ceiling with his thumb.

But he doesn't like the captain at all, does he? the forester asks anxiously. And the thing with the geese doesn't end well either.

Who then inherits the forest? insists the servant.

Yes, I do not know ... says the forester, confused. He still has the sister children in Hinterpommern, but ...

Doesn't he have a grandchild? asks the servant.

Who -? The forester's mouth is open. Do you really think so? But Miss Violet is only fifteen ... The servant's stare does not change, and the forester considers aloud: Admittedly, she is the only one he takes on the decency, that much must be true ... And when he measures the wood, she always has to come along, too, with folding rule and ruler - oh God, Mr. Wheels, and nobody knows that yet, and the madam may not know it herself yet ...

And you wanted to mingle with the uniforms, Mr. Kniebusch, the servant Räder notes with disdain.

But before the forester could still protest, there is a hasty clatter in the corridor, and Weio comes in.

Thank God, we made it after all. I could and could not leave! Armgard cried to Mama that you were always so mean to her, Hubert - are you really so mean -?

No, Hubert answers seriously. I'm just strict with her, and I don't mess with women's rooms at all.

God, Hubert, how serious you look again! Like a carp from the ponds. Do you actually drink a lot of vinegar? I am also just a woman.

No, Hubert explains. Once you are a lady, and then you are my master, so commoning with you is out of the question, madam.

Thank you, Hubert. They are really great. I think you are bursting with conceit and pride once again.

She looks at him very amused with her slightly protruding, shining eyes. Suddenly she becomes serious, she whispers mysteriously: "Is it true what Armgard told Mama, that you are an ogre?

The servant Räder looks at the curious girl with his fishy eyes unmoved. Not a trace of color rises in his gray, wrinkled cheeks.

But Armgard did not say that in front of your ears, madam, he states steadfastly. There you were listening at the door again.

Violet is not the least bit embarrassed either. The forester is amazed to see how familiar the strange couple is with each other. The wheel is even smarter than I thought. I have to be even more careful of him,' he thinks to himself.

But Weio just laughs. Don't be silly, Hubert! If I don't listen a little bit, I don't learn anything at all. Mom never tells me anything, and when I asked Dad the other day in the meadow, when we saw the stork, whether it was really true, he ran all red. God, poor dad! How embarrassed he was! - And so you are an ogre?

There is also the forester Kniebusch, deflects wheels unshaken their interest.

Yes, of course. Good evening, Kniebusch. What on earth is going on? Hubert acts so mysterious, but Hubert always acts mysterious. What's the matter with you?

God, madam," says the forester miserably, for he sees with horror the moment coming when he must report. And already everything gets confused for him, and he no longer knows what he really saw and what he only suspects. And then he doesn't even have the courage to tell her all that to her face now, and maybe the Negermeier wasn't bragging, but she really loves him, and then he fell in nicely.

I don't know ... I just wanted to ask ... I felt the six-shooter again, which the cavalry captain wanted to get so much, and if the cavalry captain were still to come tonight ... He was in clover after all, but now he goes to Haase's Seradella ...

Weio looks at him attentively.

Räder, however, looks at him coldly and contemptuously. He waits calmly until the forester has completely muddled through, then he says compassionlessly: "It's because of the U-ni-form, madam! And if it weren't for me, he would have told the madam and not you ...

Fie, Kniebusch! scolds Violet. Shame on you! Always snitching and telling stories behind your back ...

And now the forester, if only to relieve himself a little, has to dig up everything from the order run through the village to the call from the pub. Then he reports haltingly, half aloud, embarrassed beyond measure, about the drunken chatter of Negermeier. He wants to beat around the bush, but he doesn't succeed. Weio like wheels are relentless researchers: No, there's something missing, Kniebusch, say everything! I'm certainly not blushing.

But fifteen-year-old Weio did become that. She stood against the wall, her eyes closed except for a narrow slit, but her lips trembled and she breathed hastily.

But she does not give in, she tirelessly continues to ask: Come on, Kniebusch, what did he say then?

And now came the matter of the letter.

Did he read it all out? What did he read out? Say every word he read out ... So, and you idiot thought I wrote this to him, him, this guy -?!

Now came the epiphany under the Haase plank gable.

What?! You saw the - gentleman and you didn't tell him anything?! Not even given a hint?! Of all the blockheads, Kniebusch, you are the biggest!

The forester stands in front of her, flabbergasted and conscious of guilt; now he also sees: he has done everything completely wrong.

The Schulze was there, let himself be heard wheels.

Right! But he could have given him the letter!

The forester did not even have the letter! (Wheels again.)

Oh yes, I am all mixed up! But Meier still has it - maybe sits with it in the jug, shows it to others ... You have to go now, Hubert!

Meier has been back in his room for a long time," Hubert said imperturbably. I told you myself that he came home drunk from the tavern after six. But I suggest the U-ni-form ...

True! Go ahead, Hubert, tell him. You'll find him, I'm sure he's still at Haase. No, don't tell him anything, just tell him I need to see him right away. But where? Say, in the old place ... But how can I leave here? Mom won't let me leave now!

Shh! The madam! warns Hubert Räder quite unshakenly.

Well, what is the plot here? says Frau von Prackwitz, standing very astonished on the threshold of the servants' chamber. I look for you everywhere, Violet, and here I find you -! She looks from one face to the other. Why do you all look so embarrassed? In a sharper voice: I want to know what's going on! Come on, Weio!

Excuse me, madam, for speaking, the servant Räder lets himself be heard. It is no longer any use, madam, we must tell the madam.

Breathless silence, desperate hearts.

Silence. Silence.

It is, madam, just out said, because of the buck!

Because of what buck?! What kind of nonsense is this?! Weio, I ask you -!

But because of the buck in the clover, which the Herr Rittmeister also spoke of, Räder says. Excuse me, madam, for having heard it. It was the day before yesterday at dinner, I just served the tench.

Raeder's dispassionate, ever-so-slightly lecturing voice shrouds everything in a gray fog.

And now the buck had suddenly disappeared, just when Herr Rittmeister was going to the hide, and Herr Rittmeister attached such importance to it, madam heard it himself ...

I still haven't heard what kind of meeting this is -!

And now the forester has put the buck out today, madam, in Haase's Seradella, and tonight it must be shot, because it keeps changing back and forth. And we thought, because the captain had left, that the young lady would surprise the captain. It was not right of us, madam, that we wanted to do it secretly ... But it was I who suggested it, that we wait until the madam goes to sleep, because we have a full moon, and it is rifle light enough, says Mr. Kniebusch ...

Now, Hubert, stop your terrible droning at last! says the madam, noticeably relieved. You are an atrocious person. For days you wish: if only he would finally open his mouth! But when you open it, you only have one wish: that you close it again quite quickly. - And you could also be a little nicer to the girls, Hubert, no stone will fall from your crown!

Yes, says servant wheels unmoved.

And you, Weio, the madam continues in her sermon, are a real goose. You could have told me this, it wouldn't have made the surprise for Dad any smaller. Actually, I should not let you go as punishment, but if the buck is only this evening in the Seradella ... But you don't leave her side, Kniebusch ... God, what's wrong with you again, Kniebusch, what are you crying about!!?

Oh, it's just the fright, madam, the fright of seeing you standing in the doorway, the old man wailed. And I can't hold it then. But it was a joyful shock, they are tears of joy ...

I think, Hubert," said the madam dryly, "that you will also get yourself ready a bit and go along. Otherwise, when they meet a wood thief in the forest, our good Kniebusch also bursts into tears of joy, and Weio can then see how she copes alone ...

Oh, Mama, said Weio, I'm not afraid of wood and game thieves.

You had better be afraid of many things, my dear Violet, Frau von Prackwitz said energetically. Above all, you should be afraid of secrecy. - So, it remains the same, Hubert comes along.

Yes, Mama, said Weio obediently. Just wait a minute, I'm about to change.

With that, she ran upstairs, but the madam was alone with the two men and properly washed their heads because of the 'sneakiness, with the child, the Weio'. She did it very thoroughly, but she was not completely satisfied with the result. As a real woman, she had the unmistakable feeling that something was wrong. However, since the Weio was still quite a child, it wouldn't be that bad in the end, and she calmed herself at the thought that Weio's misdeeds had still cleared up quite harmlessly. Her worst misdeed so far had been messing up her beautiful long hair into a bob. And such a bad crime can be committed only once, thank God.

4

The women's cell in the Alexanderplatz police prison is completely overcrowded. When this prison was built, when the cell was finished, the air capacity of the cell was also painted on the green, iron-clad door: so many cubic meters were written on it, quite sufficient for one inmate. It had been a long time since a second bed had been put in; two beds in the cell was a normal occupancy even for the oldest officers.

But then came inflation. The tide of arrestees swelled and swelled. Two more beds were placed above the two beds, thus doubling the prison's occupancy capacity in one fell swoop. But even that was no longer enough. Now, as they arrived in endless stream, day after day, in the green 'ragpickers.' of the police, they were stuffed indiscriminately into the cells. In the evening they threw a few mattresses, a few woolen blankets behind; now see how you settle in!

Petra Ledig had rarely felt more abandoned, more lonely than in the crowded cell of the prison. It would not and would not get dark.

She was probably not one of those girls from secure circles to whom the fact of being in prison meant collapse and shame. She lived in everyday life, she knew that this life remained a difficult thing to overlook for one who was poor and friendless, who never knew what else could happen to you, from which corner the wind of disaster was now blowing.

She knew, after a second, very cursory interrogation here at the Presidium, pretty much what she was accused of. She knew that these accusations were partly outdated, partly incorrect. But she didn't know what would be in it for her. It was possible that there would be workhouse, or the control ticket, or prison, weeks or months. All this was in the hands of people who were as foreign to her as people of another world to whom one cannot speak.

She was immediately taken to the doctor. But there they were, standing in an endless line in front of the door, and finally they said: No more screenings! The medical councilor went home.

So Petra had been led back to her cell, and she had found that dinner had been served there in the meantime and that the others had eaten their share. She didn't mind much, she thought she had eaten enough earlier at the station for now. Only with half an ear did she listen to the bickering of the others, who accused each other in turns. It could be true what the fat woman in the lower bed (the oldest cell inmate, already here for two days) said, that the chicken harrier had stolen her food.

But it was the same. It would have been better if they had kept quiet about it. Now the hen harrier became wild again and fell upon Petra with insults and shouting. It was not pleasant that she had come to the same cell with the chicken consecration, but that had to be endured as well. The girl wouldn't last long with all this shouting and fussing. When she had come into the cell, she had still been as limp as a wet towel. But now she was restless again; she kept pushing Petra and would have liked to hit her. Only she didn't have as much strength as before, alcohol and cocaine had done their work, Petra could keep them at bay with one hand. She did not answer her at all, yet the hen harrier screamed more and more wildly.

That was annoying. Under these constant attacks and shouting, Petra could not think as she would have liked to do. There was the matter of Wolfgang: did he come today, did he come at all? She now knew what they believed about her, surely they would tell him at the station - and what would he believe now? If she had put herself in his place, she would have come all the faster, but with him there was no way of knowing.

Petra looked around the cell. She would have liked to ask the old, gray-haired woman on the bed about visiting hours, but the hen harrier screamed worse and worse. The others, of course, didn't seem to mind or even care. The two brown-black gypsy girls with their bold, restless bird eyes squatted together in a corner on the mattress and whispered half aloud with many rapid finger gestures, looking at no one else in the cell. The long, pale girl who had the other lower bed had already crawled under the covers; only her shoulders could be seen twitching. She must have been crying. - A small fat woman had sat down on the stool and was picking her nose with a scowl on her face.

Now the gray-haired woman sitting on the edge of her bed looked up and said angrily, "Shut the fuck up, you stupid bitch! - Punch her in the mouth, Kittchen, so that she spits teeth! The title 'Kittchen' meant Petra. The old woman probably called her that because she was the only one of the cell residents to wear the blue prison garb. They had dressed her immediately upon admission.

But Petra did not like to beat the chicken consecration. There was no point, she was out of her mind with greed for cocaine or alcohol. A few times the night watch had already knocked on the cell door and offered silence. Then the hen harrier had always quickly jumped to the door and begged: Oh, please, give me a shot! A single, small! You can do it, boys! You guys like to have a tipple too! Oh, please give me one, boys ...

But the footsteps of the night watch had died away without response, at most that one half-laughed. Then the hen harrier had thrown a tantrum, drumming her fists against the iron door and shouting abuse at the guards.

But slowly the chicken consecration changed. As the time advanced, the sky behind the cell window became dull and dark, the electric light flashed above the door, it was more and more as if the girl did not quite know where she was, what was around her. She probably thought she was in hell. She ran up and down like an animal, always from one wall to the other, blind to her companions. At the same time, she muttered to herself incessantly, half aloud. Suddenly then, she stopped and screamed in a high, wailing voice, as if in wild pain.

Again the guards knocked, again their call gave the tormented cause for new, heart-rending begging, then wild insults. This time she fell down at the door; leaning her head against the iron of the door, the miserably ruffled hen harrier squatted there as if listening for something. She started mumbling: It's on, she muttered. It's crawling in my belly. Oh, so many legs! They want out, my whole body is full of them, and now they want out!

With trembling fingers she tore at her clothes, trying to free her body. Ants! she complained. Red, transparent ants! They run inside me. - Oh, give it a rest! she begged. I have nothing. I can't give you coke!

She jumped up. Give me coke! she screamed. I want you to give me coke, you hear me! You have coke!

With a faint cry, the gray-haired woman had sunk backwards; without an attempt at resistance, she lay beneath the raving woman, whimpering softly.

The gypsy women on their mattress interrupted the incomprehensible whispering and watched the robbery with a grin. The shoulders of the long girl in the bed stopped twitching. Slowly she turned her head and looked with her fearful eyes and large, pale nose at the bed opposite, ready at any moment to crawl completely under the covers. The fat woman on the footstool scolded me unpleasantly: "Oh, give it a rest! How can one think when you make so much noise?!

Petra had jumped in. It was easy to pull the slender, ravaged creature backwards, away from the one lying under her; impossible, however, to release the clinging hand from the hair of the assaulted one.

Will you be quiet, you women! the guards scolded through the door. The riffraff has got their hair! Just wait, there's going to be a fight!

Petra turned, to the door she called angrily: Come on in! The girl has a seizure! Why don't you help us?

For a moment there was silence behind the door. Then a polite voice said: We're not allowed to, miss. We are not allowed in any women's cell after lockdown. Otherwise, they'll say we have something with you.

And another voice: Who knows if it's not just a trick of yours?! We'd rather not fall for that.

And Petra: But it doesn't work like that! She is already half mad. There must be a guard here in the house. Or a doctor. Please, send a doctor.

All gone already! said the polite voice. She should have said that when she was admitted. Then she would have gone to the infirmary. You five will be able to handle the one.

It didn't look like it. The gypsy women sat silently, the fat one squatted sullenly on her stool, the elongated one had crawled under her blanket - and the old woman continued to whimper under the aching clasp of the chicken's consecration.

For a while the hen harrier had lain in bed sobbing quietly beside the old woman, now she began to cry again. At this, she tore the woman without thought, but wildly by her thin shag. The woman was also screaming now.

You must help! Petra shouted indignantly, drumming her feet against the iron-barred door. It droned. Or I'll make such a racket that the whole prison will start screaming!

It was almost time. Angry calls for silence sounded from many cells. A high female voice began to sing the Internationale.

The door flew open; uniformed and armed, but on silent felt shoes, not to disturb the prisoners' sound sleep, two guards stood in the doorway.

But we won't go in to you! said a tall blue-eyed man with a reddish-blond mustache. We tell you what to do. You are quite reasonable, Miss. - Quick, go, get a pinch of salt from the cabinet.

Petra ran, the constable ordered: You old scarecrow there on the mattress, take a wool blanket! Can also do something!! You others too!

The two gypsy girls jumped up, grinning, and did as he said.

You there, little pretty on the bed, the guard called from the cell threshold. Up with you now! Now there's coke!

With a cry of joy, the hen harrier jumped up, ran staggering toward the guards. You guys are guys -!

The old woman straightened up with a groan, groping for her hair with careful hands.

Away! shouted the red blond to the chicken consecration. Three step from the body! And after a searching look: Yes, it really does not simulate. This is a cokehead as only one can be.

Shooed back by the command, encouraged and made obedient by the promise, the hen harrier stood at attention. She looked at the men with drooping arms and a dog-like expectant look. Petra, the gypsy girls were also waiting. Only the long, pale one had completely crawled under the covers to avoid the male gaze, and the fat one muttered angrily: "Oh, get lost with your nonsense! Let one think!

Lie down long on the ground, you! the red blond ordered. Do. Otherwise, there's no coke.

The sick woman hesitated, then, with a soft, disappointed cry, she lay down on the cell floor.

Arms to the body! the guard ordered. You, don't make stories! So, now she rolls into a blanket first! Harder! Harder! As hard as you can! Oh nonsense, it does not hurt her! Show her the coke that she does not resist! -

That's what I'm talking about, stupid! Show her, she'll believe it. - Yes, my good one, my lamb! You'll get it in a minute, just be good now!

The girl moaned. Oh please, please! Don't torture me like this! Give me coke! she begged.

Just one more moment! Now the other blanket - no, rolled over in the opposite direction. Turn them over quietly like a package. This will not break it for a long time. You there, fat man on the stool, take your finger out of your nose, do something too! Get the two sheets from the upper beds - yes yes, my good one, it's almost time! Can't you see what a lot of coke that is?! You'll get your pinch in a minute!

According to the instructions of the guard, the sheets were tied tightly around the package like ropes. Willingly, the girl put up with it. It did not turn its eyes from the hand that held the salvation, the cocaine, the salt. Oh, give me! she murmured. How can you be so hard?! It's beautiful ... I can't take it anymore ...

So, said the guard after a scrutinizing look. This will hold. Well, actually it's superfluous, she'll notice it right away, but at least give her the salt ...

Yes, Coke. Please, please, coke! begged the bound woman.

Hesitantly, reluctantly, Petra held the salt on the palm of her hand under her nose. And, strangely touched, saw the transformation in the face of the tormented.

Closer! whispered the with an unwilling, serious look. Why don't you hold it under your nose? She drew it in deeply. Oh, that feels good!

Her sharp, torn face smoothed out, her eyelids drooping almost completely over her eyes in relaxation. Where there had been only black hollows under the cheekbones, soft flesh bulged again. The sharp wrinkles around the mouth disappeared, the cracked, chapped lips curved, gently went the breath ...

Oh, blessed -!

'It's only salt!' Petra thought in shock. 'Common table salt - but she believes in it, and so it makes her young again!'

And in a sudden connection of thoughts she had to think of Wolfgang, of Wolfgang Pagel, whom she had been expecting all evening, she knew it well, but always, from minute to minute - how did the others see him -? 'It's only salt!'

There - here it comes! said the guard half aloud.

The face, close under the face of the kneeling Petra, had changed frighteningly. The mouth was a black, deep cavern, the eyes wide open in shock, in anger.

You dogs! You bastards! she screamed. This is not coke! You have deceived me! Oh - oh - oh!!

Her whole body reared up, her head went up. Dark red, blue-red her face became under the effort to free herself.

Let go of me! she screamed. I want to show you!

Petra had jumped back. Such hatred, such despair struck her from the face that had just been completely redeemed.

Don't worry, little one! said the guard. It holds! Watch out, you blue, you're still the most sensible! Let her lie quietly on the ground, do not set her free, whatever she tells you. But be careful that she doesn't smash her head on the stone floor, she's capable of it. If she screams too much, put a wet towel over her mouth, but make sure she doesn't choke ....

Why don't you take them out?" said Petra crossly. I don't want that. I am not a prison guard! I do not like to torture people ...

Don't be silly, little blue one, the guard said equanimously. Are we torturing them? The addiction tortures them, the coke tortures them. Did we get her into the habit -?

Hans Fallada   -322-   Wolf among Wolves

She belongs in a hospital! Petra said unwillingly.

Do you think that's where they give their coke? the guard asked again. Go she must of it, here, everywhere. Is she still human like that? Look at her, little girl!

She really looked barely human, a trembling, frantic head, now full of rage and hatred, now crying, already despairing, now asking, as a child asks, full of faith that the one prayed for could do anything.

I will see that I get a sleeping pill for her at the military hospital, the red-blond said thoughtfully. But I don't know if there's anyone around who has the key to the medicine cabinet. Those are the times, I tell you ... So don't count on it!

You can always give her salt a few times in between, the other one interfered. She'll fall for it ten more times. Man is like that. Well, good night.

The door slammed shut. The lock cracked loudly under the keys. Now the latch clanged. Petra squatted down next to the sick woman. The now threw the head from side to side, continuously, with closed eyes, faster and faster, faster and faster .... Coke, she whispered as she did so. Coke! Coke! Good coke ...

'She always falls for salt,' Petra repeated to herself blearily. 'Man is like that.' And: 'He's right: man is like that. - But I don't want to be like that anymore. Not me!'

She looked against the door. The spy's windshield blinked like an evil eye. 'Wolf's not coming anymore,' she thought resolutely to herself. 'He believed what they told him. I don't want to wait for him now either!'

5

At the 'Schloß' in Neulohe, with the old people, with the Teschows, they had dinner at seven o'clock sharp. By half past seven they were done with that, and then the girls only had the washing up and cleaning up in the kitchen, which was done by eight at the latest. The old lady said: 'Even a servant has to finish his work one day!

Of course, there was still the evening service at 8:15, for which everyone in the castle had to appear freshly washed - except, of course, for the old Herr von Teschow, who, to the ever new annoyance of his wife, always had to write an urgent letter at this hour that could not be postponed at all.

No, it's really not possible today, Belinde! And anyway - because of you, I already listen to what old Lehnich tells us from the pulpit every Sunday. I have to say, it sounds quite nice, but I can't imagine anything right about it, Belinde. And I don't think you do either. When I imagine us flying around as angels in heaven, you, Belinde, and I - in white shirts like on the pictures in the big picture bible ...

You're mocking again, Horst-Heinz!

I preserve, no trace! - And I meet my old Elias there, and he also flutters around like that and sings forever, and then he whispers to me: Well, Privy Councillor, you were also lucky if I had told the good Lord all that about your red poppy, and what blasphemous speeches you sometimes made ....

Right, Horst-Heinz, very right!

And everything without distinction of status and simply by you, in such a kind of nightgowns and with goose flights - Yes, forgive me, Belinde, because they are goose flights. They are supposed to be swan escapes, but swan and goose are pretty much the same thing ...

Yes, just go upstairs, Horst-Heinz, and write your important business letter. I know, you're just mocking, and not even about religion, but only about me. But I don't mind, I wear that, it's even better. For if you mock religion, you would be rejected forever - but if you mock me, you are merely rude. And you can be, we have been married for forty-two years, so I am used to a rude husband!

With that, the madam rushed off to the prayer room, but the old man stood laughing on the landing and spoke: I du thunder, there I have it again and thoroughly! But she is right - and so I really want to go to one of her devotions again, tomorrow or the day after tomorrow. It does cheer her up a bit, and you should do something for your wife once in a while, even if you've been married for forty-two years. - If only she wouldn't always get the hiccup as soon as she is stirred! It's just like when someone squeaks when they're playing pool - I can't hear the squeak and I can't hear the hiccup, yet I'm always waiting for it. - Well, now I want to calculate a little bit, I am convinced, my son-in-law pays much too little for the electric current ...

With that, the Privy Councillor climbed up to his study and three minutes later, enveloped in the clouds of a brasil, was absorbed in his argumentative bills, an arguably old, but unkillable, ruffian. But the bills were so contentious because he wanted to get at his son-in-law with them.

He paid, as for everything, also for the electric current to the father-in-law much too little, as the latter found; much too much, as he himself found. Neulohe was not connected to any overland power station, but generated its own electricity. The power-generating machine, an ultra-modern crude oil diesel engine, stood with the accumulators in the castle cellar, and because it was there, it was not leased to the son-in-law for whom it mainly worked, but the old gentleman had kept it for himself, although he only burned 'three sparklers in his Katen'. The agreement about the price of electricity had also been quite simple: each of the two parts had to pay its share of the cost according to the share of consumption.

But even the simplest, clearest agreement fails where two people can't stand each other. Old Herr von Teschow thought his son-in-law was not a farmer, but a great gentleman of have-nots, who wanted to live well on the basis of his father-in-law's pocket. Rittmeister von Prackwitz found his father-in-law to be an envious, miserly fellow and, in addition, a good deal more 'plebeian' than he could bear. The old man saw his cash dwindling under inflation, and the more worthless what he had accumulated over many

Hans Fallada   -325-   Wolf among Wolves

years became, the more urgent the hunt for new money seemed to him. The cavalry captain noticed how much more difficult it was to manage the business from month to month, felt how the harvest, which had been turned into money, was melting away under his hands, worried and found it extremely filthy of the old man to keep coming with new demands, objections and reminders.

On the whole, Geheimrat von Teschow thought that his son-in-law was living far too well. Why didn't he smoke cigars like me that you can suck and suck on for an hour? No, they must be cigarettes, those coffin nails that only give you brown fingernails and are gone in three minutes. He arrived here after the war with an officer's suitcase, and there was nothing more than dirty laundry in it! Nah, Belinde, if anyone pays for his cigarettes, it's us - but of course he doesn't pay for them at all, he buys on account.

All young people smoke cigarettes nowadays, Belinde had noticed, and got her husband going all the more with this remark. Wives, husbands in general, have a special knack for such irritating remarks.

I will teach him! He's not that young anymore! the Privy Councillor had finally exclaimed threateningly, turning crimson. Mr. son-in-law should learn once again how hard money is earned!

And so the old man sat at his desk and calculated, with the intention of earning hard money. But he calculated what his lighting system would cost if he purchased it today, at the dollar rate of 414,000 marks. And he spread these acquisition costs over ten years.

Because the plant will certainly not last longer than that - and even if it does last longer, in that time I certainly want to have it written off.

It was quite a sum that was now on the paper: even if each month was only charged with one twelfth, it was still a huge number, with a lot of zeros.

He will look tomorrow morning, the son-in-law," said the Privy Councillor to himself, "when he reads this good news. Of course, he didn't have any money; he must have left what little he had in Berlin. But I'll sit on him so that he threshes quickly; and then I'll chase the threshing money from him, and he may see how he gets through the winter!'

It was actually incomprehensible that the old man had such hatred for the son-in-law. Earlier, when the cavalry captain had been an officer and had lived in some remote garrisons, and then, when there had been war, the two had actually gotten along quite well when they saw each other once. The real hatred had only arisen in the old man since the cavalry captain lived here in Neulohe as a tenant farmer, since the Prackwitz family life took place under the old man's eyes ...

The old man was not so stupid and stubborn, he saw quite well how the cavalry captain troubled and worried. Certainly, the son-in-law was a retired cavalry officer and not a farmer, therefore he handled many things clumsily and also wrongly. Certainly, he was often too mild and sometimes too heated. Certainly he wore English suits from a very expensive tailor in London, to whom he always sent his measurement, and dress shirts buttoned through from top to bottom ('Disgustingly feminine' - though no woman ever wore such dress shirts), while the old Privy Councillor wore only loden suits and hunter's shirts. Sure - and so there were ten, twenty more objections to the Rittmeister. But each separately and all together did not yet give a reason for such hatred.

The Privy Councillor von Teschow has finished his arithmetic; he will write the letter to his son-in-law later, now he reaches for the Oder-Zeitung. But he doesn't get to read, he discovers that the dollar is no longer at 414,000 but at 760,000. That should actually annoy him. He should have looked in the newspaper before he started his arithmetic. Now he has to do it all over again.

But it does not annoy him. He likes to do the new math - the son-in-law has to pay all the more!

'I'll break it after all!' he thinks fleetingly, and the hand with the pen remains still for a moment, as if startled by the thought. But in a moment she continues writing. The privy councilor just shrugged his shoulders. That was a silly thought, of course, he does not in the least set out to ruin Herr von Prackwitz. He should only pay what is due. That's all he asks. 'As far as I'm concerned, he can live over there as he likes, in silk shirts and bustles!' thinks the Privy Councillor grimly and continues writing.

Through the old castle sound the plaintive and now almost lightly fluting notes of the harmonium. Geheimrat von Teschow nods and treads the beat with his feet - accelerating: 'Faster, Belinde, faster! At this rate, people must be falling asleep.'

He is not only the Rittmeister von Prackwitz - he is also the husband of our only daughter, Belinde said the other day. Exactly, exactly; how a woman can say something like that as if it were the most natural thing in the world: the husband of the only daughter!

When the old privy councillor is walking through the village and he sees some girl, he crows loudly all over the village street: "Well, what a lovely child she is! - Well, come on over, my little sweetie, let's have a look at you! You are quite lovely, my little one - thunderclap, what eyes you have!

And he pats her cheeks and grabs her under the chin, all publicly in front of the whole village!!! And publicly in front of the whole village he goes with her to the merchant and buys her a bar of chocolate, or he enters with her at the innkeeper and lets her have a sweet. And then he grabs her once more around the waist, quite visibly, and now he dismisses her and goes into the forest, grinning with satisfaction at himself.

But he doesn't smile because of the girl who looked embarrassed and yet flattered really lovely - there is no more girl running on the green earth who can still warm his old blood. He smirks because he has once again thrown sand in everyone's eyes. Pastor Lehnich will hear it, and he will gently spit it out to Belinde, and Belinde, the poor chicken, will run around as if she had swallowed a ruler - and no one, no one will suspect anything!

Except for one - the old gentleman probably knows. She suspects it, more than that, she knows it. He hardly ever sees her anymore, and never in private. And after the first bad time, when this hit him quite unexpectedly, he doesn't bother to meet her anymore. No, the Privy Councillor knows: an old man no longer burns bright fires. A silent spark, hurriedly flitting through the covered ashes - that's all.

But if such a cavalry captain of have-nots and can-nots, but will-very-much comes - let him be told: we did not raise our daughter for you! The husband of the only daughter, yes, there you go - but why, actually? That is quite wonderfully thought out we raised our daughter, a girl like none, so that you have your pleasure?! And not even that - it is not uncommon to pass by the villa, you can already hear it: you are yelling at Evchen?! No, my dear son-in-law, we want to show you that, and now we don't mind at all that the price of electricity at our plant will be exactly eleven times as high as at the Frankfurt power plant - you should still have to pay that, no, precisely because you are our daughter's husband!

The old man paints his numbers with an angry determination. He doesn't care that there will be noise, there can't be enough noise! He will also make a hole in the park fence again so that Belinde's geese can go into the son-in-law's vetches. Belinde still calms the storms around the son-in-law. But if he does something to her geese, as he threatened, she will not calm the storms!

Privy Councillor Horst-Heinz von Teschow is on the move. He is now just in the right mood to write the letter to the son-in-law. Of course, as is part of the business: cool, concise, businesslike. (One should not mix kinship feelings into business!).

I am extremely sorry, but the increasingly difficult conditions on the money market force me, etc., etc. Enclosing lineup. Yours sincerely, H.-H. von Teschow.

Period! Ready! Deleted!! Elias can deliver the letter first thing in the morning. Then the gentleman finds him immediately on his return from Berlin. That will paint him the hangover, which he certainly brings from Berlin, firmly against the grain! Herr von Teschow already raises his hand to ring for Elias when the harmonium sounds from downstairs remind him that the devotion is still in progress. Belinde does it thoroughly once again today. Surely she has a mangy sheep in the flock that needs to be brought to repentance before bedtime. So he can't call the Elias. And he would love to see the letter on its way!

By the way, of course he knows who the mangy sheep is, Belinde told him: the poultry fairy Amanda with the red painted cheeks and the little Meier with the beaded lips. Recommend themselves as fiancées. Well, I guess they've already been through the engagement. And half the marital status on top of that! Well, let them!

The Privy Councillor grins a little, and it occurs to him that it would be much better to hand the letter over to Field Inspector Meier for the errand. This will annoy the son-in-law the most. Because he knows quite well that his father-in-law likes to have a little chat with Meier. And when he then receives such a letter through little Meier, he naturally thinks that his father-in-law has spoken to Meier about the contents of the letter. Is but of course much too fine to ask his official for such a thing, and that again multiplies still the trouble!

The old man puts the letter in his yoke pocket, takes his cane and loden hat and slowly descends the stairs. The evening service seems to be finally over, two of the girls walk past him up the stairs. They look very amused, not at all like pious edification, but as if there might have been a small incident during the devotion. Von Teschow is about to inquire, but then he prefers not to. If Belinde hears him talking on the stairs, she might join him and ask where else he's going, and offer to accompany him - nope, better not.

So he steps out alone into the park, which is already quite dark, just right for his purpose. Of course, he knows exactly where his wife's geese always look for a hole in the fence; he had it closed only the day before yesterday at her request. What you can close, you can also open again, he thinks, and rattles the slats thoughtfully. He does eventually have to find a loose one that he can tear off with his hands.

While he is so busy, he suddenly feels as if someone is watching him. He quickly turns around, and sure enough, there is something like a human shadow standing next to the bushes. The old man's bulging big eyes still see quite well, even in the shuddering -: Amanda! he calls.

But nothing answers, and as he looks closer, it's not a human shadow at all, just the rhododendron and jasmine behind it. And if it really was her, it doesn't matter to her and it must not matter to her, of course he was just checking to see if the slats were stuck. However, he forgoes loosening up for this evening and makes his way to the Negermeier's booth.

Of course, he prefers not to go into the civil servants' house - unlike his wife, the old privy councillor has not the slightest inclination to see things that offend common decency. He merely takes the stick and knocks on the open window.

Heh! Mr. Meier - put your honored head through the curtains! he shouts.

6

Poultry maid Amanda Backs would have liked to avoid attending this evening service, as she had done many times before - if otherwise for the more general reasons of boredom and whatnot, then this time because she could very well guess where the madam would be aiming her thoughts of penance and prayer. But the fat Mamsell and the black Minna did not let Amanda out of their sight.

Come on, Manding, now we'll quickly help you count the chickens, and then you'll help us scrub the pots!

I always understand train stations, Amanda said with the most popular expression of the time, and that meant exactly the same as her mother had meant with "Nightingale, I hear you warbling!

But the two simply went along, sure as death the madam had already whistled a verse to them.

Always the same! Amanda Backs scolded the few late chickens, which hurriedly, with excited clucking, headed from the meadow toward the chicken house. But I'll close the blow in your face again, and then you can see how the fox says good night to you! - And you shouldn't act so stupid at all, Minna! As for the Mamsell, with her net two hundredweight, it is already difficult with the men, and she can't help it if she stands there forever like an angel made of laundry soap! But you, with your six snotty noses who have at least ten different fathers -

Oops, Mandchen! Don't be so mean! Black Minna had protested. The madam really means it so well with us!

I always understand station, had said the Amanda Backs again and had broken off the debate. Because with the black Minna - that the madam had appointed her of all people as a guardian, that was really too ridiculous. But one knew how childishly the old madam had behaved with this shaggy, elderly woman! Whenever such an accident happened again - and the madam really only noticed it when the midwife was already there, although it was visible to every eye long beforehand in the scrawny, bony female - then the madam would fly into a rage and insult the black Minna and cast her out of her eyes and out of the Neuloh poorhouse forever and ever as completely incorrigible.

Then the black Minna screamed and made a spectacle of herself, but she also wept and loaded a little of her stuff onto a handcart - but by no means all of it, only so much that the madam had a beautiful sight to behold. But especially all their brats. And so this woman went through the village howling and singing hymnals. And in front of the lock she stopped once more, pressed the brass bell button and asked the servant Elias, with many tears, to tell the dear, good madam her blessings and her heartfelt thanks! And whether she may not kiss her hand goodbye -?

Elias, who already knew this theater, always said no. Then Black Minna cried even more bitterly and left for the wild, wide world with her fatherless children - to the bruising stone at the entrance to the castle. There she sat and cried and waited, and depending on the wrath the madam had for her, she had to wait one, two or even five hours, and sometimes even half a day.

But she knew that she would not wait in vain, and if she had not known it from experience, she would have seen it - namely on the curtains in the castle. For she pushed the old lady back and forth with trembling hands, and could not help looking at her favorite lost lamb.

But if the case was once again quite bad, and Frau von Teschow knew it from Schulzen Haase through her husband, that this time there were certainly three men in question, and perhaps there were even five, not to mention those, which the black Minna concealed out of 'sympathy' (for the black Minna precisely distinguished between 'sympathetic' men and petty hangers-on in her dealings) - then the gracious one hardened her soft, world-inexperienced heart and considered all this Sodom and Gomorrah and remembered how often the black Minna had already vowed her betterment.

And she let the curtain out of her hand and said to her friend, the old Fräulein von Kuckhoff, who always lived with her: No, Jutta, this time I won't be softened again. And I don't want to look out the window for her anymore either ...

And the old Fräulein von Kuckhoff, with the black velvet ribbon around her neck, nodded energetically with her old little bird of prey head and said in her flowery but clear way: Certainly, Belinde - after all, a camel also drinks up a well.

Yes, and then surely not half an hour passed that there was a soft knock on the door and old Elias reported: Hold to grace, madam, but I am to report it: now she makes herself free.

And right, when then the two ladies each rushed to a window, there sat then this poor, homeless person on the bruiser, had unbuttoned the blouse and approached her youngest sin fruit.

Then the madam said with a sigh: "I think, Jutta, we cannot justify this new nuisance.

And Jutta replied darkly: "It is not the worst fruits that such wasps gnaw on! which Frau von Teschow took as an approval of her intentions.

No, Elias, I'll go myself, she said hastily, because even if Elias was already high in his sixties, whether he was up to such a sight remained uncertain. So the old woman of Teschow personally went down to the sinner, who hurriedly closed her blouse when she only saw the madam step out of the castle. Perhaps she realized that this feeding was just an act; Black Minna could not feed at all and had raised all her children with the bottle. But the madam did not need to know that.

So the two of them moved back into the poor people's cottage, and the old woman walked along beside the ridiculous cart, and it did not occur to her that people might mock or laugh at her. But she softened her heart and made it humble, remembering how she too had once almost succumbed to temptation when the dashing Lieutenant von Pritzwitz had wanted to give her a kiss behind the door now more than forty years ago - and yet she had been as good as engaged to Horst-Heinz then!

And then, when she crossed the threshold of the people's cat with the black Minna, she was ready to understand everything and to forgive everything, and even if she was not stupid enough to take the sinner's tears completely at face value, she still thought in her heart: 'A very little bit honestly she means it after all, and a very little bit sorry she is - and what do I know, how much repentance God demands of us!'

This is how the old woman of Teschow thought and this is how she acted - and even Amanda Backs could have found this quite nice and friendly, if only the good heart of the gracious woman had been so sweetly forgiving to all sinners. But people's hearts are all strange, and why should the old woman's heart be any different? What she forgave a sly wench like Black Minna ten times over, she would not even forgive a young girl.

And certainly not the Amanda Backs! For she was impudent and shameless in her words; she laughed merrily at all men; wore skirts so short that they were no longer skirts; never cried over her mistakes; never repented and never sang a pious song, but very loudly terrible hit songs like: What are you doing with the knee, dear Hans -? and What a woman dreams in spring ...

No, the Amanda probably knew what was in store for her in tonight's devotional! But she was particularly disgusted that Black Minna had been assigned to supervise her, and for a moment she seriously considered locking the two of them up in the henhouse and ducking out to play henpeck - it would have been a marvelous joke!

But as cheeky and impudent as Amanda was with her mouth, she was also deliberate and prudent in her actions - which is what a poultry mistress has to be. For poultry is the most difficult livestock of the world, ten times more difficult than a circus full of wild animals, and parries only a prudent nature. Yes, out of Meier's window last night, Amanda had bragged in her rage and could have threatened her madam with leaving - but in the end she was sincerely fond of her little, bulging-lipped Hansel, and the Garden of Eden itself would have seemed barren to her without her Negermeier.

So she didn't slam the door of the chicken coop - she just chased out the two unwinged chickens and with Putt and Schnutt brought her people to rest and counted the heads and found that she didn't lose one. Then she said quite unmistakably: So, you chickens, and now that you have helped me so mightily, I will scrub your pots.

God, Mandchen, moaned the fat mamsel and cracked her fish-leg corset, if you didn't know that you were just kidding ...

And how do you know that?! Amanda Backs asked very belligerently, and belligerently she walked between the two silenced, belligerently bobbing in her short skirt.

For she was very young, and the bitter years of her childhood had not been able to rob her of the appetite for life and the freshness of her youth, and being young was fun for her, and war was fun for her, and love was fun for her - and if the madam imagined that she could drive this fun out of her with singing and praying, then there had been a Uhl!

Such thoughts as Amanda's may help quite well over the scrubbing of even the sootiest pot, for an evening devotion in the Neuloh castle she was not right. There they sat for quite a while now, the usual crowd, quite a handsome crowd. For the lady not only insisted that all those who were in her employ came to these services with all their children, but also that anyone from the village who wanted to have a few meters of wood for free in winter, or who wanted to gather berries and mushrooms in the Teschow forest in summer, had to earn the right to do so on many an evening. Old Pastor Lehnich often did not have as many parishioners in church on Sunday as the madam had in her prayer room night after night.

And you, Amanda? Frau von Teschow had asked, and Amanda had risen from her sinful thoughts, stared around and knew nothing about anything. The geese on the back bench, the fourteen-, fifteen-year-olds who laughed at everything, had of course immediately started to gniggle. The madam, however, had mildly asked again: And your verse, Amanda?

Oh yes, they were doing 'row singing'! Each person had to name a verse from the hymnal, which they then all sang together. This often went wildly with evening songs, death songs, praise songs, penitential and cross songs, Jesus songs and baptismal songs. It was mostly fun for everyone, though, and brought some momentum to the sleepy evening boredom. Even the madam got red cheeks at her harmonium, so quickly did she have to turn the pages of her music book and so nimbly jump from one melody to another.

You go your own way ... Amanda shouted quickly, before the gniggle turned into laughter.

The madam nodded: Yes, you should do that, Amanda!

Amanda, however, bit her lips that she had just named such a song beginning and made it so easy for the madam. She was a little red when she sat down.

But at least there was no pause, because Mrs. von Teschow knew this song from her head. In a moment the harmonium started, and in a moment everyone sang. And now it was the turn of the black Minna next to Amanda, and the hypocrite naturally chose again: Out of deep distress I cry to you ...

And already they were singing again.

Amanda Backs, however, now allowed herself no more dreams, but sat upright and alert, for she did not want to be laughed at again. Nothing happened for quite a while. The singing went on and on - at the end without any swing, because the people got bored and because even the tired madam on the harmonium missed her mark more and more often and got out of time. Then the harmonium began to whistle strangely, to flute and groan, the goslings on the back bench gnawed again, and Frau von Teschow blushed until she had taken her instrument to the curb anew.

'She's getting tired,' Amanda thought. 'Well, it's not much at all anymore. Perhaps by now she has run out of steam to make a long chatter about the story, and I'll quickly get to my Hansen's Corner!'

But of this Amanda Backs had no idea, how warm an old woman can be made by the sins of others, how she can revive under the missteps of her sisters. For a moment, of course, it looked as if the madam wanted to call it a day. But then she came to her senses. She stepped in front of her small congregation, cleared her throat, and said a little hastily and a little sheepishly: Yes, dear children, now we could say our final prayer and each of us could go home and go to sleep, knowing that we have concluded our day well. But do we really -?

The little old woman looked from one face to the other, her embarrassment already gone. She had also already suppressed the stirrings of her evil conscience, which told her she was up to something she had been strictly forbidden to do.

Yes, do we really -? When we look to Neulohe, and now even to Altlohe, where they may still be sitting in the tavern, we can probably be satisfied with ourselves. But when we look inside ourselves, what about us -? We human beings are weak, and each of us sins every day. So it is good to confess it publicly again and again, and to say before our gathered fellow Christians what we have sinned. Only the sins of one day - and I myself want to make a start ...

With that, the old woman of Teschow quickly knelt down, and already she prepared herself with silent prayer for her loud confession of sin. But a barely suppressed movement went through her flock, for there was not one among them who did not know that Pastor Lehnich and even the Superintendent in Frankfurt had strictly forbidden the gracious lady to confess her sins in public. For it is completely against Christ's and Luther's spirit and smells of the Salvation Army, Baptism and especially of the reprehensible auricular confession of the Catholic Church!

But if none of those gathered got up and went out to protest - and the old Fräulein von Kuckhoff or the servant Elias were the people to do that unabashedly - it was just because one was as anxious as the other to hear what was coming. For there is really hardly anyone who hears about the sins of others without tingling. Everyone hoped that it would not hit him behind the gracious lady, and everyone quickly reviewed the sins of the last time, secret and obvious, and thought that it would probably not be that bad with him.

But one of them, who knew that she would certainly be among the two or three who were later called by Frau von Teschow, and who knew that this entire transgression of pastoral and superintendential prohibitions was only for her sake - one of them sat stiffly and rigidly there and did not let it show. Sullen and annoyed, she listened to the stammering of the old woman, who must have been very excited, because she threw everything in confusion and again and again the hiccup went up in her throat that everything would have laughed without the great tension. She did, however, list as her sins that she had re-read the bad novel in the paper after all - Hickup! - and that she is impatient against her dear husband - Hickup! - and called him 'rude' - Hickup! Hickup - and that she had again had margarine kneaded under the butter for the servants ... Hickup!

Amanda Backs listened to this and drew an impatient, annoyed, dismissive frown. There the people sat and listened to this silly stammering, ten times more eager than they had listened to God's Word, and yet it was all a lie! The madam did not say the right thing either, so piously she did. They had all tasted the margarine, they didn't need to be told. The novel thing was nonsense, and how often she quarreled with 'her dear husband' was known to everyone in the house. All eye-blinding and hustle! She had better confess publicly that she had made all this fuss just to spite her, the Amanda Backs - that would have been a real confession of sin! But she didn't even think of that!

Still - the mamsel had really turned bright red cheeks with excitement and was puffing out of her thick chest like a steam boiler, and the fish leg was cracking around her. And Minna had stupidly and dozily opened her mouth as if she expected roasted chickens!

Amanda Backs also got red cheeks, but not from excitement and shame, but from defiance and anger. Now the madam, in her shamelessness, really began to talk about last night, that she had surprised a girl - alas, a girl from this house! -that she surprised it, how it climbed in the dark to a man in the room -! (Hickup!)

A formal jolt went through the whole assembly, and Amanda saw faces grow dumb and rigid with amazement and expectation: here it comes!

But it did not come yet, but now the madam, interrupted by many a swallower, complained that she had let anger get the better of her and had scolded the girl heatedly and threatened her with dismissal, instead of considering that we are all sinners and that even this erring sheep must be led with patience into the shepherd's fold. Ruefully she confessed that she had neglected her duty, because this young girl had been entrusted to her care, and she asked that HE might strengthen her with long-suffering and patience in the fight against evil ...

Completely contemptuous and very angry, Amanda listened to this talk, and if she had first made one decision, she now made another. And hardly had Frau von Teschow said the last Amen and stood up, and had not even had time to indicate with word and finger the next to kneel on the penitential and prayer bench - when Amanda already rose with her cheeks flushed, but with eyes that were quite dark with anger, and she said that the madam need not bother, she already knew who was meant by all this talk, and so there she stood, and whether the madam was now satisfied -?!!

After these words, however, the Amanda Backs went around like a real fury and attacked the black Minna, who pushed and pressed with her hands on the Amanda's back so that she would step forward properly in front of the congregation: "Will you take your dirty paws off my clean dress? I will not be pushed to the front - and certainly not by you! And with the dear God and with repentance and penance this theater has already nothing at all to do!

With this angry attack Amanda had made her opponent, Black Minna, small, and now she turned to the assembly again and said (for now she was on the move): Yes, she was the one who had climbed into a window last night, and so that they would also know in detail - it had been the window in the officials' house, the one of Inspector Meier! And she wasn't ashamed of it at all, and she could point to at least ten here in the meeting who were going into still completely different windows, to still completely different guys -!!!!

And with that she raised her finger and drove it towards the black Minna, who crouched down on her bench, shrieking. And Amanda raised her finger again, but before she had even pointed it, the bench at the back of the dark corner where the goslings were sitting, all in an excessive hurry to hide and duck, toppled over.

Then Amanda Backs started laughing (and unfortunately, unfortunately, quite a few people laughed with her), but suddenly her laughter turned into crying. Angrily she shouted, "You'd better pay a decent wage!

And with that, she ran out of the hall into the dark park, crying groundlessly. -

In the hall, however, not only the bench had fallen over, but the old gracious lady had also collapsed a lot. Trembling and sobbing pitifully, she sat in her armchair, and this time even her old friend Jutta von Kuckhoff stood mercilessly in front of her and said sternly: You see, Belinde, he who touches bad luck defiles himself!

But the people made that they came out of the prayer hall. Now, of course, they looked very quiet and almost embarrassed, but unfortunately there was no doubt that they would find their way back to their home. But about whom it would then go, that could also not be doubtful - the Amanda

Backs it was certainly not, because she had emerged as a winner from the battle!

She, of course, who was now still running around the park, very upset and crying, did not feel that way at all and scolded herself as an ass and a stupid nut for having messed up her own and Hänsecken's business so badly. Once she stopped because she saw something driving along the fence, and it was the old privy councilor. She was about to take heart and ask him for mercy, but the experiences of her young life warned her to ask anything from anyone.

So she continued to walk through the park and gradually she became calmer. She washed her face in the cool water at the pond and went to her hen's corner. However, she arrived just as the Privy Councillor knocked on the window and called for Inspector Meier. And I heard a woman shriek in fright inside at the corner of the hen.

7

Outside, the last evening twilight quickly fades into darkness. It's nine o'clock over. The lanterns are already burning in the streets. Mrs. Pagel, long widowed, stands at the window of Wolfgang's room. She looks out into the gardens, which are now almost completely dark. But behind it flames and flashes, a reddish glow lies over the city - does she consider under which lamp the son may now sit, squandering the stolen money?

She turns into the room, where in the glow of the light the girl Minna is packing a suitcase, and says impatiently: "Close it, Minna! He can come after the things at any moment!

The girl Minna does not look up from the little bags into which she pushes the carefully unblocked shoes. He is not coming after all, madam, she says.

Mrs. Pagel is getting angry - Minna's answer almost sounds as if she has to be talked out of an eagerly awaited visit! She says briefly: You know quite well what I mean, Minna. Then he just sends someone for the stuff!

Minna continues packing, very calmly, without all haste. The wardrobe trunk would not have had to give gnä' Frau also. Now when madam goes to Ems in the spring, you don't have a decent suitcase!

Stupid person! says the madam and looks out of the window. - You can't see the road - because of the dense treetops - but in the deep silence here you can hear every step, every approaching car.

Should the bathrobe also go in, ma'am? Minna asks.

How -?! asks Ms Pagel. Oh, the bathrobe. - Of course. Everything that belongs to him is packed.

Minna makes a mucky face. But then I still have to get on the floor, she says, and get the boxes of books. I don't know if the houseman is still up. I can't manage the boxes on my own.

The books have time, says the old woman, annoyed by these constant difficulties. You can ask him if he wants them when he comes.

He's not coming after all, madam," says the old girl Minna, monotonously but opinionatedly.

This time Mrs. Pagel didn't listen, this time she doesn't have to be annoyed by the girl's stubbornness. She listens to the street, half leans out the window, she listens, she listens ... one step ...

The girl, even if her back is turned, has sensed that something is going on. She pauses in packing, a bathing suit in her hand, she turns, sees the listening figure, says pleadingly: Madam -!

Wolfgang -?! shouts out of the window. Doubtful at first, then sure: Wolfgang! Yes, wait, boy! I'm coming! I'll catch up with you in a minute!

And she drives around, her face flushed, her eyes under her white hair shining and flaming as ever.

Come on, Minna! The keys! The young gentleman is waiting downstairs! Run!

And without paying attention to Minna's imploring words, she runs ahead of her into the dark hallway. She turns on the light, grabs some keys from the board next to the mirror console at random, and runs down the stairs, followed by Minna.

At the front door she tries. The keys do not want to fit. Feverishly she calls out: "Hurry up, Minna! Just quickly - maybe he'll change his mind again, he was always weak!

Minna, who has become mute, presses the handle and the front door, which was not locked, opens. Mrs. Pagel walks through the narrow front garden, she pushes open the iron door to the street: Wolfgang. Boy! Where are you?!

The lonely night walker, an oddball who instead of bars and business has longed for fresh air and the smell of greenery, pulls up in surprise. He sees an old, white-haired, very excited lady in front of him in the flickering light of the lone gas lantern, behind her an elderly girl, a bathing suit in her hand. He foolishly asks: Excuse me?!

The old lady stops and turns so suddenly that she almost fell. The elderly girl with the bathing suit gives him an annoyed look and walks behind. Now she grabs the old lady under the arm and together they disappear into the next house.

'Don't lock it,' the lone walker notes to himself. 'Twisted chickens to scare you like that!'

He sought an even quieter street for his refreshment.

The two old women climb the stairs slowly, without a word. Minna feels that the hand of the gracious woman on her arm is trembling as if in a convulsion. She notices how difficult it is for her to climb the stairs. The floor door is open, the forecourt is brightly lit. They go into the apartment. Minna closes the door. She is not quite sure where the madam wants to go, whether to the young gentleman's room or to her own room. It would be better if the madam lay down after all the excitement. But Minna, the stubborn, bull-headed Minna has learned one thing in her life that most women never learn, namely that talking has its time and silence its time. Now is the time for silence.

She walks gently down the hall with the madam, and a gentle tug on her arm tells her that the madam wants to go back into the young gentleman's room. When the two enter, the wardrobe trunk is in front of them, wide open. A drawer is pulled out, on top of it lies the young gentleman's blue and white striped bathrobe.

Mrs. Pagel stops at this sight. She clears her throat and then says dryly: Take out the bathrobe, Minna!

Minna does it, she puts the bathrobe on the sofa.

Take it all out! says Mrs. Pagel even more angrily. You need to start packing again, Minna. I can not do without the wardrobe case in any case.

Wordlessly, Minna sets about unpacking. The madam stands by, with a stern, hard face. She supervises Minna. Perhaps she waits eagerly for a hesitant grasp, for the slight hint of opinion. But Minna's wooden face remains expressionless, her grips for laundry and clothes are not too quick and not too slow.

Suddenly, Mrs. Pagel turns around.

She still wants to quickly escape through the door into her dark room. But she doesn't get that far anymore. The plunging tears obscure her view, she leans in the doorframe, crying without support.

Oh, Minna, Minna, she whispers, sobbing. Am I now to lose him too, the last thing I still love -?

But the old girl, who all her life, in the kitchen, in the servants' quarters, has thought and worked only for the madam, who has always been fetched and who has always been sent away, just as her mistress felt, and who is forgotten again in this hour - but the old girl grasps her mistress' hand imploringly. It whispers insistently: "He'll be back, ma'am. Certainly! Wolfi is coming back after all!

8

Sophie Kowalewski, the former maid of Countess Mutzbauer, had spent the evening at the Christian Hospice quite pleasantly. First, until it was time for dinner, she had rummaged through her things - it was a nice feeling, after all, to be the final owner of everything she had taken from her mistress. That was not little - Sophie could say of herself that she was not only rich, but also precious. Neulohe would burst with envy if it got to see all this.

By itself, the patterning became changing clothes. After all, she had to wear something appropriate for dinner at this hospice. With the instinctive adaptation for her surroundings that was Sophie's forte, she chose a blue costume. She put on a yellowish raw silk blouse to go with it. The skirt was perhaps a bit too short for really devout people, but that couldn't be helped. Sophie did not own any longer skirts, but she firmly resolved not to cross her legs. She corrected the too low neckline of the blouse with a light, colorful silk scarf.

Just a very tiny bit of lipstick, just a hint of red on the cheeks -: Sophie finished and descended into the dining room. The sayings on the walls, some burnt wood, some painted cardboard, delighted her. On the tables, with the ugly but lavishly turned legs, were tablecloths of gray waffled paper. Where the tablecloth had gotten a stain, a paper napkin had been placed over it again. That was thrifty, practical, and as befitted the third in the bunch, fundamentally ugly - Sophie thought.

The soup was thin and came from a cube, on the pods for this the flour was not spared, the pork chop was small, and the fat smelled. Sophie, the spoiled Sophie, ate this food with fervent pleasure. She enjoyed being a guest of the pious. So that's how they lived, they put each other through such hardships, just to despise the earthly and to be on good terms with the dear God, who didn't exist at all!

With particular interest, however, Sophie eyed the serving hall daughters. She tried to find out if they were improved fallen girls and if they liked their current job. If they had fallen once, Sophie decided, it must have been a very long time ago, they were so elderly. And morose they all looked, actually: this could not be - contrary to the saying above the sideboard - a very fat green pasture.

By the time Sophie had eaten, it was half past eight; impossible to go to bed now. For a while she stood irresolutely at the window of the dining room and looked out onto the rain-damp Wilhelmstraße. She had only ever gone out west, maybe they could check out the downtown establishments for once? But no! - She was determined to go to bed early tonight and to be extremely solid throughout her entire vacation - going out tonight was out of the question under any circumstances. Thankfully, she spotted a door marked Writing Room and now knew how she would spend her evening. She had to tell her friend Hans that his sister would be visiting him soon.

In the very bare, scantily lit writing room sat only a white-haired gentleman dressed in a long black lap skirt - surely a pastor. At her entrance, he pulled up from his newspaper in confusion, or from his nap over the paper, and stammered something. Decidedly he was embarrassed, probably he was in doubt whether he should be alone in a room with such a nicely dressed girl.

As Sophie slid past him with a daughterly smile - at least she thought she did - and climbed the swivel chair in front of the desk, she thought to herself that this old sprayer looked rather soft. Pastor Lehnich in Neulohe was of a tougher ilk. She had an accurate memory of how hard that one could hit if you hadn't learned your hymnal verses, or even more so if you had been drafted with 'boys'.

Neither softness, nor age, nor piety, however, seemed to prevent the white-haired gentleman there from peering up from the newspaper and at her legs every nostril. Sophie angrily pulled her skirt down as far as it would go - about to her knee. She thought it was wrong of a pastor. Otherwise, she always enjoyed it when the gentlemen peeked at her legs. But for a pastor this was not suitable, a pastor had other things to do than to find her legs pleasant, for this he did not get his salary.

When she caught the old man for the third time, she gave him a sharp look. Immediately he blushed, munched something and left the reading room in a hurry.

Sophie sighed. She didn't mean it that way again, enjoyed all alone this writing room was abundantly gloomy.

In any case, however, the letterheads bore the imprint 'Christian Hospice'. That was gratifying. She assumed that such a letter would be treated with respect in the penitentiary, that such a letter would certainly get her the desired and longed-for permission to visit. As a precaution, she immediately slipped a dozen such sheets and envelopes into her purse; they would surely come in handy again.

Of course, even the most pious imprint could not relieve her of the effort of writing; as in the morning, it was a heavy work in the evening - she sat over it for a long time.

But finally, she was done. She hadn't written very much, just four or five sentences. But they were enough to prepare Hans Liebschner (and the prison administration) for the visit of the 'sister'. How Hans would grin at this letter! How nice the visit would be when he saw her - he could do such a thing fabulously! - would treat her completely as a sister. She already felt his naughty sibling kiss before the eyes of the policeman - or what ran around as a guard in such a penitentiary. By now it had become half past nine, there was nothing left to do, at best one could go to bed. Slowly she undressed. Now she was wide awake, even though she had been tired for ages during the day. Not a trace of need for sleep. And outside under her window the cars were grinding and honking. She saw it literally - while she undressed sullenly - how the men now entered the bars ridiculously grave or with badly played nonchalance, nodded briefly to the girls and climbed onto their high stools - ordering their first cocktail or whisky.

But no! Today would not go out under any circumstances! So it was a good thing that on the nightstand next to her bed there was a black booklet with red trim. It bore the golden imprint: The Holy Scripture.

Since her confirmation, Sophie had not had a Bible in her hand - and at that time her occupation with this book had also been limited only to the learning of verses commanded by Pastor Lehnich and - more frequently - to the search for seductive passages. Tonight, however, she had time for once, so she took the Bible, and to do it right, she started over. (If it appealed to her, she would pack this excellent free read in her suitcase for the vacations).

Sophie was curious to find out what was actually true about this famous book. The creation story found only their moderate interest - because of them! It might have been that way, or it might not have been that way, it didn't matter. The important thing was that you were there yourself - and you were, thanks to the creation of Adam and Eve in the second chapter and the Fall in the third.

This, then, was the famous fall from grace with which educated men so often soured on a girl in the bar (while they were still pretending to be fine). Sophie found everything again, it was all there: the tree of knowledge, the apple, which is why I'm sure they still said 'kidding' today, and the snake. But Sophie did not agree at all with the depiction in the Bible. Whoever read correctly what was written there could immediately see that God had never forbidden the woman to eat from the tree of knowledge. Yes, he had forbidden the man, but before the woman was created. That was a fine thing to do, to punish the woman for something she had not been forbidden to do at all! Such a thing looked like the men!

'If that's how it starts,' Sophie thought angrily, 'how can it go on? It's all a hoax! You have to be stupid to fall for something like that! And this is what the brothers are still telling you today! Well, someone else should come to me with something like that!'

Annoyed, she folded the book closed. 'Take it on vacation? Out of the question! That I have to be angry forever! That's why they leave the thing so exposed here - no demand for it!'

She turned off the light, she was in the dark.

Her anger passed, but it was too warm under the covers, the air behind the closed windows was too oppressive. She stood up and opened it. She heard the trains ringing; whenever they turned into Krausenstraße, they rang. She heard the footsteps of pedestrians, sometimes isolated, very loud - sometimes many, a confused, varied sound. The cars came and went, they whirred and honked, they hurried on ...

Now her body began to itch; she scratched here, she scratched there. She threw herself here, she threw herself down. Then she forced herself to lie still; she took her fall asleep position: on her right side, under her right cheek both hands. She closed her eyes. Sleep was very close.

But immediately she remembered that she was thirsty; and she had to go up and drink a glass of water that tasted stale. She lay again and waited for sleep. But there was no sleep for them, there seemed to be no more sleep for them at all. For nothing she imagined how tired she had been in her chamber this morning, in the crushed dress, her mouth insipid from all the liquors, her feet burning - how she had struggled with sleep as she wrung the few lines from herself to Hans while in her back the cook, the oaf, snored. In vain, no sleep came. She started counting to a hundred. Like them, thousands lay in their beds, hunted, restless. They were the ones whose last money was spent. They were the ones who, in the hangover of the morning, had vowed never to go out again, to sleep thoroughly, night after night. They were those who had grown tired of the eternal hunt, who had given up searching night after night for something whose name they did not even know. Like Sophie Kowalewski, they tossed and turned restlessly in their beds. It was not the thirst for alcohol, not the desire for hugs that kept her awake, eventually driving her up again. They could not be alone, nor could they rest. The blackness of her room reminded her of death. They had heard and seen enough of death, four years had been spent dying outside and inside all the time. They died soon enough - far too soon. But now they were still alive, and so they wanted to live!

Like the others, Sophie Kowalewski got up and hurriedly got dressed, as if she had the most urgent appointment, as if she could not miss something very important at any price. She quickly goes down the stairs and steps into the street.

Where should it go? She looks up and down the street. It doesn't really matter where it goes. Inside, she knows: it's the same everywhere. But she remembers wanting to check out the downtown eateries once. So she walks slowly (suddenly, being among people, she has a lot of time) towards the city center.

9

A long, quiet walk through the Tiergarten had cleared the head of Studmann's former receptionist. He had also given Rittmeister von Prackwitz the opportunity to paint a picture of Neulohe for his friend, as it lay far back in the Neumark, almost on the Polish border, completely encircled by forests. Prackwitz did not intend to portray Neulohe as rosier than it was; he did not want to deceive his friend. But it was quite natural that in the midst of this staggering, corrupt, mad city, Rittergut Neulohe rose more quietly and more purely, every face familiar, every person ultimately clear - and neither plant nor animal infected by the tumult of the times.

It was easy for von Prackwitz to say, in view of the facades of the buildings, which were garishly painted with marble store fittings, illuminated signs, and picture signs at the bottom, but were crumbling and decaying at the top: "Thank God my buildings still look a little different! Not pretty, but solid, unflattering red brick.

When they saw the burnt lawns, the weedy beds of the zoo, for the maintenance of which there was no more money (as much money as there was), he could say: We also had it very dry. But a pretty good crop has grown anyway. Uncalled!

In the Rosarium rose bushes stood plundered, also broken down. There seemed to be florists who met their needs here rather than in the market hall. We also have theft, but thankfully not yet vandalized!

They sat down on a bench. The dry air had already absorbed the rain moisture again. In front of them, with its bushy islet, lay the New Lake. Above them silently stood the crowns of the trees. From the zoological garden sounded indistinct animal roar.

My father-in-law, said Herr von Prackwitz dreamily, has reserved his eight thousand acres of forest for the time being. But as filthy as the old man is in many ways, he grants hunting permission generously - you could shoot many a nice buck there.

Yes, Neulohe, in the darkening evening, became a quiet island far away from the world, and Herr von Studmann was not at all insensitive to such a message. In the morning, he had still dismissed any thought of escaping to the countryside. But then the afternoon had come with its many experiences and had proved that this time could finish even the nerves of a four-year-old front-line fighter. It was not even so much the grotesque, embarrassing incident with the Reichsfreiherr Baron von Bergen. Fortunately, completely insane people did not run around so often in the history of the world that one had to include collisions with them in one's life calculations.

But this incident had exposed in a saddening, agonizing way the steely cold mechanism of the hotel gear, to which von Studmann had hitherto given strength, zeal, work. He had believed that through the most scrupulous performance of duty he had earned, if not attachment, then respect. He had had to experience that the fallen man had been granted only shameless, impudent curiosity from the last elevator boy up to the top general manager. If the spirited Privy Councillor Schröck, with his somewhat unusual views on the mentally ill, had not stepped in, he would have been deported with the greatest speed, without any consideration, like half a criminal.

So, however, he had been intercepted before his exit, Mr. General Director Vogel, in spite of all the gray abundance, had squirmed smoothly between on the one hand and on the other hand, a severance pay - paid in noble currency, of course - had been handed over to him first, warmest recommendations had been assured to him -: Yes, I even believe, my dear colleague, that this small, in itself quite unpleasant incident still turns out to be completely to your advantage. If I understood Privy Councillor Schröck correctly, he expects very high demands from you - the highest!

No, said Herr von Studmann on his zoo bench out of deep thought. Of course, I don't want to suck any honey from the moral inferiority of this little fruit.

How -?! von Prackwitz asked, driving up. He had just been talking about wild boar hunting. No, of course not. I understand that completely. You don't need it either.

Forgive me, said von Studmann. I was still here with my thoughts. Berlin. It is actually pointless work that has been done here. Something like cleaning: you wash yourself off, and the next morning everything is dirty again.

Of course, agreed the cavalry captain. Women's Room Work. With me ...

Forgive me, I couldn't be with you either without doing something. Really something to do ...

You would be a great help to me, von Prackwitz said thoughtfully. I spoke to you this morning about these political-warlike entanglements. I am sometimes a bit alone - quite at a loss.

There are, the lieutenant continued his thought aloud, so many people running from their jobs now. Working, doing anything at all, has suddenly become meaningless for them. As long as they got a fixed, tangible value for it in their hands at the end of the week, of the month, even the dullest office work had meaning for them. The fall of the Mark opened their eyes. Why are we actually alive? they suddenly ask themselves. Why do we do what? Anything? They don't see why they should do anything just to get their hands on some completely worthless paper rags.

This devaluation is the most infamous fraud on the people ... von Prackwitz said.

This afternoon, von Studmann continued, was an eye-opener for me. - If I really went to you, Prackwitz, I would have to have real work. Work, you see!

Von Prackwitz racked his brain.

'Horses to ride,' he thought. 'but my few crocks already have more movement than they would like. - Writing on the office? But surely I can't put Studmann behind the payroll!'

He suddenly saw the manor office in front of him with the green-painted, old-fashioned strongbox, the size of which was disproportionate to its contents, the ugly spruce shelves full of outdated law collections -: 'A disgustingly dusty and dilapidated place', he thought.

Von Studmann was much more practical than the Rittmeister. I understand he helped him, are there volunteers on many manors?

They exist!" confirmed Prackwitz. A terrible society! They pay pension - otherwise nobody would take them -, keep their own riding horse, stick their nose into everything, understand nothing, touch nothing, but can talk enormously smart about agriculture!

So not, decided von Studmann. And what else is there?

Many things. For example, farm stewards who dispense feed, supervise feeding and milking and grooming, keep stock books, do duty at the threshing machine. Then there are field managers who are outside, plowing and fertilizing and ordering harvests, just all the field work, have to be everywhere ...

Riding horse -? asked von Studmann.

Bicycle, replied von Prackwitz. At least with me.

So you have a field inspector?

Tomorrow I'll put him out, a lazy, boozy guy!

But not because of me, Prackwitz! I can't become a field inspector with you right away! You say: Studmann, fertilize this rye for me. Damn it, it should turn sour on me, I don't have the slightest clue after all - except about natural fertilization, which would be insufficient, I'm afraid.

The two gentlemen laughed heartily. They got up from their bench, von Studmann's growler was gone, Prackwitz was sure the friend would come to him. They discussed the project at length, very thoroughly, as they went along. They agreed that von Studmann should come to Neulohe as something in between an apprentice, a confidant and a supervisor.

You're going first thing in the morning, Studmann. You packed your things in half an hour, if I know you. - Now I'd have to get a decent guy who could supervise and drive the people I hired today - and the harvest would go great! Oh God, Studmann, I'm so glad! The first happy hour, I do not know how long! Listen, now we're going to eat somewhere nice, it'll do you good after that miserable binge. What do you think about Lutter and

Wegner? Beautiful! - Now another man, preferably also from the Kommiß, former Spieß or something, who can deal with people ...

They went to the basement at Lutter and Wegner. The man from the commissary, whom Rittmeister von Prackwitz needed, was sitting at the corner table. He had not been a spit, but he had been a flag officer. At the time he was quite drunk.

10

But that's Fahnenjunker Pagel!

There sits grenade bagel!

This was shouted by von Studmann and von Prackwitz.

And immediately, with almost eerie clarity, they both saw a scene that had made this very Pagel unforgettable to them among the many figures of the World War. That is, it had no longer been the World War, but that last, desperate attempt by German troops to hold the Baltic against the onslaught of the Reds. It had been in the spring of 1919, it had been that wild attack of Germans, Balts and Latvians that finally liberated Riga.

In the motley detachment of the cavalry captain von Prackwitz, there had also been the young Pagel at that time, hardly older looking than a tall schoolboy. Perhaps he really was already seventeen, more likely only sixteen years old, dropped out of the Kadetten-Anstalt Groß-Lichterfelde, he, who had been destined for an officer's career, was thrust into a raging, embattled world that no longer wanted to know anything about officers. Then it had come about of its own accord that the uprooted, senseless man had wandered further and further east until he finally landed with men whom he could still call comrades and did not have to address as comrades.

Touching and ridiculous at the same time had been the joy of the downy-cheeked man, who had never smelled powder before, to be among battle-hardened old people who spoke his language, wore his uniform, gave and took orders - and then actually carried them out. Nothing could tire his zeal, nothing his eagerness to get to know everything in the shortest possible time: machine gun, mine launcher, and the one, only tank platoon.

Until it went to the attack, until the foreign machine guns also began to hack to the own ones, until the first shells howled away over them to die further behind. Until the eager child's play of the schoolboy became serious. Prackwitz as well as Studmann had seen the young Pagel turn pale, suddenly he had become quiet. With each shell howling hollowly away over him, he had pulled his head between his shoulders and made a deep bow.

The two officers had communicated with a glance - without a word. They hadn't said anything to the boy either. From him, green in the face, with sweaty forehead and wet hands fighting against his fear, a bridge had been built to those incomprehensibly distant August days fourteen, when they themselves had heard this howling for the first time, had pulled their heads between their shoulders for the first time. Everyone went through this once, everyone had to fight the battle with the bastard in them once. There were many who never quite came to terms with him. But most of them remained winners, and from then on it did them no harm.

With the young Pagel it was doubtful. You could have spoken to him now, yelled at him, he wouldn't have heard anything. He heard only the howling in the air, he looked here, there, like one frightened in a dream, he hesitated in proceeding. Now he looked back.

Yep, Pagel, it's safe, the damn Reds are shooting in, the impacts are closer and closer. Sure, Squire Pagel, now we're getting haze!

And there it is already in the ranks, the first grenade! Mechanically, Studmann and Prackwitz throw down - but what about Pagel? The young pagel stands there, stares, looks at the earth funnel, he moves his lips as if he said something incantatory -.

Throw it down, Pagel! cries von Prackwitz.

Then everything is upturned earth, dust, fire, smoke - the bang of the explosion tears the air.

'Sheep's head!' thinks von Prackwitz.

'What a pity!' thinks von Studmann.

But - and it is not to be believed - there stands, shadow in fog and haze, still the figure, motionless. It becomes clearer, the figure makes a leap, grabs something from the ground, shouts angrily: Ow damn! drops it, takes the cap to grab, rushes to Prackwitz, knocks his heels together: Report obediently, Herr Rittmeister, a grenade blast! And completely unmilitary: miserably hot!
-

He had - forever - gotten the bastard in him under control, the young Pagel.

Forever?

This scene, this somewhat silly and yet heroic act of a bloody young man, was clearly before the eyes of the two when they saw Pagel sitting there, apparently a little drunk, at the corner table with Lutter and Wegner when they called out: But that's the grenade pagel!

The grenade pagel looked up. With the cautious gesture of the drunken man, he first pushed back his glass and bottle a little before standing up and saying without any surprise: "Officers!

But stand at ease, Pagel, said the cavalry captain with a smile. With the gentlemen officers it is over. You see, you are the only one of us who still wears a uniform.

At your command, Herr Rittmeister, said Pagel stubbornly. But I don't do service anymore.

The two friends communicated with a quick glance.

May we join you at the table, Pagel? von Studmann asked kindly. It's pretty crowded down here, and we would have liked something to eat.

Please. Please! said Pagel and sat down quickly, as if standing had long since become difficult for him. The two also sat down. A time passed choosing the food and wine and ordering.

Then the cavalry captain raised his glass: "Here's to you, Pagel! Here's to the old days!

Thank you most obediently, Herr Rittmeister! Lieutenant! Here's to the old days, yes.

And what do you do now?

Now? Pagel looked slowly from one to the other, as if he had to think very carefully about his answer first. Yes, I do not know myself exactly ... Something ...

He made a vague hand gesture.

But you must have done something in the four years since then! von Studmann said kindly. Started something, engaged, aligned - how?

Sure, sure! Pagel politely agreed. And asked with the clear-eyed malice of the drunkard: If I may take the liberty of asking, Lieutenant - you have aligned a lot in these four years -?

Von Studmann paused, wanted to get angry, then laughed. You are right, Pagel! I have not aligned anything. As you can see me here, six hours ago I netted another complete shipwreck. And I really wouldn't know what to do with myself if the cavalry captain didn't take me to his estate - as a kind of apprentice. Prackwitz has a large estate in the Neumark region.

Six hours ago shipwreck, repeated Pagel, completely overhearing the good. Funny thing.

Why is that funny, Pagel -?

I don't know ... Maybe because you're eating duck with wine cabbage here now - maybe that's why it seems funny to me.

As for that, said von Studmann, now mischievous in his turn, you also sit here and drink a stone wine. - By the way, enjoyed in such quantities much too heavy, duck would also be better to you.

Of course, Pagel readily agreed. I've thought about it too. Only, eating is terribly boring, drinking is much easier. And besides, I still have plans.

Whatever you intend to do, Pagel, Studmann said lightly, food will be more useful than drink.

Hardly, hardly! replied Pagel. And as if to prove it, he drank his glass empty. But this demonstration made no impression on the others, their faces were skeptical - so he added by way of explanation: "I still have a lot of money to spend.

You certainly won't be able to spend much more money on drinking, Pagel! von Prackwitz intervened. He had long been annoyed by Studmann's wimpy attitude, which tended to encourage this young fant. Gosh, don't you realize that you're full to the brim?!

Von Studmann waved his eyes away, but to his surprise Pagel remained calm. Possible, he said. But that doesn't matter. The easier I get rid of my money.

So women's stories! exclaimed von Prackwitz angrily. I'm not a moralist at all, Pagel, but drunk like that, in this state, no, that's nothing!

Pagel did not answer. Instead, he had refilled his glass, emptied it thoughtfully, and refilled it. Prackwitz made an angry move, but von Studmann did not agree with his Rittmeister at all. Prackwitz was a great guy, a decent guy, but he was certainly not a psychologist, he could not observe other people at all - he always thought that everyone had to feel like him. And if things didn't go his way, he immediately boiled over.

No, just as Pagel had filled his glass and quickly emptied it and filled it again, Studmann had been reminded very embarrassingly, but no less vividly for that reason, of a certain room with the number 37. There, too, the glasses had been filled this way and emptied that way. Studmann also remembered very clearly a certain eye expression of fear and insane impudence that he observed there. He wasn't at all sure that Pagel, nonsensical as he was drinking, was drunk at all. It was certain, however, that the questioning of the gentlemen was not pleasant for him; he would have preferred to sit alone. Studmann, however, had no intention of being influenced by this indifferent or hostile mood of Pagel's; he felt they had met the former Fahnenjunker in a dangerous position. As in those days, one had to keep an eye on him. And von Studmann, who had suffered a defeat in the afternoon, vowed not to fall for any bluff that night, but to throw the hand grenade in the shape of a champagne bottle in time - there were many possibilities and types for such throws.

Pagel now sat quietly smoking, seemingly pensive, not quite aware of the presence of the other two. Studmann informed Prackwitz half aloud of his intention, von Prackwitz only made an impatiently defensive movement, but finally agreed.

When the cigarette was finished, Pagel again tilted the bottle over the glass, but nothing flowed from the neck, the bottle was empty. Pagel looked up, he avoided the gaze of the other two, he waved his eyes at the waiter and ordered another bottle of stone wine and a double cherry brandy from him.

Impatiently, von Prackwitz wanted to say something, but Studmann put his hand on his knee imploringly - and the cavalry captain remained silent, albeit unwillingly.

When the waiter brought the drink he had ordered, Pagel demanded the bill. Either the waiter was striking out violently in view of the guest's condition, or Pagel had been drinking here for hours: the bill was very high. Pagel pulled a bundle of banknotes out of his pants pocket, took a few, gave them to the waiter and refrained from handing them over. The waiter's unusually submissive thanks revealed the amount of the tip.

The two gentlemen communicated again by glances, one angry and the other urging calm. But they still said nothing, instead they continued to watch Pagel, who now pulled bundles of banknotes out of all his pockets and bags and packed them on top of each other. Then he took his paper napkin, wrapped it around the pile, searched in his pocket again, brought out one end of string, and tied up the pack. Now he pushed it to one side; as if leaning back after work done, he lit a cigarette, tipped the cherry brandy and poured a glass of wine.

Now he looked up. His gaze, strangely dark and fixed from such bright eyes, was on the gentlemen with a slight sneer. Studmann was clear at the moment he was looked at in this way that Pagel was only acting. Both the drinking and the apparent disregard, like the challenging exposure and wrapping of the money - all theater, performed for them both!

'The boy is completely desperate,' he thought, strangely touched. Maybe he wants to tell us something or ask for help - but he can't bring himself to do it yet - if only it weren't for Prackwitz ...'

But the white-haired, hot-tempered Prackwitz had already been unable to hold on to himself. It's a mess, Pagel! he shouted angrily, the way you handle the money! This is no way to handle money!

Studmann had the impression that Pagel was pleased with this outburst, even though he remained calm.

If I may be so bold as to ask, Herr Rittmeister, he said with a heavy tongue, but ever increasing politeness, how do you handle money?

How?! shouted the cavalry captain. His forehead veins swelled and his eyes reddened with anger. How to handle money?! Neat way to handle it!!! Herr Fahnenjunker Pagel!!! Neatly, conscientiously - as befits, understand? You don't carry it loose in your pockets, you put it in a wallet -.

It's too much, Herr Rittmeister, Pagel said apologetically. It doesn't go into any wallet.

You don't carry around that much money at all, sir! the cavalry captain shouted in bright anger. (They were already peeking from the next tables.) That's not decent. You don't do things like that!

No? Pagel asked like an obedient, inquisitive student. Studmann bit his lips to keep from laughing out loud. Von Prackwitz, however, was too humorless to realize that his ensign was playing a little joke on him.

Pagel said apologetically, "As soon as I've finished my wine, I want to see about getting rid of this stuff as quickly as possible.

He drank. Now a mischievous, very boyish smile slid across his face. Studmann thought he looked like he did that first day in Courland no thought of a resemblance to the Reichsfreiherr Baron von Bergen. Pagel reached for the money pack, hesitated, and then with quick decision held it out across the table to the Rittmeister: "Or do you want it, Herr Rittmeister?

Rittmeister Joachim von Prackwitz half jumped up from his chair, his face turning dark red. This was an insult, a thoughtfully inflicted insult, and it made it ten times worse that it came from a former ensign. An officer, and among all officers especially a Rittmeister von Prackwitz, may well take off his uniform, but he still retains the old concepts and views. Von Studmann and von Prackwitz were good friends, nevertheless - the friendship had been established under the rank ratio Rittmeister-Oberleutnant, and it remained so. If the lieutenant wanted to say something unpleasant to the cavalry captain, it had to be done with careful observance of all the forms that belonged between superiors and subordinates. Pagel, however, was not even the Rittmeister's friend; he had said something very unpleasant, indeed something insulting, virtually without any preparation and without any preservation of form. So the Rittmeister von Prackwitz cooked.

Something terrible could happen. Von Studmann put his hand firmly on the Rittmeister's shoulder, forcing him back to his chair. He's senselessly drunk, he said half aloud. And sharply to Pagel: Apologize right now!

The boyish smile on Pagel's face slowly faded. As if he was not quite clear what was actually happening, he looked broodingly at the angry cavalry captain, then at the money pack in his hand. His face became somber. He put the pack back on the table beside him, reached for the glass and drank hastily.

Sorry ... he then suddenly said sullenly. Who today still attaches importance to such faxes ...?!

I have, Herr Pagel, exclaimed the cavalry captain still very angry, kept my old ways of life, may others find them obsolete and bad. I put a lot of emphasis on these faxes!

Lieutenant von Studmann suggested perfectly clearly: Let him, Prackwitz. He's overwrought, he's drunk, and maybe he's up to something bad.

I am not interested in him! shouted the cavalry captain angrily. I love to let him!

Pagel had glanced quickly at the lieutenant, but had not answered.

Von Studmann bent over the table and said kindly: "If you would offer me the money, Pagel, I would take it.

The cavalry captain made a gesture of stunned astonishment, but Pagel hastily grabbed the money packet and pulled it closer to him.

I won't take it away from you, said the lieutenant, a little mockingly.

Pagel blushed, now ashamed. What would you do with the money? he asked sullenly.

Keep it to you - up to a better hour.

This is unnecessary - I don't need any more money.

Exactly what I assumed, the lieutenant calmly confirmed. And he asked, emphatically indifferent: Why did you actually get shipwrecked six hours ago, too, Pagel?

This time Pagel turned completely red. With an almost agonizing slowness, the blush spread from his cheeks all over his face. It crept under the high, wrinkled collar of the tunic, rising to below the hairline above the forehead. Suddenly you saw how bloody young this person was, how terribly he was now suffering from his youthful embarrassment.

Even the angry cavalry captain looked at his grenade pail with different eyes.

But the latter, embittered by the embarrassment so evident, asked defiantly: "Who told you that I was shipwrecked, Herr von Studmann?

And Studmann: I had understood you that way, Pagel.

And Pagel: Then you have misunderstood me - I - But he broke off unwillingly, his blush betrayed him too visibly.

Of course you are in a bad way, Pagel, von Studmann said gently - we can both see that, Herr Rittmeister as well as me. You're not a habitual drinker after all. They drink for a reason. Because something went wrong for you, because you - well, you get the idea, Pagel!

Pagel turned his wine glass in his hand. His posture was more relaxed, but he did not answer.

Why won't you let us help you, Pagel? the lieutenant asked again. I also had the Rittmeister help me this afternoon without hesitation. I was also quite unpleasantly fallen ...

He smiled at the memory of his case this afternoon.

He had no memory of him, but Prackwitz had described it to him quite drastically, how he had rolled at the feet of the guests. Studmann was aware that his 'case' was substantially different from Pagel's - physically, actually, only, not so much psychologically. But this little exaggeration did not bother him.

Perhaps we can advise you, he continued with gentle but insistent persuasion. It would be even better if we could help you energetically in some way, Pagel, he said very forcefully. When we advanced on Tetelmünde at that time, you fell down with the machine gun. You did not think for a moment to accept my help. Why should not apply in Berlin what applied in Courland -?

Because, Pagel said gloomily, we were fighting for a cause then. Today, it's every man for himself - and against everyone.

Once a comrade, always a comrade, said von Studmann. You remember, don't you, Pagel?

Yes, of course, Pagel said. He lowered his face as if thinking. The two looked at him waitingly. Then Pagel raised his head again. A lot could be said against it, he said very clearly with his slow, labored pronunciation. But I do not like I am terribly tired. Can I meet you somewhere, tomorrow morning?

With three words, the two friends had reached an understanding. We will leave tomorrow morning shortly after eight from the Silesian station, heading for Ostade, von Studmann said.

Good, Pagel said. I will then also be on the track - maybe ...

He looked in front of him as if everything was done. He didn't ask any questions, he didn't seem to care why you were driving, where you were going, what came next.

This cavalry captain doubtfully shrugged his shoulders, unsatisfied by this half promise. But Studmann did not give in.

That's something, Pagel, he insisted. But not quite what we would like. - You are up to something, Pagel, you said something earlier about becoming moneyless ...

Women's stories! muttered the cavalry captain.

It's almost twelve. Between now and eight o'clock tomorrow morning you have something planned, Pagel, the outcome of which seems so uncertain to you yourself that you may not give us a firm promise that you do not want us to be there either ...

Wretched women ... muttered the cavalry captain.

I am, Studmann said more hurriedly when he realized Pagel wanted to answer, of a different opinion than the Rittmeister. I don't think there is any dubious womanizing behind it. You're not the man for that kind of thing.

Pagel lowered his head, but the cavalryman gasped.

I would be grateful, we would be grateful, if you would allow us to spend just the next few hours with you.

It's nothing special, said Pagel, now overcome by the other's careful persistence. I just want to make a sample.

The former lieutenant smiled. A question to fate, eh, Pagel? he said. God's court, invoked by the former Fahnenjunker Pagel. - Oh, how enviably young you still are!

I don't find myself so enviable! growled Pagel.

No, of course not, you're quite right, Studmann hurried on. As long as you are young, you think youth is just a mistake. - Only later do you discover that youth is happiness. - So, how about it, are we coming along?

You do not prevent me from doing what I want?

No, of course not. They should act as if we were not there. The Herr Rittmeister also agrees?

Rittmeister von Prackwitz only grumbled softly, but this agreement alone was enough for Pagel.

So, for my sake, come along! Something revived him. You may even find it interesting. It's - well, you'll see. Let's go ...

They set out.

Chapter 07

- Sultry full moon night -

07 01

Amanda Backs stood in the bushes breathing rapidly. The Privy Councillor squawked in his bruised old man's voice in the highest tones: "Well, Mr. Meier, what kind of voice have you acquired? You're whistling like a woman!

Negermeier's head went out the window. That's just, Mr. Privy Councillor, he said, explaining, because I came up from my sleep like that. I always have such a high voice in my sleep!

I don't care," said the old man. The main thing that your wife believes in the high voice later. - I have a letter here, Mr. Meier.

Yes, Privy Councillor, will be taken care of.

Just you wait, young man! You'll be back in your poses soon enough! - Give the letter to my son-in-law!

Yes, Privy Councilor. First thing tomorrow morning when he gets off the train.

Nah, that doesn't suit me. Then his wife is there, it's a business thing, you see, Mr. Meier -?

Yes, Privy Councilor. So I give it ...

Just you wait, young man! Why don't you make the bed creak? The bed creaks just out of boredom - or what?

Yes, Privy Councillor ...

There you go! - And you won't catch a cold here at the open window, as cool as you are used to. - Do you actually always sleep shirtless, Mr. Meier -?

Privy Councillor, I ...

You'd better say Jawohl, Privy Councillor - that's your safest bet, isn't it? They think I can't see in the dark. I can see in the dark just as well as an old tomcat, got it?!

It was so hot, Privy Councillor, excuse me ...

Of course I apologize, my son. I'm sorry you're hot tonight. Where you haven't run in, and afterwards you're still watering your nose - how can you not be hot?!

Privy Councillor ...!

Well, what's the secret council -?! You know what, son, I've been thinking about this. I'd better have my Elias carry the letter over, I almost think you'll have too much butter on your head tomorrow to even think about the letter ....

Pleading: Mr. Privy Councillor -!

So, good evening, Mr. Meier, and you'd better put on a nightgown. I think I saw the Amanda in the park earlier ...

The old man shuffled away; Amanda stood in the bushes, her heart pounding hard. She had always known that her Hänsecken was not much good and ran after every woman's skirt. She had thought she could keep him in line if she was always there for him .... Nope, is not, for ours such a thing is not enough!

Little Meier was still leaning against the window. Once more he had begged quite miserably: But Privy Councillor ... As if the Privy Council could help anything, and as if it would have changed anything if the letter had been entrusted to him after all ...

Amanda could see him lying in the window quite well from her seat. God, he was so stupid, you Meier! Why did she always fall for such stupid, wimpy guys -?! Which were also no good at all! She did not understand. She was sad.

Now the women inside started whispering and whispering. Hansel half turned around and said roughly: Oh, shut up!

This pleased Amanda again; the fact that he was so hostile to the other girl showed that he did not care much for her. He shouldn't have talked to her like that, she always gave him something on the roof right away. But she would have liked to know who the other one was - it wasn't anyone from the castle, they had all been in prayer.

Get dressed quickly! she heard Hansel say. When Amanda comes, there is a hell of a racket! I can use that just yet.

Amanda almost laughed out loud. Stupid as always! The noise was outside his window, but he didn't look, he didn't notice anything. Hänsecken was always terribly clever afterwards! But she would have liked to get it for the wench - everyone in the village had to know that she went with Hänsecken. Not to mention those on the farm!

The one inside seemed to really hurry up, Amanda heard her rumbling in the parlor. Now her head was next to Hansen's.

Just close the window and turn on the light. I can't find my stuff, she scolded.

('Just who is it -? When someone whispers like that, you can't guess who it is at all!')

Shh! Meier made so loud and sharp that even Amanda flinched in her bush. Can't you shut up -?! If I turn on the light, they'll think I'm awake!

Who is supposed to think about that? Probably your Amanda?

(Whether it was the Hartig -? That would be the height! The Kutschersche with her eight children steals a boyfriend from a young girl! But then there was something!)

None of your damn business! Get the hell out of here!

But my stuff ...

I do not make light. I don't care how you get along!

Scolding, the second head disappeared from the window. Amanda was now almost certain it was the Hartig. But almost sure is not quite. She was in no hurry, Hänsecken still caught her, first she had to catch the wench! She had to catch them - and if she was going to stand here all night! Before their eyes, the came out - either out the door or out the window, so just be patient!

It was funny - but after Amanda had gotten so thoroughly angry in the prayer room, now that there was much more occasion, she couldn't really get angry at all. Not at all on Hansel corners. He was a sheep and remained a sheep, and if she didn't take care of him, he just did stupid things. But she wasn't really that angry at the wench either. Amanda wondered to herself. But maybe once she knew who it was and talked to her, she would still get angry. She hoped she would still get going -! She should not imagine that she let herself be deprived of anything that belonged to her!

So she stood and waited patiently and impatiently, just as her thoughts were going. Until she finally saw - not without amusement - that the visitor climbed out of the window scolding her. The pleasure, however, came from the fact that this climbing out of the window proved once and for all that Hänsecken did not care much for the woman's room, nor did she have any power over him. Because if he was even too lazy to unlock the front door for her -!

The woman did not linger long over a fond farewell, nor did she look around, but headed straight for the corner of the house in the courtyard.

'Now then!" thought Amanda Backs, and headed for it. In the inspector's room, the windows were closed with quite a bit of noise, and that did get Amanda going a bit now. Because closing the windows on such a warm night could only mean that Inspector Meier did not want any more visits - and Amanda was referring to herself.

You, wait a minute, Hartigen! she called out.

You, Mandchen? asked the coachwoman, peering at the other one. What you scared me! Well, good night. I have to go on. I'm in a hurry.

Take me with you! Amanda said and hurried beside her across the yard, towards the coachman's apartment. I have the same way as you!

Did you?" asked Mrs. Hartig, walking more slowly. Yes, someone like you, on your feet from morning till night - the madam won't easily get her back!

I also don't get off my feet as easily as some others, Amanda said full of meaning. Well, go to, your husband will be waiting for you!

But the Hartig remained standing. It was in the middle of the yard. On the right were the pigsties, where it still rustled sometimes (the stall doors were open because of the heat), on the left was the dunging area. The two women, however, stood in such a way that Amanda could just see the light in the coachman's apartment, at one end of the courtyard; Mrs. Hartig, however, looked over to the other end, where light was now also burning behind the inspectors' windows - and that must have really annoyed her that he had now turned on the light after all.

Mandchen is not a form of address for me at all! Amanda Backs finally said belligerently after a long silence.

I can also say Fräulein Backs, if you prefer," Hartig admitted peacefully.

Yes, Miss, it sounded back. I am not a woman yet - I can always go where I like!

You can, confirmed the coachwoman. Such a poultry maid as you are, any dominion will gladly take.

Now, do we want to talk about it or do we not want to talk about it?! Amanda shouted angrily and stamped her foot.

The coachwoman was silent.

I might as well talk to your husband about it, Amanda said threateningly. I heard, he was really wondering last time because you have such plaid kids!

Checked children! laughed Hartig, but a bit forced. How funny you can talk, Mandchen, one just has to wonder!

You are not supposed to say Mandchen! Amanda ordered angrily. I don't like hearing that from you!

I can also say Miss Backs.

Then do it too - and anyway, it's a shame when a married woman takes away a girl's boyfriend!

I didn't take him away from you, Mandchen," said Hartig pleadingly.

You did -! And such a one, who has eight children, you have your part away, you should think!

God, Mandchen! said the coachwoman peacefully, you just don't know what it's like when you're married. You think of it all quite differently.

Don't make any speeches, Hartigen! Amanda shouted threateningly. You can't get me the sweet way.

Once you have your feast, the hardy readily explained, you think it's over. But then you feel so funny again ...

How funny -? Don't give me any rhubarb!

God, Mandchen, I don't do that either! You know how it is when you feel so strange, and you have a tingling sensation all over your body, and you have no peace about anything, and everything always has to happen quickly, as if you can't wait - and suddenly you've been standing there for a full quarter of an hour, the bucket of pork potatoes in your hand, and you don't know anything about anything....

I have nothing to do with pork potatoes! Amanda Backs said dismissively. But she wasn't actually that dismissive anymore, she was more thoughtful.

No, of course not! said Hartig hurriedly. And she added, because now she could probably dare: With you it is then the chicken potatoes ...

But the poultry maid did not feel this malice at all. You'll have your husband for that, she said with newly awakened severity, if you get so weird. You can't get in our way anymore!

But, Mandchen, that's just what you don't know beforehand! exclaimed Hartig eagerly.

What do you not know beforehand?

That the own man against it does not help at all! If I had known as a young girl what I know today, I would never have married, believe me!

Is that really so, Hartigen? Amanda Backs asked, deeply thoughtful. Don't you like your husband at all?

God, yes, of course - he's quite nice so far. And quite neat too. But sooo not. Not for a long time.

So you like Hänse - the Inspector Meier better -?

God, Mandchen, the things you think too! I already told you, I'm not taking him away from you!

Amanda's voice sounded very angry: So that's where he started, I mean, the Meier?

Hartig was silent for a while and considered. But she decided to tell the truth after all. No, Mandchen, I don't want to steal anything from you. I wanted it first - and that's what a man feels. And then he was also a bit thin ...

So, duhn he was also! But I still understand station - if you do not like him at all?

Yes, you know, Mandchen, I don't know either, but when you get that tingling feeling, and you're curious, too ...

But you shall not -! Amanda lashed out for a tremendous final punitive sermon, though it would have been much milder than she had intended. Because in the end she understood the Hartigen quite well ...

But Amanda broke off.

Across the courtyard came walking one after the other three figures: first a man, then a woman, then another man ...

Quietly and gently, they walked across the courtyard in the dark, without a word - and Amanda Backs and Mrs. Hartig, they stared.

When the foremost man reached the women, he involuntarily stopped and asked in a sharp, commanding voice: Who is standing there -?!

At the same time, the two women were illuminated by an electric flashlight held by the woman in the middle. (For the moon was not yet high, the stable buildings still intercepted its light).

I, Amanda, Amanda Backs said calmly, while the coachwoman involuntarily put her hands in front of her face, as if she had been caught doing something forbidden.

The man in front said again, and silently and gently the three of them passed the two women - across the courtyard, around the corner of the inspector's house - and Hartig could see that there, during their dispute, the light had gone out again.

Who was that?" asked the coachwoman in amazement.

I think it was the madam, Amanda said thoughtfully.

The madam, in the middle of the night, with two men! shouted the Hartig. I'll never believe that in my life!

Hans Fallada   -376-   Wolf among Wolves

The one in the back may have been the servant, Amanda continued to ponder. I don't know the one in front. He's not from here - I haven't heard that voice yet!

Funny ... said the Hartig

Funny ... said the Backs.

What business is it of his that we are standing here? Amanda asked aloud. Is not even from here and sends us to bed!

Exactly! echoed Hartig. And the madam lets him command quietly ...

Where the heck did they go? Amanda asked, staring toward the end of the yard.

To the castle? suggested Hartig.

I wo! Why around the back? The lady doesn't need to go to the back of the castle! Amanda said dismissively.

Then there is only the inspector's house ... said the Hartig trying.

I was just thinking the same thing, Amanda admitted frankly. But what do they want there, so funny, three in a row, and so gently - as if no one should see them ...

Yes, it was funny, Hartig admitted. And suggested: If we sow once -?

You're finally going to your husband! Amanda Backs said sternly. If anyone looks at the inspector's house, it's me.

But I would like to know, Mandchen ...

You're supposed to say Miss Backs. What are you going to tell your husband anyway, where you've been for so long? And your children ...

Oh ... made the hardy indifferent.

And anyway, you leave my Hans in peace now! Once again it does not go so well! If I catch you again ...

Hans Fallada   -377-   Wolf among Wolves

Certainly not, Mandchen, I swear to you! But you also tell me tomorrow ...

Good night! Amanda Backs said shortly and walked towards the dark inspector's house.

The coachwoman stood a moment longer, watching her enviously. She considered how good such young, unmarried girls had it, and how they didn't even know it. Then she sighed softly and walked toward her home, toward the flurry of children and the man who was surely scolding her.

2

After the shock in the evening devotion, Mrs. von Teschow had felt a deep need for rest. She didn't want to see or hear anything anymore, quickly she wanted to go to bed.

Guided on one side by her friend, Fräulein Jutta von Kuckhoff, on the other by the servant Elias, she had staggered upstairs to the large, three-striped mahogany bedroom. Fräulein von Kuckhoff had undressed the trembling, sobbing one, and now she lay in the wide mahogany bed, small to look at, like a child, with the dry, tiny bird's head, a white bed bonnet over her thin hair, a wide-meshed knitted bed jacket draped around her shoulders.

She wailed: O my Lord and my God - Jutta, what a world! God forgive me for judging - but what a shameless youth! Oh, what will Lehnich say -?! And first Superintendent Kolterjan?!

Every thing is good for something, Belinde, Jutta said wisely. Don't get any more upset! - Are you still freezing like that?

Yes, Mrs. von Teschow was still freezing. Fräulein von Kuckhoff rang for the servant Elias. He got the order to get two hot water bottles from the kitchen.

The servant wanted to leave.

Ah, Elias!

Please, madam?

Why don't you tell Mamsell to brew me another cup of peppermint tea? Yes - and quite strong. And with lots of sugar.

Yes - oh God!

Yes, ma'am.

The servant wanted to leave.

Ah, Elias!

Please, madam?

I'd rather have her make me mulled wine, not peppermint tea. Peppermint tea always bumps so! But without water, only red wine. Red wine already contains a lot of water. Oh God - and a little bit of nutmeg. And a carnation. And a lot of sugar. Right, Elias, you're getting this right for me?

Yes, ma'am.

And - ah - Elijah, just a moment! Tell her to put a little shot of rum in it - I really feel very sick - not much. But you have to taste it, of course, not so very little, Elias, you understand -?

The servant Elias, soon to be seventy, with the smooth head, understands. He waits another moment and is about to leave, when the faint call of the sick under the door reaches him once more: Ah, Elijah!

Please, madam -?

Oh, Elias, please, come closer ... You can once inquire in the kitchen ... but not as if it's coming from me, by the way ...

The servant Elijah waits silently. The madam must be very sick again right now, she can hardly talk. Surely it would be good if she could get her mulled wine quickly, but he can't order it yet, Frau von Teschow still has something on her mind.

Elias - why don't you ask - but unobtrusively! - - whether they - you know! - has gone to bed. Yes, ask once, but unobtrusively ...

For a while, the sick woman is still very ill, and Fräulein von Kuckhoff has a lot to do, with good sayings, wise coaxing, warming the cold hands between hers, stroking the aching forehead. But then the hot-water bottles arrive, the mulled wine comes, smelling strongly of rum: the smell alone invigorates Frau von Teschow. Sitting up in bed, lips tightly pinched, she hears the message that 'she' has gone out.

It's good, Elias. I am very sad. Right good night, Elias. I will probably hardly be able to sleep.

Elias makes an appropriately sad face to this parting remark, also wishes a good night and then sits down in the anteroom. He still has to wait for the Privy Councilor to take off his boots. Then his service is over.

But the wait will not be too long for old Elias, he has his occupation. From his pocket he pulls out a thick, formerly brown, now almost black wallet, and a long list with many numbers, names, words. From the wallet comes a packet of brown banknotes, the list is opened, and now they compare, mark, write.

The old madam is having a bad evening today, but the servant Elias is having a good one: today he managed to buy up five new old brown red-stamped peacetime thousand mark bills.

Like many Germans, namely older people, who experience the hellish wonders of inflation, Elias refuses to believe in a general devaluation. Something must remain for a man who has saved diligently for fifty years; it is impossible for the whirlpool to swallow everything.

A simple consideration says that 'real money' from the time before the war must also have remained 'real'. This is already proven by the sentence on the bills that they will be redeemed for gold by the Reichsbank. And gold is still right. Incorrect, of course, is money spent during the war or even after the war. During the war, the fraud already started with the linen shirts made of paper and the leather shoes made of cardboard.

When old Elias felt the first signs of inflation, he started buying up thousand mark bills. There were always people who needed money, he got some. There were always people who could not think as well as old Elijah. Yes, Elias had heard that the Reichsbank in Berlin was no longer giving gold for these thousand mark bills. But, of course, that was just bluff, calculated on the stupid. The Reichsbank wanted to get its own bills cheap - to save the scarce gold. Elias, however, was not stupid, he did not give his bills to the Reichsbank cheaply. He waited, he could wait - one day he did get gold for it, just as it was clearly printed.

That's how it started with the Elias - in the beginning it was a capital investment. But then it was added that this also had its science - the old Elias discovered in his old age the delights of the collector (without knowing it).

There were so many different brown thousand mark bills! One thing we learned right away: only those with the red stamp were any good. The ones with the green one were all from the war and post-war period - you were not allowed to collect them! But there were now bills with one red stamp and some that bore two red stamps! There were banknotes that did not have a fiber stripe, and then came bills with a blue fiber stripe on the left and bills with a blue fiber stripe on the right! There were bills with eight signatures, but also some with nine, and some were even signed by ten men! Then there were bills with the letters A, B, C, D, and some with seven-digit numbers, and some with eight-digit numbers. It was always exactly the same brown thousand mark bill, nothing changed in the picture and writing - but what a bewildering amount of differences!

The old servant Elias writes on and compares, he has long since ceased to collect only brown thousand mark bills, he collects differences, marks, characteristics. His big, round, smooth head turns all red at this. He beams when he finds a new way to play that he doesn't have yet! He is firmly convinced that these differences are secret characteristics, made by connoisseurs for connoisseurs. They certainly mean something; whoever knows how to interpret them will win a lot of gold with them!

The old privy councilor may laugh at him. As smart as the old man is, he doesn't know anything about these secret things! He believes what people tell him on the banks, he believes what the newspapers say. Old Elias is not so devout - but today he is already richer than his master, he owns well over a hundred thousand marks! Gold money! Money like gold!

Today he is very happy: he has three brand new bills among his new purchases. He never knew that there were such old thousand mark bills, his oldest one was from 1884. Oh, he will think twice about exchanging these bills for gold one day when the time comes! They are so beautiful, these bills with the solemn figures that he has heard signify industry, commerce and traffic.

Industry, trade and transport, he whispers, staring at the bills with emotion.

Everything that the people work, he considers. Only agriculture is not there - and that's a pity!

What would he want with gold? For over a hundred thousand marks of gold he can not carry around. He only has to worry about gold - but this paper is so beautiful!

He is happy, the old servant! Bill after bill is carefully folded before being returned to the bag. The banknote presses in Berlin chase and rush the people into an ever more agonizing frenzy - they have given them luck, great luck! Beautiful bills!! -

+++

The mulled wine had done its job. Fresher Mrs. von Teschow sat between the cushions, to her friend she said: If you would read me something, Jutta?

From the Bible -? asked Fräulein von Kuckhoff readily.

But that was not a good suggestion tonight. The evening devotion with the conversion of the sinner was unsuccessful. So the Bible, along with its God, was a little out of favor.

No, no, Jutta - we must finally get on with Goethe!

You're welcome, Belinde. Please, the keys!

Fräulein von Kuckhoff got the keys. Upstairs in the closet, among the hats, lay well hidden a beautiful, thirty-volume, half-leather Goethe - under lock and key - the confirmation gift from Frau von Teschow to her granddaughter Violet von Prackwitz. Violet's confirmation was a long time ago, but there was still no telling when she could be given the Goethe.

Fräulein von Kuckhoff took the seventh volume from the cupboard:

The poems - Lyrical. I.

He looked strangely swollen. Next to the tape on the table, Fräulein von Kuckhoff placed scissors and paper.

Kleister, Jutta! warned Frau von Teschow.

The friend also added the pot of paste, opened the book and began to read the poem of the goldsmith's journeyman at the designated place.

After the first verse, Frau von Teschow nodded her head approvingly: "We're in luck this time, Jutta!

Wait and see, Belinde, said Fräulein von Kuckhoff. One should slaughter the pig before praising its bacon.

And she read the second verse.

Good, good! nodded Frau von Teschow and also found the following verses praiseworthy.

Until you got to the lines:

The little foot kicks and kicks;

Hans Fallada   -383-   Wolf among Wolves

That's when I think of the cradle,

The garter I think also probably with,

I give it to the dear girl ...

Stop, Jutta! called Frau von Teschow. Again! she said plaintively. What do you think, Jutta? she asked.

I told you so right away, explained Fräulein von Kuckhoff. The cat does not leave the mouse!

And that wants to be a minister of state!" Mrs. von Teschow was outraged. The ones from today are no worse. What do you say, Jutta? But she did not wait for the answer. The verdict was in. Tape it up, Jutta! Tape it good and tight - if the child would read it!

Fräulein von Kuckhoff was already plastering the lewd poem with paper and paste. There's not much left, Belinde, she said, lifting the ribbon examiningly.

It's a disgrace!" Mrs. von Teschow was outraged. And something like that wants to be a classic! Oh, Jutta, I would rather have bought a Schiller for the child - Schiller is nobler, not so carnal for a long time!

Remember the old saying, Belinde: no ox without a horn. Schiller is also not for the young. Think of Kabale and Love, Belinde. And then this woman person, this Eboli ...

Right, Jutta. Men are all like that. You don't know how much trouble I had with Horst-Heinz ...

Yes, said the Kuckhoff. Good pig loves his dirt. - Well, I'll keep reading.

Gottlob was followed next by the poem of the saving Johanna Sebus. This was now noble again, but it remained quite unclear why the poet always called Johanna Sebus Schön- Suschen.

He should have written Schön-Hannchen, shouldn't he, Horst-Heinz?

For the Privy Council had just entered. He watched the two women at work, grinning with amusement.

Hanne will have been too ordinary for him, the Privy Council suggested after a close examination of the case. He walked up and down the room, book in hand, on socks and in shirtsleeves.

But why Suschen?

I think to myself, Belinde, Suschen is an abbreviation of Sebuschen. And, Sebuschen, you know, Belinde - what do you think, Jutta? The Privy Councilor was serious, only the wrinkles in the corners of his eyes twitched. Busen - Buschen - Sebuschen - it also sounds offensive, how -?

Tape it up, Jutta, tape it up! If the child would get these ideas! exclaimed Mrs. von Teschow excitedly. Oh, it just remains nothing! - Horst-Heinz, you have to put out the backs right away!

Right now I'm just going to bed. Besides -

I'm going," grumbled the Kuckhoff. Let me lock up the Goethe first!

- moreover, the Backs is already out. I saw them in the park earlier.

You know quite well what I mean, Horst-Heinz!

If I know what you mean, you don't have to tell me anymore, Belinde. And with a threatening clearing of the throat: Fräulein von Kuckhoff, I call your attention to the fact that I am now getting out of my pants!

Horst-Heinz. Give her time, she has to say good night to me first!

I'm going already! Good night, Belinde, and don't worry about the devotion anymore! Sleep well! - Are the cushions lying correctly? The hot water bottles ...

Miss von Kuckhoff -!!! Now come the underpants, and then I'm in a shirt! You're not going to put a Prussian Privy Councillor of Economics in your shirt....

Horst-Heinz.

I'm leaving right now! Sleep well, Belinde, good night and the sherbet powder ...

Suschen - Buschen - Sebuschen -! cried the privy councilor. He was left with only his shirt. But he was reluctant to drop this last shell ... Every evening the same theater with the two old chickens! Oh, those women! he cried.

Have a good night, Privy Councillor, said Fräulein von Kuckhoff with dignity. And he created people in his image - that was a long time ago ...

Jutta! protested Mrs. von Teschow weakly against this denigration of her Horst-Heinz, but the door fell shut behind her friend, and not a moment too soon.

What happened to the evening service? asked the Privy Councillor, diving into his nightgown.

Don't dodge me, Horst-Heinz, you have to fire the Backs tomorrow!

The bed heaved a huge sigh of relief under the old man. It's your poultry mistress and not mine, he said. Do you actually want to keep the lights on for much longer? I want to sleep.

You know that I can't stand excitement - and when such a person becomes insolent ... You could do me the favor once with pleasure, Horst-Heinz!

Did she get cheeky in the evening devotions? inquired the Privy Councilor.

She is indecent, said Mrs. von Teschow angrily. She always climbs up to the inspector in the window.

I think tonight, too, said the Privy Councilor. Your devotion must not have worked yet, Belinde ...

She just has to go. She is incorrigible.

Hans Fallada   -386-   Wolf among Wolves

And then the fuss with your poultry starts again. You know how it is, Belinde. None has ever had so few chicks leaving, nor have there ever been so many eggs. And food she needs less than any other!

Because she is in cahoots with the inspector!

Right, very right, Belinde!

She just gets much more food than she writes on!

That can only be good for us, it is our son-in-law's grain! - No, no, Belinde, she is capable and has a happy hand. I would not give her notice. What business is it of ours what she does at night?

But the house should be clean, Horst-Heinz!

She goes to him in the official's house, he doesn't go to her here in the cottages!

Horst-Heinz.

Well, what else, Belinde? It is true after all!

You know quite well what I mean, Horst-Heinz! She is so outrageous!

It is, the Privy Councillor admitted with a yawn. But that is actually always the case. The most capable people also let themselves be told the least. The little guy, Meier, her boyfriend, you can kick his butt for hours, he just gets more and more polite ...

With her husband, Mrs. von Teschow usually did not hear a rude word at all, so she also overheard the butt.

So tell Joachim to kick the guy out. Then I can keep the backs.

If I tell my son-in-law to throw out his civil servant," the old man said thoughtfully, "he will certainly keep him for the rest of his life. - But take comfort, Belinde, I think Amanda's boyfriend is flying tomorrow .... And if he doesn't, I'll praise him a little - then he'll have to pack his bags the same hour!

You do that, Horst-Heinz!

Hans Fallada   Wolf among Wolves

3

Man is not entirely free from the characteristic of attributing his faults to other creatures: there is no truth in the story of the ostrich that buries its head in the sand out of fear; but it is certainly true that many a man closes his eyes to the approaching danger and then claims that it is not there.

Inspector Meier had only turned on the light after Mrs. Hartig had left because he wanted to find something to drink. The completely depressed skull, the flop with the old privy councilor (on whose benevolence he had always counted), the approaching avenger Amanda - all this evoked in him nothing but the desire to drink. He just 'didn't want to think about all that dirt anymore'.

After securing the windows against a raid by Amanda, he stood quietly for a moment in his rather desolate looking room with the bed rumpled apart and clothes strewn about. It looked just as desolate in his skull, plus a sharp pain stabbed against his forehead from the inside. Scraps of thoughts came out of the darkness and had passed before he could even recognize them. He knew he didn't actually have anything to drink in the booth, no cognac, no Korn, no bottle of beer - but if you were like he was now, there was always something to drink, you just had to think of it.

He frowned from the effort of thinking, but all he could think of was that he could go to the inn again and get a bottle of liquor. He moved his head discouragedly. He had already thought about that, that he didn't want to be seen there because of the impending bill. Besides, he wasn't wearing anything - even that old, clever carrion, the privy councilor, had noticed that. The others would notice too if he went to the inn like that!

He looked down at himself, he started to smile gloomily. A nice dirt, such a guy! A body for the fire tongs!

The shame is not in the shirt - he said aloud a phrase he had once heard and kept because it seemed to him to justify any shamelessness.

Hans Fallada Wolf among Wolves

But now he had to look for his shirt, and he began to push the clothes back and forth on the ground with his feet, hoping that the shirt would appear. But it didn't come out, instead he poked a splinter into his sole.

Swine, wretched, he scolded aloud, and by swine he remembered the pigs, but by pigs he remembered the cattle dispensary in the office. When he thought of the livestock pharmacy, he first thought of Hoffmann's drops. But they were too few to drink with effect, plus there probably weren't any in the pharmacy!

Hoffmann's drops - since when did they give Hoffmann's drops to pigs -?!!! On a lump of sugar, eh?! He had to laugh at this stupid idea, it was too stupid, this idea!

He turned sharply, suspicion and fear on his face. Was there someone laughing at him in the room?! It sounded exactly like someone was laughing at him here! Was he alone at all? Had the Kutschersche already left? Had the Amanda already come or was she just coming? He looked around slowly, stiff-eyed - the path between seeing and recognizing was so arduous. For a long time he had to look at an object until the brain reported: 'Cupboard!' Or: 'Curtain!' -'Bed, no one in it!' - Later: 'No one under it either!'

Laboriously, slowly, he came to the conclusion: there really was no one in the room. But how was it with the office? Was there someone in there watching him? The door to the office was open, the dark room next door was as if someone was lying in wait ... Was the outer door to the office locked at all? Drawn the curtains? Oh God, oh God, so much to do, so much to take care of, he still hadn't found his shirt either! Did he never come to bed -?

With hasty, staggering steps, naked, Negermeier walked up to the office and rattled the outer door. The door was closed, he had known, the curtains were also closed. Who told such nonsense?! He turned on the light and looked at the curtains hostilely - of course they were closed -, all dull smoosh, only made to fool him. The curtains were closed and they stayed closed - someone should come and touch his curtains! It was his curtains, his!

He could do what he wanted with it - if he tore it down now, it was his business alone!

In supreme excitement, he took a few steps toward the unfortunate curtains - and the livestock dispensary, a brown-painted, spruce cupboard, came into his field of vision.

Hello, there you are! Finally! Negermeier grinned with satisfaction. The key was in, the door had learned to parry and opened at the first push, and there we have, in two packed compartments, the whole salad. At the very front is a brownish bottle, it also says something on the sticky note - but who wants to read such pharmacist's claw?! Well, it's printed, but it's the same dirt!

Negermeier takes the bottle, pulls the stopper and smells into the neck of the bottle.

He's about to do it again. High up into his nose he draws the ether vapor, and so he stands there while his body begins to tremble quietly. An unearthly clarity enters his brain, realization and insight such as he has never felt fill him - he breathes in and breathes out - this is bliss!

His face becomes sharper and sharper, his nose more pointed. Deep wrinkles furrow the skin. The body begins to tremble. But he whispers: Oh, I understand everything! Everything! The world ... Clarity ... the happiness ... blue ...

The ether bottle falls from his trembling hands, hits the floor hard and breaks. He stares at it, still intoxicated. Then he quickly goes to the counter, turns off the office light, enters his room, again turns off the light, gropes his way to his bed and throws himself down.

He lies motionless, with his eyes closed, completely surrendered to the moment of the luminous figures moving in his brain. The figures become paler, gray mist blows over them. Blackness draws in from the edges of the brain, it gets darker and darker - suddenly everything is black: Negermeier is asleep.

4

You must know who has the key to the house, the lieutenant scolds angrily.

The three are standing in front of the dark official's house, the servant Räder has pressed the handle, but the front door is locked.

Mr. Meier has the key, of course, says the servant.

There must be another key, the lieutenant insists.

Madam, don't you know who has a second key?

Although the situation is quite clear, the lieutenant persists in addressing Violet as 'Gracious Miss'.

The second key will have dad, says Weio.

And where does your father have the keys?

In Berlin! In response to an annoyed gesture: "Dad's in Berlin, Fritz!

He won't have dragged the key to this place with him to Berlin! - And I have to go to the meeting!

If we went after -!

And meanwhile he runs on with the letter! - Is he even inside?

I don't know! says the servant Hubert, offended. I have nothing to do with Herr Meier, Herr Leutnant!

The lieutenant expires with impatience, annoyance, anger. Always those darn chick flicks that get in the way. He absolutely can not use women in this matter! And how helplessly this Weio now stands by! Not a bit different from this stupid servant! Let him do everything on his own! What will she ask again now -?

She says: There's a window open upstairs, Fritz.

He looks up. Really, there is a window open at the top of the gable!

Great, madam! Now we are about to pay the Lord a little visit. You, heh, young man, I'll lift you here on the chestnut tree - from the branch you can easily get into the window.

But the servant Räder steps back. If the madam will forgive - but I would rather go home now.

The lieutenant curses: Don't be silly, man - with the madam around!

I was happy to help you, madam, says the servant Räder with unwavering firmness and knows and hears no lieutenant at all, and I hope you will not forget it. But now I really have to go to bed ...

Oh, Hubert, begs Weio, do me this favor! Once you have unlocked the front door for us, you can go home immediately. It's just a moment!

It is, in a way, a punishable act, pardon me, madam, the servant modestly objects. And just now two women were standing by the manure pile. I'd really rather go to bed ...

Oh, let the silly Kaffir go, Violet! shouts the lieutenant angrily. He's as scared as a whole company with dysentery! Go away, young man, and don't hang around in the bushes!

Thank you very much, madam," says the servant Räder with unfaltering politeness. I wish you a good night then.

And sure, unwavering step (he doesn't know a lieutenant) he disappears around the corner of the house.

The lieutenant scolds him. Truly, Violet, I would like to be once on Sunday, what he imagines all week! - So, now help me up the tree. If the log wasn't so miserably slippery from being so wet, yes, I could do it on my own. But I think what this idiot can do, so can you ...

While Weio helps her lieutenant up the tree, the servant Räder walks across the estate, hands in the pockets of his jacket, quietly fluting to himself. He has his eyes everywhere, and so he sees very well the figure that wants to pass him in the shadow of the horse stable.

Good evening, Miss Backs, he greets very politely. Still out so late?

You are still on your way, Mr. Wheels! the girl answers belligerently and stops.

Yes, me too! says the servant. But I think it's time to go to bed now. What time do you get up in the morning?

But Amanda Backs overhears his question. Where did the lady go with the gentleman, Mr. Räder? she asks curiously.

Everything in order! says the unadolescent Hubert educationally. I asked you what time you get up in the morning, Miss Backs?

If the Amanda had not been a real woman, she would have answered 'At five' and then could have demanded the answer to her question. But now she says: That can't be of any interest to you, Mr. Räder, when I get up! and thus makes the debate unmanageable.

But finally, after some back and forth, Mr. Räder then learns that Amanda's time of rising is based on sunrise, because the chickens wake up at sunrise. And he hears that now in July the sun comes up around four, so Amanda has to be out by five at the latest.

He finds that this is rather early; he himself does not get up until six, indeed, often later.

Yes, you! Amanda says rather contemptuously, because basically a man who cleans rooms is contemptible. And now he thinks she'd better go to sleep.

And where did the lady go with the gentleman so late? Amanda asks pointedly. She's only fifteen, she should be in bed by now!

Yes, I don't know when the lady will go to bed, says Räder. That is, well different!

Amanda is not giving it up yet. And what kind of gentleman was that, Mr. Räder? I don't even know him.

But the servant Räder thinks he has done his duty. The madam must be in the house with her lieutenant now. That's all he can do to protect them from spies.

No, you probably don't know the gentleman, he confirms. A lot of gentlemen come to us. - So good night!

And before Amanda can ask another question, he has moved on. She stares after him angrily before deciding to go home. As clever as he is, the young wheelman, the feeling arose in her that he had led her around by the nose. And since Mr. Räder is a very natural person, who otherwise never talks to her, he will not have led her to gas for nothing, so completely without purpose. There is something behind it!

Thoughtfully, Amanda continues. She leaves the courtyard, turns the corner of the dark inspector's house, and stops, pondering, in front of her friend's windows.

Earlier, the windows were open, then he closed them. But earlier, when she looked over from the courtyard for a moment, there was a light burning in the window; now there is no light. Amanda tells herself that this is all perfectly all right, that her Hänsecken is asleep now, that it is best to let a man who is tired sleep, and that letting him sleep is the best thing she can do, especially in view of the discussion with Hartig. There's really no point in stirring this thing up again - it's not in her nature at all. Hartig will not get involved with the Hänsecken again - Amanda is firmly convinced of that.

So she could let him sleep and could also go to sleep herself, she can also need sleep - and solid! But her fingers are so itchy, she feels so funny, the bed doesn't even beckon yet, even though she longs for it. She usually knows what she wants, but now, even though she wants to let him sleep, she would also like to drum her fingers against the windows, just to hear his angry, sleepy voice, to know it's all right.... Her is so, her is also different again ...

'Oh, come on! I just drum!' she decides to herself right now. Then she sees a small, round white light in Hansen's room, as if from a flashlight. Involuntarily, she quickly steps aside, although she has seen by the light that the curtains are drawn. Just such a glow of light was directed at her earlier, when she was standing with Hartig by the manure pile. Just such a one!

She stands there pondering, racking her brains as to what the electric flashlight, the madam, and the unknown gentleman are doing in her hen's corner room so late and so secretly. She sees the light wander, go out, light up again, wander again ...

But she is not the person after that to stand idly in front of a window and brood for a long time. She quickly goes to the front door and carefully presses the handle. Leaning her shoulder against the door, she gives in.

Quietly, Amanda steps into the dark hallway and pulls the front door closed behind her again.

5

The lieutenant had reached the dark hallway of the inspector's house via the gabled parlor and the attic stairs. A flash of his flashlight showed him that the key was thankfully inside the front door - he unlocked it, and Weio scurried in to join him.

The office door was locked, but Violet knew what was going on: the double key was in the tin letterbox by the office door, which could be easily pushed open - a convenient arrangement for Meier, so he didn't have to get up in the morning when the yardmaster went to get the stable keys from the office. The two stepped into the office. Here it smelled narcotic, the lieutenant lit up the remains of the bottles and said: chloroform or alcohol - he won't have done anything to himself, the guy? Don't step on the broken pieces, Violet!

No, he hadn't done anything to himself. Already the hearing reported it: Negermeier snored and rattled, that it could frighten one. Violet put her hand around her friend's arm and now felt born in this desolate, smelly, humid room.

Even more: she found this whole nocturnal excursion, this fuss about a letter of hers 'fabulously interesting' and the Fritz 'outrageously dashing'! She was fifteen, her appetite for life was great, and Neulohe was outrageously boring. The lieutenant, of whose existence her parents knew nothing, whom she herself knew only by his first name, whom she had met on her walks through the forest and whom she had liked at first sight, this hurried, often completely absent-minded, mostly cool and brash man, from whose coolness it broke now and then, always surprisingly, like consuming fire - this lieutenant seemed to her the epitome of all masculinity, wordless heroism....

He was completely different from any man she had ever known. Even if he was an officer, he in no way resembled the officers of the Reichswehr who had asked them to dance at the balls in Ostade and Frankfurt. They had always treated her with the utmost politeness, she had always been the 'madam' with whom they chatted seriously and noncommittally about hunting, horses and, at most, the harvest.

With Lieutenant Fritz, she had experienced nothing of politeness. He had strolled through the forest with her, chattering away as if she were some girl; he had taken her arm and held her under, and had let go of it again as if this had not been a favor. He had handed her his dented cigarette case with an indifferent request, as if the strictly forbidden smoking understood itself, and then he had taken her by the head while burning the cigarette and kissed her - just as if that was part of it ... Just don't get in line! he had laughed. Girls who line up, I find simply disgusting!

She didn't want him to find her 'just disgusting'.

You can warn a young person about dangers and maybe even protect them from them - but what about the dangers that look like the dear everyday life, like the most natural thing in the world, that don't look like dangers at all -?! Violet never really had the feeling with Lieutenant Fritz that she was doing something really forbidden, that she was in serious danger. At that time, when it happened and yet something like an instinctive resistance, a panic horror wanted to overtake her, he had said so honestly indignant: I beg you, Violet, don't make any stories! I can't stand this silly, goose-stepping attitude to death! Do you think any girl is any different?! That's what you're here for in the world! So please -!

She might have asked, but then she knew she was just being silly. She would have been ashamed not to do what he wanted. Precisely because he attached so little importance to them, because his visits were so irregular and short, precisely because all his promises were so unreliable (I was going to be here Friday? Don't be silly, Violet, I really have other things to think about than you!), precisely because he was never polite to her, precisely because of that she had fallen for him almost without resistance.

He was so different. Mystery and adventure surrounded him. All his faults became advantages for her because the others did not have them. His coldness, his sudden greed that just as quickly went out, his non-committal forms that just sat on the skin, his complete lack of respect for anything in the world - for her it was all practicality, mad love, masculinity!

What he did was right. This windy fellow who drove around the country with a noncommittal mission to mobilize the country people just in case, this cold adventurer who was not concerned with the goal of the fight but only with the fight, this lansquenet, who would have fought for whatever party, if only there had been unrest - because he loved the unrest and hated the calm, in which he immediately sat there empty, hollowed out, no longer knowing what to do with himself - this dashing Hans in all alleys, he was the hero!

And he could have set a world on fire - he remained the hero for them!

How he now shines the flashlight in his hand, her slightly trembling fingers around his upper arm, on the rumpled bed with the naked man on it, how he says to her indifferently: "You'd better look away, Violet! and pulls a blanket over the naked man; how he growls: "Pig! and then tells her to sit down on a chair next to the bed: "Watch out if he wakes up! I'll quickly look through his things! - this camaraderie, which is lumpiness, which barely conceals inconsideration, lack of respect, crudeness - everything she finds splendid!

She sits in her chair, it is almost completely dark, the moon barely penetrates through the gray-yellow curtains. The one in bed gasps, snores, moans, she can't see him, but now he tosses and turns as if sensing enemies in his sleep. The one behind her is working between things, half cursing; it's hard to find anything in an unfamiliar room with a flashlight in hand. He rustles, bumps into chairs, suddenly the light dances against the window and goes out. Now the rustling starts again ...

Yes, she has to be in bed on time in the evening, occasionally she is allowed to go to a ball until eleven, at the latest twelve o'clock, or with special permission, accompanied by forester and servant, to go to the decorum. In the afternoon, one day after the other, her mother speaks to her in French and English - "So that you stay up to date, Weio! You will have to play a role in society later - unlike your mom, who is just a sharecropper's wife! - Oh, how blasé, how mendacious, how flat the world seems to her at home! Here she sits in the stinking inspector's room, life tasting of blood and bread and dirt. It is by no means, as parents, teachers, pastors claimed, a gentle, friendly, polite affair, dark it is ... a wonderful dark ...

And out of the darkness comes a mouth with gleaming white teeth, the canines are pointed; the lips are narrow, dry, so bold - O mouth, man's mouth to kiss, beast's teeth to bite! Out of the darkness, towards me -!

The parents, the grandparents, Old and New Rohe, Ostade with the garrison, the autumn market in Frankfurt on the Oder, the Café Kranzler in Berlin narrow world, obedient world that stands eternally silent. One sits at a marble table, the waiter bows, dad and mom discuss whether the taller daughter can still take a cream puff with whipped cream, the cheeky guy at the next table fixes her, and the taller daughter looks away - orderly world that has long since ceased to exist, stagnant ruin!

For another life has dawned, in which all this no longer applies, it hunts, glows, flashes - oh, infinite fire, mysterious adventures, glorious darkness, in which one may be naked without shame! Poor mom who never knew this! Poor dad - so old with your white temples! I live, I tumble, I dance - ways upon ways, and what ease to whirl along them, always new ways, always different adventures! Stupid, ugly negermeier, good for nothing but to give a quarter of an hour a little tingle, and to be punished long, hard!

Is this the wipe? the lieutenant asked, lighting up a damp, smudged rag. The guy drowned him in booze!

Oh, please, give it to me! she exclaims, suddenly ashamed of her stupefied scribbling.

But he: Thank you, no, child! That you send him on his travels again, and I can run after him! - He already has it in the bag. - And I'll tell you this, Violet, you're not writing to me again! Never! Not a word!

I was so longing for you! she cries and throws her arms around his neck.

Yes, of course. I understand, I understand everything. - Tell me, you don't keep a diary?

I -? Why -? A diary -? No, of course not!

Well -! I think you are sohlst! I will have to revise your room once!

Oh yes, please!!! Please!!! Please, Fritz, come into my room once, it would be wonderful of you if you had been in my room once.

Hans Fallada   -399-   Wolf among Wolves

Beautiful! Beautiful! That can be arranged! But now I have to hurry, to the meeting, they will already scold!

Today - will you come to me today? After the meeting? Oh, please, Fritz, do it!

Today? It's out of the question! I have to come back here after the meeting - talk to the guy, see if he hasn't told others about the letter ...

He thinks.

Yes, Fritz, give him a good smack on the roof! He must be afraid, otherwise he will go on talking about everything. He is too disgusting and mean ...

And you yourself recommended him to me as a messenger! But the lieutenant catches himself, breaks off. There is no point in holding a mistake made against women, in picking a fight with them. It always gets rampant right away. Another, much more terrible thought occurred to the lieutenant. He can't just talk about the letter; he knows other things too, maybe Kniebusch didn't keep his mouth shut ...

No, I absolutely have to talk to him later! he says again.

It is as if she had guessed him. And what do you do with him then, Fritz?! If he betrays you -?

The lieutenant stands very still. Even this small, stupid goose has come to the thought, has felt the danger, from which the 'thing' is always threatened, which all fear: Betrayal. Hardly anything is said already, except for the closest circle hardly anyone knows exactly what it is all about, what is planned. One makes a suggestion, general phrases. There is enough discontent, hatred, despair in the countryside. The banknote press in Berlin hurls a new wave of bitterness into the country with every new surge of paper money - all it takes is a few words, the restrained clang of weapons ... almost nothing!

But one doesn't need to be so bright, one doesn't need to know much, it's enough if he tells the district administrator: there's someone driving around the country and couping the people. He even heard today that the weapons will be counted in the village ...

The lieutenant lets the glow of his lamp fall on the sleeper's face - it is not a good face, not one that can be trusted. He already had the right instinct when he didn't want this fellow with him.... But there was this Violet. She had suggested him, he would have been such a convenient, unobtrusive messenger between them. He alone always had access to the knight master's house and was always to be met in the fields, in the forest ... And things went wrong on the first errand! Always these women's stories - always this long-haired riffraff had to come in between! They had nothing on their minds but their so-called love!

The lieutenant turns around briefly and says crossly: "You're going to bed right now, Violet!

She is quite startled by his tone. But Fritz, I wanted to wait for you here! And then I also have to talk to the forester, because of the buck ...

Here -? Don't be ridiculous! How do you think that when the guy wakes up, or someone comes in here ....

But Fritz, what do you want to do?! Now when he wakes up and he realizes his letter is gone, my letter I mean, and he has a rage at us and runs off and tells everything to grandpa or mom....

So, please, stop already, Violet! Please!!! I will take care of all that. I'll take him on after the meeting - and thoroughly, I can tell you -!

But if he runs away before -?!

He does not run away! He's drunk!!

But if he runs away before -?!

For God's sake, shut up now, Violet! the lieutenant almost shouts. And since he himself got a fright, whispering: So, please, be reasonable now. You can't possibly wait here. Watch out for me in front of the house - I'll be back in about an hour.

They go together. They feel their way through the dark room, across the dark hallway. Now they are out again.

It is night, full moon night, peaceful, the air is very warm.

Damn moon! Everyone can see us! Go into the bushes there. So in one hour ...

Fritz! Calling after him: Fritz!

What? Will you shut up?!

Fritz -! No kiss at all -?? Not a kiss?!

Oh damn! O cursed! And loud: Later, my child, later we'll make up for everything.

The gravel crunches. The lieutenant is gone. Violet von Prackwitz is standing in the bushes where Amanda Backs was standing. Like them, she has her eyes fixed on the windows of the inspector's house. She is a little disappointed - but also proud again of this post.

6

The forester Kniebusch wandered slowly through the nocturnal forest, the triplet on his back. The full moon was already quite high, but down here, among the logs, its glow only made visibility more uncertain. The forester knew the forest as a city dweller knows his home; he had walked here at all hours of the day and night. He knew every bend in the path, every juniper bush that appeared - ghostly as a ghostly man - between the tall pine trunks. He knew that the rustling just now came from a hedgehog hunting mice - but even if everything was familiar and known to him - now he did not like to walk through the forest.

The forest had remained the same since time immemorial, but the times had changed, and with the times the people. Yes, there had been wood thieves in the past as well. But these had always been the same questionable characters, whose acquisition was dark and whose reputation was even darker. They had been caught, they were what they were, and because they were like that, they wandered off to the Kashott. There was no need to get angry with them, in the end they always had the trouble and the damage from their thievery.

But had that happened in the past, that a whole village, man by man and house by house, had gone to steal wood? One ran and watched and fretted to death, and when one was finally caught, it became either a fear of revenge or a shame that such a man had gone among the thieves.

In the youthful days of forester Kniebusch, during his first years of service in the Neuloh forest, there had also been a notorious poacher here: Müller-Thomas, who later hanged himself in the cell of the Meienburg penitentiary. There had been a long war to the death with the guy; cunning had fought cunning and violence had fought violence, but it had still been a battle of equal means somehow ... Today they went hunting in packs with army pistols and carbines! They drove up the game where they found it, they spared no pregnant, no nursing mother animal - they shot at pheasants, yes, at field fowls with the bullet! If they had still been interested in the hunt like the miller Thomas or in the roast to satisfy their hunger - but they simply murdered out of lust for murder, murderers that they were - murderers and spoilers!

The old man is now out of the high forest, walking on a narrow aisle between spruce spars. The little trees are fifteen years old, they should have been thinned for two or three years - but there are no people to get! Thus, the clearings have become an unspeakable thicket, a barrage and thorn of branches, broken trunks, the cross and crossways - even in the daytime you can't see three meters into it! Now in the moonlight it stands there like a black wall ... Whoever has an enemy coming this way need only sit down in this thicket, he cannot miss his man at all!

The forester says to himself in vain that no one can expect to see him coming along this aisle; it is a stalk entirely out of order, and if he had kept his mouth shut, there would not have been this stalk either! No one can ambush him in the cuddle!

And yet he goes quieter. He knows where the mossy strip of grass runs, on which it is possible to walk so gently, and if a twig cracks under his footsteps, he stops and listens and his heart beats. He has long since put the pipe in his pocket, because you can smell tobacco far away in the forest. He keeps the triplet ready to shoot, because even an unsafe shot is better than none. He is a very old man, he would have liked to retire long ago. But that could not be, now he has to walk at night between the spruce spars, because a stupid young girl can not fit her heart and letters. It is quite a nonsensical way, he does not get the buck in front of the can after all. And if he gets it in front of the rifle, he doesn't hit it. And if he does put it on the blanket, it doesn't matter - the madam doesn't, the captain doesn't, none of them would have been surprised if Miss Violet had told them: their stalk was in vain. 'You see!' is the most the cavalry captain would have said. 'If you had stayed in bed smarter, Weio!' And would have laughed at her just a little.

But no, they didn't think of that. They really sent him off on that buck, he had to run while the three of them got the story straight with that darn guy, Inspector Meier! To whom did they owe all their science? But to him alone! Who had taken this stroppy, windy lieutenant out of Schulzen Haase? But he alone! And then this young snoot said very snobbishly: We can't use you here, Kniebusch. You go and shoot the buck! But don't give me any dog-ears here between the bushes! I'll go sledding with you, Lord!

Miss Violet had stood by, she had heard every word of this lofty speech. It would have suited her to be a little grateful, but no, she had only said: Yes, do that, Kniebusch, and make a little effort so that I have something to show Dad tomorrow!

There was nothing left but to say "Yes, madam!" and return to the woods! So you would never really get to know what happened to Field Inspector Meier that night! He would certainly not open his mouth, the servant Räder would also keep quiet, the lieutenant would be blown away tomorrow, and the madam was also not in favor of telling, as much as she liked to be told something.

So what came out of this carefully considered show-off that was supposed to bring in so much?! A night stalk through the forest and the eternal hatred of the little Meier! And he could be a real poisonous toad when he was angry!!!

Forester Kniebusch stops, sighing softly, he dries his forehead - it is hot, very hot! But it's not the sultry, rain-sodden heat of the stagnant air here in the forest that makes him so warm, it's the anger at himself that heats him up. For the thousandth, for the ten thousandth time in his life, he resolves not to see or hear anything that does not concern him, not to talk about what he is experiencing. Only to go his way for himself, the few years he still has life, not to be smart and wise and clever and calculating ahead - nothing more!

As if to put a dot under this immovable resolution, like the amen in the church, suddenly a shot echoes through the forest!

The forester pulls up, he stands there and listens without lifting his foot. It was a rifle shot: the crack was sharp as a whip crack. And it was the rifle shot of a poacher - because who else should be in the forest at this time -?

Both of these are certain, but the forester cannot be quite so certain as to the direction from which the shot came. The high forest wall around the shelter throws the sound here and there, it plays ball with it. But the forester would almost like to swear that the sound came from where the forester is on his way: from the seradella loft of Schulzen Haase! Where the six branch! Another had shot at the buck of the madam!!!

The forester is still standing on the same spot where he was standing when the shot was fired. He's not in a hurry, inside he's all steely with determination. He is a man, he does exactly what he wants - nothing else! Slowly he hangs the triplet over his shoulder, slowly he pulls the half-length pipe out of his pocket. He stuffs it and - after a brief hesitation - flares the match. He draws hard, then presses out the match between the tips of his thumb and forefinger, folds the nickel lid of the pipe shut, pressing the tobacco gently once more, and sets off. Purposeful, steely with determination, he moves away step by step from the spot where the shot was fired! What does not burn you, do not blow. Period. Amen.

However, some people are virtually haunted by news, whether they like it or not, while others wander through life and hear nothing. You always get the bread when it is stale. In fact, in the afternoon the forester had not done the least to get science from the letter of the madam. On the contrary, he had rejected Meier's gossip with disgust, he had not wanted to hear about this disgusting boast - and already he learned everything about the letter!

The forester, so comfortably smoking away from the poacher, the old Kniebusch, grinning at his own cunning, quite calmly determined to walk the less dangerous parts of the forest so slowly, until he can assure completely credibly that all the effort and all the patient stalking had been in vain, there was no buck to shoot, this old scaredy-cat Kniebusch was condemned to shoot his buck after all - and now even without a rifle!

The news from which he so eagerly stalked away came quietly and hurriedly cycling down the hollow path between the tall fir trees that no moonbeam could illuminate. The forester went up the hollow way fuming.

The impact was violent. But while for the old forester Kniebusch soft sand was lying there enough to spare his old bones, a strong boulder had been waiting for the cyclist: he first hit it with his shoulder, which elicited a strong curse from him, although he did not even know that his collarbone was breaking at that moment. Then he scraped his jaw along the rather grainy outside of the stone. The skin came off and the raw meat burned like fire. But the fallen cyclist hardly felt that, because in the meantime his temple had made acquaintance with a protruding, sharp-edged stone bulge - and a temple is just as sensitive as sleep: from rough disturbances both are easily injured. The cyclist said again, already quite absent-mindedly: Uch, and was no longer heard.

The good forester Kniebusch sat in the sand and rubbed his thick leg, which had taken the brunt of the collision. He would have liked to see the other get on his bike and ride on, he, the Kniebusch would have raised no objection and asked no questions, so steely was his resolve not to get involved again.

He peered in the darkness for the other. But since it was far too dark to see anything at all in the gorge between the firs (only someone who knew the forest like the back of his hand could dare to pedal down this pitch-black hollow path), the forester gradually imagined that he saw something. But what he thought he saw was a dark figure sitting on the sand, rubbing his body just as he was.

So Forester Kniebusch sat quietly and peered. He was now quite sure that the other was also sitting and peering, that the other was also sitting and just waiting for him to leave. At first the forester was undecided, but then he considered the case and realized: the other was right. He, as the authority, so to speak, had to go first and thereby express that he waived the prosecution of the case.

Slowly, quietly and carefully, the forester stood up, always keeping a close eye on the black spot. He took a step, another step - but on the third step he fell a second time, and of course just over the man he was walking away from. The black spot had been nothing at all; right next to his very latest news the forester sat down, yes, partly even on it!

He would have liked to get right back up and start running, but he had sat down in the frame of the fallen bicycle, and that had given some

Hans Fallada   -407-   Wolf among Wolves

confusion with clothes, pedals, chain, can strap, and saddlebag, not to mention the pain of hastily sitting down on the thin steel bars and jagged pedals.

So the forester sat there, quite shaken up, physically as well as mentally, and if at first he had still thought: 'I must go!', he could not help but gradually notice that the body on which his arm lay was somewhat more motionless than it would have been with a conscious, waiting person.

It took quite a while before the steely resolve gave way to other resolutions. But finally Kniebusch brought himself to turn on his electric flashlight. But once that had happened, and the cone of light had fallen on the pale, one-sidedly battered face of the unconscious man, things moved more quickly, and from the realization that this was the notorious Schubjack Bäumer from Altlohe, defenseless as a lamb given into his hands, to the decision to put this wretched ruffian and poacher in the pokey - was only one step.

While the forester, with rope and straps, made a package out of the beamer, such as no packer of a department store can make better and safer, he thought about the fact that with this 'arrest' he would reap great fame, not only with the old privy councilor and young cavalry captain. Because Bäumer was an arch rascal, a ringleader, a chief thief, a poacher and completely a stake in every owner's flesh - all of which was clearly proven by the six-shooter in his backpack and the carbine on his bicycle! But much more important than this fame was for the old Kniebusch that in this risk-free way he got rid of his most dangerous enemy for a long time, who had often threatened him with a beating if the forester should dare to search his wooden cage. That this dangerous enemy, who was strong for three, was so defenselessly given into his hands, this had to be truly a providence of heaven, which rightly overturned and softened every steely resolve. And so the forester tightened and tied the knots with such heartfelt pleasure as if he had just experienced the greatest stroke of luck in his life.

Miss Jutta von Kuckhoff could of course have told him that you should only praise the bacon when you have slaughtered the pig.

7

Wolfgang Pagel looked up and down the dark street near Wittenbergplatz. Few hurried pedestrians still passed them. It was shortly after midnight. Back there, where the square widened in a whitish glow, some male individual was leaning against a house wall, wearing a slouch hat and smoking a cigarette and, despite the summer heat, with his hands in his pockets - everything as it should be.

That's him, said Wolfgang and nodded. Suddenly he froze - he was so close to his goal. Tension and expectation had gripped him.

Who is that? asked von Studmann, rather uninterested. It was a boring thing to be dragged through half of Berlin at night, dead tired, to finally be allowed to look at a guy with a slider cap.

The Peeping Tom! said Wolfgang, without any feeling for the tiredness of his two companions.

Your knowledge of Berlin in all honor! scolded the Rittmeister von Prackwitz. Highly interesting, no doubt, that such a guy is called a Peeping Tom - but won't you finally explain to us what you are actually up to?!

In a moment! said Pagel and peered further.

The Peeping Tom whistled and disappeared out into the brightness of Wittenbergplatz. Very close to the three gentlemen a key cracked in a house gate, but no one appeared.

They locked the front door; it's still the old house, number seventeen, Pagel explained. Now comes Schupo. In the meantime, we want to walk around the quadrangle once.

But the cavalry captain became rebellious. He stamped his foot and shouted heatedly, "I refuse, Pagel, to go along with this nonsense any longer unless you explain to us right now what you are up to. If they are light-shy things, then thank you very much! Frankly, I long for a bed, and Studmann will be no different.

What is a peeping Tom, Pagel? Studmann asked gently.

A peeping Tom is someone, Pagel readily explained, who peeps to see if the Schupo is coming and if the coast is clear at all. And who just quickly locked the front door, that was the tugboat, he drags the guests up ...

So it is something forbidden! the cavalry captain shouted even more heatedly. Thank you very much, my dear Mr. Pagel, I will not take part in this! I don't want to have anything to do with the police, I'm old-fashioned in that again ...

He broke off, for the two Schupos had approached. They strolled side by side, a stocky tall one and a fat short one, the storm strap of the chako under their chins; softly clinked the little chains on which the rubber shillelaghs hung. The noise of their iron-shod shoe soles echoed off the walls of the house.

Good evening, Pagel said half aloud, politely.

Only the tall one who passed closest to the three turned his head a little. But he did not answer. Slowly the two guardians of order passed, down the street. Furthermore, the noise of their shoe nails resounded into the silence of the three. Then the Schupos turned onto Augsburg Street, and Pagel made a small, relieved movement.

Yes, he said, and felt his heart beat more calmly again, for he had feared there might be some last-minute obstacle. Now they're gone, now we can go right up.

So let's go home, Studmann! said the cavalry captain angrily.

What's up there? Studmann asked, nodding his head toward the dark house.

Nightclub, Pagel said, looking toward Wittenbergplatz. The Peeping Tom emerged newly from the brightness and came slowly down the street, hands in his pockets, cigarette in the corner of his mouth.

Fie Deubel! shouted the cavalry captain. Stripped women, adulterated champagne, nude dances, I'm telling you! I said it as soon as I saw you! Come on, Studmann!

Well, Pagel? asked Studmann, without paying attention to the cavalry captain. Is that so?

I don't know! Pagel replied. Roulette! Just a little roulette!

The Peeping Tom had stopped five paces away from them under a lantern and looked profoundly into the light, Mucki, say Schnucki to me! fluting. Pagel knew the guy was listening, he knew he, the worst customer of all gambling clubs, had been recognized, he trembled that he would be denied entry.

Unwilling of the delay, he waved the money package in his hand.

Roulette! the cavalry captain shouted in amazement and took another step closer. Yes, is that allowed -?!

Roulette! said von Studmann also surprised. And with this nepperei you ask questions to the fate, Pagel -?!

It is played fair, objected Pagel half aloud, his eye on the peeping tom.

There has never been anyone who admitted to being deceived, Studmann objected.

I used to play roulette when I was a young lieutenant," said the captain dreamily. Maybe you'll take a look at it sometime, Studmann. Of course, I do not bet a penny!

I don't know! Studmann said hesitantly. It must be a rip-off. All that gloomy makeup. - Do you understand, Prackwitz, he explained somewhat sheepishly, of course I also took part in games of chance now and then. And I would not like to ... God knows, once you've tasted blood there, and in the condition I'm in today ...

Yes, of course ... said the cavalry captain, but did not go.

So, are we going -? Pagel asked the two undecideds.

The two looked at each other questioningly, wanting, not wanting, afraid of the tease, even more afraid of themselves.

You can have a look at it, gentlemen! said the peeping Tom and strolled closer, pushing his cap carelessly out of his face. Excuse me for butting in.

He stood there, his pale face raised toward them. The small, dark mouse eyes ran musingly from one to the other.

Viewing costs nothing. No play money, gentlemen, no checkroom, no alcohol, nischt von Weibern ... Just solid game ...

So, I'm going up now, Pagel said firmly. I have to play today.

He went hastily - he couldn't wait any longer - to the front door, knocked, was let in.

Wait, Pagel! the cavalry captain called after him. We are also coming soon ...

You should really go with your friend, the peeping tom said persuasively. He's bright, he knows what's being played. There is no evening where he is not deported with his winnings ... We all know him ...

The cavalry captain called out in astonishment.

Of course, we don't know what his real name is; gentlemen don't introduce themselves to us. We just call him the Pari-Panther because he always plays the Pari-Chance ... But how! He is a player, still and still! Every one of us knows this one. Let him go ahead, he will find his way even in the dark, I'll light you up ...

So he plays a lot? von Studmann inquired cautiously, because the Pagel case interested him more and more.

Much -?! said the Peeping Tom with increasingly unmistakable respect. The man never misses a night out! And always he serves the cream! A rage we sometimes have at him -! But he's cold, I tell you, I couldn't be as cold as that man! You just have to marvel at how the man can break up when he has enough in his pocket! I'm not really allowed to let him up, they're so loaded on top of him! Well, it doesn't matter today, because you are there, gentlemen ...

Von Studmann started laughing heartily.

Without understanding, the cavalry captain asked, "Why are you laughing like that?

Oh, forgive me, Prackwitz, Studmann said, still laughing on. I always like to hear such a nice compliment. Don't you understand: they let the smart, the cold pagel up because he brings us stupid ones. - Come on, now I feel like it too. Let's see if you and I can't be smart and cold too.

And still laughing, he grabbed the cavalry captain under the arm.

The peeping tom also laughed. I've made a mess of things. Well, you don't take it amiss, gentlemen. And since you're not like that, maybe give me a little tip while you're at it. I don't know, the way you both look: with a knighthood in your pocket, you won't come back down the stairs either ...

He deftly lit up Prackwitzen's wallet on the landing, looking for a tip.

He really trusts us to come out without a penny, Studmann, said the cavalry captain angrily. What a jinx!

A little bit of grumbling still helped in the game, the peeping tom said. And gently coaxing: Well, another little bill, Baron. I see you haven't heard our sentences yet. Whereas I always have one foot in the Alexanderplatz police prison, so to speak!

And what about me?" the cavalry captain wanted to flare up, very annoyed that he was again reminded of the illegal nature of this enterprise.

You?! said the peeping Tom pityingly. Nothing will happen to you! At most, those who gamble get rid of their money. But he who tempts to play must hum. I am tempting you, Baron ...

A dark figure came down the stairs.

Psst, Emil! These are the two gentlemen to the pari-panther. Jeleite them up, ick jeh span. I have today so 'n dußlijet Jefühl in the stomach, it could still jeben!

The three were already climbing higher. In hollow whispers the Peeping Tom called after them: You, Emil! Listen again!

Yes, what? I told you not to make any noise!

I've already cashed them in! Don't milk me for the second time!

Oh, get out of here - you'd better tighten up dufte!

Come on, Emil! Keep tensioning even if the mast breaks!

He disappeared into the dark regions.

8

Wolfgang Pagel was already sitting in the playroom.

In some mysterious way, word of the large sum of money the pari-panther had exchanged for gambling tokens had filtered from the forecourt to the rapacious croupier and his two assistants, giving him a seat near the head of the table. Yet Pagel had only put in a quarter of his money with the sad constable. He had stuffed the rest of the bills carelessly and hastily back into his pockets and had entered, rummaging with his hand between the leggy, cool tokens in his skirt pocket. Quietly, with a pleasantly dry sound, the tokens rattled.

This sound immediately evoked the image of the gaming table: the somewhat carelessly stretched green cloth with the flat embroidered yellow numbers under the electric light, which always seemed particularly still and white above the gaming table despite all the noise around it - and now the purr and clatter of the ball, while the wheel whirred softly.

With a deep, as if relieved breath, Wolfgang sucked in the air.

The playroom was already very full. Behind those sitting on chairs, despite the early hour, there were again two dense rows of players. Wolfgang had only a vague idea of all those white, tense faces.

A croupier's helper led him - a favor he had never enjoyed before - to the chair that had been cleared for him.

As Pagel walked past a woman, he suddenly smelled her perfume with almost overwhelming strength, a scent that seemed strangely familiar. He would have liked to think about the game now, but to his chagrin he discovered that he was quite distracted. His brain certainly wanted to find the name of the perfume. A lot of words like houbigant, mille fleurs, patchouli, amber, mystic, juchten popped into his head. Only when he sat down did it occur to him that he probably didn't even know the name of this perfume, that it had only seemed familiar to him because it was the perfume of his enemy, the Valuten vamp. He thought he remembered that this woman had smiled at him.

Pagel was now sitting. But he still forbade himself to look at his surroundings and the playing surface. Slowly and carefully, he placed in front of him a pack of Lucky Strike he bought at Lutter and Wegner, a box of matches, and a silver cigarette holder, a kind of little fork that you slipped over your little finger with a ring, and that was supposed to keep your fingers from turning yellow. Then he counted off thirty tokens and placed them in piles of five in front of him. He had quite a few more tokens in his pocket. Still without looking up, he played with them, delighting in the dry clatter as in a beautiful music that entered him without any resistance. Then suddenly - the decision had arisen in him as surprisingly as the first lightning bolt drives out of a thunderstorm sky - then suddenly he placed a whole handful of tokens, as much as he could just grasp, on the number 22.

A quick, dark look of the croupier met him, the ball rattled, rattled endlessly - and the sharp voice sounded: Twenty-one - unequal - red ...

'Maybe I'm wrong,' Pagel thought, strangely liberated. 'Maybe Petra is only twenty-one.'

Suddenly he was in good spirits, his absentmindedness had disappeared. Without regret, he saw how the croupier's rake raked his bet, it disappeared - and darkly he felt as if he had bought his freedom from her with these chips sacrificed on the years of Petra's life, could now - without any consideration for her - play as he wanted. He smiled faintly at the croupier, who looked at him intently. The croupier returned this smile, almost imperceptibly, his lips barely curling under his ruffled beard.

Pagel looked around.

Directly across from him, on the other side of the table, sat an older gentleman. The face was so sharply cut that the nose in profile looked like the blade of a knife, its end was like a threatening point. The motionless face was frighteningly pale, in one eye sat a monocle, over the other hung limply the probably paralyzed eyelid. The gentleman had whole stacks of tokens in front of him, but also banknote packets.

The croupier called, and the gentleman's long, thin, very well-groomed hands hastily grabbed tokens and money with their upturned tips. They spread the sentences over quite a number of numbers. Pagel followed these hands with his gaze. Then he looked away quickly and contemptuously: this pale gentleman with the controlled face had completely lost his head! He played against himself, betting simultaneously on zero and numbers, equal and unequal.

Eleven - unequal, red, first dozen ... shouted the croupier.

'Red again!'

Pagel was convinced that Black would come now; with a quick decision he put all his thirty tokens on Black and waited.

It took an endless amount of time. Someone took back his bet at the last moment and then bet again after all. A deep, deadly unwillingness seized Wolf. It was all going too slowly, this whole game that had filled his life for a year suddenly seemed idiotic to him. There they sat around like children, waiting breathlessly for a bullet to fall into a hole. - Of course, she fell into a hole! In one or the other, it was the same! Then she ran and purred, oh, if only she would stop running, if only she would fall, that it would be over! The monocle opposite gleamed treacherously and wickedly, the green cloth had something sucking - that he would only be rid of his money -! What silliness to have starved after this game -!

Pagel was out of money. Under the rake of the croupier escaped the thirty chips, seventeen had been called. Seventeen, also quite a number! Seventeen and Four was still better than this silly game. For Seventeen and Four, you needed some brains. Here one had only to sit and await his judgment. The stupidest thing in the world - something for slaves!

With a jerk, Pagel stood up, pushed through those standing behind him, and lit a cigarette. First Lieutenant von Studmann, who had been standing unconcerned against a wall, asked with a quick look at his face: Well? Ready yet?

Yes, Pagel said sullenly.

And how did it go?

Moderate. He smoked greedily, then asked, "Shall we go?

Gladly! I don't want to see or hear anything from this company! - I'm going to loosen Mr. von Prackwitz right now! He wanted to watch for a moment on a lark ...

For fun! - So I'm waiting here.

Hans Fallada   -417-   Wolf among Wolves

Studmann slid in between the players. Pagel took his place against the wall. He was limp and tired. So this was the evening he had always hoped for, the evening with the big gambling capital, where he would be able to bet as he pleased. Things never came together! Today, when he could have played as long as he wanted, today he didn't feel like playing! 'Then we lack the cup, then we lack the wine,' it sounded in him.

So it was finally over with playing, he felt it, he would never want it again. So tomorrow morning he could calmly go to the country with the cavalry captain, as a kind of slave bailiff presumably - he missed nothing here in Berlin. Not a chance! You could do one thing, you could do something else: everything was equally pointless. It was thought-provoking to observe how life melted away under one's hand, made itself meaningless, as it were, and emptied itself (just as the ever more hurriedly flowing, flowing money made itself meaningless and became empty): in one short day mother and Peter, no, Petra!, were lost, and now also the game .... This matter has become rather contentless... Truly, you could just as easily jump from a bridge under the next light rail train - it was just as sensible and pointless as anything else -!

Yawning, he lit a new cigarette.

The Valuten vamp seemed to have been waiting for just that. The woman approached him. Will you also give me a -?

Wordlessly, Pagel held the package out to her.

English -? No. I can't take them, they're too heavy for me! Do you have any other -?

Pagel shook his head, smiling faintly.

That you like to smoke them! There's opium in there!

Opium is no worse than coke, Pagel said challengingly, looking at her nose. She could not have snuffed much today, the nose was not white. Of course, one had to think of the powder, of course, the nose was powdered ... He looked at her with a calm, matter-of-fact curiosity.

Coke! - Do you think I coke?

Something of the old enmity made her voice sharp, though she was now making every effort to please him. And she looked really good. She was tall and slim, the breast in the wide-cut dress seemed small and firm. Only that this woman was evil could not be forgotten, evil: stingy, greedy, quarrelsome, coked up, cold. Urböse - Peter hadn't been evil, or had he, Petra had been evil after all. But one had not noticed it so, she had been able to hide it for a long time, until he had come on it to her. No, Petra was also done for.

So you don't do coke? I thought! he said indifferently to the Valuten vamp and looked around for Studmann. He would have been happy to go. This well-built cow bored him to death.

Just once in a while, she admitted. When I'm jaded. This is also no different than taking a pyramidon, don't you think? You can also ruin yourself with Pyramidon. I once had a friend who took twenty Pyramidon a day. And this is ...

Given, my darling! said Pagel. I am not interested. Don't you want to go play for a while?

But it was not that easy to get rid of. Nor was she the least bit offended; she was only ever offended when she wasn't meant to be.

You're already done with the game? she asked.

Yes, he said. No more valutas to collect. Completely broke!

Little teaser! she laughed silly.

He looked at her, she did not believe him. She had heard something about the contents of his pockets, she would never otherwise waste so much time and kindness on a shabby fellow in a tunic, since for her only cavaliers in tails came into question -!

Do me a favor! she suddenly shouted. Put once for me!

What good is that going to do?" he asked angrily. This Studmann remained endless, and he did not get rid of the goose! I think you know with the game without me!

For sure you bring me luck!

Possible. But I don't play anymore.

Oh, please - be nice to me for once!

You hear me, I don't play anymore.

Really not -?

No!

She laughed.

And Pagel angrily: Why are you laughing so stupidly?! I do not play anymore!

You - and not play! I think rather ...

She broke off, giving her voice a gentle, persuasive tone: Come on, darling, sit down for me once - I want to be very nice to you then too ...

Thank you very much for your kindness! said Pagel roughly. And breaking out: God, can't I get rid of you at all?! Go away, I tell you, I'm not playing anymore, and I already can't stand you at all! - Disgusting you are to me! he shouted.

She looked at him intently. Now you're looking lovely, laddie. I never saw how pretty you actually were - you always sat like a stockfish at the game! - She cajoled: Come, darling, sit once for me! You bring me luck!

Pagel threw the cigarette away and bent very close to her. If you say one more word to me, you fucking whore bitch, I'll punch you in the face so hard you'll ....

He was trembling with senseless rage all over his body. Her eyes were very close to his. They were also brown - now they blurred in a surrendering dampness.

Go for it! she whispered devotedly. But bet once for me, sweetie ...

He turned with a jerk and quickly went to the gaming table. He grabbed von Studmann by the elbow. Breathing quickly, he asked, "Are we going or not going?

I can't get rid of the captain! Studmann whispered back just as excitedly. Just look!

9

Most reluctantly, Rittmeister von Prackwitz had accompanied his former ensign on his mysterious journey through nocturnal Berlin; very reluctantly, he had already endured his company and challenging chatter at Lutter and Wegner's, hardly forgiving him the insult with the offered money. Quite inappropriately, he had found his friend Studmann's interest in this rather dawdled and flabby young fellow, whose rich financial possessions seemed at least questionable. If that little incident with the retrieved shrapnel in the battle before Tetelmünde seemed a little ridiculous to Herr von Studmann, but certainly - and even more so for such a young lad - quite heroic, for Herr von Prackwitz the ridiculous outweighed anything heroic - and a character capable of such extravagances could only appear suspicious to him.

The good Rittmeister Joachim von Prackwitz - he only found other people's extravagances suspicious, about his own he thought perfectly benevolently. From the moment he heard it was not some dirty, naked female stuff - his horror! In the same moment the two Schupos with their nail-shod shoes had lost all warning, the dark house had taken on something inviting, the cheeky 'Peeping Tom' had been shrouded in humor, and Fahnenjunker Pagel had turned from a seducer and dubious fruit into a real guy and worldly-wise lad.

When the cavalry captain had stood on the small bourgeois forecourt, with the clothes hooks hung far too full, when the mustachioed gentleman behind his folding table had asked in a friendly manner: "Tokens, gentlemen? and when the cavalry captain, after a quick, orienting look, had asked: "Old service, huh? Where?", and the moustachioed man had answered with hacking: "At your command! Nineteenth Saxon Train - Leipzig, the cavalry captain had felt in the best of moods and completely at home.

No thought of the forbidden nature of such a game had yet dampened this good mood; animatedly, he had had the use and value of the tokens, which were new to him, explained to him - in his day, one had only jeutted against cash or, at best, against visiting cards with a number written on them. If he had remembered his ensign at all, he would have remembered him most favorably. But no thought of this young person crossed his brain yet.

He had found the game and the company of players far too interesting for that. It was with regret that he had to admit that the company here was nowhere near as first-class as that in an officer's mess of peace. There was, for example, a fat, red-faced man sitting at the gambling table, muttering incessantly half aloud to himself and placing bets with thick, jewel-encrusted fingers - looking at his bacon neck with many folds, there could be no doubt that this was some kind of brother or cousin of the cattle dealer from Frankfurt, whom he never liked to let into his house. By the way, this brother had also fooled him a couple of times, the one in Frankfurt, of course. Hostilely the cavalry captain looked at the fat man, so here remained the profits unjustly taken from the landed property - and not even with decency this guy was able to lose! The fear of every loss, which he nevertheless challenged anew with every new assignment, was clearly noticeable to him.

The cavalry captain was also disturbed by the large number of women crowding around the gaming table - women, in his opinion, had no business playing jeu. Jeu was an all-male affair, only a man could muster enough cold-bloodedness and brains to jeu with success. They were also very elegant, but a bit too extravagantly dressed or rather undressed for his taste. This manner of presenting a pair of young breasts, as it were in a wide-open silk case, to every observer for inspection, made him think of the streetwalkers he hated so much. Surely such wenches had no access here, but to be reminded of them already was embarrassing!

There were also pleasant things to see, for example, an elderly, white-skinned gentleman with a strangely sharp, pointed nose and monocle - where this gentleman played, where this gentleman took a seat, where this gentleman was a guest, a Rittmeister von Prackwitz could also sit down.

It was significant that the cavalry captain did not see the flag boy Pagel sitting right next to him at all; his otherwise sharp eye noticed shabbily dressed figures only with difficulty!

As far as the roulette was concerned - and the cavalry captain politely and gratefully took a seat on a chair that seemed to have been vacated for him willingly, but only at a higher hint - as far as the roulette was concerned, it was difficult to find one's way around it. There were a surprising number of possibilities - moreover, they were played with an almost unseemly haste. The cavalier had hardly realized how the stakes were distributed before the disc was whirring, the ball was running, the croupier was shouting, chips were raining here, drought was breaking out there, past, on, bet, spin, run, whir, shout - confusing!

The cavalry captain's own experience with roulette lay far back in his lieutenant years. They had been sparse enough even then; the game had not been played more than three or four times. This was due to the fact that it was particularly strictly forbidden, even more strictly than all other games of chance, it was considered particularly dangerous. Actually, the young officers at that time had known only one game of chance, called 'God's Blessing at Cohn's', which was considered relatively harmless. After all, it had become so dangerous for the Rittmeister, then still an unmarried young lieutenant, that after a turbulent night he had had to travel head over heels to his father, a possibly even more hot-tempered gentleman of general rank. There, within half an hour, he had experienced rage, disinheritance, and repudiation, but finally the two of them - after copious outpourings of tears - had signed a whole series of bills of exchange with a blackish gentleman, for which they received so much money that the gambling debt could be covered by the skin of their teeth. Since that time, the cavalryman had not played again.

So now he sat confused in front of the green cloth, looked at the numbers, looked at the inscriptions, rattled quietly with the tokens in his pocket - and did not know what to start, as much as he would have liked to start.

But when von Studmann asked him, "Well, Prackwitz, do you really want to play? - he replied angrily, "You don't? What did we put tokens in for -?!

And he bet on red.

Of course, red came. Before he had quite come to his senses, a heap of brands fell dryly pattering on his. The unsympathetic guy looking like a ruffled vulture shouted something, again the game wheel spun. The cavalry captain was undecided what to bet now - there was already the decision again.

Again, red had come, now he already owned a whole mountain of tokens.

He withdrew it, looked around, as if awakening: the best man at the gaming table was still the gentleman with the monocle. He watched the long, thin, slightly upward-curved fingers distributing heaps of marks on the various numbers and on the intersections of number fields with incredible speed, and without thinking twice, he imitated this gentleman. He also bet on numbers, on intersections of number squares, but out of a sense of chivalry (so as not to disturb the other) he avoided the squares occupied by the other.

Again the croupier called out something, again tokens went to the ones he had set, while other heaps disappeared under the rake and fell with a quiet clatter into a bag at the end of the table.

From now on, the cavalry captain was enchanted. The rolling of the ball, the croupier's exclamations, the green cloth with the numbers, inscriptions, squares and rectangles, on which the multicolored chips were always arranged anew - all this held him completely captive. He forgot himself, forgot the time and the room he was sitting in. He no longer thought of Studmann and the questionable Fahnenjunker Pagel. There was no more Neulohe. He had to be quick, the eye, even quicker than the hand, had to spy out free fields on which tokens were to be thrown; the winnings had to be fetched in a hurry, it had to be decided what had to remain standing.

For a moment there was an unpleasant pause due to the fact that the cavalry captain, as he realized to his surprise, was completely without tokens. Annoyed, he fumbled in his jacket pocket, annoyed because he now had to skip a game. The fact that he no longer had any tokens, however, did not evoke in him any thoughts of a loss he had suffered; only the delay disturbed him. Fortunately, it turned out that he had been observed; an adlatus of the croupier already held more chips ready for him. And with complete absent-mindedness, which did not at all allow the thought to arise that he was giving away money here, and in fact almost all the money he was carrying, he pulled the bills out of his pocket and exchanged for them beige tokens.

Shortly after this unintentional, annoying break in the game, just when the cavalry captain was in the most beautiful sitting, von Studmann suddenly arrived and whispered over the shoulder of the player that Pagel had now had enough and wanted to leave.

Quite irritated, the cavalry captain asked what on earth young Pagel was to do with him? He was sitting here excellently and had not the slightest intention of going home yet.

Quite astonished, von Studmann again asked back whether the cavalry captain really wanted to play -?

Von Prackwitz was - almost certainly - of the opinion that that heap of marks on the intersection of the numbers 13, 14, 16 and 17, which had just won, had been placed by him - a woman's hand adorned with a pearl ring had reached after it and taken the heap away. Von Prackwitz met the gaze of the croupier, who looked at him calmly observing. Very irritated, he asked von Studmann to finally go away and leave him in peace!

Studmann did not answer, and the cavalryman played on. But it was not possible to concentrate on the game, he felt, without seeing it, that Studmann was at his back, watching his setting.

He turned around with a jerk and said sharply: "Lieutenant, you are not my nanny!

This word, which reopened an old antagonism from wartime, did its work: Studmann made a very slight, apologetic bow and withdrew.

When the cavalry captain looked back at the green cloth with a sigh of relief, he saw that in the meantime the last of his tokens had also disappeared. He cast an annoyed glance at the croupier, it seemed to him as if a smile crept into the ruffled mustache. Von Prackwitz opened the inner compartment of his wallet, which was secured with a double clasp, and removed seventy dollars from it - all the foreign currency he still had. The croupier's assistant stacked piles and piles of tokens in front of him with tremendous speed. The cavalry captain hurriedly put them in his pocket without bothering to count them. For a moment, when he realized that many faces were looking at him scrutinizingly, he had the vague feeling: what am I doing -?!

But it was more the words that sounded in him than their meaning. So many brands gave him security, pleasure filled him. He thought kindly: 'That foolish, eternally anxious Studmann -!', moved almost smilingly in his chair and began to sit down again.

But this good mood did not last long. More and more irritated, he watched bet after bet disappear under the croupier's rake, almost not even hearing the dry pattering down of the won tokens on the fields he occupied. More and more often he had to reach into his pocket, which was already no longer bulging. It was not yet the thought of loss that irritated him, it was the incomprehensible rapidity of the game ... Nearly already he saw before himself the moment when he would have to get up and give up this pleasure which he had hardly tasted before. With the number of bets, he thought, his chances of winning must increase - more and more hastily he distributed tokens all over the playing field.

That's no way to play! said a serious voice next to him disapprovingly.

How -?! the cavalry captain went up and looked indignantly at the young pagel who had sat down on the chair next to him.

But here the young pagel was not uncertain and embarrassed. No, you don't play like that! he said again. After all, you are playing against yourself.

What am I doing?! said the cavalry captain, wanting to get very angry, to tell the young fellow thoroughly, just as von Studmann had done before! But to his surprise, the anger that usually lay in wait did not come; instead, embarrassment seized him, as if he had behaved like a foolish child.

If you bet red and black at the same time, you can't win," Pagel said reprovingly. Either red or black wins - both never.

Where did I -? the cavalry captain asked in confusion, looking over the console. But just then the croupier's rake drove in between, the tokens rattled ...

Take it! whispered Pagel sternly. You have had a lucky break. That there is yours - and there - and there - madam, I beg you, that is our stake!

Some woman's voice said something very excitedly, Pagel paid no attention. He continued to order, and like a child, the cavalry captain followed his instructions.

Hans Fallada   -427-   Wolf among Wolves

So - and this time you won't bet anything - we want to see how the game goes first. What other brands do you have? - That's not enough for a big hit - wait, I'm still buying ...

You wanted to leave, Pagel! the obnoxious teacher's voice of Studmann was heard.

Just a moment, Herr von Studmann, said Pagel, smiling amiably. I just want to quickly show Herr Rittmeister how to play properly. - Please, fifty to five hundred thousand and twenty to one million ...

Studmann made a gesture of despair ...

Really just a moment, Pagel said kindly. You can believe me, I don't enjoy gaming at all, I'm not a gamer. It is only because of the cavalry captain ...

But von Studmann heard no more. He had turned angrily and walked away.

Pay attention, Herr Rittmeister, Pagel said. Now red will come.

They waited anxiously.

Then came - red.

If we had set now -! complained the cavalry captain.

Patience only! comforted Pagel. First you have to see how the hare runs. Now you can't say anything definite - after all, black is very likely to come.

But it came red.

Look! said Pagel triumphantly. How good that we had not set! But now we will start soon. And you shall see - in a good quarter of an hour ...

The croupier smiled imperceptibly. Von Studmann, at an angle, cursed the moment when he had approached the young Pagel at Lutter and Wegner.

Chapter 08

- He gets confused at night -

08 01

In her bush outside the door of the officer's house, Violet von Prackwitz stands guard; inside the office, another girl, Amanda Backs, steps out of hiding. She has by no means understood everything that the two of them, the lieutenant and the madam, negotiated with each other. But many things could be guessed - she had heard before about the lieutenant who travels through the country and gathers people for some coup; and a saying goes through the German lands at that time, gloomily threatening: Traitors fall to the Feme!

It is not pleasant to have to think of your loved one as a traitor, and Amanda Backs may be as solid a piece of rabble as can be devised, she would never be a traitor. She loves and she hates, without inhibitions, out of her strong, unbreakable nature, but she could never betray. That is why she continues to stand by her Hänsecken, despite everything she knows about him. He is also just a man, and with men, with all of them, there is not much state to be made - a girl must take them as they are!

She quickly darts over to his room, kneels down next to his bed and shakes the sleeper vigorously. But it's not that easy to shake him out of his drunken stupor. Amanda has to resort to strong means, and when even the wet washcloth doesn't want to miss anything, she just pulls him by the hair with one hand, while she puts the other one carefully over his mouth, so that he can't get loud.

This cure really helps - the little field inspector Meier wakes up from the raging pain, because she tears and tugs at his hair with all her not small forces. As humans are, and as Negermeier in particular is, he first instinctively defends himself: Negermeier bites the hand that lies over his mouth.

She suppresses her scream and hastily whispers in his ear: Wake up! Wake up, Hansel! It's Amanda!

I can tell, he grunts angrily. If you knew how fat I have you women! Never can you leave one in peace -!

He wants to rant on, smouldering, with his head swollen up and the wildest hair ache ... But she's afraid of the eavesdropper outside, and her hand settles firmly over his mouth anew. In a moment he bites again -!

But now their patience is over. She yanks her hand out of his teeth and strikes, blindly, in the dark as it hits. Her feeling, however, guides her correctly, she hits excellently, the blows fall on him hail-deep, right, left - there, this must have been the nose! And now the mouth ...

And at that, she moans half-loudly, breathlessly, entranced by this beating in the dark on something soft, moaning: Do you want to be reasonable! Do you want to cower! They'll beat you to death if you don't!

(She is well on her way to getting this herself).

Breathless, almost completely disillusioned, cowardly, without resistance - now little Meier begs: But yes, Mandecken! My Mandchen! After all, I want to do everything you want. But now let - oh, no, take care a little bit ...!

Panting, her chest flying, she stops. Will you parry, you fool?! she moans with angry tenderness. The lieutenant was here -!!!

Where - here? he asks stupidly.

Here, in this parlor! He was looking for something - he took a letter from your jacket.

A letter ... He still doesn't quite understand. But then slowly, not yet completely clear, comes the memory. Oh, that one -! he says contemptuously. Let him keep it, the rag!

But Hansen, be reasonable! Think about it for a moment, she asks. You must have done something wrong - he's so angry with you! He still wants to come back - tonight.

Just make him come back! he boasts, despite an uncomfortable feeling creeping up on him. I already have the monkey in my pocket, him and his fine Fräulein von Prackwitz ...

But Hänsecken, she was here too! She was looking for the letter with ...

The Weio -?! The madam - the daughter of the owner of the bread roll -? In my room?!! Where I lay drunk and naked in bed - o wei, o wei! O Weio!

Yes - and now she stands guard outside your window so that you don't run away!

I and run away! he says boastfully. But he involuntarily muffles his voice. That's what they want me to do, run away! That would so suit the two of them! But, no, I'll stay, I'll go to the cavalry captain tomorrow morning and tear them in with their fine lieutenant ...

Goosebumps, why don't you stop with your nonsense! He wants to come back, tonight. He will not let you go to the cavalry captain tomorrow...

What do you want him to do? He can't tie me up!

No, he can't tie you up ...

And when I tell the cavalry captain about the letter!

Oh, leave that stupid letter alone! You don't even have it anymore! He has it!

But the Kniebusch can testify ...

Nonsense, henpeckers! All nonsense! What kind of witness is the forester Kniebusch, if he is to testify against the madam?

Little Meier is silent for a moment, he really starts to think. Then he says more meekly: "But he can't want anything from me! He has so much dirt on him himself!

Hans corners, but yet just because! Because he's dirty, he wants something from you! He's afraid you'll talk...

What do you want me to talk about? I will keep my mouth shut from the stupid letter ...

But it's not just the letter, Hansel! she calls out in despair. There is still the other thing, the coup -!

What kind of coup -? he asks, puzzled.

Oh, Hansel, don't pretend! You don't have to pretend in front of me! The coup you want to make - he's afraid you'll tell!

But I don't know anything about his stupid coup, Mandchen! exclaims the dairyman. My sacred word of honor, Mandchen! I have no idea what the brothers are up to!

She thinks for a moment. She almost believes him. But then again her feeling says that everything he tells is indifferent, that he is in danger and that is why he must leave immediately.

She says very seriously, it doesn't matter whether you really know something or not. He thinks you know something. And want to betray him. And he has a grudge against you because of the letter. He wants to hurt you, believe me!

What can he do to me -?! he says wanly.

But Hansel, don't pretend! You know, and it was also in the newspaper the other day, and there was also a picture, all of them with white hoods, so that you can't recognize them as they hold court, and underneath it said: Feme Court. - Traitors fall to the feme, henpeckers, that's what they say!

But I am not a traitor, he says, but he says it just to say something, says it without right conviction.

She doesn't even go into it anymore. Hansen! she asks, why won't you go away? He has now gone to the village, to a meeting, and I want to get them away from the window. Now you can still go well - why do not you want?! You don't care so much about me that you want to stay where you even got involved with Hartig today. (She couldn't bring herself to say anything about it, but already she's sorry). And, look, tomorrow the cavalry captain is coming back, and you only did crap while he was away, and you also got drunk in the jug during working hours - why don't you want to leave voluntarily, when he is kicking you out -?

I don't have a penny of money, he says sullenly. Where should I go -?

Well, I thought, if you sit down here somewhere in a village in a small inn, to Grünow perhaps - there is a nice inn, I know it from dancing. And on Sunday I'm off, so I'll come over and visit you. I still have some money, I'll bring it to you. And then you look for a new position so gently, there are always some in the newspaper, but not so close to ...

On Sunday in Grünow, I also know someone who kicks at the moon! he says grumpily. And who can wait for his money, that's me!

But Hansel, don't be so stupid -! I don't have to offer it to you if I don't want to come! So, aren't you going -?

You're suddenly in a big hurry to get rid of me - who do you have on your mind now?

You have just cause to act jealous - yes, to act, for you are not the least bit jealous!

He is silent for a while, then he asks: How much money do you have?

Oh, it's not much, because of the devaluation of money. But I can always pass on to you, I will now already make sure that the madam pays me stable value - in Birnbaum they should already get their wages in rye ...

You and wage in rye ... The old woman never thinks of that! You're always imagining nonsense! He laughs contemptuously, he needs to feel a little on top again. You know what, Mandchen, you better go right now and get your money. I can't sit in the pub without any money. And you send the Weio away at the same time. I still have to pack, I can't do it in the dark! Oh God! he suddenly groans. Lugging two heavy suitcases all the way to Grünow - only you could come up with such nonsense!

Oh, henpeckers! she consoles him, "It's not so bad, as long as you get away in one piece! Always remember that! And I also wear a while, I do not need to lie down anymore. How fresh do you think I am when I wash myself cold from top to bottom in the morning -?

Well, he says grumpily, if you're just fresh, that's the main thing. So are you going or not going?

Yes, I will go now. But it may take a while, first I have to get rid of Miss. - And, aren't you, Hansel, hurrying a bit? I don't know when the lieutenant will be back.

Oh, him! says Negermeier contemptuously. He shouldn't brag like that! How long do you think a meeting like this takes? At least two, three hours! Farmers don't let themselves be talked around that quickly!

So hurry up, Hänsecken! she admonishes him once again. I am also back very quickly! - Kiss, Hansel!

Get the hell out of here, he says angrily. You think only of your smooch, and with me it's a matter of life and death! But that's how you women are! Always just your so-called love in mind - yes, slice!

Oh, you knucklehead, she says and yanks him by the hair, but tenderly this time. I'm just glad you're getting out of here! Finally you can work properly again. It's crazy, but when it sits in your bones like that, and you have to look and think forever.... What are you already -? You're nothing at all - don't you think I know that? But that's why it won't be any different if you know that too. A pure monkey show is life, and you are certainly the biggest monkey of all ...

And with that she presses a kiss on him, he may want or not, and goes out of the parlor, almost chipper, almost amused.

08 02

The field inspector Meier did not wait long to see if Amanda had really guided the gnädige Fräulein away from her guard post. He took only a cursory glance out the window into the moonlight outside and, seeing no one, switched on the light. Like all unimaginative people, he could not imagine the danger that threatened him. Everything had still gone quite well in his life, with stubbornness one got far, and so it would go well again this time.

Actually, it wasn't such a bad prospect to play the reindeer for a while now - and he even suddenly had his plans for the future! What a lieutenant is good for! He had a lot of things to do tonight before he left here, in fact he really had to fix it. But that doesn't really work either, for one thing his head is still stupid and dizzy, and then putting on the city-fair outfit with shirt, collar and tie makes quite a bit of trouble. Meier notes that he has a dodder. 'Must be from the ether,' he decides. I've never gotten a dodder from boozing. Filthy stuff!'

Sighing, he sets about packing. It's quite a task to pick out your seven plums from a trashed, untidy room and squeeze them, dirty and crumpled as they are, into two suitcases. They went in once, he has acquired nothing here in Neulohe, so they have to go in again! With pressing, squeezing and choking he finally makes it - breathing a sigh of relief he locks the suitcases and ties up the straps - his next one, who gets to fluff and wash the stuff, has nothing to laugh about!

Hans Fallada   -435-   Wolf among Wolves

(I wonder how much money Mandchen brings him? Efficient girl, the Mandchen, a bit much indication, but otherwise quite nice! No, it won't bring in a lot of money, a lot of money can be driven on a wagon - but it can be used as an allowance).

Cursing wildly, little Meier discovers that he is standing in the room in socks - and the shoes are in the suitcase! Damn dirt! He is so used to going into the longshanks at the very end of his dressing routine that he didn't think about the shoes. Of course, he puts on the pointed low shoes, the reddish tango shoes to the city dress. But in which suitcase are they? For a moment, he has quiet misgivings when his longshanks look at him from the opened first suitcase - after all, the way to Grünow is quite long with two suitcases in the fins, and the tango shoes are quite tight. But the thought of what kind of figure he would cut in front of the girls in Grünow, in a city suit and long shoes, decides: it must be the low shoes!

Of course, he finds it only in the second suitcase. He gets them on pretty hard. 'They widen when you walk!' he consoles himself.

Negermeier marches, this accomplished, into the office. He picks his papers out of compartments and folders; he sticks the employee insurance policy half a year in advance, just in case. There are enough stamps in this stable, and if the stuff is devalued afterwards, it does no harm.

Now he carefully writes himself a police sign-out, Mr. Hans Meier goes 'on a trip'. The head of the estate stamp is pressed under it - so, the putty is also in order.

But a moment's reflection convinces Meier of the correctness of the sentence that twice sewn is better kept, and so he immediately writes a second sign-off. On it, Meier has become a Schmidt, sorry! -: von Schmidt, Hans von Schmidt, occupation administrator, also traveling. 'So, you gobshites, now you're supposed to find me!'

Meier grins with great satisfaction. The satisfaction of one's great cunning drives away head pressure and hair ache - it is a glorious thing to be smarter than the others and to fool them! Cheers!

Meier flips open the typewriter and sets about typing a testimonial for himself on a letterhead from the Neulohe estate administration. Of course, he is the pearl of all officials, knows everything, can do everything, does everything - and honest, reliable, hardworking he is also! It is a delight to get all this in writing. From the lines of this testimony rises a Meier as Meier would like to know him, as Meier would like to be a Meier, a blameless, capable Meier with a beautiful, promising future, truly suitable for an administrator position, in short, the Meier of all Meiers!

This testimony is actually too beautiful - it is not quite understandable why one would ever let such a civil servant go, one would have to keep him until the end of his life! But the clever, the wise, the witty Meier is also up to this situation. He writes down 'Because of giving up the lease' - you see, there are no queries from the new boss to the old one. Has yes given up the lease, do not know where he has now moved. Now still stamp of the estate administration, signature: Joachim von Prackwitz, Rittmeister a. D. and Rittergutspächter - another stamp of the head of the estate for signature authentication - stamps are always good. Knorke looks the thing - on it catches the most polished fox!

Put the papers in the wallet. We put the stamps we have in stock right along with it, you can always use stamps - what should the stuff be here for? The money cabinet doesn't groan very loudly, as I said, it's not overly much, but it's enough for a while. And if Mandchen still diligently zubuttert, I can live a few weeks fat! God, I am the right swollen Oskar, on the right the papers, on the left the money - bosom, bosom, my child, must have! Bust is the big fashion - nope, actually not at all! But from me bust is always nice. Now still the strongbox closed, it looks better tomorrow morning ...

Leave 'n open, darling! Always leave it open, young man - it looks better. The Rittmeister will be in the picture first thing in the morning! the lieutenant calls from the door.

For a moment, Meier's face contorts. But it's really just a moment. I'll do it just the way I want, he says cheekily and closes the door. And by the way, you have no business here at night ... Earlier you stole a letter from me in my room ...

Youngster! says the lieutenant threateningly and takes two steps closer. But he is somewhat stunned by this fabulous impudence. Youngster, do you see this?

Of course I see the thing, Meier explains, and barely a tremor in his voice betrays how uncomfortable he is with the sight of the gun. And I could have taken such a gun, because in the thrust lie enough. But I always think it will work out that way, too. - I knew you were coming! he adds somewhat boastfully.

So, you knew that -? says the lieutenant quietly, looking intently at the small, ugly, mischievous person.

You want to be a conspirator?! You want to stage a coup? sneers little Meier and already feels quite safe and on top again. And you don't even realize that a girl was standing here in the next room the whole time, here in the office, like you were in my room. And she listened to everything you and the Weio talked about - yes, you are amazed!

But it doesn't look like the lieutenant was amazed. So, he says calmly, there has been a girl hidden here? And where is the girl now? In the next room again?

Nope! says Meier boldly. Not this time. We are completely among ourselves, so you do not need to be embarrassed. Your Miss Bride is going for a walk with my Miss Bride. - But you can imagine, of course, he adds warningly, seeing an unrestrained movement of the lieutenant, what my girl

Hans Fallada   -438-   Wolf among Wolves

will tell tomorrow if something happened to me. - Or do you want to shoot us both to death?! he says boldly, rejoicing in his impudence and laughing.

The lieutenant throws himself into a chair, crosses his brown gaiter legs and thoughtfully lights a cigarette. You're not stupid, my boy, he says. The only question is whether you are not too smart. - Is it okay to ask about your plans?

You may! says Meier readily. Now that he has convinced the lieutenant that it is wiser not to harm him, his only desire is to part on good terms with the man. I'm getting out of here! he says. I've already called it a day - well, you saw it earlier at the safe ... He looks at the lieutenant, but the lieutenant does not flinch.

That is my right that I took the money. First of all, I still get salary, and then, what do you think, what he paid me here for a disgraceful wage by the devaluation!?!! If I take a little, it's nowhere near as much as the cavalryman stole from me.

He looks at the lieutenant as if he should agree.

But he just says: I'm not interested in that. - Where do you want to go?

A little further away, says Meier and laughs. I think the neighborhood smells sour. I thought Silesia or even Mecklenburg ...

Beautiful, says the lieutenant. Quite reasonable. Silesia is not bad. - But where are you going now?

Now -?

Well, says the lieutenant a little impatiently. That you won't be leaving tomorrow morning from the county seat, where everyone knows you, I can actually guess. So where do you want to go now?

Now -? Oh, just here to a village nearby.

So, to a village? Which one, for example?

What's it to you, anyway?" Meier asks, because this questioning, behind which there is something hidden, makes him quite nervous.

Oh, that concerns me a bit, my boy," the lieutenant answers coolly.

Why -?

Well, where, for example, sits one who knows about my relations with Fräulein von Prackwitz. In Silesia, no one is interested in that, but here in the vicinity, he might get the idea of making money out of his science.

I would never have thought of that! Meier is outraged. No, I'm not such a pig after all! You may be quite sure of that, Herr Leutnant! I'll keep my mouth shut, I'm a gentleman in these matters!

Yes, I know, says the lieutenant impassively. So - what is the name of the village?

Grünow, says Meier hesitantly and actually doesn't know why he shouldn't mention the name when the lieutenant already knows everything.

So, Grünow, says the lieutenant. Why Grünow in particular! You mean the Grünow near Ostade?

Yes, that's what my girl suggested to me. She wants to come to my dance there on Sunday.

Do you want to dance there too? I suppose you want to stay there longer?

Just a few days. Monday I'll take off - from Ostade. You can count on it, Lieutenant.

Yes, can I? says the lieutenant thoughtfully, stands up and walks toward the drawer that Meier indicated to him earlier. He pulls it open and looks at its contents. Well, you've got some pretty nice blunderbusses there, he says patronizingly. You know what, Mr. Meier, I'd pocket one of those after all.

But he fights back. What am I supposed to do with that? Nah, thanks a lot!

You're walking through the forest, Mr. Meier, and there's enough riffraff around now. I would take the thing with me, Mr. Meier, I never go without a firearm. Better is better!

The young lieutenant - he has become quite talkative, so concerned is he for the life of his friend Meier.

But he remains defensive. Nobody is going to hurt me! he says. No one has ever hurt me. The old thing just tears your pockets.

For my sake! Do what you want! the lieutenant suddenly says angrily and lays the pistol open on the cabinet.

He nods briefly to the little Meier, says good evening, and is already out of the office before he can answer.

Funny, Meier says, staring at the door. He was really funny at the end. Well, he consoles himself then, these brothers are all like that. First bragging big and then nothing behind it.

He turns around and looks at the gun.

Nah, he decides, I don't want to have anything to do with those things. It can go off in your pocket. - Where is Mandchen? I'll have to take a look. A little bit she can carry the suitcases well ...

He goes to the door.

Nah, first put the gun away again. It's going to look so stupid tomorrow morning otherwise.

He has the gun in his hand, and again he hesitates.

'Actually, he's right,' it shoots through his head, 'a gun is always good.'

He goes to the door, turns off the light, steps out of the official's house. With each step he notices the weight of the pistol in his back pocket.

'Funny - gives a sense of power, doesn't it, a thing like that,' he thinks, not displeased.

08 03

Field Inspector Meier has only a few steps to go when he sees the two girls sitting on a bench. Next to them stands the lieutenant, talking. At the sound of footsteps, the lieutenant looks up and says, "Here he comes!

His standing close to the girls, his whispering with them, this announcement - everything annoys little Meier. Adding to this, he says irritably: "If I'm disturbing you, I can leave again.

No one seems to have heard him, no one answers.

You three must have a sweet secret together?" Meier says challengingly.

Again no answer. But now Violet stands up and says to the lieutenant: Come -?

For my sake," exclaims little Meier irritably, "you can call him you. We know - and about a lot of other things!

Surprisingly peaceful, the lieutenant takes the arm of the young lady and wordlessly walks away with her, into the park.

Meier calls mockingly behind him: Good night, ladies and gentlemen! Wishes a pleasant rest!

The lieutenant turns and calls out to Amanda, "So just talk him through it. Coaxing always helps!

Amanda nods thoughtfully.

Irritated, Meier drives at them: What else do you have to nod at the monkey?! What do you even have to talk to that guy for?!

She says calmly: You also think everyone else is a monkey but you!

Like this! So I am a monkey in your eyes!

Hans Fallada   -442-   Wolf among Wolves

I did not say that!

Don't talk! Just now you said it!

No! And after much thought: The madam is quite right.

What is the Weio right about -? She can only talk nonsense - a seven-month-old like her!

That it is better not to get involved with someone like you!

So, that's what she said? Meier almost croaks with rage. The injured vanity chases the bile into his blood, almost trembling he says: And your guy, the lieutenant - is he something better than me? How -? You think so?! What a pig! Waving a revolver in my face in my office! But I told him about it! Let him come at me again, the stupid bacon hunter, now I have a revolver too! And I - I don't just threaten like the monkey - I shoot!

He pulls the pistol out of his pocket and waves it in the air.

Have you gone mad? Amanda yells at him angrily. Put that thing back in your pocket! Driving me in the face with something like this, I love it right now! You think that impresses me -?!

He winced at her angry, contemptuous rant. Somewhat embarrassed, admittedly still completely defiant, he stands before her, the pistol in his hand with the barrel lowered to the ground.

She orders: Now you go back inside right now and put the money back in the cash register! Ugh, I can take a lot, and I'm not disgusting at all, but stealing money from the cash register - no, thanks! Not me! Not with me!

Meier has blushed - admittedly, she can't see it.

So, did he clap you that, the fine boy who -?! he shouts angrily. Let me tell you something, it's his business and it's none of your damn business! I have to settle this alone with the cavalry captain. If I take my salary, you have nothing to say to me, understand?

Hans! she says more gently. You have to put the money back in the cash box or we're finished! I can't stand that kind of thing.

But I don't give a shit if we're over or not! I am glad that we are finished! What do you think you're good for?! Do you think I care about you! I had the hardy ones in bed tonight, yes, the hardy ones, there you have it! And such an old woman with eight children - I still prefer her ten times better than you ...! Ow, damn it!

It was a very unflattering blow, from all their forces, it sat in the middle of his face - Meier really staggers.

You pig, you! she says breathlessly. You miserable bastard!

You hit me -? he says quietly, half unconscious with pain. You hit me - you pathetic chicken girl hit me, the inspector -?! Now you should see ...

But he himself sees almost nothing. It spins before his eyes, in the moonlight her figure fades, and suddenly she is there again ... Now, now he sees them clearly ... She hit him!

He quickly raises the pistol and squeezes off with a trembling finger ...

Unbearably loud the shot whips into his ear ...

Amanda's face, growing larger and larger, comes very close to him, white and black in the moonlight....

You! she whispers. You, Hansel, shoot me ...

And now it becomes very quiet between the two. Only the other's hasty, jerky breaths are heard by each. For a long, long time they stand like this ...

The shot has long since faded. His sound went out of her ears, other sounds came for it, alleviating ... they hear again the soft wind in the tops of the trees ... Now, at the back of the barn, a halter chain slowly rattles through the ring ...

Mandecken, Negermeier says. Mandecken ... I ...

Hans Fallada   -444-   Wolf among Wolves

Off! she says in a hard voice. All the way out!

She looks at him again.

Shoots me - and then he says Mandecken ... It is as if this thought takes her breath away anew. I wonder what he would have said if he had met me - ?

And the grave danger in which she had been hovering, the incomprehensible salvation overwhelmed her so suddenly that she burst into a low, whimpering cry. So crying, she runs away from him, her shoulders hunched ...

Under the light hem of her skirt he sees her coarse legs moving faster and faster - she walks, she runs, she hurries away from him.... She turns into the path to the castle, now he doesn't see her running anymore, he only hears her crying, this suppressed, pitiful wailing - and now that is gone, too ...

Meier stands there for another moment, staring after her. Then he lifts the pistol, which still hung heavily in his hand, and looks at it. He moves the wing of the safety - so, now the gun is secured, nothing can happen with the thing ...

With a sullen shrug, he shoves it into his back pocket and hastily heads for the office to retrieve his suitcases.

08 04

The lieutenant and Weio are sitting on a bench in the park. They don't sit there like lovers - or maybe they do sit there like lovers, but like a balky one, namely far apart, namely without a word.

To be offered such a thing by the coward! she said at the end of her argument. I don't understand you!

Of course you don't understand me, Schafel, he answered very condescendingly. That's only good. Because then he doesn't understand me either.

To run away from the guy - what he will imagine now! Where I can not smell him!

Don't get so close to him! he said bored. Then his smell does not bother you.

Please, Fritz, when did I get too close to him?! she shouted indignantly. Fritz, that was mean of you!

But Fritz did not answer anymore, and so silence broke out among them.

The bang of the gunshot disturbed this quarrelsome silence. The lieutenant pulled up from his thoughts.

It shot! he shouted and ran off.

Who -? she asked, getting no answer and running after them.

Over the park meadows lying in the moonlight the run went, their long, damp grass wetted the stockings; then through bushes, across the paths, in the middle of flower beds! The boxwood of the path edges makes them stumble. Weio gasps breathlessly, wants to shout and can't because she has to keep running.

Now the lieutenant stops and tells her to be quiet. Over his shoulder away, she peers through between the lilac and snowball bushes. Just then she sees the poultry maid disappear crying to the castle, Inspector Meier stands motionless in front of the official's house.

Did not hit them, thank God! whispers the lieutenant.

Why is she crying?

The fright!

The guy has to go to jail! says Weio emphatically.

Don't be stupid, Weio! What he would talk out then, huh? You would have liked that, wouldn't you?

Well, and now?

Now we will wait and see what he does.

The small, dark figure walks quickly towards the official's house, all the way into the bushes they hear the sound of the door being forcefully slammed shut. Field Inspector Meier is gone.

Now he's gone, says Fräulein von Prackwitz unhappily, and from now on I'm allowed to be especially polite to him so that he keeps his mouth shut in front of Papa.

Wait and see, Violet, says the lieutenant.

You don't even have to wait long. Barely three, four minutes. Then the front door opens again, and out steps little Meier, a suitcase in his right hand, a suitcase in his left hand. He doesn't even take the time to close the front door again, blackly yawning its opening - Meier, however, marches, a little hindered, nevertheless at a brisk pace towards the courtyard, out into the world - off!

Get lost! whispers the lieutenant.

Thank God! she breathes a sigh of relief.

You won't see him again ... says the lieutenant, suddenly silent, as if what he has said already annoys him.

Let's hope so, she replies.

Violet! says the lieutenant after a while.

Yes, Fritz?

Stop here for a moment, will you? I just want to check something on the office.

What do you want to look up?

Oh, just so ... What it looks like there.

Why? We could care less about that.

Hans Fallada   -447-   Wolf among Wolves

So let me already -! Sorry - so, here you wait!

The lieutenant hurriedly walks over to the officer's house. He enters, feels his way across the dark forecourt, switches on the light in the office. He doesn't look around for long - he heads straight for the drawer with the firearms. It is half open, but that is not enough for the lieutenant, he pulls it all the way open and looks very carefully at its contents.

No, the nine-millimeter mouser is not among them. He pushes the drawer shut again. He thoughtfully extinguishes the light and walks out across the dark forecourt into the moonlight, to her.

Well, what does it look like inside? Violet asks a little mischievously. He must have done a quick tidy up?

What should it look like -? - Oh, yes, of course pigsty, still pigsty, that's what it looks like, my little sheep.

The lieutenant is strangely tidy.

She uses this right away: You, Fritz ...

Well, Violet -?

Do you also remember what you wanted today -?

Well, what did I want? Give you a kiss? - Come on then!

He gets her by the head, and for a while they are busy until she is completely breathless against his chest.

So, says the lieutenant, and now I must hurry to Ostade!

To Ostade -?! Oh, Fritz - you wanted to check with me whether I wasn't keeping a diary -!

But Schafel, but not today -! I really have to go full steam ahead - I have to be in Ostade by six!

Fritz -!

What?

Is it not possible at all -?

No - today completely excluded! But I will definitely come. The day after tomorrow, maybe tomorrow already!

Oh, you always say that! Tonight you also didn't say anything about the fact that you have to go back to Ostade right away -!

I have to, but I really have to ... Come on, Violet, take me all the way to my bike. Please, please, don't make stories now, Schafel ...

Oh, Fritz, you ... what are you doing to me ...

08 05

For a long, long time, Petra had sat frozen.

Exhausted, the sick enemy also lay still for a long time, until restlessness overcame her anew. She had hurled all the insults she knew into Petra's face; spitting at her, she had recalled with a whoop of the most wicked triumph how she had once been taken out of a car cab by her -: Away from the fine pisser, and your umbrella went down too, you carrion!

Mechanically, Petra had done what had to be done: had given a little water, put a poultice on the forehead, a towel over the mouth, which was nevertheless pushed back again and again. However much the other scolded and scolded, sneered and sought to hurt, it no longer affected her, just as the quieter sounds of the city after midnight no longer affected her. The city outside, the enemy inside - both were none of their business.

A feeling of utter abandonment had blown at her with its icy breath, freezing everything inside her. In the end, it was every man for himself - what the others did, said, did, it was nothing. A single, only human being on itself, the earth swings through the eternities of time and space its course, always only one alone on itself!

So Petra sits, thinks and dreams, Petra, unmarried single. She proves to her heart that she will not see the wolf again and that it must be so, and that

Hans Fallada   -449-   Wolf among Wolves

this is just the order and that she has to be content with it. So she will sit and think, dream and prove many a time in the days and weeks to come. Even if love, which longs, cannot prove anything, something like consolation, like the faintest memory of happiness, lies already in the fact that it can sit and dream like this.

That's why Petra is almost unwilling when a hand rests on her shoulder and a voice takes her away from her dreams with the words: "You, Kittchen, tell us something! I can not sleep. My head hurts, so your girlfriend pulled my hair, and I also have to think about my business all the time. What are you thinking about?

It's the fat, elderly woman from the lower bed that the hen harrier fell over earlier. She moves to a stool next to Petra, looks at the girl with her dark, mouse-like eyes and whispers, tired of sitting alone and brooding, pointing at the sick girl: "She can show off like a bag of mosquitoes! Is it true what she says about you, Kittchen?

Suddenly Petra is pleased that the woman has spoken to her, that there is some entertainment in the long night. Suddenly, she does not dislike the woman at all, if only because she looks without hatred at the sick woman who has caused her enough pain.

Therefore Petra answers quite willingly: Some things are true and some things are not true.

The woman asks: But that you go on the street, that's not true -?

A few times ... Petra begins hesitantly.

But the old woman understood immediately. Noah, noah, my little one," she says, graciously. Ick am also raised in Berlin! I live on Fruchtstraße. After all, I have also been through these times, which are times like there have never been before! I know the world, and I know Berlin too! You used to get one when you were hungry for cabbage - what?

Petra nods.

Hans Fallada   -450-   Wolf among Wolves

And that calls so 'ne bitch go on the line! And that's why she ratted you out! She ratted you out, didn't she?

Again Petra nods.

There you go - it's such a food envious beast, you can tell by the neese! Those who have such a thin neese, they are always sharp and begrudge no other nothing! You don't have to think about it, it's not her fault that she's stupid, she didn't choose her neese either. - And what else do you do?

Sell shoes ...

Well, I know that, that's also a bread with tears for the young things. There are such a life journey, when the fur itches, then they run from one shoe store to another, and always just try shoes, and then poke the young girls with the shoe tip - well, of course, you know all that too ... Or -?

Yes, there are such, says Petra, and we know them already. And those we don't know, we can see it on their faces, and then no one wants to serve them. And some are even worse, they not only prick, they also talk to it, as mean as no girl from the hustle ... And if you resent it, they complain, the saleswoman serves badly - and they have a real joy when the manager snaps at you ... There is no point in defending oneself, after all, one is not believed that such a fine gentleman uses such mean words ...

We know, child," the old woman said soothingly, for the memory of many a dishonor inflicted had come back to Petra that she had spoken almost heatedly. We know all that! Do you think it's any different on Fruit Street? It's no different there. And if it's not a shoe store, then it's a pastry store or ice cream parlor - the last one is bitten by dogs everywhere. - But surely it will be over with the shoes now that you're sitting, or will they take you again when you come out?

After all, it was already long gone with the shoes, Petra reports. Almost a whole year. I was living with a friend, and just today no, yesterday at noon, we were going to get married.

No such thing! the old woman wonders. And of all things, on such a special day, the little poisonous toad has to interfere with her ad! Now tell me really, child, what did you do that was so bad that they put you in jail clothes right here? They actually only do that with the brides of the robbers, where they think they are bunking off in civilian clothes! But if you don't want to, don't. I don't like to be spanked either, and I always notice it when you get dizzy... So it happened that Petra Ledig told the rather miserable story of the collapse of her hopes to an elderly woman, completely unknown to her by name, between one and two o'clock in the night, exactly at the hour when her wolf thought he had finally won the great 'victory' of his life, and how she was now all alone in life again, and actually did not really know why and why not.

The old woman listened to all this very patiently, nodded her head sometimes, shook it vigorously sometimes and said: We know all that! and: That exists! or also: One should tell that to the dear God times, but he got his business in the last five years also over and hears on the ear badly ...

But when Petra had finished and was staring silently at the sick woman on the floor, or even just in front of her, or at all the debris, the extent of which she had only now become quite aware through her own narration, so that she really no longer understood at all why and why and why and where - then the old woman gently put her hand on her arm and said: "Child - so Petra is your name and he always called you Peter -?

Yes, said Petra Ledig rather perplexed.

So I will also say Peter to you, even if he doesn't deserve it. And I am Mrs. Krupaß, Mother Krupaß they say to me in the Fruchtstraße, and so you should also say ...

Yes, Petra answered.

And what you told me, I even believe you, and that is more than the police chief himself can tell you. But if it's like you say (and it is, I can tell), you'll be out of there today or tomorrow - because what can they want you for? Nothing at all they can want you! You're healthy, and you didn't go on the street, and you're also in the registry office - don't forget to tell them that, the registry office always attracts them ...

Yes, said Petra.

Well, today or tomorrow you'll get out, and they'll find you some clothes from the charity, so you'll get out - and then what will you do?

Petra only shrugged uncertainly, but she was now looking at the speaker quite attentively.

Yes, that is the question. Everything else is tin, kiddo. Thinking back and feeling resentful and regretful - it's all tin. What do you do when you get out - that's the question!

Of course, said Petra.

For gas or the Landwehrkanal you are not, as you look, and then you would like to get the worm quite, huh?

That's what I want! Petra said resolutely.

And what about the shoes? inquired Mother Krupaß. Do you want to start that again?

I can't get a position again, Petra said. I have no testimony about the last time, and from the last position I just stayed away, overnight. All my papers are still there, I told you, it came so quickly with Wolf ...

I know, I know, said Mrs. Krupaß. You get the papers again, papers are always good. So with the shoes it's nothing more, and even if it were something, it's not enough, and then the other just comes back, and whether you want that right now -?

No, no, Petra said hastily.

No, of course not, I know that. I'm just saying. And now here's another one, child - you know what, child - I'd rather call you child, and not Peter - Peter is not on my lips. So, there's your friend now, how about that, kid?

He stayed away!

That's him, you're right. And he probably won't be back either. He'll think he'll get in trouble for his shenanigans if he inquires too much about you with the police, and maybe he'll think you ratted him out ....

Wolf doesn't think so!

So, then he doesn't think so, also good, said Mrs. Krupaß docilely. He can be just as fine a cavalier as you say, and I don't say a word against it, and he still stays away. Men are no different. Do you want to go look for him now?

No, said Petra. Do not search ...

What if he comes to visit you tomorrow?

The old woman shot a quick, dark look at the girl. She saw Petra get up and walk back and forth, and now she even stopped, and it was as if she was listening out into the prison. Then the girl shook her head discouragedly and walked up and down again. Stopped against the wall, leaned his head against the stones, stood like that for a long time.

That is so, said the Mrs. Krupaß finally reporting. Then the constable knocks on the door and says: Single, come along, visit! And then you go after it, shuffling as you are now, in your blue putty. And then you come into a room, there's a wooden fence in the middle, and he's standing on one side, all dressed up, and you're standing on the other side, all dressed up, and there's a constable sitting in the middle watching you. And then you talk to each other, and when the constable says: Time's up, then he goes back out into the open, and you go back to your cell....

Petra has long since turned around and looks at the old woman with a pale face tensely. When she doesn't speak any further, Petra moves her lips as if she wants to say something, ask something, but she says nothing, she asks nothing.

Yes, Kittchen, says Mrs. Krupaß suddenly in a hard, angry voice, now just tell me, what have you actually done that you're traipsing into the cell again? And what is so praiseworthy about him now that he can go outside again?

It is very quiet in the cell. Finally, however, Petra says wearily: He can't help it ...

Nope! says the old lady triumphantly. It's not his fault that you were always hungry and that you had to wait forever, and that he beat up your clothes, and without him you wouldn't have come here at all. He can't help that! He has worked the pelt of the paws with card shuffling, a restless night worker is that jewesen -!

Petra wants to say something.

Silence! screams the old lady. I'll pull your tooth out! You are stupid! He had his vajniejen with you - and when he didn't feel like vajniejen anymore, he left and thought: now another film, let the first film take care of itself! So wat lieb ick, ich sage dir, so wat stir mir die Galle um! Don't you have any honor left in your body, girl, that you want to stand there in the visiting room like a primrose pot with a pink napkin and beam at him - just because he really comes to visit you! Is this marriage, I ask you, is this companionship? Is it just friendship? Mere bedriddenness is det, I tell you! Shame on you, girl!

Petra stands very still and white in the cell. She is shaking all over. Of course, she has never had her star stung or her tooth pulled before, she has never seen her relationship with Wolf in this light - all the veils that love drew over it have been torn apart. 'Stop!' she wants to shout. But she does not call it.

It may well be, Mrs. Krupaß continues more peacefully, that he is quite a good man, as you say. He's doing something for your education, you say - fine, let him do it if he enjoys it. It would be better if he did something for your heart and something for your stomach, but of course he doesn't feel as

Hans Fallada   -455-   Wolf among Wolves

smart there as he does with the books. A good man, you say. But, child, that's not a man, maybe it should become one! What is a man in bed, that is far from being a man, believe 'ner old woman. You young girls are just imagining things! And if you go on like this with him, with spoiling and always-parenting, and mother is also in the background with a nice, fat money bag - then it will never become a man, but you will become a dunghill, God forgive me for my words!

She really snorts with effort and bitterness, again and again shooting sharp glances at Petra, who stands pale and still against her wall.

Now Mrs. Krupaß says more calmly: "I'm not asking you not to see him again at all. Only now let him manage on his own for a while. You can wait and see what he does for a year or even half a year (I'm not like that!). Whether he continues with the gimmick - lazy! Or whether he crawls under with mother - oberfaul! Or if he bends another one - then he never had anything real in mind with you. Or whether he starts working at something sensible ...

But I must at least tell him what has become of me, or write to him, Petra asks.

To what? What helps to say or write? He has seen you for a year, every day, if he doesn't know you then all the writing is useless. And he can ask at the police station - they'll tell him you're here, they don't make a secret of it. If he comes here and looks at you - well, then you just go down and tell him: "Well, my dear Spitz, I want to prove myself first, and you should also prove yourself first...". And besides, I'm going to have a baby, you say, not like, we're going to have a baby.... Because you get it and you should keep it, and I want the child to have a real man for a father, who can also take care of a bit of snacks, you know, something to eat, something against the hunger, so that you don't just fall over in the street, in dealing with you, you know....

Mother Krupass! Petra asks, because the old woman is already getting angry again.

Well, child, she resents, you can tell him that, it won't take the gold off him, a man needs to hear that, it's only good for him....

Yes, says Petra, and what do I do half the year -?

You see, child, said the Krupass delightedly, that was the first intelligent word you said this evening. And now you sit here comfortably next to me on the bed - the old bitch there must be asleep - and now we'll have a real talk. We don't talk about men at all anymore, a real woman shouldn't talk about men so much at all, they're just imagining things, and they're not that important ... What you're supposed to do in that one year? This is what I want to tell you -: you shall represent me!

Ah! said Petra, a little disappointed.

08 06

Yes, you say ah!, said old Mrs. Krupaß quite kindly and groaningly crossed one leg over the other, revealing that she was not only wearing quite unfashionably long, wrinkled skirts (and there was even a petticoat under the skirt), but also completely impossible, thick, home-knitted woolen stockings, now in the middle of summer.

You say ah, child, and you're right! Because how can such a pretty young thing represent such an old broom like me - and like 'ne old whorehouse mother and Schlafbosten I also still look, what -?

Petra shook her head sheepishly, but still smiling.

But you're not right, child. And why aren't you right? That's why, because you wrote on the checkout pad by the shoes and you can calculate, and eyes you also have in your head that see what they look at. That's what I said to myself as soon as you came into the cell, sigh, I said, finally one that has eyes to look at again, not those piercing eyes like the calves today: everywhere and nowhere ...

Do I really have such eyes? Petra asked curiously, because her mirror had not yet given her the idea that she might have different eyes from the others, and Wolfgang Pagel had not yet told her that either, although he had been able to feel her eyes now and then.

If only I told you! declared the Krupass. I have learned on eyes in the fruit street, where I have fifty, sixty people walking, and they all lie to me with their mouths, but they can't lie with their eyes! And I'm sitting here in this wretched bug hutch, brooding and pondering what it's going to take me this time, and I'd like to think three months, but it's going to be half a year already. Killich also says half a year, and Killich is seldom wrong and must know, because he is my legal counsel ...

Petra looks a bit questioning, but the old woman nods her head energetically and says: "That will all come. You will learn everything in its own time, child. And as you said 'ah' earlier, you can say 'no' later, I don't care. Only, you don't say it ...

She looks so sure and so energetic, and yet again good-natured, that Petra first of all really gives up all misgivings that want to rise to her with such pious providence into a prison sentence.

But Mrs. Krupaß continues: "And there I sit and think: six months in jail is all right so far, you need some rest - but what about the business, especially in these times? Randolf is real, but he is weak in arithmetic, and now that everything is about to go into the millions, and then only a slate and chalk - that won't do, child, you can see that too!

And Petra sees it and nods her head and shakes it, just like Mrs. Krupass wants it, although she doesn't see clearly yet.

Yes, so there I sit and ponder about deputies, which is a nice word, except that they all steal like hungry ravens, and no one thinks about the old woman in the pokey. But here you come in, child, and I see you and your eyes. And I see what's going on with you two, and I hear what she throws at you - and then the attack on me and the pulling of my hair and the wrapping in blankets - and everything done properly, without anger and yet not like Salvation Army ...

Petra sits very still and doesn't pull a face. But it is good for every person to have his actions recognized a little bit, and it is especially good for a beaten, pushed around person.

Yes, I thought, that's right, that would be something for you. But of course, such a thing is in putty, such a thing is not handed. Just get it off, Mother Krupass. She's still mending shirts when you're long gone. - And then I hear what you tell, and it is not the possibility, I think, they must have sent the child to you directly from heaven into your abandonment....

Mother Krupass! Petra said for the second time.

Well, of course, Mother Krupass, how else? says the old woman quite happily and slaps Petra roughly on the knee. Did I give you a good beating earlier, huh?! Come on, it doesn't matter. They gave me so much juice in my youth, and later still, not too scarcely, as the boys fell in the war, and my Oller picked himself up out of melancholy. But not with me in the Fruchtstraße, there he was already in Dalldorf, which is now called Wittenau - let one, I think, sauer macht lustig ...

She leans forward, looking at Petra with her busty eyes. But I am not very funny, child, do you understand? That's just the way it looks - on the whole, I find the operation pretty lame ...

And Petra nods her head in complete agreement, and it is quite clear to her that the operation does not mean the Alexanderplatz police headquarters. She completely understands the attitude of Mother Krupass, that one can find life quite miserable and yet not hang one's head. After all, she has a pretty similar attitude, and when you discover such sympathy, you are always pleased.

Yes, but I'm still running the business, it keeps me alive. And if you don't keep yourself alive and create something, child, that's nothing, you rot alive. And the way you did it, always sitting in the furnished room, and maybe once in a while, when it's a lot, a little washing up for the furnished slumbering mother, that's no life, girl, everyone has to become stupid and gloomy ...

And again Petra nods her head, and again she finds that Mrs. Krupaß is quite right and that it is quite impossible to return to the old life at the Pottmadamm. And now she would just like to know what kind of work Mrs. Krupaß has kept so fresh and lively, and she wishes with all her heart that it is some kind of work that is decent and responsible.

And then Mrs. Krupaß says: "And now I want to tell you, child, what kind of business I have. And when people turn up their noses at it and say: it stinks! - it's a good deal after all! And it has nothing to do with jail, because it is a decent business - only my stupidity has to do with jail, because I am a greedy person, a money-hungry person. I can't help it, and a hundred times I say to myself: leave it, Auguste (my name is Auguste, but I don't use it), leave it, you earn enough money as it is, deliver it - I can't help it! And then I fall in - and already the third time! And Killich says yes, it will take six months.

Now she sits there very collapsed, the money-grubbing Mrs. Krupaß, and Petra can see that what she said earlier about the six months of rest was only a hoax, that Mrs. Krupaß is not at all hardened, but has a hellish fear of these six months in jail. And she would like to say something comforting to the old woman, but she still doesn't know what it's all about. Nor can she get the slightest idea of Mrs. Krupaß's business, which is going well but smells bad, and which is supposed to be decent again after all.

So Petra Ledig prefers to remain silent and wait. And after a while, Mrs. Krupaß pulls herself together again and says with an almost apologetic smile: "God, now I'm sitting there moping too. But that's what you get when you boast about being funny and all. But now you shall hear, child! Do you know what a product business is?

Petra nods a little and has an idea of a musty, smelly basement.

You see, child, I have, and you don't have to pull your nose at it, it's a good business and nourishes you, and you don't have to put up with insolence from old pleasure seekers in the process. Waste paper and old iron and bones and rags, and skins I also have ... But not with a small handcart to the garbage dumps, no, I have a large yard, with a truck, and six men work for me. And then there is Randolf, who is my supervisor over the campground, a bit düsig, but real, as I have already told you. And then they come to me, fifty, sixty hand trucks every day. I pay what is right, and they know that too, that Mother Krupass pays the right prices. And now at all it becomes more every day where everyone goes with 'n n handcart, because the work is less and less ...

But Mother Krupass, I don't know anything about that! says Petra shyly.

You don't have to, my girl. Randolf knows everything and knows everything, except that he can't calculate and is slow. You should calculate and write and pay out money, and I have great confidence in you, child, but it will be all right. And in the evening you call the spinning mills and factories, what they pay for everything, each their stuff, I still tell you the numbers and names of the people, and then you pay, quite real. And then it goes to the factory with the truck, deliver, and then you get money, and the paper we load when we have enough for a wagon. Randolf tells you everything. This then also gives money again. It's fun, kid, when you take the money, and nowadays any kid can trade at all, where the dollar is always rising ...

Petra looks at the old woman, suddenly, seeing her eagerness, her shining eyes, it all doesn't seem quite impossible to her anymore. It's work after all - what do you mean stinky rags?! It is something like a future after all.

But then she remembers that Mrs. Krupaß is in prison and that there must be a catch to the whole thing, and her joy gently fades.

Hans Fallada   -461-   Wolf among Wolves

But the old woman keeps talking, and what she talks rekindles the joy of fresh. And do not think, she says, that it is otherwise a break with me. All real and solid. Proper business records and with the tax office no more trouble than anyone. And a cottage on the square, tiptop, fine with egg, with flowers and arbor, just as it should be. Randolf lives downstairs and I live upstairs, three rooms with bathroom and kitchen - great! And Randolfen cooks my food, and so she shall cook it for you. I like to eat something - she cooks not bad! - And I thought to myself, you live in my apartment and sleep in my bed; and in the bathroom you wash ... But in the tub you do not bathe, there the enamel of broken or becomes streaky, with the enamel I know alone. You must promise me in your hand that you will not touch the tub! - You don't get so dirty that you have to take a bath - the dirty work is done by Randolf and the men ...

Again Petra nods and now she would like very much that it would become something - but there is still the one, the one point.

And tomorrow morning Killich comes here to the consultation hour, which is my legal counsel, and that's a sly dog, I tell you, child! I will say to him: Killich, Mr. Killich, Mr. Attorney Killich - tomorrow or the day after tomorrow or today, someone will come to you in the office hours, Petra Ledig is her name, she is my deputy. You see, it's not what she wears on her body that is welfare or care, look her in the face, and if she shits on me, Killich, then I don't believe anyone in the world anymore, not me and certainly not you, Mr. Killich ...

Mother Krupass! says Petra, putting her hand on the hand of the other and is firmly convinced that it really can't be that bad with the crimes of the old people.

Well, what, my girl?! What then, what then?! It is so! And then Killich goes with you to Randolfen and tells him that you are like me, with money and disposal and housing and food and command quite like me, and what you need in clothes and linen and things, you buy. And at the city bank, where I have my account, you can also sign like me, Killich will make everything ready for you ...

But Mother Krupass ...

Well, but what -? You get food and you get clothes and you get an apartment and you can have your child with me (but hopefully I'll be out by then), but there's one thing you don't get: you don't get a salary, you don't get money. And why not? Because you just give it to him! You're so dusky, I know that, I'm a woman myself for that. When he comes and makes a loyal puppy dog look, you give him what you have. But what you do not have, namely my money, you do not give him - for that I know you now! That's why you don't get a salary - not out of curmudgeonliness you don't! And now say, child, do you agree or do you disagree -?

Yes, Mother Krupass, of course I agree. But there is still the one thing, the thing ...

What kind of thing?! Don't make me stories, girl! With this guy? We're not talking about that guy anymore, let him become a guy first!

No, your business, Mother Krupass, your -!

What, my thing?! I have told you everything, child, and if that is not enough for you ...

No, your thing, the thing you are sitting for! Petra exclaimed. The thing for which you want to get half a year, Mother Krupass!

I and want, child! What a good girl you are!!! You have a concept of what I want, I really have to say -! So: the matter is none of your business, you have nothing to do with it and the business has nothing to do with it, only my happiness has to do with it. So: when we sort rags, I'm usually there to make sure that nothing made of cotton flies between the linen rags, because linen is expensive and cotton is cheap, don't you understand?

Yes, said Petra.

There you go! said the old woman with satisfaction. Head remains head. And as I stand there, and the rags fly through the air, I see something blinking with my greedy raven eyes. I sneaked up, and there's a real dress shirt in between, and the goofball who threw it away - but it must have been the goofball's girl who wanted to make a little money with linen rags (many people do that nowadays, because the wages don't go there and don't come back) - had three diamond buttons stuck in the front of the board! No Pofel, I see the same, real diamonds, and not small! Well, I pretend I don't see anything, but I quietly pooh-pooh them out. And then at home I rejoice. Wonderful - I am so, about such a thing, and if's now even cost nothing, I can be happy like a child! I know I'm not supposed to, I've already fallen for it twice with something like this, but I can't help it. I always think, no one has seen it, do not deliver it, you have your little joy at it ...

She looks at Petra and Petra looks at the old woman, and Petra is very relieved, but Mrs. Krupaß is very distressed.

And that's the mean thing about me, child, that I can't let it go. That I do not get this under, about it I am annoyed again dead! Killich also says to me: What are you doing, Mrs. Krupaß? You're a rich woman, you can buy yourself a six-pack of diamond buttons, don't do that! - And right he is, but I can not leave it! I can't handle it, I can't handle it, I can't handle it. What would you do in such a case, child?

I would deliver them, says Petra.

Deliver? The beautiful knobs?! Nah, so stupid! She wants to get excited again, but she comes to her senses right away. Well, let's not talk about it anymore, I get annoyed enough without talking. What more do I have to say? One of my people must have seen it, they are all greedy, and the Crimean is already there and is quite polite. Well, Mrs. Krupaß, how's that again with a little misappropriation? he says and still grins, the monkey! Did you perhaps put it back in the mirror cabinet? Open it! And I really put the buttons in there again like last time, the man is right, and he's not a monkey at all! The monkey is always just me! Well, what is not born a criminal, will not be one for the rest of his life!

Krupass sits there, lost in thought, and Petra can see that even now, despite all the self-knowledge, despite the fear of the six months, she regrets the loss of the buttons. And Petra almost wants to smile at the childish, foolish old woman. But then she thinks of Wolfgang Pagel, and even if she immediately wants to say, 'That's something different than buttons!' - she still thinks, 'Maybe I'm just imagining that it's something different. What the wolf is to me, the buttons are to Mother Krupaß!'

And now she remembers that it is over with the wolf for the time being, and she thinks of the little house on the produce storage yard, of which she can already form a proper idea (fire beans grow high on the arbor), and she knows now quite firmly that there is no more pot-madam and no more overheated yard room, no more screaming of the cut sheet metal from the factory on the ground floor, no more idle waiting, no more bed rest because of lack of clothes, no more courting for a few rolls. - But instead cleanliness, order, a scheduled day with work, food and rest ... And this prospect so overwhelms her that happiness almost touches her with a cry. She swallows once, she swallows again, but then she comes to her senses. She approaches the old woman, gives her her hand and says: Well, I do, Mother Krupass, and gladly! And I also thank you beautifully!

08 07

A long time, an immeasurably long time, for almost an hour the cavalry captain and his squire had played together. With whispers they had communicated to each other, Pagel had listened to the suggestions of the cavalry captain and had followed them, or he had not followed them, just as he judged the game.

The ball had run and rattled, the wheel had whirred, the croupier had called, hurried to move in and reset. Time ran hastily, it ran, it had always been filled - and that one moment when the ball seemed to pause at the edge of a hole, undecided whether it should fall in or run on - that one moment when time seemed to stand still with the breath, with the heart in the chest - that one moment always passed far too quickly.

Young Pagel, as he set in a controlled and calculating manner, had not been a bad teacher for Herr von Prackwitz; the cavalry captain saw, while Pagel explained the odds to him with a few half-words, how senselessly, how childishly he had played before. Now that he had a clearer view of the playing field, could already judge that the pale, sharp-nosed gentleman with the monocle, as controlled as he looked, was playing like a fool after all - now the cavalry captain could already make more sensible suggestions, which, as already mentioned, were often not followed by the ex-flag lieutenant.

A quietly irritated, later really bitter mood slowly grew stronger and stronger in the cavalry captain. Young Pagel played with varying success, but on the whole he was on a declining streak despite scoring a few goals. If it may not have come to his consciousness, the cavalry captain probably noticed how the ensign had to keep replenishing tokens from his tunic pocket. The boy had every reason to follow his, the elder and former superior's, advice! Ten times the captain of the cavalry had it on the tip of his tongue to say: 'Now, for once, do what I tell you! - Now you've lost again!'

If the cavalry captain swallowed this sentence again and again (with great difficulty), it was not because the young pagel could, after all, play with his own money as he pleased. Pagel was undoubtedly playing with his own money; the cavalry captain was merely a tolerated spectator, with only three or four tokens in his pocket and hardly any money up his sleeve. Mr. von Prackwitz was very clear about this. But this was not what prevented him from duly calling the Junker to order as his superior. Rather, it was the dark fear that Pagel might abandon the game at the slightest incident and want to go home. He trembled at this, it was the worst thing he could think of - not to be allowed to sit here anymore, not to be able to watch the rolling of the ball, not to hear the croupier's voice announcing the big blow at last, at last, maybe already at the next game. This apprehension alone, only darkly and barely conscious to him, was what kept the explosive cavalry captain constantly holding back. After all, it was questionable how long even such a strong inhibition could hold him back as his bitterness continued to rise. An argument between the two was inevitable. But, of course, this dispute turned out quite differently than expected.

The game you indulge in requires the complete attention of its followers. The eye that has strayed for only a moment has already lost track. The context is torn - incomprehensible is now why there the marks pile up, here the players have extinguished eyes. The game is a relentless God - only those who surrender to it completely, it gives all the delights of heaven, all the despair of hell. The half, the lukewarm are also spat out here - as everywhere.

It was hard enough for Pagel to continue unperturbed with the constant chatter of the Rittmeister. But now, right before his eyes, which were following the course of the ball, a white, very perfumed woman's hand with many boasting rings appeared, a hand holding a few tokens, as a voice ingratiatingly asked: So you see, darling, I told you! Now set for me too, as you promised me -! -

That's when young Pagel's patience ran out! Driving wildly around, he stared at the hold-smiling Valuten vamp and snarled: Tell them to go to hell!

He almost choked with senseless anger.

What Rittmeister von Prackwitz had observed in this incident was this: a young, very attractive-looking lady had wanted to make her bet, perhaps somewhat clumsily, over the shoulder of the flag junkie, and had been shouted at by him for doing so in the rudest, most insulting manner.

The cavalry captain hated rudeness towards women, he touched young Pagel by the shoulder and said very sharply: "Herr Pagel, you as an officer -! Immediately ask the lady to excuse you!

The croupier at the top of the table saw this clash, not without concern.

Although he knew the Valuten vamp quite well, he was not aware of anything ladylike about this wench. After all, it was impossible to have a loud argument in such a forbidden gambling club. There were the neighbors in those once stately tenements of the West. There were the owners of the apartment themselves in their marital bedchamber, who had only been driven by the hardship of the inflationary period to give up their good room for such a light-shy purpose. There was the porter downstairs in his box, who had received money, as a sure sleeper, but who had just received it - all of them could make a loud argument curious, suspicious, fearful.

So the croupier gave his two assistants a warning, pointing look. And these two helpers immediately rushed to the battlefield, one to the white-nosed Valuten vamp, to whom he suppressedly whispered: "Don't give us any trouble, Walli! while he said loudly: "But here you are, madam, chair? The other pushed up to the angry Pagel, who had jumped up angrily, gently but irresistibly removed the cavalryman's hand from Pagel's shoulder, for he knew that nothing makes an angry man angrier than when he is held down. At the same time, he anxiously pondered whether or not, if the young man in the shabby tunic continued to show off, a strong hook to the chin would be disliked in this distinguished company.

The croupier himself would also have liked to act as an arbitrator, only he could not yet leave the gaming table. In a half-loud voice, he asked the players to take back their stakes until the little disagreement between the gentlemen there was settled. At the same time, he thought incessantly about which of the two disputants there he would have to throw out the door. Because one of them had to go out, that much was clear.

The table in front of the croupier was now almost empty, and the gamekeeper was just about to carry out his intention, namely to ask the young pagel (who of course was not known to him by name) politely or forcibly, whatever, to step outside the door, when the tense situation unfortunately resolved itself in a way that did not fully correspond to the croupier's intentions.

The Valuten vamp, or rather Walli, who had really been able to buy a few letters of snow from a late-arriving gambler in the last hour and who had snorted up her entire acquisition at a nonsensical pace, wanted, unpredictable as addicts are, to find the angry Pagel only funny this time. Delightfully funny, heavenly, comical, to fall in love funny! She wanted to burst out laughing at his erratic, angry gestures, she asked the bystanders to join in the laughter, she pointed her finger at him: "He's too cute, that boy, when he's angry! I have to give you a kiss, darling!

And even when Pagel, senseless with rage, scolded her in front of the whole company whore slut, damned! this also only increased her merriment. Almost sobbing with hysterical laughter, she screamed: Not for you, Schatzi, not for you! You don't have to pay me anything!

I told you that I would hit you in the face! Pagel shouted and struck.

She shrieked out.

The tone of the conversation between the two, the way they insulted each other, had long since led the croupier's assistant to the conviction that a hook to the chin must be just as appropriate here as at home in Wedding. He also struck - but unfortunately into the staggering back Walli, who sank down without another sound.

Both von Studmann, who had been smoking inattentively and sullenly as a wall-holder, and the croupier were late. The Valuten vamp, suddenly looking very yellow and pointed, lay on the ground, senseless. The assistant tried to explain how everything had come about. Von Prackwitz stood there frowning and chewing his lip angrily.

Studmann asked rather dictatorially: So now I guess we're finally going -?!!!

Pagel stood there breathing rapidly, very white, and visibly did not listen to the cavalry captain, who now agitatedly and sharply reproached him for his uncavalier behavior.

Hans Fallada   -469-   Wolf among Wolves

The croupier saw the game evening threatened, many guests, and especially the more elegant, more solvent ones, who adored the view that one may transgress the laws, but only if all forms are respected, were preparing to leave. With three words he informed his people: the unconscious girl was carried into a dark adjoining room, already the disc was again whirring, the bullet rattled and jumped; magically, softly, seductively the green cloth glowed under the shielded lamp. The croupier sang: Here are two more inserts on the table ... Make your game ... Two gentlemen have forgotten their bets ...

Many turned back.

So let's go after all! von Studmann shouted again impatiently. I really don't understand you guys ...

The cavalry captain looked at his friend sharply and crossly, but he followed as Pagel walked wordlessly out the door.

In the hallway, the sad constable sat at his little table. The cavalryman fished in his pocket, fished out the two or three tokens he had left, threw them on the table, and called out in a tone that was meant to sound unconcerned: There -! For you, comrade! Everything I own!

The sad constable slowly raised his bulging eyes to the cavalryman, looked at him, shook his head, and placed three bills on the tabletop for the three tokens.

Herr von Studmann had opened the door to the dark stairwell and was listening down.

The man at the change table said, "You'll have to wait a moment. You will be illuminated immediately. He just went down with some gentlemen.

Pagel stood pale and weary in front of the greenish dressing room mirror, looking at himself thoughtlessly. He thought he heard the clatter of the ball inside, now the croupier shouted, he heard it clearly: Seventeen - Red - Unequal ...

Of course: red, his color. Its color! In a moment he would descend the stairs to go to the country with the cavalry captain, inside they would play his color, but for him it would be over with playing.

The cavalry captain said in a tone that was supposed to imply that everything that had happened was forgiven and forgotten, but which sounded quite irritated again: "Pagel, you still have some badges to change. It's a shame about that!

Pagel reached into his pocket and blindly gathered all the chips into his hand with his fingers.

'Why doesn't this guy come to let us out?" he thought. 'Of course they want us to keep playing!'

He tried to count how many tokens there were with his fingers in his pocket.

'If it's seven or thirteen, I'll play one last time.' 'I haven't really played at all today,' he thought, strangely bleary-eyed.

There had to be more than thirteen, he couldn't get the number out. He pulled the hand with the tokens out of his pocket and met the gaze of the cavalry captain. This look seemed to point to the door, to want to say something.

'It's not like it's seven or thirteen,' he thought gloomily. 'I have to go home!'

He remembered that he no longer had a home. He looked at the door. The unsuspecting von Studmann had stepped into the stairwell and was making a suppressed hello for the candlestick.

Pagel looked at the chips on his hand, counting them. There were seventeen. Seventeen -! His number -!!

At that moment, an incomprehensible feeling of happiness trickled through him. He had made it - the big chance was there! (O life - glorious, inexhaustible life!)

He approached the cavalry captain and said half aloud, glancing at the open door to the stairwell, "I'm not leaving yet. Still playing.

The cavalry captain was silent. Very quickly, he blinked his eye once - as if something had flown into it.

Wolfgang stepped up to the change table, he pulled a banknote packet, the second one, out of his pocket and said: Tokens - for everything!

While being counted and enumerated, he turned to the Rittmeister standing silently by and exclaimed, almost triumphantly: "I will win a fortune tonight! I know that -!

The cavalry captain moved his head gently, as if he knew this too, as if it was actually self-evident.

And you -? asked Pagel.

I have no more money with me, the cavalry captain replied. He sounded strangely guilty, looking almost fearfully at the open door.

I can help you out - play on your own account!

Pagel held out a money pack to the Rittmeister.

No, no, said the cavalry captain defensively. It's too much - I don't want so much ...

(Neither of them remembered at that moment the scene at Lutter and Wegner, since the young Pagel had also offered money to the Rittmeister and had been rejected with the most contemptuous indignation).

If you really want to win, Pagel stated emphatically, you have to have enough working capital. I know this!

Again the cavalry captain nodded. Slowly, he reached for the money packet. -

When von Studmann returned from the stairwell, the forecourt was empty.

Where are the gentlemen?

The constable made a movement with his head to the door of the playroom.

Von Studmann stamped his foot angrily. He went against the door. But he resolutely turned around again, thinking angrily: 'but I'm not even thinking about it! I am not his nanny! As much as he would need one ...'

He walked to the hallway door.

Right next to him a door opened, the girl with whom Pagel had had the argument stepped out.

Can you take me down the stairs? she asked tonelessly, indistinctly, as if she were talking in her sleep, as if she were not quite herself. I feel sick, I want to get some air. . .

Von Studmann, the eternal nanny, offered her her arm. But certainly. I was going to go anyway!

The constable took a silver-gray cloak from the wardrobe and hung it over the woman's bare shoulders.

The two descended the stairs without a word, the girl leaning heavily on Studmann's arm.

08 08

Of course, the peeping tom, and the same one who had shined the light up at the gentlemen, had been standing downstairs at the door and had just not let himself be called. Because every player who wants to leave must be given the opportunity to reflect for a long time.

But now that von Studmann appeared in the hallway with the girl on his arm, into which the glow of a gas lantern fell from outside, he was completely up to this situation as well. The Valuten vamp, the Walli, he knew, and that money and love often play together Ringelreihe or Bäumchen confused, was also not new to him.

Car? he asked, waving his tipped hand jovially and explaining before von Studmann could even answer: Wait Se one here. I'll get one from Wittenbergplatz.

With that, he disappeared, and von Studmann had time to think about the captiousness of his situation, here in the dark, unlocked hallway of an unknown house, with an unknown girl on his arm. Upstairs, however, was a gaming table - and now all that was needed was for a man from the security and lock company to come -!

It was all quite embarrassing once again, and today had fully met von Studmann's need for embarrassing situations! It was a cursed life in those days; a man could never know what would happen in the next quarter of an hour, whether what was valid would still be valid.

Studmann had been honestly pleased when he had met his old regimental comrade this morning. Prackwitz had behaved with fabulous decency; without his intervention, nothing of a Privy Councillor Schröck would ever have reached Studmann's ears, but he would have been pretty much sent away in disgrace. The prospect of leaving this hellhole for the quiet countryside with Prackwitz had also been very nice - and now this same Prackwitz was sitting up there, squandering his money in the most stupid way - and had already called him 'nanny'!

He didn't need a nanny - truly, he needed one, and he needed one now! When von Studmann thought of the two of them now sitting in the playroom again, when he remembered young Pagel's nonsensical money packages, and the vulture nose and the bird-of-prey look of the gamekeeper came very clearly before his eyes, he knew that he - nanny or no nanny - had to climb the stairs at once and put an end to this suicidal gambling.

But this girl, this unfortunate girl on his arm -!

It didn't seem quite in its right mind - no wonder, by the way, after the hard blow! It trembled, tore at his arm, chattered its teeth, whispered something about 'snow' again and again. From snow! - in a stinking, muggy, humid heat that was to die for! It remained clear that Studmann had to go upstairs immediately and free the friend, but it was equally necessary to take this girl somewhere safe first - to relatives. He would have liked to know her address, but she did not listen to his questions, answered only once gruffly that he should leave her in peace, she did not want, her apartment was none of his business!

Meanwhile, a car pulled up outside and stopped. Studmann was unsure if it was the one meant for him. The Peeping Tom did not let himself be seen, the girl whispered of snow, von Studmann stood irresolute.

Eventually, the Peeping Tom did slip out of the car and into the front door. I am sorry that you had to wait. To me it was like the air smelled sour. You know - the gambling department of the Krimpo! The boys can't get a good night's sleep, the cabbage steam keeps them so lively!

He whistled: And I sleep so badly and I dream so hard ...

Well, now you quickly, Count, into the rocking bag! Don't forget me either! All right. Wieda money, of which the Olle knows nothing. Well - and where to now, madam -?

He waited in vain.

Von Studmann looked dubiously at the girl leaning next to him in the corner of the carriage.

In de Mulle, Walli? the Peeping Tom suddenly roared. Where are you now?

She mumbled something about being satisfied.

The Peeping Tom to the chauffeur: So, get lost, man! Kurfürstendamm down! She'll perk up ...

The car started as Studmann was annoyed that he had not gotten out.

Later, in his memory, it was as if they had driven hours and hours. Streets up, streets down, dark streets, streets shining with light, empty streets, streets crowded with people. Now and then the girl knocked on the window, got out, went to a pub or talked to a man on the street ...

Slower she came back, said to the chauffeur: Go on! And the car started again. The girl sobbed, her teeth chattering louder, then whispered torn away.

Excuse me? asked von Studmann.

But she did not answer. She did not pay attention to him at all, for her he was not there. Long ago, he could have gotten out, gone back to the playing club. If he remained seated, it was not for her sake. He was not such an unconditional admirer of womankind as Rittmeister von Prackwitz, he knew very well who he was sitting next to. Yes, he also knew now, he had guessed, what the girl was hunting for. He had remembered that 'snow' had also been mentioned once in the hotel. A toilet tenant of the hotel café had suddenly led it. Of course, the man had flown, even the most modern hotel could not accommodate the wishes of its guests at this crazy time - but at least von Studmann knew about it.

No, if he was still sitting, if he was still driving, if he was waiting more and more anxiously each time to see if the girl's demand would finally be successful - it was because he was fighting for a decision. As soon as the girl would succeed, he would decide, one way or another. He would!

The remark of the tense about the gambling department of the Krimpo had brought von Studmann on the thought, careful inquiries with the chauffeur of this cab had made him sure - it would be the best to call this gambling department once. To have the gambling club excavated. What he had heard earlier about these things, what the chauffeur confirmed to him, was always that the players had little to fear. Their names were ascertained, in the worst case they got a small fine - that was all! Those who were hard touched were the birds of prey, the exploiters, the gamekeepers - and that was only right!

Again and again Studmann told himself that this solution was the best.

'What's the point of me going up there again?' he pondered again and again. I'm just having a fight with Prackwitz, and he's just playing on! No, from the next cafe call the police! I know that would be the most salutary lesson for Prackwitz, there is nothing he hates more than to be noticed - and if his personal data were to be ascertained by the police, that would drive away all desire to play! He still thinks he's in the casino - and yet it's all crooks and cheats ... It will cure him!'

Nothing, not a word could be said against these considerations, they were correct. The gamekeepers were punished, but the reckless Prackwitz together with young Pagel, who seemed to have lost all direction, they were warned. And yet von Studmann continued to struggle to find the strength to carry out this decision. It resisted within him to do the right thing because it was uncompassionate. You didn't bring a friend into contact with the police - even with the best of intentions. He put it off, first the girl should be taken care of.

He looks at her expectantly, but again she has nothing. She whispers: long with the chauffeur.

That's too far, Frollein, he hears the man say. I've got relief.

She whispers more insistently, finally he gives in.

But Frollein, if det again nischt is ...

They drive, endlessly, endlessly. Deserted, almost dark streets. Broken lanterns, for thrift only one in six or eight burns.

The girl next to him automatically whispers to herself. Oh God - oh God - oh God, on and on, and after each 'oh God' she bangs her head against the back of the car!

Von Studmann sees himself picking up the phone in the booth of a café: Please, give me the police headquarters, gambling department ...

But maybe they don't even have a cell, and he has to make calls at the buffet; people will think he's a plucked gambler out for revenge ... It looks very indecent, but it is the decent, it is - the - An-stän-di-ge!!! Studmann keeps telling himself. In the past, people had it better, because decent things also looked decent. This afternoon he had been decent too; he could have beaten that rascal to death by a baron, and for his decency he rolled down the stairs drunk - cursed life!

If only he were in the countryside with the rescued Prackwitz - in the calm, in the peace, in the long-lasting patience!

Finally the car stops, the girl gets out, hesitantly walks towards a house, once she stumbles and interrupts her way with scolding. Von Studmann sees only dark house fronts in the uncertain, flickering light. No local. No man. Something like a store, drugstore apparently.

The girl knocks on a ground-level window next to the store door, waits, knocks again.

Where are we? von Studmann asks the chauffeur.

At de Warsaw Bridge, the man says unhappily. Do you pay the tax? That costs a lot of gold!

Studmann says yes.

The window on the ground floor has opened, a pale, fat head over a white nightgown has appeared, it seems to whisper angry imprecations. The girl pleads, begs, a kind of howling wail penetrates to the car.

He won't give us anything, says the chauffeur. Well, so in the middle of the night from 't bed. And there is jittchen ooch for it. So eene does not hold the flap. - There you go, that's what I said!

The man angrily: No! No! No! screamed and threw the window shut. The girl stands there for another moment; her crying, desolate yet angry, can be heard all the way to the car. Von Studmann, the nanny, is standing by - he can already see the girl falling. He gets out of the car, wants to help her ...

But there she is already with him, with many, very quick, very short steps.

What is this? he shouts...

But she has already snatched the walking stick from his hand, runs back to the window before he can take it away from her again - all wordlessly, sobbing quietly. This quiet sobbing is particularly ghastly. And now she has smashed the window pane with one blow. Clinking, loudly rattling, the glass clatters onto the pavement ...

And to this the girl screams: Schieber! Fat pig! she screams. Are you giving out the snow?!

Let's move back, sir! suggests the chauffeur. If the Schupo didn't hear that! See, now the windows are already getting light ...

Really, windows light up here and there in the dark house fronts, a faint, high-pitched voice cries out: Quiet!

But there is already silence, because the two there at the shattered window only whisper to each other. Now the pale-faced man no longer scolds, or only quietly.

Jaha! says the chauffeur stretched. Who gets involved with such first once, must do what se want! It's ejal whether the Schupo comes and closes his store, the main thing, she can continue to do coke. Let's go, Mr. -?

But once again, Studmann can't bring himself to do anything like that. Even if the girl acted irresponsibly, meanly, he can't drive off and leave her here on the street, where police can turn around the next corner at any moment. And then he wants his verdict: if she gets her coke, he has to go to the next open café. Again he sees himself, the phone in his hand: Please the gambling department of the criminal police ...

It all just doesn't help. You have to save Prackwitz, you have your obligations ...

Now the girl comes back, and von Studmann doesn't even need to ask whether her path was successful. Just from the way she suddenly looks at him, the way he is there for her again, the way she addresses him, it is easy to see: she has been given coke and has also already snorted it.

Well?! she asks challengingly and holds out his cane to him. Who are you? - Oh, you're the friend of the young man who hit me. Nice friends you have, I must say, punching a lady in the face!

But no, says von Studmann politely. It wasn't the young person, who is not my friend by the way, who hit you like that - it was someone else, one of the two who always stood by the gamekeeper.

Curlywilli you mean? Oh, don't give me that crap, I was confirmed yesterday! Your friend was the one who brought you - well, I'll get that boy!

Don't we want to drive? suggests von Studmann.

He can't deny it, suddenly he is dead tired, tired of this women's room and its insolent, rabble-rousing tone, tired of wandering haphazardly around this giant city, tired of all the mess, the dirt, the bickering.

Of course we're going, she says immediately. Do you think I type all the way to the West?! Chauffeur, to Wittenbergplatz!

But now the chauffeur revolts, and since he does not need to talk as a cavalier, and since the gentleman has agreed to pay for the fare, he does not mince words. He tells her thoroughly what he thinks of such an old coke that breaks windows; he announces that he won't go one step further, not for the life of him!, he explains that he would have put her out long ago, if it weren't for the Lord ...

This rant makes little impression on the lady. She is used to scolding, arguing is in a way her life element. It makes her fresh, and the poison she has just taken fires her imagination, so that she is far superior to the grumpy, slow chauffeur. She'll have his driver's papers taken away, she'll report him to his haulier, she has a friend, she'll memorize his car number - he shouldn't be surprised if his tires are slashed tomorrow morning -!

Endless, silly babbling, wild straw threshing, the voices rise louder. Deathly tired, von Studmann stands by - he wants to intervene, to put an end to it, he protests, but he has no momentum, he can't get up against them, he's too tired. When will this end? Windows are already getting light again. Already again voices call for calm ...

But I do ask ... says von Studmann weakly, and again is not heard.

Suddenly the noise is over, the quarrel is over, and the chatter has not even been pointless: the parties have come to an amicable agreement. The train does not go all the way to Wittenbergplatz, but it does go one step further, to Alexanderplatz.

That's where I have my garage," explains the chauffeur, and this explanation prevents von Studmann from thinking any further about this destination, Alexanderplatz. Otherwise it would have occurred to him that Alexanderplatz is home to the very police headquarters whose gambling department he must call immediately now that the girl has her way.

But von Studmann doesn't think about anything anymore, he is glad that he can get back into the car, that he can finally sit comfortably in the padded corner of the car again. He is really infinitely tired. It would be nice if he could take a nap now. Nowhere does it sleep so well as in a gently shaking car. But he fears that the distance to Alexanderplatz is not worth falling asleep, and that afterwards you will be all the more tired.

So he prefers to light a cigarette.

You may offer a lady a cigarette! says the girl crossly.

Here you go! says von Studmann and holds out his case to her.

Thank you! she says sharply. You think I need your stubby cigarettes?! I have some myself. You should be polite to a lady -!

She digs out a case from her pocket, commands fire!, smokes, and says somewhat erratically: What do you think I'm going to do to your friend!

He is not my friend! says von Studmann mechanically.

He should still think of me, the boy! Kiebig becomes the carrion, hits 'ner lady in the face! And again quite abruptly: Why does he have so much money tonight? Otherwise he never had anything, the little pisser?!

I really don't know, von Studmann says wearily.

Well! she says with joyful emphasis. If the club won't take his money, I'll make sure he gets rid of it. You can count on it, he won't keep a penny for all I care!

Dear Miss! von Studmann asks rather desperately. Wouldn't you let me smoke my cigarette in peace? I have already told you, the Lord is not my friend.

Yes, you and your friends -! she says angrily. Beat a queen! But I'll let him go up - your friend!

Von Studmann remains silent.

Even angrier: Don't you hear -? I'll blow up your friend!

Silence.

Scornfully: Do you even know what that means: to blow up?! I'll squeal on your friend!

The chauffeur's voice sounds through the open glass window: "Why don't you punch her in the face, sir! Always in the face - what else does not belong to such a one. Your friend was quite right, sir, he is right, he knows! Always push, until the olle Schandschnauze times stops. Where you make all the expenses with the car, and then still unjebildete Redensarten von wejen Verpfeifen ...

Again the fight between the two arises, alternately the glass pane to the driver's seat is torn open and pushed shut again, the narrow cab echoes with the shrieking and shouting.

'He'd better watch the controls a bit,' Studmann thinks. 'Well, it doesn't matter, if we pull up somewhere, at least this noise will be over.'

But they don't drive against anything, they stop normally at Alexanderplatz. The girl climbs out of the car, ranting on and on, bumping against his legs. Then she shouts once again back into the car: And such a thing now wants to be a cavalier! And runs across the square toward a large building lit only in a few windows.

There she goes! says the chauffeur who was looking after her. But it beeps for quite a while when the guard lets it in. She's doing what she said she would, and she's got dirt on her own, still and still. If they ask her if she's on coke, she'll be in in a minute! Maybe they keep them right there, well, I should be happy!

What is that? von Studmann asks thoughtfully, looking at the large, almost dark building under whose doorway the girl has just disappeared.

Well, sir, the chauffeur wonders. You're probably not from around here, that's the presidium! The police headquarters where she's going to rat out your boyfriend!

What does she want there? asks von Studmann, suddenly becoming more alert.

Well, yes - squeal on your friend!

But why -?

Ick jloobe, you have jeschlafen, Lord, with the noise! Because he stuck one on her, even I understood that!

No, says Studmann, suddenly very agitated. Because of what? You don't walk into police headquarters because of a slap in the face!

Do I know that? asks the chauffeur reproachfully. What your friend ate out?! But you also asked so strangely, about the gambling club and so on - she will probably want to make lamps at the Krimschen!

Stop! von Studmann shouts wide awake and jumps out of the car to follow her. For just as determined as he was a while ago to denounce the gambling club, he is now equally convinced that the denunciation of this vicious girl must be prevented.

But stop! cries the cab driver, who sees his fare, and a lot of fare, running away. And now comes for the restless, impatient, feverish Studmann an endless negotiation, a never-ending calculating, until he finds out what he actually has to pay. The price times so-and-so, calculated with a pencil, and calculated three times differently, and then the surcharges ...

Finally, von Studmann is allowed to walk across the square, and now he has to negotiate again with the guard, who doesn't understand what von Studmann actually wants, whether he's looking for a lady or the gambler's office, whether he wants to make a report or prevent one - and that's it.

Ah, the calm, the level-headed - ah, the thoughtful retired first lieutenant and retired receptionist von Studmann! He has completely lost his head at the thought that someone wants to report his friend and young Pagel to the police for illegal gambling - and yet he himself had the same thought just half an hour ago -!

Finally, however, he gets permission from the post to join the Bureau, and it is also described to him how to go in order to get to the 'night stand', because that seems to be his destination, not the players' department, as he has believed so far. But of course he didn't listen carefully to the description and gets lost in the monstrous, only sparsely lit building. He runs over corridors and stairs, hollowly the sound of his feet runs with him. He knocks on doors behind which no answer is heard, and on others from which he is sent on ungraciously or grumpily or sleepily. He runs and he runs, and in his fatigue it is as if he is running in a dream that will never end. Until he finally stands in front of the right door and hears the sharp voice of the bad girl inside.

And at the same moment it occurs to him how nonsensical it is that he is standing here; that he cannot say a word to invalidate the report, no, that he still has to confirm it. After all, it is a gambling club, and it is forbidden gambling. Rather, he has to run as fast as he can to the gambling club and warn them and get them out before the police arrive.

Again he turns back, again he wanders through the presidium and finally finds his way out and creeps guiltily past the post. He knows he has to hurry to get ahead of the police, and fortunately he remembers that he's right by the light rail here, and that he can get to the west faster by light rail than by any car. And he walks over to the city train station and wanders around the closed counters until he remembers that there are no trains running at this hour of the night. That he has to take a car after all. And he also finally finds a car, and breathing a sigh of relief, he lets himself sink into the upholstery.

But it's about to go up again. He can't give himself up to rest, he has to sit and listen -: didn't the car of the raiding party just trill -?

He sits and he listens, and suddenly the ludicrousness of what he has been doing all evening suddenly comes to him, and he sits rigidly there and thinks, startled: 'Is this still me, Lieutenant von Studmann, who never lost his head in the war?

And it is as if he has completely slipped away from himself, as if he is no longer himself, but a completely different one, a hateful, fidgety, senseless, contradictory other. And he beats his fist against his chest and says: Cursed time! Damn time, stealing from the people themselves! But I want to get out of all this - I'm going to the country, and I'm going to become a human being again, as true as I am of Studmann!

And then he sits again and listens to see if the raiding party trills, thinking, 'I have to get there first - I can't let them fall in!'

08 09

Confident of victory, Wolfgang Pagel enters the game room with the cavalry captain beside him. He holds the seventeen chips from the first game loosely in his closed hand. He shakes them quietly, they rattle wantonly and happily.

As he walks toward the gaming table, as he has so many times in the past year, a deliciously dry, hollow feeling in his mouth, he knows that this time he is approaching the game very differently than ever before. Always, always he misplayed, devised idiotic systems that were bound to fail. Like today, he must do it, wait for an inspiration and then set. Wait until inspiration comes again, perhaps wait endlessly, but have the patience to wait, and then immediately sit down again.

Yes, very nice! Very! he says, answering the cavalryman who has asked something, and he smiles kindly at this answer. The cavalry captain looks at him in amazement, probably he answered some nonsense, but it doesn't matter, he is now quite close to the game table.

At this time the table is more densely besieged than ever. It's getting down to the last hour, they close here at three, at the latest half past three in the morning. Everything from players exhausted, overtired, standing on the walls and smoking, sitting irresolutely on armchairs and sofas - that now crowds around the table. The escaping time offers once again the prospect of great profit - use it! When the city awakens in a few hours, you will be rich or poor - wouldn't you rather be rich -?!

The incident from earlier is long forgotten, no one pays attention to Pagel.

He sees no way to get close to the table, so he walks all the way around it to its head end. With a movement of his shoulder, he squeezes himself between the croupier and the assistant. The assistant, Lockenwilli, the stocky thug from Wedding, wants to protest angrily against this impropriety - a quiet word from the croupier tells him not to.

Wolfgang Pagel quietly shakes his seventeen tokens in his hand, he wants to bet them - a thin, mocking smile under his beard, the croupier instructs the old player that betting is not allowed when the ball is rolling.

Time - long, stagnant time Wolfgang must wait. Then finally the ball comes to rest, a number is called out, winnings, ridiculous, trivial, unimportant winnings are dealt out and pocketed - and now Wolfgang's hand lowers on the green cloth:

Seventeen tokens lie on the number seventeen.

The croupier looks at him briefly from the side and smiles faintly. With his call he drives the players to action one last time, he grasps the cross, the disc begins to spin purring, the ball runs ...

His game begins - it begins the game of Wolfgang Pagel, Fahnenjunker a. D., ex-lover of a girl named Petra Ledig, currently unemployed - it begins that game for which he has been waiting for a year, no, a lifetime, for which he has actually become what he became; for the sake of which he quarreled with his mother; for the sake of which he took a girl to himself, who shortened the waiting time for him, but who now also left when the time came. We bet seventeen, seventeen tokens on the number seventeen ...!

Attention, we are playing! Seventeen brings thirty-six times the profit - endlessly the ball runs, clatters, clatters ... We would still have time to calculate in millions and billions what we will win when the seventeen has come ... the bullet rattles like this - if it were made of bone, we could say, this is how the bones of the dead rattle in their tombs, but we live, we live and play ...!

Seventeen! shouts the croupier.

Yes, isn't he shouting it? It is the hour of judgment - the goats will be shorn, but the righteous - they will be crowned! It pelts down from Marche, a rain, a flood, a deluge! Into the bags with it -!

Wait! I want to sit too - is there no chair free for a player like me?!

What do I put -? I need to be quiet, think ... I bet red. Red is right, I worked that out once, long, long ago! See, there is already a chair -!

Here, son, this is ten dollars, good American dollars - remember how you wanted to punch me in the face earlier? Heh - heh - heh!

I shouldn't be so loud, I'm disturbing the others? Let the others die! What do I care about the others with their paltry stakes? They play to win, to hoard dirty paper money, I play for the sake of the game, for the sake of life.... I am the king!

Red!

He sits there and stares, suddenly darkened, suspiciously. Are these enough brands? He can no longer leave them in his pockets, he piles them up in heaps of ten in front of him, and his hands, trembling with excitement, immediately knock the heaps over again. They all want to cheat him here, steal from him, he is only the Pari-Panther, a Garnichts in a shabby tunic! This dog, the croupier, has always treated him like a thief - he will get even!

And he bets again and wins again, and happiness returns to him again, it is so easy for him! Blessed exhilaration, never felt before, when you fly along like a cloud in the summer sky, below the heavy, dark earth with the lowly people and their heavy, cramped faces - but you fly along, blessed clouds, blessed gods - O happiness!

What fell there? What trickles? What falls?

Hans Fallada   -488-   Wolf among Wolves

Like a stream, the tokens that he can no longer retrieve slide merrily under his arms to the ground. Let them fall, happiness smiles at me! Let others bend over for it ...!

Let them collect, we have enough and we will get more!

How gloomy the croupier looks, how his beard bristles! Yes, today we'll bag you, my son, bald as a rat you'll slip into your hole - soon you'll have no more stamps and will have to hand over the paper money, today we'll get it all!

What does the cavalry captain want? He gambled it all away? Yes, you have to know how to play, do it like me, Rittmeister, I showed you! Here you have paper money, American dollars, 250 dollars, no, ten went off for Curly Willy, 240 that is! Yes, tomorrow morning we will settle it, but in half an hour already this money, on the detour via the croupier, will be with me again!

The game turns -? The ball no longer rolls the way he wants -?

Yes, it's just the way it is: you shouldn't give money away under the game, it brings bad luck. He sits there scowling, trying the pari chances again, the triple chances. He plays carefully, prudently. But the brands between his arms lose, the regiments become thin. Again and again the army of the beaten rattles under the croupier's rake, the gamekeeper smiles again.

And the players don't look at Pagel anymore, they don't pay attention to him. Unabashedly they make again over his shoulder away bets. He is no longer a gifted player, he is a player like everyone else: luck smiles at him once, but then forgets him again, he is the ball of luck, not his bedfellow.

What has he been doing all this time? How long has he been sitting here?

Already he is fishing in the pockets, the stream has dried up. Does he immediately forget every lesson that fate gave him? Seventeen he must bet, seventeen tokens on seventeen - that's what it's called!

Seventeen -!

Hans Fallada   Wolf among Wolves

And the patter of the stamps!

And the intoxication comes back, the bliss of flying, world distance and sun! He sits there, his head slightly bent forward, a forlorn smile on his lips. He can bet however he wants, now the current is flowing again. And now it comes as he expected: the tokens run out. Now the bills are already coming at him, more and more. They crackle, dully they look at him -: ridiculous paper marks, precious pounds, delicious dollars, rich, fat guilders, nutritious Danish crowns - robbery from the wallets of fifty, sixty guests! Everything flows to him!

The croupier looks deathly gloomy, as if seized by a disease, suffering nonsensical, unbearable pain. Hardly he can still control himself, twice already the curlywilli ran for new money on the forecourt, the daily cash must approach - soon it goes to your wallet, croupier!

He mumbles something about closing, but the players contradict, they threaten ... They hardly play anymore, but they watch the duel between croupier and pagel. They tremble for the young person - will happiness remain faithful to him? He is one of their own, the born gambler, all their losses he avenges the old, evil bird of prey, the croupier. This young person does not love money, as the croupier does - he loves the game! He is not an exploiter!

And young Pagel sits there, smiling more and more, calmer and calmer. Torn away, the cavalry captain whispers at his shoulder, Pagel only moves his head with a negative smile.

The cavalry captain shouts: Pagel, man, call it a day! You have a fortune!

No, the cavalry captain is no longer embarrassed to shout in this room, but Pagel just smiles numbly.

He is here, and he is very far away. He wants this to go on forever, timelessly through eternities - that's why we live! The wave of happiness carries us, we swim liberated!

Unspeakable voluptuousness of existence - this is how a tree must feel, which after days of tugging, agonizing sap rise unfolds all its blossoms in one hour! What else is the croupier -?! What is money -?! What is even game -?! Keep rolling, little ball, roll, roll - is that how I thought the bones of the dead rattled?

Drums and trumpets! Red? Red, of course, and red again. And again red. But now we take black - otherwise life doesn't taste good, without a little black in between, life doesn't taste good. More banknotes - where should I leave them all? I should have brought a suitcase - but who can know such a thing in advance -?

What does Studmann want again? What is he shouting? Police -? What should police - why does he need police? - What are they all running -? Stop, let the ball run out - I win again, I win again, again and again! I am the eternal winner ...

There are already the policemen! Now the players all stand as silent as their own ghosts. What does the funny man with the stiff hat want? He says something to me. All play money is confiscated, all money? But of course it is all play money - money to play with, otherwise there would be no point - to what else?!

You want us to get ready and come with you? Of course we'll come along; if there's no more playing after all, we might as well come along. Why is the cavalry captain arguing with the blue one? There's no point in that! If you can't play, nothing matters!

Come on, Herr Rittmeister, be peaceful. You see, Studmann is also coming along, and he hasn't even played. Let's go!

How deathly pale the croupier looks! Yes, it's bad for him. He was losing - but me, I was winning like never before in my life! It was beyond glorious! Good night!

At last I can sleep peacefully, I have achieved what I longed for, sleep forever. - Good night!

08 10

In a small meeting room of the Alexanderplatz police headquarters, a pitiful, sparkly light bulb was burning. It cast its reddish glow on the sullen, slouched, awkwardly silent, sleeping or eagerly chattering figures of the sistas in the gambling club. Only the gamekeeper and his two assistants had been taken away separately - otherwise they had all been herded into this room as they had stepped from the police transport car, the doors had been locked from the outside to save guarding - done! Now wait your turn!

From time to time, at long intervals, the door to an adjoining room opened, an overtired-looking, yellowish, wrinkled clerk waved his finger at the person standing at first - he disappeared and did not come back. Then, after endless time, the next one was beckoned.

It was busy at the presidium, there was a shortage of officers, of police officers. The murder of Chief Constable Leo Gubalke had given rise to a series of raids, and unfortunately there was no lack of targets for these raids: ring clubs had been dug up; nests of fences had been visited; nightclubs had been visited; nude dance halls had been combed through; doss houses, hour hotels had been checked; the waiting rooms of the railroad stations, the homeless asylums had been revised ...

Incessantly, from the square, one could hear the excitable, nervous trill of the patrol cars driving out or returning home with new droves of suspended persons. All the rooms, all the halls were crammed - exhausted secretaries, half-asleep scribes, gray-looking stenotypists kept pushing new sheets into the typewriters, folding yellowish file paper, interrogating in hoarse voices so low that they could hardly be understood.

Brawl

Fornication

Adverse fornication

Light theft

Pickpocketing

Burglary

Mortuary

Begging

Street robbery

Prohibited carrying weapons

False Play

Prohibited gambling

Stolen goods

Counterfeit money distribution

Narcotics

Pandering, both light and heavy

Blackmail

Pimping

... an endless list, the tedious, deadly menu of crimes, vices, misdemeanors, transgressions.... The officers almost nodded in behind their machines, over their logs ... Then suddenly they started screaming until their voices completely failed them again ... And an unceasingly rising tide of lies, excuses, distortions, palliations, denunciations ...

Hans Fallada   -493-   Wolf among Wolves

(And in the Reichsdruckerei, in fifty, in a hundred auxiliary printing works, the paper money presses rushed, prepared the new day, the new abundance of money, generously poured out in beguiling abundance on a starving, lumpen people, who lost all sense of honor, every decency day by day more and more ...)

It's hell to pay! yelled the Rittmeister von Prackwitz, jumped up and raced across the room for the tenth time. The fact that he had to avoid half a dozen other peripatetic people did not improve his mood at all. Panting, he stopped in front of his first lieutenant. How long do you think we have to wait here -?! Until the gentlemen rest, huh?! It is outrageous to arrest me ...

Silence. Quiet! asked von Studmann. By the way, I don't think we are arrested at all.

Of course we are under arrest! the cavalry captain shouted even angrier. The windows are barred and the doors are locked - you don't call that being arrested -?! Ridiculous! Then I would like to know what an arrest looks like with you, yes, please -?!!!

Quiet, Prackwitz! von Studmann asked once again. Your excitement doesn't improve anything.

Quiet, of course, quiet, said Prackwitz suddenly sullenly. That's easy for you to say - you don't have a family, you don't have a father-in-law. I would like to see how calm you would be if you had the Privy Councillor Horst-Heinz von Teschow as your father-in-law!

He won't find out anything, the lieutenant comforted. I tell you, all we have to do is identify ourselves and they'll let us go. Nothing is done.

Then why won't they let me?! Here I have my papers - here I have them in my hand! I have to leave, my train is leaving, I have a transport of people! - You, listen, you! Mr. Anyway! he rushed at the clerk, who had just emerged from the next room. I demand to be let in on the spot. First they take all my money ... Afterwards, afterwards, said the clerk indifferently. Calm down a bit first. Come on now! And he waved at a fat man.

I should calm down first, von Prackwitz said excitedly to Studmann. That is just ridiculous! How can I calm down with this kind of operation!

No, really, Prackwitz, von Studmann said seriously. Get it together. If you keep raving like this, we'll be the last to go. And then I ask you one more thing: do not yell at the officials ...

Why shouldn't I yell at them -?! I'm going to breathe on them! Keeping me here for hours -!

For half an hour.

By the way, they are used to yelling at each other. They are all old sergeants and constables - you can see that.

But you're not here as their superior, Prackwitz. It's not their fault you got caught gambling.

No, they don't. But please look at the pageboy, this lively young man! Sitting there as if the whole mess didn't concern him, looking and grinning like a Buddha. - Why are you grinning like that, Pagel -?

I'm just thinking about it, Pagel said with a smile, how crazy everything got today. For a year I have been struggling for a bit of money - today I get it, masses and masses, slosh! it is confiscated and gone it is -!

And you still laugh about it -? Well, you have a taste for the ridiculous, Pagel ...

And then one more, Pagel continued unperturbed. Today at noon I was going to get married ...

You see, Pagel, said the cavalry captain triumphantly, suddenly in a brilliant mood, "I saw it in your eyes right away at Lutter and Wegner's, that you're in trouble because of women's stories...."

Hans Fallada   -495-   Wolf among Wolves

Yes, Pagel said. And tonight I heard that my future wife is arrested for something and that she was taken to the Alex ... And now I'm sitting here too ...

Arrested for what, the cavalry captain asks curiously, because the reflections on events do not interest him as much as the events themselves.

But von Studmann shakes his head and Pagel remains silent.

The cavalry captain comes to his senses: "Excuse me, Pagel, of course it's none of my business. But why you are sitting here grinning so happily for this very reason, I frankly don't understand. The thing is most sad ...

Yes, Pagel says approvingly. This is it. Funny she is. Very funny. If only I had won the money twenty-four hours earlier, she wouldn't have been arrested, and we would be married now. Really very funny ...

I wouldn't think about it anymore, Pagel, suggests von Studmann. Thank goodness that's all over and done with now. In a few hours, we'll all be on the train together, heading to the country ...

Pagel is silent, and the cavalry captain is silent this time, too.

Then Prackwitz clears his throat. Give me a cigarette, Pagel, he says mildly. My throat is so dry. Nah, better not give me one - I already owe you so much ...

Pagel grasps the air laughing: that's all gone ...

But the cavalry captain protests: But, man, don't talk like that! You lent me money! Do you even know how much you gave me?

It doesn't matter, Pagel says. I am not supposed to have any of the money, as has now been shown.

Gambling debts are debts of honor, Herr Pagel! explains the cavalry captain sternly. You will get your money back, you can count on it! Of course, it won't work right away, first we have to get the harvest in and start threshing ... How is it, are you now coming with -?

Oh, just to wait for the money ... Pagel says sullenly. I would like to finally start something real. I feel so stupid, all empty ... if I only knew what! Yes, if you had real work for me, Herr Rittmeister -?

Of course I have work for you, man, says the cavalry captain excitedly. You have no idea how I have longed for a few reliable people -! Giving out fodder and paying people and distributing deputat and every now and then a control walk through the fields at night - you can't imagine all the things that are stolen at my place! If you could rely on a few people, that you don't keep running from one place to another because you keep thinking, now you're going to be cheated again....

And forest and fields, von Studmann adds hopefully. Trees, animals - no half-world, no stone building blocks with fallen down facades, no cocaine, no gambling club ...

No, that of course, says the cavalry captain eagerly, you would have to promise me in your hand, Pagel, that you will not play while you are with me. Because that is quite impossible ... He breaks off and blushes. Well, of course, he then says a little poltriguously, it also works without promises. I really can't take one away from you. So yes -?

In any case, I'll come to the track tomorrow morning and let you know, Pagel says hesitantly. Eight o'clock, Silesian - that's how it was, wasn't it -?

Prackwitz and Studmann look at each other. Again the cavalry captain makes an angry, almost furious gesture. But Studmann asks kindly: "Has your question to fate still not been answered, Pagel? And when Pagel remains silent: Because the game was your question, wasn't it, Pagel?

But I won, Pagel says defiantly.

And sit without anything on the Alex! laughs the cavalryman mockingly. Be a man, Pagel! he speaks admonishingly. I find this swaying ghastly. Pull yourself together, man, work something! Stop playing around!

You are worried about the girl? asks Herr von Studmann gently.

A little, Pagel admits. It is really so strange that I am now also sitting here on the Alex ...

So do what you can't help doing! the cavalry captain shouts angrily. On my knees, I will not ask you to come to Neulohe!

In any case, I'll see you at the station at eight! von Studmann nods hurriedly, because shouting has become loud, a rant, people are shouting. Through the open door of the negotiation room comes a stocky man, running at doors, windows, grabbing, looking, shaking his head, shouting: Gang! Mouse hook! Naughty company, stealing from the police ...!

He bangs on the door: "Officer, unlock the door! Hello, Tiede, make sure that no one escapes -!

Bustle, shouting, laughter.

Blues come in from the outside, the door is open. The fat detective superintendent storms up and down: Put everyone in rows! Scanning! Are you quiet, my boy! Also look under the tables and benches -!

It turns out that one or a few sistas didn't know how to use the waiting time at police headquarters more usefully than unscrewing the bronze door and window hardware. No more latches, no more window handles, no more lock hardware. The looted police headquarters - it grins, it laughs. Even the blue ones are laughing, now even the commissioner starts to smile ...

What a cheek - has anyone heard of such a thing! And of course the guy is already gone, or the guys, because there must have been a few, one can't hide it at all. - Have stood with me in the interrogation room and I do not notice anything -! Well, if I catch you! I have to check the personal data right away ...

Just a moment, Commissioner, exclaims Studmann.

Very ungracious: What do you want -?! You heard me, I don't have time now! Recognizing: Oh, it's you, man! Excuse me, Lieutenant von Studmann! - The light is so bad! What are you doing in our store, old Baltic,

Iron Division?! - Well, come along with me, of course, you'll get your turn in a minute. Just a few formalities, you'll probably get a ticket. Well, don't let any gray hairs grow over that, the devaluation pays for itself. - These are your friends -? Very pleasant, Herr Rittmeister. Very pleasant, flag boy. Allow me to introduce Commissioner Künnecke, formerly a constable with the Rathenow Hussars. - Yes, so we meet again - miserable times, eh? And so you are the young man who made the monstrous Rebbach -? Unbelievable! And just then the evil police has to trill in between! Yes, the money is down the drain, we don't give it back, what we have we keep, huh! - But just be happy, money like that never brought happiness to anyone - thank your Creator that you're rid of it! - Nah, the door handles, no, something like that - what do you say, Tiede -? They're going to give us a good run for our money tomorrow, our colleagues! I still have to laugh. Was good bronze - there they get 'nen bag money at the scrap dealer! - So, and now the personal data. Mr. von Studmann - Profession?

Receptionist ...

You -?!! O God, O God, O God -! Where have we come to -? Receptionist! You - receptionist! Excuse me, Lieutenant ...

Please, please - I am also a retired receptionist, now an agricultural apprentice ...

Agricultural apprentice, that's better. In fact, that's very good. Land is the only thing to do today. When born -?

08 11

In front of a door covered with steel plate there is a table, an ordinary spruce table. On the table is a package of sandwiches next to a thermos flask, at the table sits an old man in police uniform reading a newspaper through a klemmer in very dim overhead light. When the man hears a slow step coming down the aisle, he lowers the newspaper and looks across the Klemmer to meet the arrival.

Hans Fallada   -499-   Wolf among Wolves

The young man slowly approaches. At first it looks as if he wants to pass the door and the table, but then he stops. Excuse me, he says, is this going to the police jail?

It can be done, says the official, carefully folding his newspaper and placing it on the table. But when the young man hesitates indecisively, he adds: But it is only a door for official use.

The young man still hesitates, the old one asks: Well, what's on your mind? Do you want to turn yourself in?

Why ask? Pagel asks back.

Yes - says the old man stretched. It's now four o'clock - at this hour sometimes someone comes who can't rest because he's done something wrong, and turns himself in. But there you have to go on standby. I'm just an outside guard.

No, Pagel says slowly. I did not eat out anything. Again he is silent. Then under the calm gaze of the old man: I would just like to talk to my friend. Because it's in there. And he points with his head to the door.

Now?! the old man exclaims almost indignantly. At night between three and four?!

Yes, says Pagel.

Then you must have done something wrong that you can't get any peace -?

Pagel remains silent.

Nothing can come of this. Now there are no visits. And anyway -

Is it not possible at all? Pagel asks after a while.

Out of the question! says the other. He considers, he looks at the boy. Finally he says: And you know that quite well. You're only standing here like this because it doesn't give you any peace ...

Hans Fallada   -500-   Wolf among Wolves

I happen to be here at the Presidium. I didn't come all the way here.

But you came to this door on purpose, didn't you? You didn't find them easily, now, at night?

No, Pagel replies.

There you see it, says the old man. It is with you just like with those who come to turn themselves in. They all say they don't come because of a guilty conscience - a guilty conscience doesn't exist anymore. But why do they come at two, three in the morning?! This is a special time, when man is alone with himself, when he suddenly has completely different thoughts than during the day. And here they come.

I don't know, Pagel says blearily. He really knows nothing. He just doesn't want to leave without at least asking her if it's really true. Sometimes he says to himself that the official must have told him the untruth, it's impossible, he knows Petra! And then he says to himself again that an official does not tell him anything incorrect, that he has no interest at all in telling him anything incorrect, that it must be true. Alas, the game is over, the frenzy has faded, victory became defeat - how alone he is now! Peter, Peter - there was someone next to him after all, something alive attached to him - shall all be lost?

I want to leave tomorrow morning, he says pleadingly. Is it impossible to make it tonight? After all, no one needs to notice anything.

What do you think?! shouts the old man. There are night guards inside, too. No, it is quite impossible. He thinks for a moment, looks at Pagel scrutinizingly and then says again: And anyway ...

What does that mean: and anyway -? Pagel asks a little angrily.

And in general, we don't actually have visitation permits, the official explains.

And inauthentic -?

Not really either.

That's how Pagel says.

We are police prison here, says the old man in a need to explain the situation. In the remand prison, the examining magistrate can give permission to visit, but here with us, there is no such thing. Most of them only stay with us for a few days.

A few days ... Pagel repeats.

Yes. Maybe you'll ask around Moabit next week.

That's quite sure that I can't see her here tomorrow morning? There are no exceptions made?

Certainly not. But of course, if you know anything, that her friend is innocent, and you tell that to the commissioner tomorrow, she'll come out, that's clear.

Pagel is silent, thinking.

But you don't look like you have that kind of message, do you? You don't come to me in the night with a message like that. You just want to talk to your girlfriend like this, right private?

I wanted to ask her something, Pagel says.

But then, write her a letter, the old man says complacently. If the letter doesn't say anything about what she's here for, then it will be handed to her, and then she may answer you.

But I want to ask her something just because of the thing!

Yes, young man, you will have to be patient. If you want to inquire about the matter, you are not allowed to do that even in the remand prison. Until the matter has been adjudicated, it must not be discussed with her.

And how long can that take? Pagel asks in despair.

Yes, it all depends on the thing. Did she confess?

That's just it. She confessed, but I don't believe her. She confessed to something she didn't do.

The old man reaches for his newspaper very angrily. Now you go to sleep, he says. If you want to persuade a confessor to withdraw her confession, you can wait quite a long time for visitation. And then you are not allowed to write to her, that is, she does not get your letters. That's even more beautiful! And I'm supposed to stoop to secretly paying you a visit here. No, now you go home. Now I have enough of it.

Pagel stands again hesitantly. Then he says pleadingly: But that does happen, it does happen that someone confesses to something that he has not done at all. I have read that many times.

So, have you read this? the old man asks almost venomously. Then let me tell you, young man, that someone who confesses to something wrong has always done something much worse. Yep, one confesses to a burglary because he committed a murder at the same hour. That's how it is. And if your friend has confessed, she will probably know why. I would be very wary of telling her what to do. Otherwise she will fall in much worse! Very angrily, the old man, now already through the pinch again, squints at Pagel. But he is thunderstruck. The old man's words, meant quite differently, have shed new light on Peter's confession. Jawohl, jawohl, something confessed to avoid something worse, disease and road confessed to avoid Wolfgang. Prison better than community. Over, over! Faith lost, trust lost for good - away from him, away from the world, out of the unbearable into the bearable! A high profit in turn lost. Blank, all ...

Thank you, too, Pagel says very politely. You really gave me some good advice.

And slowly he walks down the corridor, away from the gate, pursued by the suspicious looks of the old man.

It is just the right time to pick up your things from Fir Street. At this hour, the mother certainly does not expect him. At this time she is fast asleep.

Hans Fallada   -503-   Wolf among Wolves

He is sure to find a cab on Alexanderplatz. Thank God that Studmann helped out with money, Studmann, the non-player, the only capitalist, Studmann, the helpful one, Studmann, the providence of the rained-up chickens, the relief fund of the burnt-out ones. - Seriously, by the way, dealing with Studmann must be pleasant, it's almost as if you can look forward to Neulohe and Studmann.

Chapter 09

- A new start on the new day -

09 01

In a hotel room, on a bed, lie a girl and a man. The man sleeps close to the wall, in the bed, which is not wide, quietly whistling breath through his nose. The girl has just woken up, her chin resting on her folded arms, lying on her belly, blinking at the two window rectangles, which are already bright.

The girl hears: the sound of express trains entering a station; the groaning thump of a locomotive; chirps of sparrows; many pedestrian footsteps, hurried, hurried, hurried; now the room with everything in it shakes from a fast-moving, heavy vehicle - it must be a bus, the girl thinks - and now, unfamiliar sound among so many accustomed ones, a steamer hoots very close, two, three times, demanding, impatient ...

The girl, Sophie Kowalewski, has remained true to her decision: to say goodbye, she went for a stroll in the old town, and now she has landed in a hotel on Weidendammer Brücke - hence the steamer's hoot, steamers sail on the Spree - or is this not the Spree at all -?

Quietly, cautiously, not wanting to wake the man, Sophie Kowalewski slips out of bed, walks as she is to the window and lifts a corner of the curtain. The sky is a brilliant blue over the iron arches of the bridge.

'Wonderful weather I will have in Neulohe', Sophie thinks. 'Great thing: to lie under a tree at the entrance to the forest and stew ... no madam ... Swimsuit error message ... And in the evening, when the moon comes up, completely naked in the cold crab pond in the middle of the forest ...'

She lets the end of the curtain go and quickly starts washing and dressing. She just rinses off a bit, gargles fleetingly - she can still do all that thoroughly in the hospice, she has time enough until her train leaves. A joyful tension, something like the foreboding of a near happiness fill them ... Neulohe, the old, overgrown lilac bush behind the firehouse, where she got her first kiss, oh God! She will also put on fresh clothes at the hospice. All this stuff disgusts them ...

Sophie Kowalewski is finished, her little bag in her hand, and stands peering indecisively at the bed. She takes two steps in that direction and says half aloud, very carefully: You, Bubi ...

Nothing, just the soft whistling through the nose ...

Nothing.

Once again: I'm going now, Schatzi ...

Nothing, just the soft whistling through the nose ...

It is not a sudden inspiration when Sophie now looks sharply at the sleeper's clothes, which lie thrown untidily over the chair. Besides, the whole time she has been awake, she has been thinking that at least the travel money to Neulohe could come out of this stupid night. She has to watch her money a bit now, there is no fresh money in Neulohe. She quickly reaches the chair, grabs her wallet (she has already been watching where he puts it tonight), opens it ...

There's not much money in the bag - heck, there's actually very little in it for a man who spent many millions on champagne last night! Sophie hesitates for a moment. She takes a look at the clothes, and with the woman's eye she sees that they must be carefully spared, but not at all new clothes, perhaps the man has scraped together all his money for this big exit. There are such men, Sophie knows it, they save and save, they promise themselves the world from such an evening, a happiness such as they have never experienced ... Then they wake up the next morning, disillusioned, desperate, drained ...

Hesitantly, Sophie stands, purse in hand. Her gaze goes back and forth between the few bills, the clothes, the sleeper ...

'That little bit of money doesn't help me either,' she thinks. Already she wants to put the bills back in the wallet.

'But Hans would laugh at me!' she suddenly thinks. 'Hans is not that stupid. You have to take everything with you, he always says. The decent ones are the stupid ones. No, it's just fine with him, he'll pay better attention next time ...'

She takes the money. And once again a reflection: 'At least I would have to let him have the fare. Surely he must go to his office. That he at least gets to his office on time!'

And again the other voice: 'But what's it to me if he's at the office on time?! Who ever took care of me the way I came home?! On the street the gentlemen cavaliers left me standing, they were too lazy to unlock the front door for me, they put me out of the cab once they had their way! What do you mean fare?!'

She is duly proud of her decision. With angry determination, she stuffs the meager money into her purse. You're right,' Hans would say. And I am right too! Those who do not take will be taken away. If you don't bite, you get bitten. Good morning!'

And light-footedly, gleefully, she runs down the stairs.

09 02

It's already light - even in the forest. The small former field inspector Meier trudges furiously along the aisle: the suitcases are too heavy, the shoes pinch, he has too little money, the way to Grünow is much too far, he is unslept, his head hurts like seven monkeys - there are only modest things he can think of.

The most humble of all suddenly stands, as if shot out of the earth, on the path; it is the lieutenant.

But he is quite friendly. Tomorrow, Meier, he says. I did want to tell you Atjüs.

Meier stares at him suspiciously. So Atjüs, Lieutenant!

Go ahead. Take your bags and move on, we have a piece of common ground.

Meier, however, remains standing. I'm quite happy to go alone, he says.

But! But! says the lieutenant with a laugh. His laugh sounds fake, Meier thinks, and his voice flickers. Surely you will not be afraid of me, where you even carry a pistol in your pocket.

It's none of your damn business what I'm carrying in my pocket! Meier yells irritably, but his voice is shaking.

Actually, yes, the lieutenant admits. But it is important for me, because now I do not come under suspicion.

Why not come under suspicion -? stammers Meier.

If you are lying dead in the woods somewhere here, Herr Meier, says the lieutenant very politely, but bitterly serious.

I - dead - ridiculous ... stammers the little Meier ashen-faced and peers into the face of his counterpart. I didn't do anything to you, Lieutenant!

He peers imploringly and fearfully into the other's eye, but there is nothing to be read in it, nothing at all, it glitters coldly.

Your pistol and my pistol have the same caliber, the lieutenant explains mercilessly. You are a giant, Meier, that you have pocketed the pistol ... And now you have also freshly shot the barrel ... But I hit the target better than you, Mr. Meier. And I'm standing so nicely to your right now, close shot at twenty centimeters in the right temple ... Every shooting expert says suicide, my dear Mr. Meier. And at home the looted cash box ... the shot at the girl - no, no, Mr. Meier, don't worry about it, there's no doubt about it: everything points to suicide.

The lieutenant talks and talks, he acts very superior, but he is probably not as calm as he acts. It is something else to shoot someone in battle or in passion, something else again to slaughter a victim in cold blood based on rational considerations. He neatly enumerates to himself once again that he is not 'risking' anything, that he is not endangering the cause, but saving it from a traitor.

And yet he silently wishes - shooting experts to one side, risks to the other - that Meier would hastily reach for the pistol in his back pocket: a quick shot, with which the lieutenant beats him to it, is so much easier than the calm, cold-blooded shot into the gray face, which has already become so small and pointed.

But Meier is not even thinking about the gun in his own pocket, he stammers: Lieutenant, I swear to you, I will never say a word about you and Miss Weio .... And also not from the coup ... I'll hold it, Lieutenant, I'd always be afraid that you'd catch me, you or one of your men, I'm a coward after all ... Please, do not shoot! I - swear to you by everything I hold sacred ...

His voice failing him, he swallows and stares fearfully at the lieutenant ...

But nothing is sacred to you, Meier, says the lieutenant. He still can't make up his mind. You are a complete pig, Meier.

Little Meier, the Negermeier, has been staring breathlessly at the other's lips; now he whispers hastily: "I can change after all! Believe me, Lieutenant, I can still become different, I am still young! Say, please, say yes! I turn around, I go back to Neulohe, I confess to the cavalry captain that I stole the money.

Let him send me to prison, I'm happy to go, I want to improve, it should be quiet hard ... please, please, lieutenant!

The lieutenant shakes his head darkly. Oh, if only he hadn't started chatting with this guy in the first place! If only he had gone off right away, without a word, but now ... it's getting more and more disgusting! He is not completely depraved, the lieutenant, he doesn't fool himself either, he knows that he alone has dragged this young brat in. He has to die because he, the lieutenant, couldn't resist flirting with the little Prackwitz ... It's bad, but it doesn't help, now the Meier knows far too much, he's too dangerous, even more dangerous since he saw the death-threatening pistol pointed at him.

Take the suitcases, Meier, we're going for another walk!

No trace of resistance, Meier obediently takes the suitcases like a sheep, looks questioningly at the lieutenant.

Up there, along the aisle! he orders.

Meier with the suitcases goes ahead. He squared his shoulders as if that could prevent the dreaded shot from behind. The suitcases are no longer heavy, the shoes no longer pinch, he walks hurriedly as if he could run away from the death that walks behind him.

'If only it were over first!' thinks the lieutenant, his eyes attentive to the one ahead. 'But this aisle here is really too walked on. Better they don't find him for three or four days, when there is no trace of me ...'

These thoughts disgust him, they have something so unreal, something of a desolate dream. But here goes the man in front of him, it is still a living man, so it is not a dream, any minute it can become truth ...

Now left in, up the climb, Meier!

Obedient like a sheep, disgusting! Yes, up there on the heights he will do it, he must do it ... a traitor remains a traitor forever, traitors do not change, they do not improve ... it must be ...

What does the Meier have? What is he shouting? Has he gone crazy?

Now he starts to run, he screams louder and louder, he throws the suitcases at the lieutenant's feet ...

He pulls up his pistol - too late, he has to shoot at close range so that suicide is believable ...

We are coming, Mr. Forester! Yes, sir! Meier shouts and runs.

There stands the forester Kniebusch, next to him lies a man tied up in blueberry weed and moss.

Thank God that you are coming! I really couldn't drag him any further, gentlemen. For hours I've been dragging the guy ...

Forester Kniebusch is all talkative, finally he is relieved from this being alone with the dangerous guy!

It's Bäumer from Altlohe - you know, Meier, the worst of the lot! I have made a very good catch, Lieutenant, this man is a criminal!

The lieutenant is standing leaning against a tree, he is quite white in the face. But he calmly says: Yes, you have made a good catch, forester. But I -?

He stares hatefully at the little Meier. He returns the look - defiantly, triumphantly ...

Well, good morning and good work! says the lieutenant suddenly, turns around and marches back down the forest path to the aisle. When he arrives at the two suitcases lying discarded there, he can't help it: he steps emphatically first on one, then on the other suitcase.

Well! says the forester in amazement. What's wrong with him? Why is he so funny? Did he have trouble with his meeting? I have ordered all properly after all. Do you understand that, Meier?

Oh, yes! says the little peasant. I understand that. He's really mad at you!

Hans Fallada   -511-   Wolf among Wolves

To me! the forester wonders. But why?!

Because you didn't shoot the buck, the buck, you know, for the gnädige Fräulein, you know! says Meier. Come on, Kniebusch, let's go to the yard together, and I'll hitch up the hunting car, and we'll get the guy and my suitcases ...

Your suitcases -? Are these your suitcases? Are you traveling?

Ah, i wo ... These are the lieutenant's suitcases. I'll tell you everything already. Come on, we'd better walk side by side, one behind the other, because it's not easy to talk...

09 03

The car cab stopped in Tannenstraße. It is difficult to persuade the chauffeur to come up and touch the things ...

Det saren Se so, Jüngling, det jetzt keener unterwejens is. The thieves here in Ballin, they are always unterwejens. Now more than ever. And who's going to buy me a new Jummi that's not even available?! Surely not you!

+++

Well, I mean, because it's still up to the Silesian, for a Molle and a Korn, as they say, but a coffee is me lieba! - Quiet shall I be -? Ick bin so quiet, like 'ne Rejierung when se Jeld steht jeht! The brothers don't hear you, but you've lost your money, so you'll eat a broom on it!

+++

Hübschet house - een bißchen düster ... Central heating is probably not? Aba Jas, Jas hamm Se doch? The Jas in the house saves the press coal and the rope to Uffbammeln ... Yes, I'm already quiet, but you're not as quiet as I am! - With the lock now, for example, I would have fumbled more quietly ... You press want french, young man, kleena rent arrears, what -?

Hans Fallada   -512-   Wolf among Wolves

+++

Well, don't blow yourself up, I was in the field too; when you blow at me, I scream so loud that the pictures slide off the wall. You see - immediately you are peaceful ... So - and det is nu your sojenannte Bude, huh? Knorke with 'nen small grain, so ha 'ck dat nich bei Muttern ... And such a suitcase - we'll have to go twice, young man ...

+++

Jotte does! Who is lying on the chaise longue -?! Ha ick me scared! An old woman - and sleeps peacefully. Well, now I won't say another word, we'll let her sleep; she's had her sleep, she's been packing all night, the old woman! - But that's not a sleep post, that's your ma'am, isn't it? Well, I thought so right away! Well, I'd say goodbye to her, where she's been waiting for you all night ... Scherbeln jewesen, what -? Well, youth has no virtue, I was no different in your years ... Now I'm sometimes sorry, now that she's dead and lying in the Matthäikirchhof ... Well, everyone does the same things, that's why it's important that they don't all...

Well, come on, give me the wardrobe case quietly on my back, I'll manage the thing myself, I'll be right back ... Nope? You want to start right away with runta -? Well, meinshalben, everyone as he wants, everyone as stupid as he can, I say!

+++

Well, det is wenichstens wat! Write a few lines to the old woman, a little something nice, you understand! - Even if it's a fake - a mother is always happy, knows that the child is deceiving her, but is happy. Won't hurt me, she thinks ...

+++

There you go, let's get out of here ... Gently, young man, carefully by the door ... If we wake them up now, it will be a slice... to be caught like this while towering, det is jemein! Be careful! Watch out, you goofball! Se wake se ja! - Thank God, that would be done ... Nu quiet de hallway door zu ... Quietly, sare ick, youngling! Quiet is something else like with 'n Aweck! - Jotte doch, does your heart bubble like that? I was afraid we'd wake the old woman up. I'm funny that way. I can punch a man like you in the mouth, I don't think anything of it, but an old woman like that ...

09 04

It stinks - it breathtakingly stinks in all corridors, staircases, in all dormitories, in every cell, in the workrooms and workshops of Meienburg Penitentiary. The abort buckets, the disinfectants, the old tow that needs to be plucked, the smell of dried vegetables that have gone out, clip fish and old socks, coconut fiber and floor wax - a thick, hot, stale, stinking air. The thunderstorm also passed over the Meienburg penitentiary yesterday, but the damp, cool rain air was unable to penetrate the giant building, the white castle above the city made of cement, steel and glass.

Fie on you! Stinks once again! say the officers from the morning service, who come at three quarters of six.

Man, how it stinks in your house! says the station guard, who wakes up his calf Hans Liebschner with a strong jab to the ribs. Up, man, in ten minutes will be poured. Oh God, and it already smells so bad that all my morning coffee is coming up!

I don't smell anything, Mr. Hauptwachtmeister, Liebschner affirms and rides in his pants.

I've told you ten times that I'm a chief constable, not a head constable, the old man grumbled. You won't get anywhere with me the sweet way, Liebschner ...

And I would so like to achieve something with you, Herr Hauptwachtmeister, Liebschner cajoles with grinning, exaggerated eye-rolling.

And what would you like to achieve, my son? The official leans against the door, rocks the heavy steel plate back and forth with his shoulders, and looks at his calf factor, not without benevolence. You are a real gallows bird!

I want so much to go on field work, on harvest command, Liebschner begs. If you would enter me for that, Chief Constable?

Why is that, man? You stand here nothing but Kalfaktor!!

But I can't stand the air! the prisoner complains in a pitiful voice. I feel so dizzy in my head, I can't eat anything at all, and then I always feel so sick from the stench....

And just a moment ago you didn't smell anything! Nah, son, I want to tell you what's yours. You feel like building towers, you want to go to the little girls, don't you? - Nothing will come of it! Here you stay! - Quite serviceably, it is also unlawful for a penitentiary inmate to be placed on outside work before serving at least half of his sentence.

The prisoner knots his shoes silently, with his head bowed. The chief constable continues to bob his steel door, contemplating the lowered, shorn skull.

Chief Constable ... says prisoner Liebschner and looks up determinedly. I don't like to rat on anyone, but what must, must. I can't stand it in the cell anymore, I'm going crazy ...

You don't go crazy that easily, son!

But I know a guy who has a steel saw, and you swear to me that if I tell you his name, I'll be on field work....

Nobody here has a steel saw!

Yes, you can - especially on your station!

Hans Fallada   -515-   Wolf among Wolves

Nonsense - besides, I don't send on field command, the labor inspector does that.

But if you put in a good word for me, I'll come out.

Long pause.

Who has the saw -?

Do I come on external command -?

For my sake - who has the saw?

Quietly, Mr. Chief Constable, please, quietly! I'll say it in your ear. Just don't rat me out - they'll beat me to death if I get on the work floor.

Quietly the prisoner whispers at the ear of the constable. He nods, asks in a whisper, listens, nods again. Down below, the bell strikes, from station to station the call resounds: Kübeln! Bucket!

The constable straightens up. All right, Liebschner, if it's true, come on command. - What a bloody mess - I'd have been in it! - So come on, man, dalli, bucket! Bißchen fix that we are quickly through with the stench!

09 05

In the Meienburg penitentiary the morning bell strikes at six o'clock, in the Alexanderplatz police prison in Berlin it is half past six before the prisoner is allowed to get up, knows that the night is over, and something happens again - perhaps even to him.

Petra is awakened by the hurried tinkling, for a moment she still has, opening her eyes, the shadow of Wolf's face in front of her. It smiled - then much tore into blackness, an old woman (Wolfgang's mother?) told her hard and high many evil things ... Out of the blackness emerged a tree, defoliated, with bulky, threatening branches - a verse Wolfgang often hummed sounded on her ear: 'He hangs on no tree, he hangs on no rope ...'

Now the eyes are wide open. The gypsies are already chattering again in their corner, with many gestures, squatting on their mattress; the tall one is still lying in her bed, her hunched shoulders twitching, so she is crying again; the small fat one is standing in front of the palm-sized cell mirror, wetting her index finger in her mouth and running it smoothly over her eyebrows. Mrs. Krupaß, however, sits upright in her bed and braids her puny braids - and the blanket package lies motionless on the floor ...

Outside the windows, above roofs, divided by bars, the sky is dull blue and gently sunlit - a new day, goodbye, to new work! There is hardly any water left in the jug - how to wash?

The old woman nods: Listen, kid, what we agreed tonight, it's gonna stay that way, huh? Or have you changed your mind?

No, says Petra.

I have a feeling you'll be out today, all of a sudden. If we don't see each other anymore, you go to Killich - lawyer Killich at Warschauer Brücke - do you keep that -?

Attorney Killich, Warsaw Bridge ... repeats Petra.

Beautiful. So go there right away! - What do you look like? Still thinking about that guy?

No!

Na! Na!

But I think I was dreaming about him!

So - well, there's nothing you can do about it for the time being. That gives itself over time, the dreaming. Don't eat fried potatoes in the evening, tell Randolfen to always give you cold cuts. Fried potatoes in the evening, and especially with onions, that drives the dreams, you do not have to eat such things, child, understood!

No, says Petra. But I am not that sensitive.

Hans Fallada   -517-   Wolf among Wolves

What do you want to do with a guy like that? There are enough guys, there are far too many - go away with them! Always cold cold cuts and a glass of Patzenhofer's Helles, it's easier to fall asleep. Well, you'll make it, I'm not afraid of it!

Me neither!

Now go and check on your sick person, I can tell you're really jittery about it. What is a sheep, remains a sheep. You never learn either! - You, child!

Yes? asks Petra and turns around once again.

When he stands across the street and whistles and waves his finger - there you are, running from my nice floor and from the good, fat food and the bathtub and from the bed - as you stand and walk you run to him, what - ?

With newly awakened suspicion, she looks at Petra out of her old eyes.

But Mother Krupass, Petra says with a smile, now he doesn't come first after all, now I always think of it first!

She looks at Mrs. Krupaß for another moment, then nods at her and now sets about unwrapping the enemy, the hen harrier, the sick one.

09 06

The servant Hubert Räder is already up and at work when Weio arrives at the villa with his cheeks flushed.

Morning, Hubert! she calls. God, do you clean so crazy again -?! Mom has told you not to do that so many times!

Women don't know anything about that! Räder states unruffled and looks at his work with a serious but approving eye.

Since the Herr Rittmeister is returning today, his room must be thoroughly cleaned. The servant Räder proceeds in such a way that he first sweeps, mops, waxes, polishes and dusts one side of the room - only then does he begin with the other half. He drives Mrs. von Prackwitz to despair, who keeps explaining to him that the clean side is always covered in dust from cleaning the other half ...

Yes, madam, said the servant Räder then obediently. But if I am called away to another job, the Herr Rittmeister at least have a clean site on which Herr Rittmeister can live ...

And, more stubborn than a mule, he continues to cleanse in his own way.

Again he said: "Women don't know anything about that," and added emphatically: "Madam has already sneezed twice, madam!

Yes, Hubert, says Weio eagerly. It's all right. I'll go straight to my room and wash up a bit and change. And I also quickly turn a turkey in my bed, as if I had lain in it. - Oh God, no! I don't even need that, I don't even need to have been lying in bed when mom and dad hear what all happened tonight -!

Make you fast, says wheels and moves the floor polisher with loving deliberation. When the madam has sneezed, she always gets up right away.

Oh, Hubert, don't be so stupid! exclaims Weio reproachfully. You're bursting with curiosity too! - Think to yourself, the little Meier has run away with the cash register. But now he is back. And old Kniebusch has arrested Bäumer, but he doesn't have him here yet, he's lying tied up in the forest, and coachman Hartig has harnessed, and now they're out, Hartig and Kniebusch and Meier, to get him - but he's unconscious. - Don't stand there so stupidly, Hubert! shouts Weio angrily. Why don't you let go of the floor polisher - What do you say to that, Hubert?!

You have said you to me twice, madam," says the servant Räder coolly. You know, the cavalry captain doesn't want that at all, and I don't really like it either ...

Hans Fallada   -519-   Wolf among Wolves

Oh, you old blockhead! she cries. I don't care what I say to you! I don't address an old haddock as "you" either. Yes, you are - an ole haddock you are! An old stockfish! You better pay attention to what I'm telling you, you've been there too! That you do not talk everything away when mom asks you ...

Excuse me, madam, I was not there! When something wild like that happens, I'm not there. I also have to think about my reputation. I am a manorial servant - I have nothing to do with cashier thieves and with poachers. It's just like uniforms - I don't get involved!

But Hubert! says Weio reproachfully. You know mom said you should go. They're not going to pull us in after all.

I'm sorry, madam, I can't do it. - Would you please get off the Persian, I need to comb out the fringe. I wonder why people make such fringes in the carpets in the first place? Always they look untidy and messy, just so you have more work ...

Hubert! says Weio very pleadingly and is suddenly very meek. You're not going to tell mom that you didn't go because of the wild stories -?

No, madam -! says Hubert, smoothing his fringe. I already got a nosebleed on the farm and wanted to follow and did not find you because you went the way by the sheds, and I went up the aisle by the wild food place ...

Thank God! Weio breathes a sigh of relief. You're a decent guy after all, Hubert!

And I would even think for a moment, Hubert continues unruffled, what you want to tell the madam. I would not speak so much of Inspector Meier - and what about the poacher, the beamer -? If the forester has caught him, madam must have been there -! What did you arrange with the forester?

But nothing at all, Hubert! He went right back out into the woods - with the inspector!

Look! And did you shoot the buck or did he shoot it? Or is he not shot at all -? After all, it was as if I had heard a shot, today against tomorrow.

Oh Hubert, Hubert - that's just the greatest thing, I haven't told you yet! There really the small Meier shot at the poultry mamsel, the Amanda Backs -!

Madam," Hubert says sternly, turning his expressionless fish eyes on her. I haven't heard that, I don't know anything about anything so wild ...

But he didn't hit them after all! But he was so dumb!

Now go to your room and get changed, says Hubert Räder and is as excited as he can be. No, you have to get out of here now, I have to clean up here, you are disturbing me ...

Hubert, don't get cheeky -! If I want to be here, I'll stay here ...

And I would think carefully about what I say - and best not tell anything at all, but reversed with me when I got a nosebleed ... But you can't do that - and so this afternoon there will already be the most beautiful talk going on, and tonight we have the police in the house ... But I took care of myself, I have two bloody handkerchiefs, and at half past one I knocked at the Armgard and asked her what the clock was, because my alarm clock had stopped, but it had not stopped ... So I don't know about anything, and I haven't talked to you here either - since I got a nosebleed, I haven't seen you ... Good morning, madam, wish to have rested well. Yes, I'm doing a thorough cleaning here, only the vacuum cleaner is broken, that was Armgard, madam, but it also works like that ... And I beg your pardon for not having accompanied the madam to the forest.... Only, I got such nosebleeds because I can not tolerate the insomnia ... I've had that since I was a kid, when I didn't get enough sleep. ...

Please, Hubert, stop it now. I say it yes, if you open your mouth once - And you, Weio, still in your hunting dress - may one say Weidmannsheil or was the Ansitz in vain -?

Oh, Mom, the things we have experienced! It was great! Yes, the buck is shot, but not by me, but, think about it - but you never guess -, the Bäumer shot him - but you know, Mama, the poacher from Altlohe, about whom Grandfather always scolds so ... And Kniebusch has arrested him, the Bäumer of course, but we also have the Bock ... And now they went to the forest to get him, but he is unconscious. And Inspector Meier ...

May I go on in here now? the servant interrupts Räder with quite unusual emphasis.

And the madam: So, Weio, come over to me. You have to tell me all this in detail ... And you were present at something like that, afterwards I still get a fright ... But dad will also be happy that the beamer is done. Why is he unconscious -? Did Kniebusch shoot him then? I always say to father, Kniebusch is better after all ...

They are gone - the servant Räder stands there and nods seriously. For the time being everything is going well, for the time being the madam is still talking ...

But when the cavalry captain comes and asks -? What then?

09 07

Rittmeister von Prackwitz hurriedly jumped out of the autodroshke, paid and ran up the steps to the entrance hall of the Silesian Station. It was still a good half hour before the departure of the train, but he still had to take over his convoy from the agent, settle the accounts with the man, have a collective ticket issued ...

In spite of the all-night sleep, the cavalry captain felt enterprising and hopeful - it was good that he did not go back to Neulohe alone, no longer without friends. And then something of the air of the East was already blowing here at Schlesischer Bahnhof. At Alexanderplatz, one thought only of Berlin, felt only the giant city - here at Schlesischer Bahnhof, one thought of fields and harvest ... It was necessary to bring in the Neuloh harvest well -!

As if struck by lightning, the cavalry captain stopped under the archway. He stood, staring, peering - impatiently, with a shake of his head, he dismissed a carrier ... Now he stepped back a little, full of fear of being discovered ...

It was already so, only it could happen to him: the employer hid from his workers, got scared at the sight of them!

There at the stairs they stood, a heap, a horde - the cavalry captain did not doubt for a moment that these should be his people, although the mediator could not be discovered at the moment.

Oh God! moaned the cavalry captain from a deeply wounded heart. And so what wants to doll rye with me, this wants to dig potatoes, this horde live in Neulohe ...

Young boys, with their slouch hats perched on their ears, their cigarette stubs in the corner of their mouths, with their pants infinitely wide and sharply ironed, their Chaplin sticks coquettishly in their hands ... Other boors, long-haired, either without collar or with dirty shill collars, the shirt open over the chest, the arms tattooed blue and red like the chest, torn pants, barefoot or worn sneakers ... Two street girls with almost white bleached hair, in silk flags, on patent leather high heels ... An ancient man with nickel glasses, his black frock coat hanging sadly over his scrawny loins, a botanizing drum hanging by a string from his sloping armpit ... Again a girl, some green-striped flannel blouse over breasts like flour sacks - a screaming child in her arms ...

Oh my God! moaned the cavalry captain again.

And not a piece of luggage, not a margarine box, not even a Persil box - just this one dented green botanizing drum, common luggage of all.

'Not even sixty toothbrushes would fit in that thing, let alone sixty shirts!'

And all this shuffled in high spirits, laughing, chatting, whistling hits and hooting; two were already necking, sitting on a step ... Unabashedly, passing travelers were called, taunted, begged ...

A cigarette, boss, please, give me a cigarette! And the boy took the burning cigarette from the mouth of the stunned man. - Thank you, boss, I'm not like that, we all have the same disease ...

The trip to Neulohe, bringing in the harvest: a country party, a welcome joke for this - gang!

The captain of the cavalry gritted his teeth. - And excitedly to von Studmann, who was arriving with a suitcase: "Look at this gang! And such a thing wants to work in the countryside! In patent leather shoes - with shimmy pants!

Bad! said von Studmann after a brief inspection. Just don't take them. You asked for farm workers!

The cavalry captain said a little embarrassed: But I must have people! The harvest rots me outside!

So look for others. It can't come down to one day. Let's go tomorrow!

But now, in the middle of the harvest season, there are no reasonable people. Everyone holds on to what they have. And no carrion wants to go to the country - they'd rather starve here at their cinemas.

So take these - they will be useful for something.

And my father-in-law -?! My mother-in-law -?!! I am making an immortal fool of myself, they are laughing at me, I am a finished man when I arrive with these people! They are all hookers and pimps!

Pretty run down they look - but if you must have workers! - So what are you going to do?

The cavalry captain avoided a direct answer: "I'm telling you, Studmann," he said angrily, "I didn't make it easy for myself. I'm not a farmer, my father-in-law is right about that; I read, I ponder, I run from dawn to dusk, but I do a lot of bullshit, admittedly! Simply because I do not know the twist so ... And now I have really grown something, not a bomb crop, but still quite bearable - it stands outside, it would have to go in - and now this: no people! It is exasperating!

But why don't you have people when others do? Forgive me, Prackwitz, but you said yourself earlier: they're holding them all.

Because I have no money! The others hire their people in the spring, I have helped myself for so long. I put off the commitment until the last moment to save wages ... Look, Studmann, my father-in-law is a rich man, a heavily rich man, but I have nothing. I have debts! He leased me the farm as it stands and goes, with all the inventory, I didn't need any money to do it. Until now I have always managed to get by, selling a little potatoes, a little livestock - that brought the wages and what we need to live. But now, now money must come in! Otherwise I'm done for, flat broke! And the money is there, it's in the field - I just need to bring in, thresh, deliver, and I have money! And that's where I get people like that! You would have to hang yourself!

I don't know how many million unemployed we have, von Studmann said. After all, there are more every day. But there are no workers for work.

Von Prackwitz had not listened. And I don't take people! he said with grim determination. Maybe they would even do a little bit, in the first time, as long as they have no return money and hunger. But I will not be laughed at by the whole neighborhood and dear relatives! I'm not turning my people's house into a brothel - just look at the way those two are touching each other on the stairs, disgusting - I think it's disgusting! - And I don't spoil my Neulohe; it's hard enough with the people from Altlohe ... No, I don't take them.

And what do you do instead? Since you must have people -?

Hans Fallada   -525-   Wolf among Wolves

Let me tell you something, Studmann. I'll call the penitentiary, we have the Meienburg penitentiary in our area, I'll have a penitentiary commando come. Better the Bengels, with a few real constables with them, the carbine in the fin - than these! The warden in the penitentiary can't deny me that - and maybe we'll both go to him sometime - now I have you to help me!

Suddenly the cavalry captain smiles. That he has a real friend, with whom he can talk about everything, close to him from now on, he suddenly realizes again. That's why he talked more in the last five minutes than he had in five months before.

Studmann nods, and von Prackwitz says, "Look, Studmann, my father-in-law is right again: I'm not a businessman. Then I go to Berlin in the most hurried time, leave for twenty-four hours the whole big business with the harvest, on which everything depends, to a schnook and greyhound, spend a lot of money, gamble away even more, come back with a pile of debts to you and young Pagel, and bring no people, but do what my neighbors advised me already four weeks ago: I take a penitentiary commando ...

Von Prackwitz smiles; quietly, very carefully, von Studmann also smiles.

All right, so I did it wrong again. But what next? We all do our stupid things, Studmann (my father-in-law did, too), but the main thing is that we realize our stupidities. I see them! I make them better. But I'll keep going, Studmann, and you help me.

Of course! agrees Studmann. But isn't it about time for our train? I guess you still need to talk to the mediator? And young Pagel is not there yet either!

But von Prackwitz does not hear now. Does the friend do it? Does it make the startling experience at night? Prackwitz is talkative, Prackwitz wants to make confessions, Prackwitz wants to confess.

You've been working at the hotel for so long now, Studmann, you must have something away from bookkeeping and money management and people handling. I just always start yelling right away. - We have to make it! What -? That I keep the farm! I know my father-in-law would love to have it back. (Sorry for talking so much about my father-in-law. But he's my red rag. I can't stand him, and he can't stand me). The old man can't see me managing. And now if I don't get the lease together by October 1, then I have to get out - and then what do I do?

He looks angrily at von Studmann. Then: But it's outside, Studmann, and we'll get it in, and anyway, now that I have you, we'll make Neulohe a model estate. Oh, Studmann, it's lucky that I met you after all! First, I must confess, I really got a fright when I saw you there in the black skirt making servants in front of every dressed-up chick ... What have you sunk to, Studmann, I thought ...

Here comes Pagel! exclaimed Studmann, who became hot and cold at these confessions of the otherwise so reserved Prackwitz.

'Because the good guy will bitterly regret that one day,' Studmann thinks. 'And then he resents me for speaking to him like that today!'

But von Prackwitz is like drunk, it must really make the air here at the Schlesischer Bahnhof.

You've got enough luggage, Pagel, he said very sympathetically. Hopefully you'll last long enough with me that you'll put on everything you have in there once with me. In the countryside, people work, not play! - Well, that's okay, I didn't mean it at all! By the way, I played myself! And now be so good and get three tickets second at the counter, first to Frankfurt - and then we will make our way in the last minute in the storm run ...

But don't you want to talk to the facilitator first? After all, people are ordered here ...

So get the tickets and then come right back here, Pagel. - What am I supposed to talk to the man about? He set me up, now I'm setting him up!

But that's not how you do things, Prackwitz! You don't have to shy away from the confrontation. You have every right to reject people - they are not farm workers. You don't run up the stairs secretly - like a schoolboy ...

Studmann. I am not a schoolboy!! I have to ask you ...

Like a schoolboy, I said, Prackwitz.

So in a nutshell, Studmann, I want to do it the way I think it should be done.

But I think, Prackwitz, you just wanted my advice ...

Of course, Studmann, of course! Don't pull a face. Always I like to hear your advice, only this time, you see ... Because the truth is that I told the man, people can look however they want if they only have hands to work with ...

I see.

But that he sends such a gang there -! I can't pay a few hundred gold marks in commission for that! - So please, lead the way with Pagel and I'll catch up. Let me act the way I want to this one time....

Good, good, Prackwitz, von Studmann said after a moment's thought. So this one more time. True, it is not, and it is not a good start to our cooperation, but ...

Away with you! shouts the cavalry captain. Smoker, second! Eight minutes to go. And then end with Berlin - thank God!

Very thoughtfully, von Studmann climbs the stairs to the platform next to the young Pagel.

'So let's not take it as the beginning of cooperation, let's take it as the end of Berlin!'

He is glad that he does not have to see how the Rittmeister von Prackwitz avoids paying an agency commission by running off in a storm. The sight of the cavalry captain during other assaults had always been pleasant to him. Damn times that could change a man so -!

So you did make up your mind, he says to young Pagel. That's nice of you.

09 08

Left alone, the cavalry captain stands irresolute, gnawing his lip, looking at the ticket in his hand. In an instant, with the departure of the two, his enthusiastic mood, which made any confession easy for him, is gone, now he is completely dominated by the momentary situation, which is simply disgusting.

With his brow furrowed in annoyance and his evil eyes narrowed, he peers into the hall. The people there have also become restless as the time of departure approaches; those who were sitting on the steps have stood up; groups have formed, eagerly discussing with each other; on a stair landing stands the long, bony mediator with the white, hairless skull, speaking soothingly to his harassers, scanning the hall with his eyes, peering for the entrance ...

The cavalryman retreats further behind his pillar - ah, this pack of Korah, this heap of misfortune that is supposed to have brought him! He sees no way to get through unseen - why doesn't this damn platform have more stairways -?!

'And I don't take people, I don't take them under any circumstances! I'm not going to make myself the laughing stock of the whole neighborhood! I will not be laughed at! In silk bunting and high heels to the rye doll! Not a shirt to change into, not a pair of pants! Once the gang gets wet, everything sits stark naked in the den until the stuff is dry again! Paradise conditions! No, I'd rather still be a penitentiary!'

Hans Fallada   -529-   Wolf among Wolves

The cavalryman peeks around the pillar, but bounces back. The mediator has left his elevated vantage point; on one side the girl with child in the slut blouse, on the other the old geezer with botanizing drum in the roast skirt, he strives, talking excitedly, towards the station entrance - and the cavalry captain would like to crawl into his pillar, to petrify, to dissolve, so much does he dread this trio.

And just at this moment, in this most critical of all critical moments - a somewhat rough, but not at all unpleasant girl's voice sounds at his ear: Oh, the Herr Rittmeister!

He turns around and stares.

Yes, indeed: standing before him, he doesn't know where she came from, so she has really fallen from the sky, the daughter of his bailiff Kowalewski, a girl whom he has always liked among the foolish and clumsy courtiers of the estate because of her fresh nature and her dainty beauty, and whom he has honored with many a fatherly kind word.

Sophie! he says, completely taken aback. What are you doing here, Sophie?

(The girls who worked on the estate from the age of fourteen were all addressed as "Du". And that's how it stayed - even if they, like Sophie, went out into the wide world).

I'm going on vacation to my parents! she laughs and looks at him like a daughter.

Oh, Sophie! he says eagerly. You really seem to me as if sent from heaven! On the other side of the pillar, the man with the bald head, yes, the tall one - don't look like that, Sophie! -He must not see me under any circumstances, and I must get to the train! There are only three minutes left. Can't you hold him somehow, just long enough for me to slip through the entrance hall, I've already got my card - thank you, thank you, Sophie, on the train I'll explain everything to you. You're still a great girl! - Go on!

He hears her voice just now, high, very argumentative: Don't stand in the middle of the way! I have to get to my train! You'd better touch my suitcases ...

'Great girl!' he thinks again. 'But mighty changed. A little dressed up...'

He runs, runs what he can, not at all like a cavalry captain, not at all like a bread giver - the barrier, there in front is already the barrier ...

'But maybe the guy has platform tickets! - Great shadows under the eyes. And the face has become so thick, everything fine is gone. Really puffy, yes, as if from schnapps ...'

I know, thank you, I know, the train on the left - it's not the first time I've been here! Thank you!

'Thank God, we would have made it! But I'm not sure until the train leaves ... Yes, I'm afraid little Sophie has been a bit sharp with the young guys in the village before, I heard something like that once - and Berlin is a difficult place ... I can tell you a thing or two about that ... Thank God, there's Pagel waving!' There you go, gentlemen, I've done it. - Please, Studmann, please, Pagel - stand by the window so that no one can see in, the guy is capable and still revises the compartments! I have to dry myself first, I'm practically swimming - such an endurance run in the early morning ...

So you got through unmolested? asks Studmann.

It was difficult! And do you know who helped me? The daughter of my bailiff! - She just came, is going on vacation to her parents, is a maid to some countess here in Berlin ... You could actually watch out if she still makes the train. It should leave any minute. You could ask her to come in. I'd like to know how she's doing. A splendid girl - how she understood right away, without a word!

What does she look like? Old - young? Fat - thin? Blond - dark?

Oh, she's not well off in Berlin! No, let it rather! Afterwards there's only gossip, and in Neulohe it's also embarrassing when you meet again. After all, she is only the daughter of my bailiff! Always keep your distance from people, no confidences, don't get involved with them! Understood?

Yes, sir!

Thank God, we're leaving. So, sit down comfortably. Let's burn a tobac - it's wonderful to leave this dirty town for the summer, isn't it, Studmann? What, Pagel?

Wonderful! says Studmann - and asks cautiously: one more thing occurred to me, Prackwitz -: doesn't the man know your name?

What man -?

The mediator!

Yes, of course - why?

Then he will write to you and make demands - won't he?

Oh damn! Oh damn! I didn't think of that at all! All this fuss for nothing! But I won't accept the letter, I refuse to accept it, no one can force me to accept it!

The cavalryman grinds his teeth in anger.

I am very sorry, Prackwitz, but that will hardly help anything ...

Yes, now you are sorry, Studmann! But either you should have told me down at the station - or not at all! Now that it's too late! The whole trip is spoiled for me! And it's such beautiful weather!

The cavalry captain stares angrily out of the compartment, into the beautiful weather.

Before Studmann can answer anything (and it is doubtful whether he has much desire to answer), the door from the side entrance opens. But instead of the conductor, a very elegant young girl appears. Smiling, she puts her hand to her little hat: Order executed, Herr Rittmeister!

The captain jumps up, beaming.

That's great, Sophie, that you made the train after all! I was already reproaching myself. - Gentlemen, this is Sophie Kowalewski, I already told you... Mr. von Studmann, Mr. Pagel. These gentlemen are - ahem! - my guests. - So, now sit down here, Sophie, and tell us a little bit. Would you like a cigarette? - No, of course not. Very sensible, young girls shouldn't smoke at all, I always tell my daughter that. Fräulein von Kuckhoff is right, as always: women feminine - men masculine - and that's what you mean, isn't it, Sophie?

Of course, Herr Rittmeister, smoking is so harmful! And with a glance at the two listeners: Do the gentlemen only come for the weekend or do they stay longer in Neulohe -?